DESCENDANTS

EVIE'S WICKED RUNWAY
BOOK 1

BASED ON CHARACTERS CREATED BY JOSANN MCGIBBON AND SARA PARRIOTT
WRITTEN BY: JASON MUELL
ART BY: NATSUKI MINAMI

 TOKYOPOP®

Table of Contents

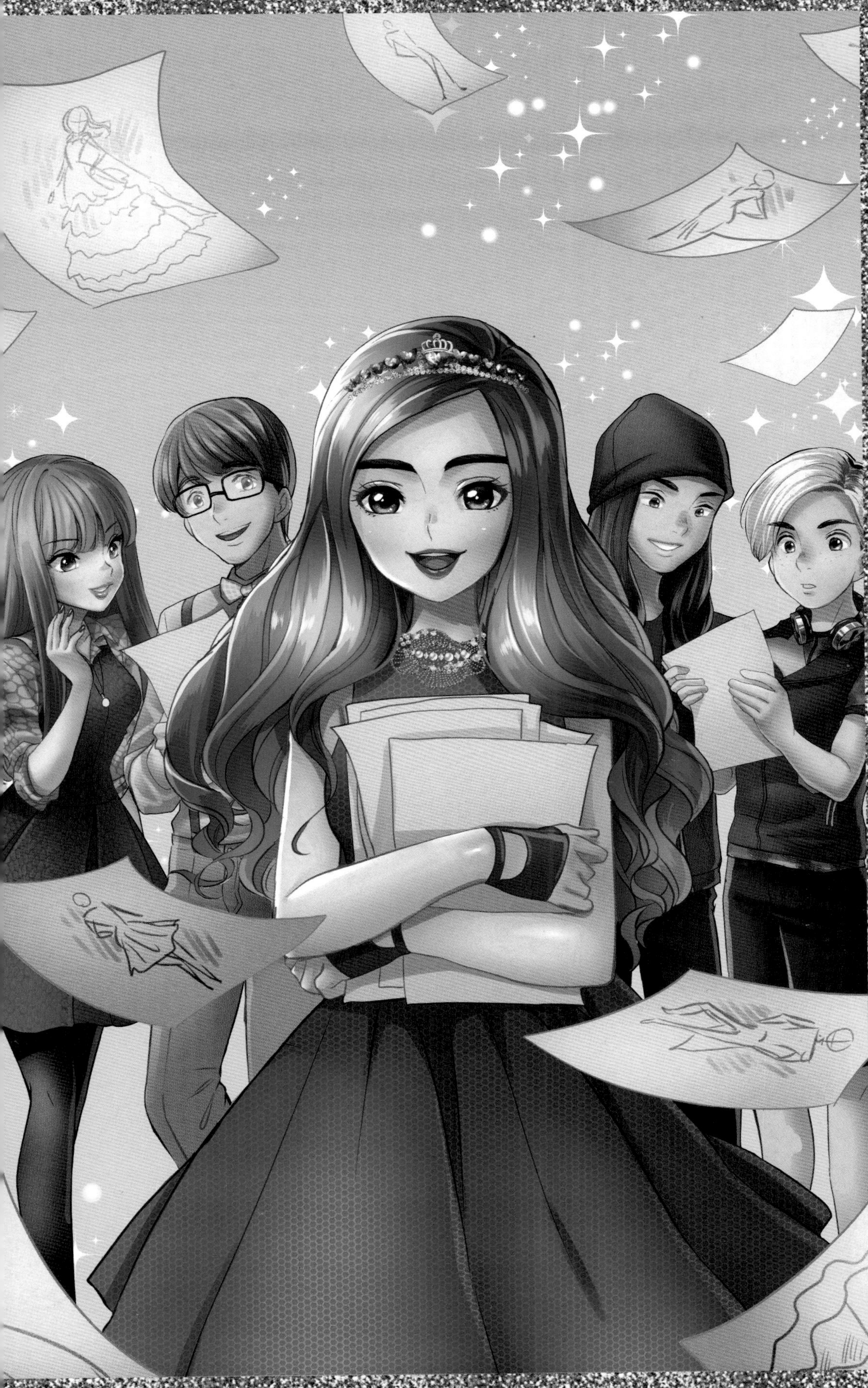

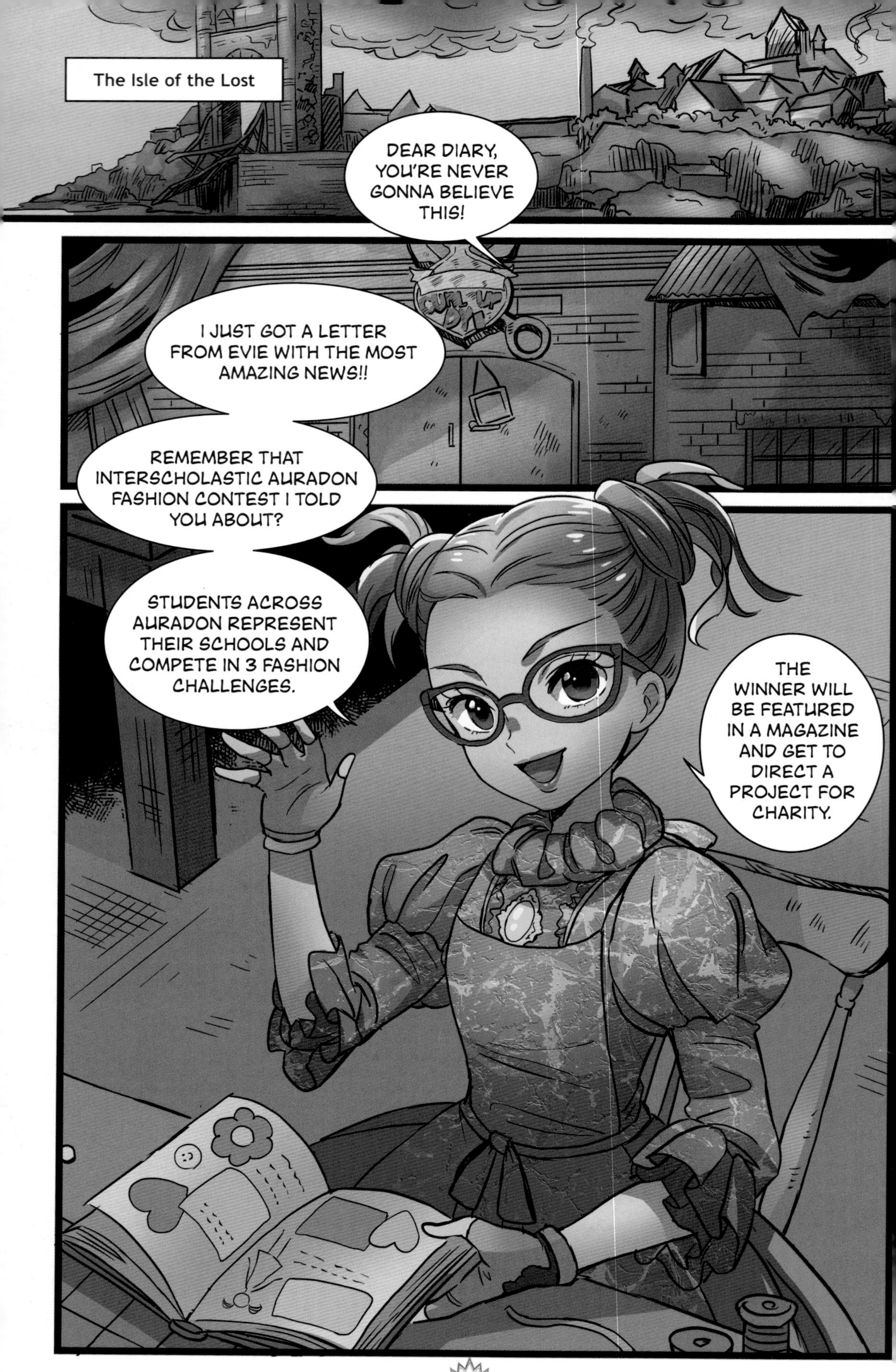
The Isle of the Lost
DEAR DIARY, YOU'RE NEVER GONNA BELIEVE THIS!
I JUST GOT A LETTER FROM EVIE WITH THE MOST AMAZING NEWS!!
REMEMBER THAT INTERSCHOLASTIC AURADON FASHION CONTEST I TOLD YOU ABOUT?
STUDENTS ACROSS AURADON REPRESENT THEIR SCHOOLS AND COMPETE IN 3 FASHION CHALLENGES.
THE WINNER WILL BE FEATURED IN A MAGAZINE AND GET TO DIRECT A PROJECT FOR CHARITY.

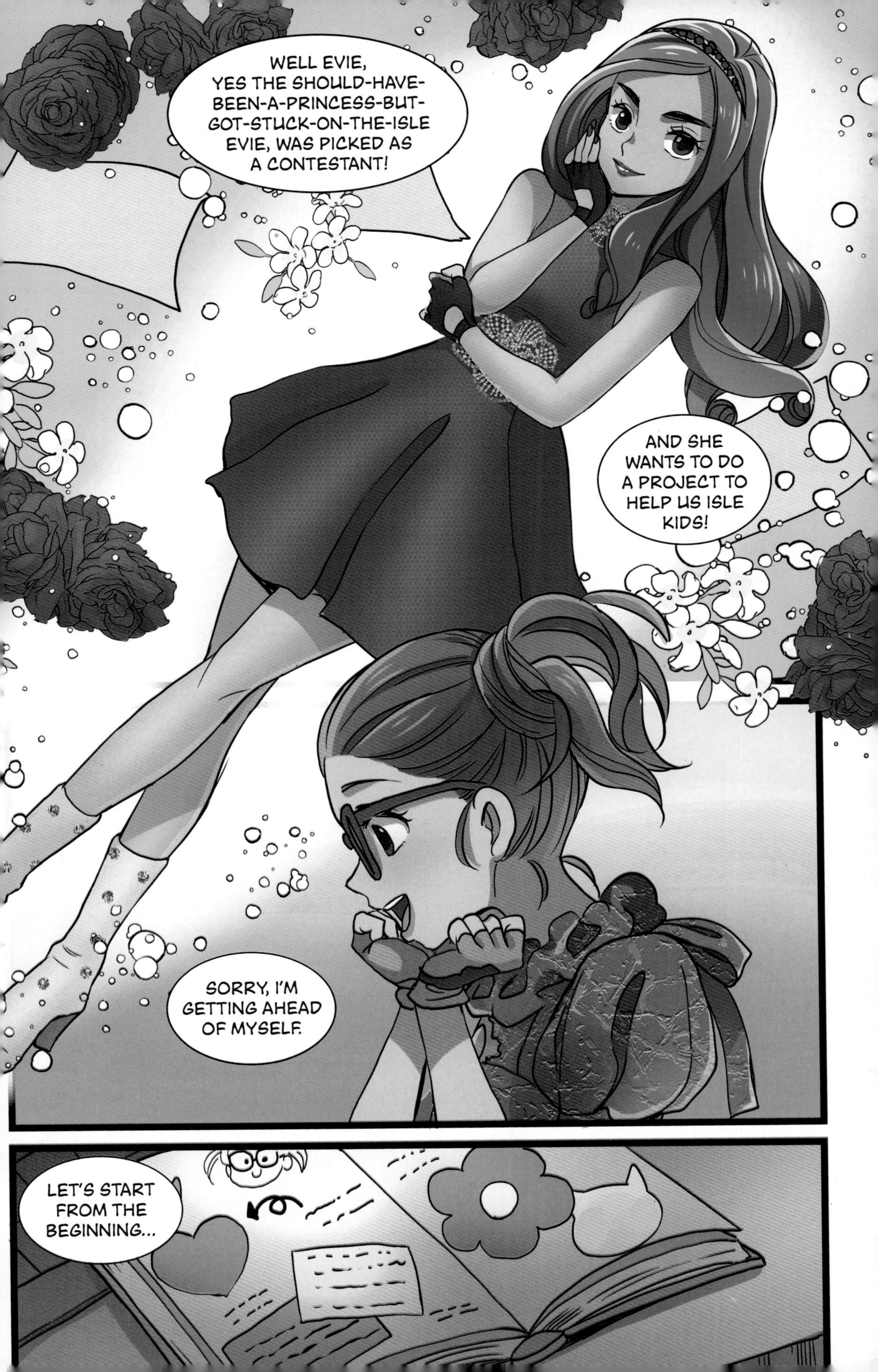
WELL EVIE, YES THE SHOULD-HAVE-BEEN-A-PRINCESS-BUT-GOT-STUCK-ON-THE-ISLE EVIE, WAS PICKED AS A CONTESTANT!
AND SHE WANTS TO DO A PROJECT TO HELP US ISLE KIDS!
SORRY, I'M GETTING AHEAD OF MYSELF.
LET'S START FROM THE BEGINNING...

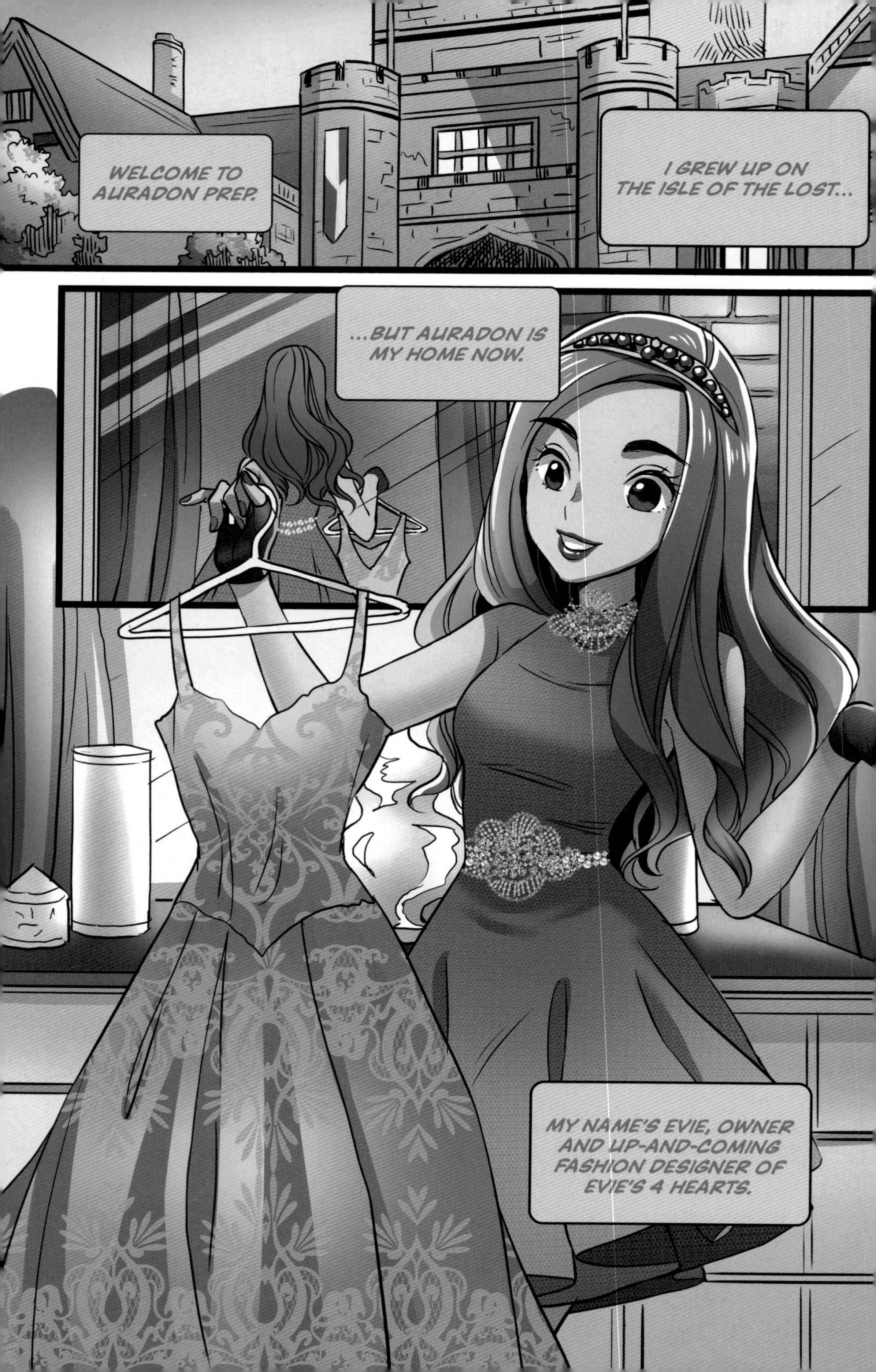
WELCOME TO AURADON PREP.
I GREW UP ON THE ISLE OF THE LOST...
...BUT AURADON IS MY HOME NOW.
MY NAME'S EVIE, OWNER AND UP-AND-COMING FASHION DESIGNER OF EVIE'S 4 HEARTS.

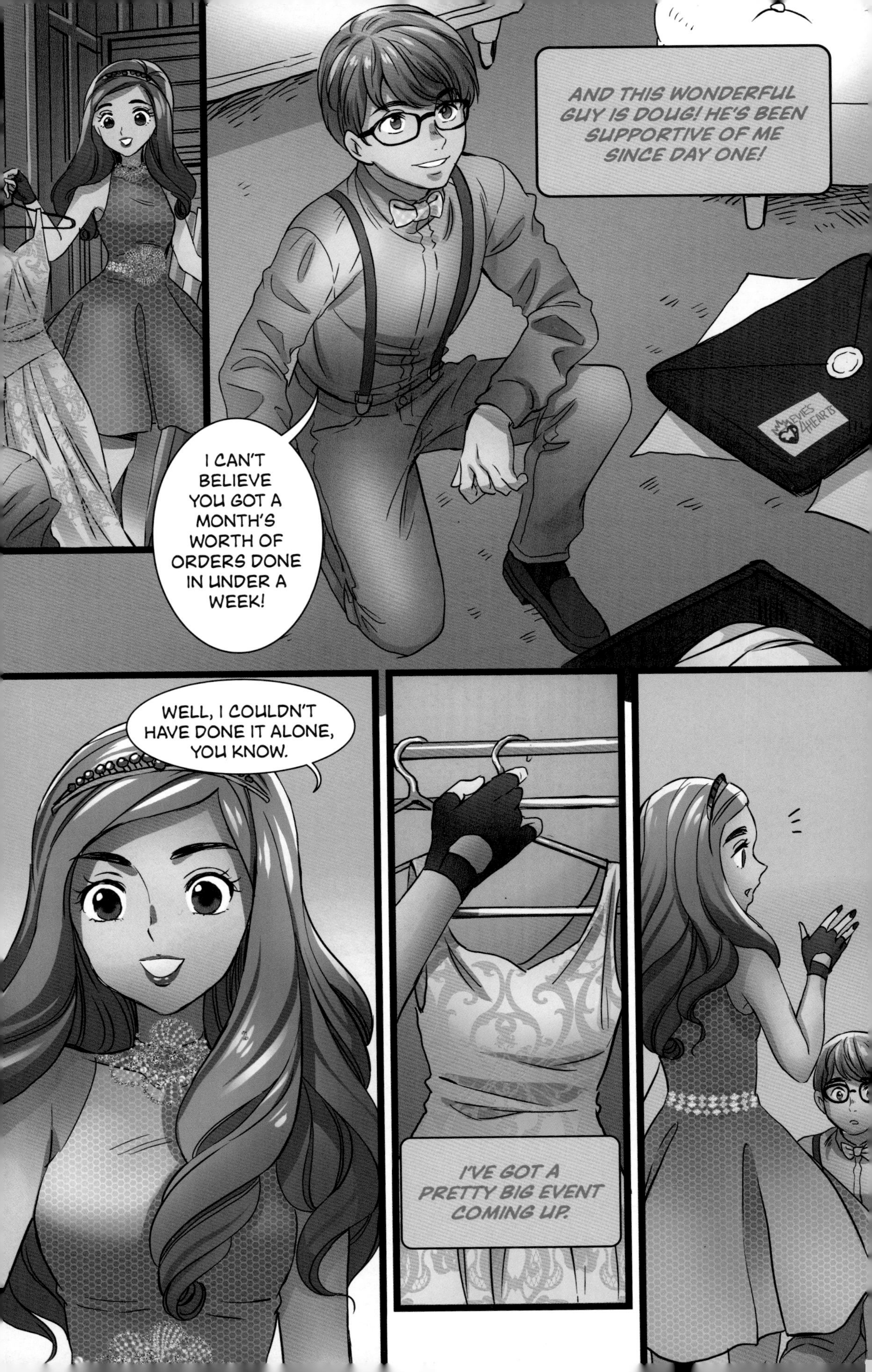
AND THIS WONDERFUL GUY IS DOUG! HE'S BEEN SUPPORTIVE OF ME SINCE DAY ONE!
I CAN'T BELIEVE YOU GOT A MONTH'S WORTH OF ORDERS DONE IN UNDER A WEEK!
EVIE'S 4HEARTS
WELL, I COULDN'T HAVE DONE IT ALONE, YOU KNOW.
I'VE GOT A PRETTY BIG EVENT COMING UP.

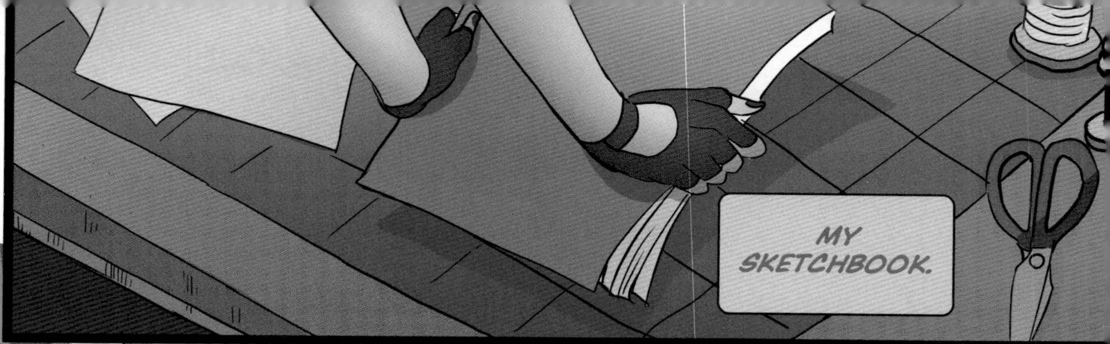
MY SKETCHBOOK.

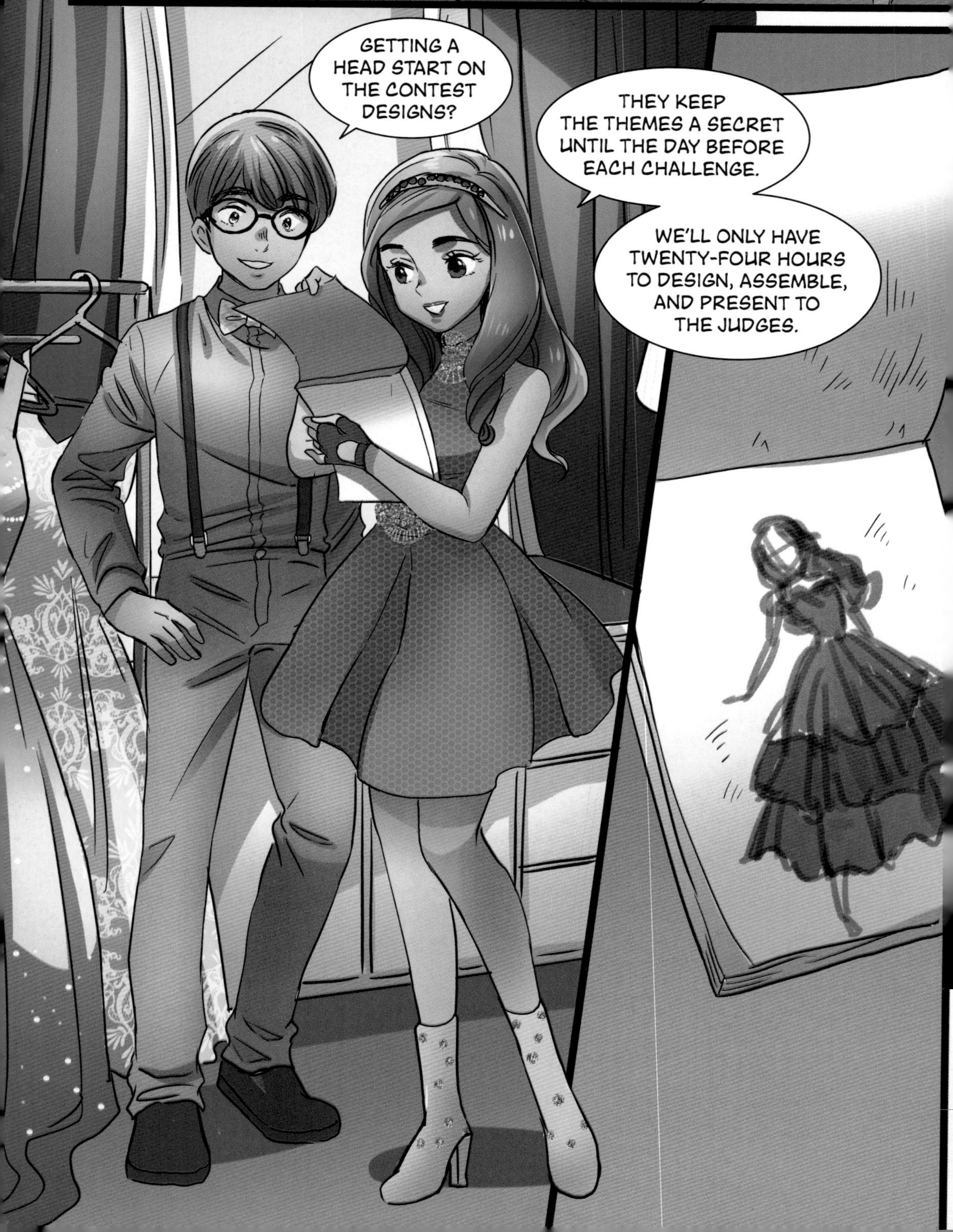
GETTING A HEAD START ON THE CONTEST DESIGNS?
THEY KEEP THE THEMES A SECRET UNTIL THE DAY BEFORE EACH CHALLENGE.
WE'LL ONLY HAVE TWENTY-FOUR HOURS TO DESIGN, ASSEMBLE, AND PRESENT TO THE JUDGES.

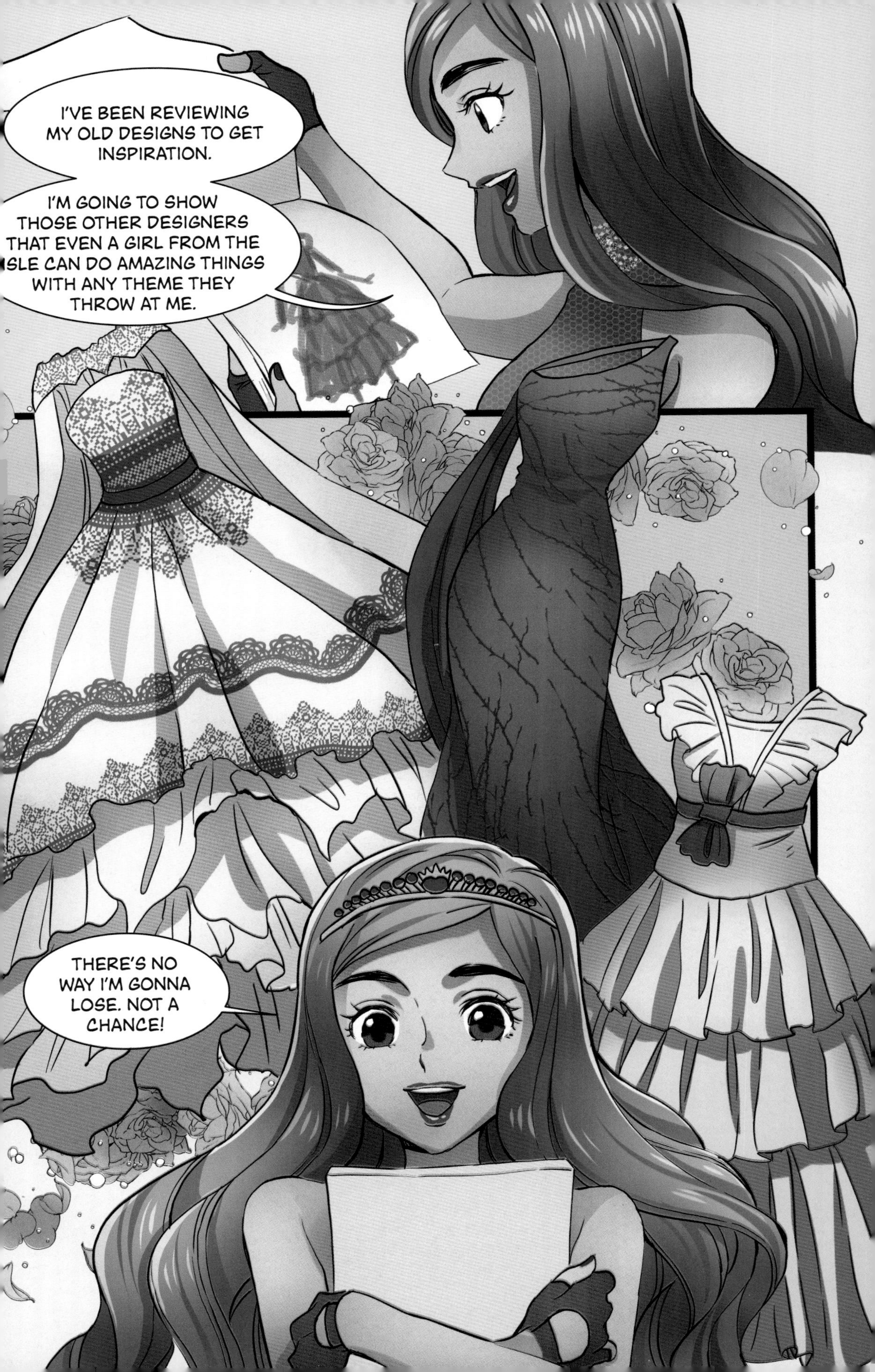
I'VE BEEN REVIEWING MY OLD DESIGNS TO GET INSPIRATION.
I'M GOING TO SHOW THOSE OTHER DESIGNERS THAT EVEN A GIRL FROM THE SLE CAN DO AMAZING THINGS WITH ANY THEME THEY THROW AT ME.
THERE'S NO WAY I'M GONNA LOSE. NOT A CHANCE!

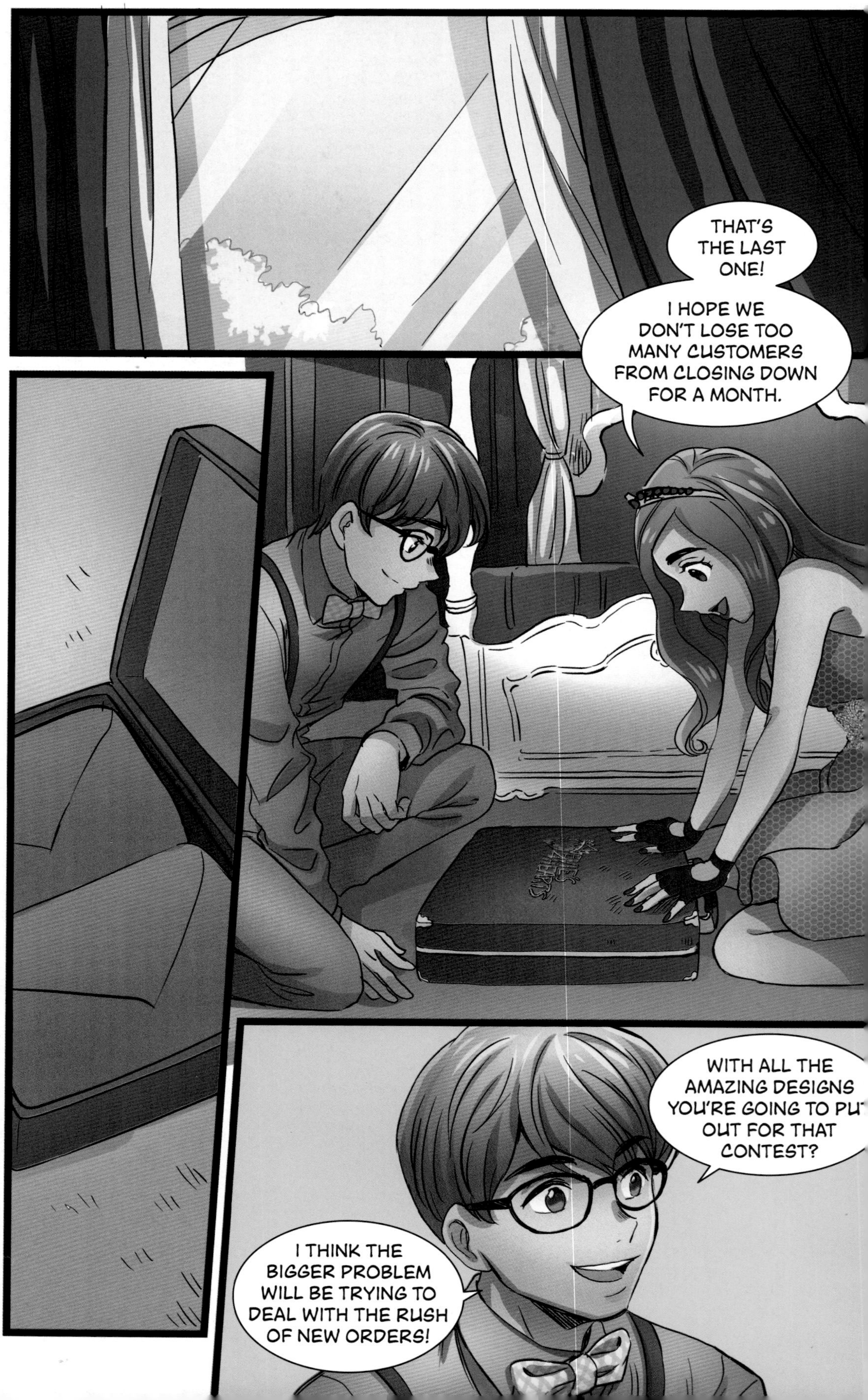
THAT'S THE LAST ONE!
I HOPE WE DON'T LOSE TOO MANY CUSTOMERS FROM CLOSING DOWN FOR A MONTH.
WITH ALL THE AMAZING DESIGNS YOU'RE GOING TO PUT OUT FOR THAT CONTEST?
I THINK THE BIGGER PROBLEM WILL BE TRYING TO DEAL WITH THE RUSH OF NEW ORDERS!

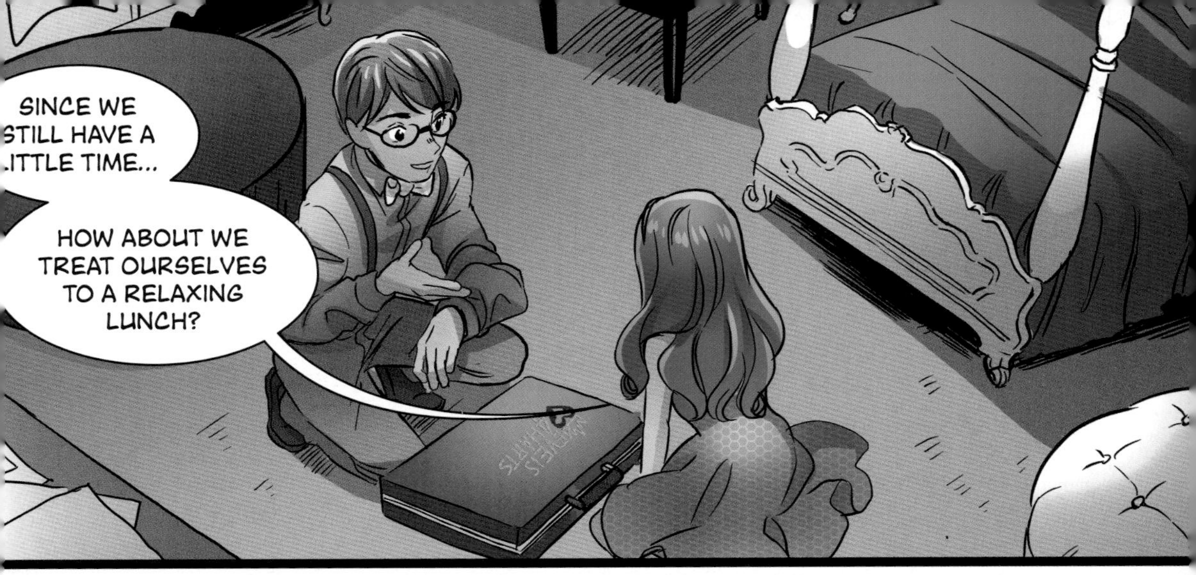
SINCE WE STILL HAVE A LITTLE TIME...
HOW ABOUT WE TREAT OURSELVES TO A RELAXING LUNCH?

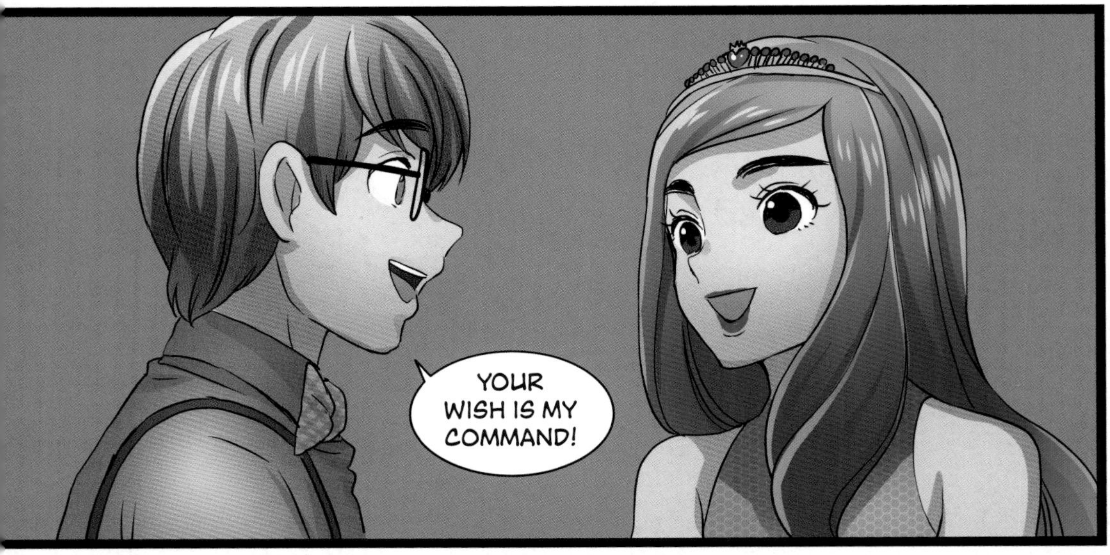
YOUR WISH IS MY COMMAND!

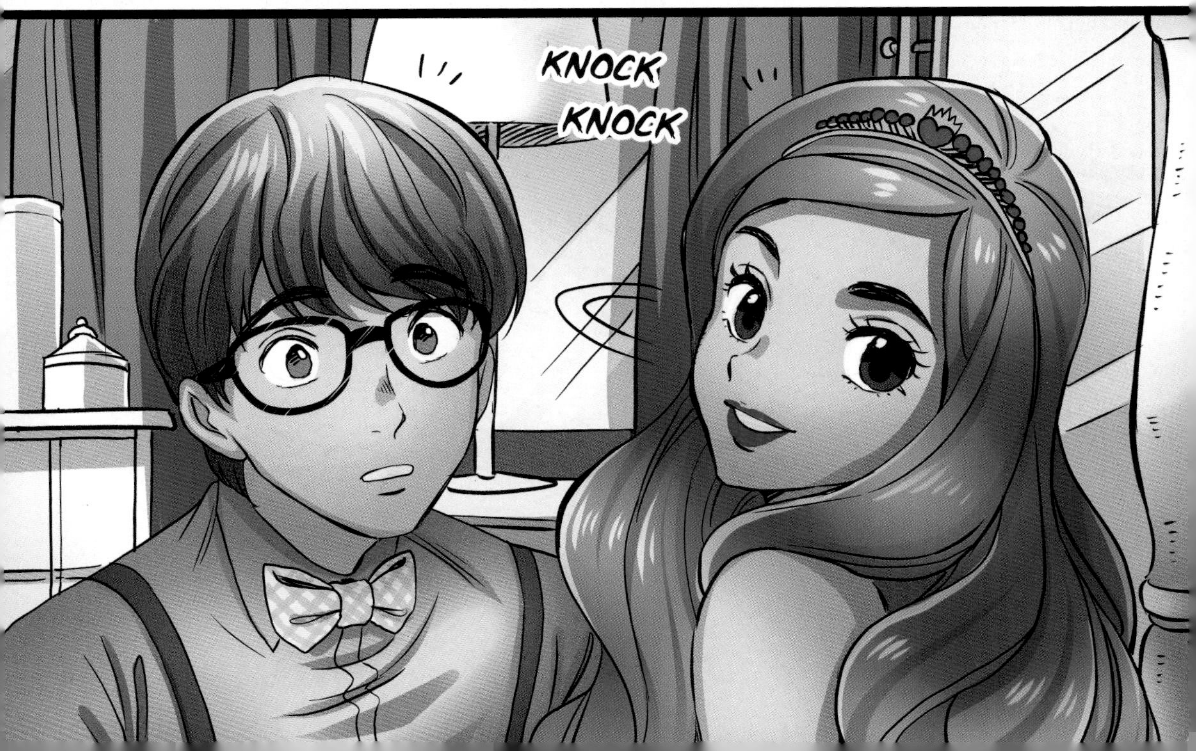
KNOCK
KNOCK

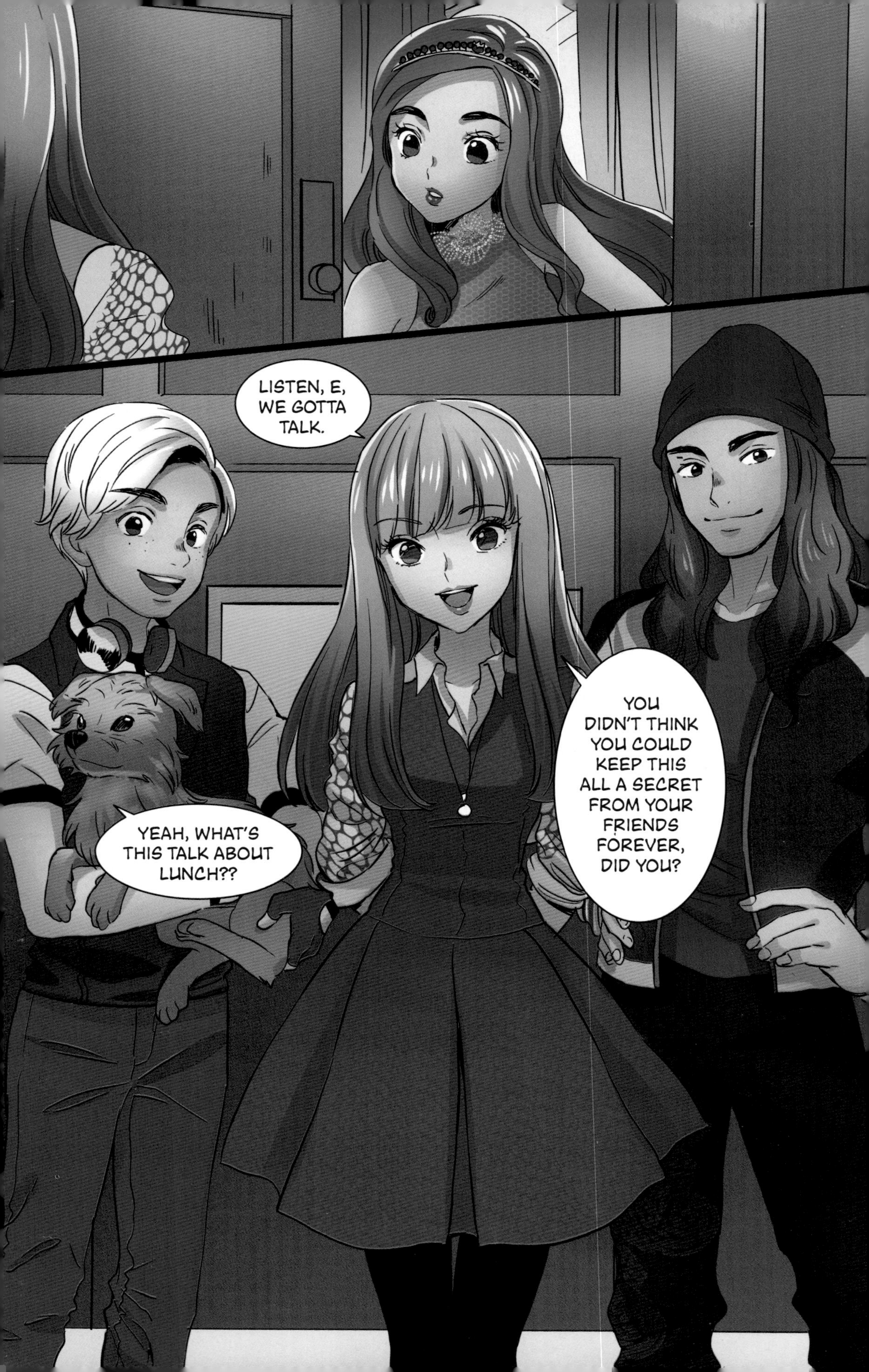
LISTEN, E, WE GOTTA TALK.
YEAH, WHAT'S THIS TALK ABOUT LUNCH??
YOU DIDN'T THINK YOU COULD KEEP THIS ALL A SECRET FROM YOUR FRIENDS FOREVER, DID YOU?

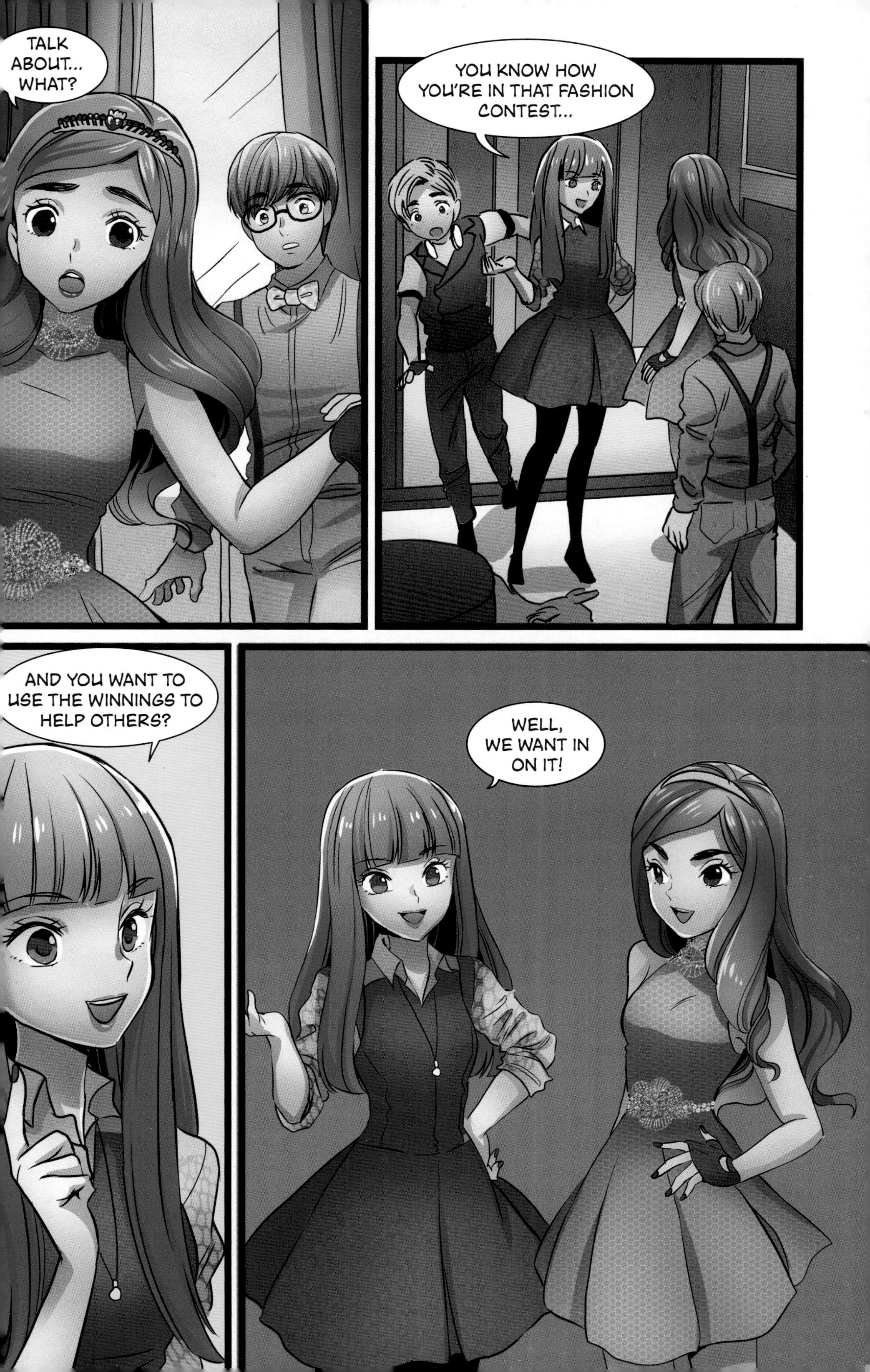
TALK ABOUT... WHAT?
YOU KNOW HOW YOU'RE IN THAT FASHION CONTEST...
AND YOU WANT TO USE THE WINNINGS TO HELP OTHERS?
WELL, WE WANT IN ON IT!

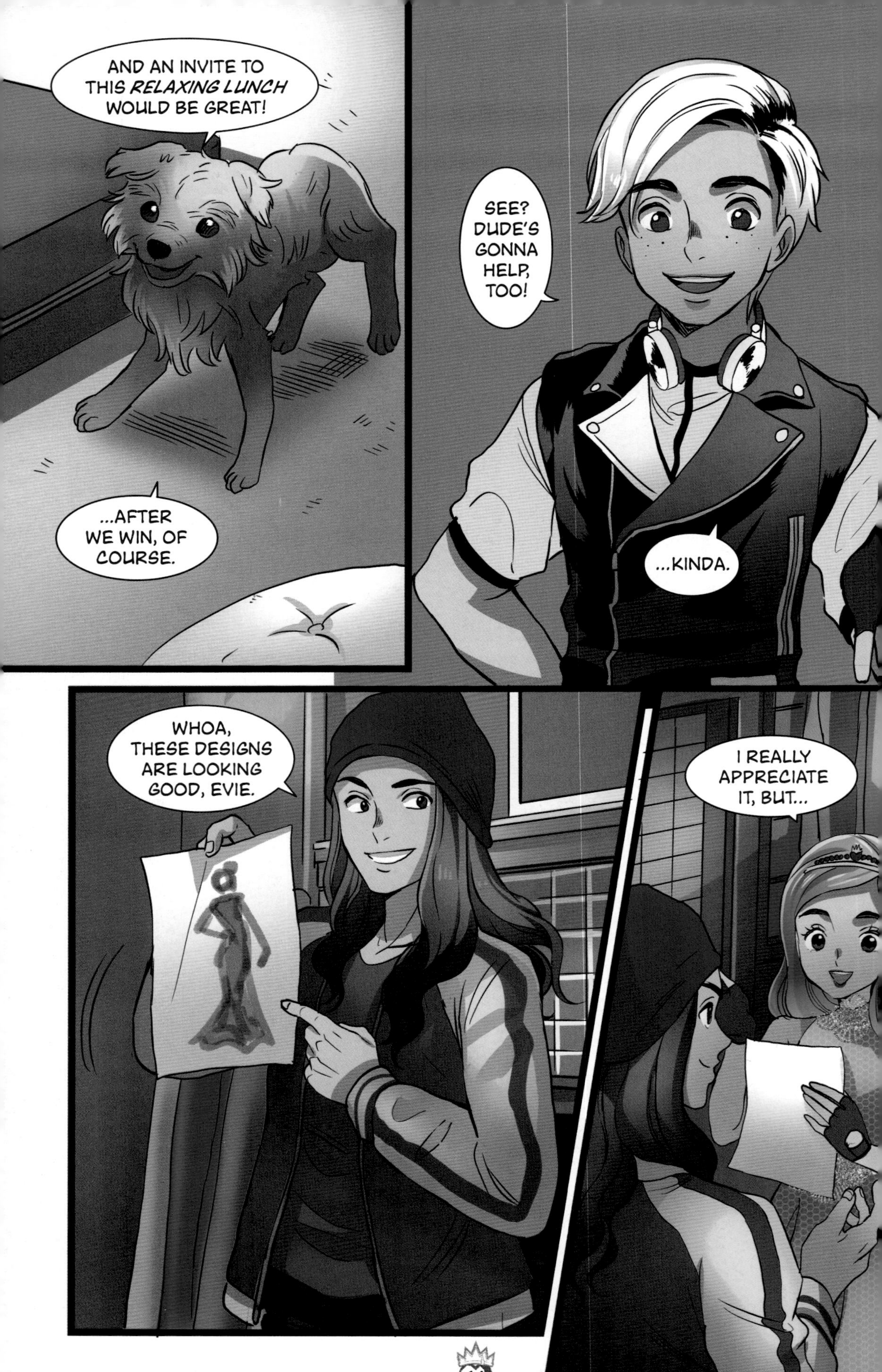

AND AN INVITE TO THIS *RELAXING LUNCH* WOULD BE GREAT!
...AFTER WE WIN, OF COURSE.
SEE? DUDE'S GONNA HELP, TOO!
...KINDA.
WHOA, THESE DESIGNS ARE LOOKING GOOD, EVIE.
I REALLY APPRECIATE IT, BUT...

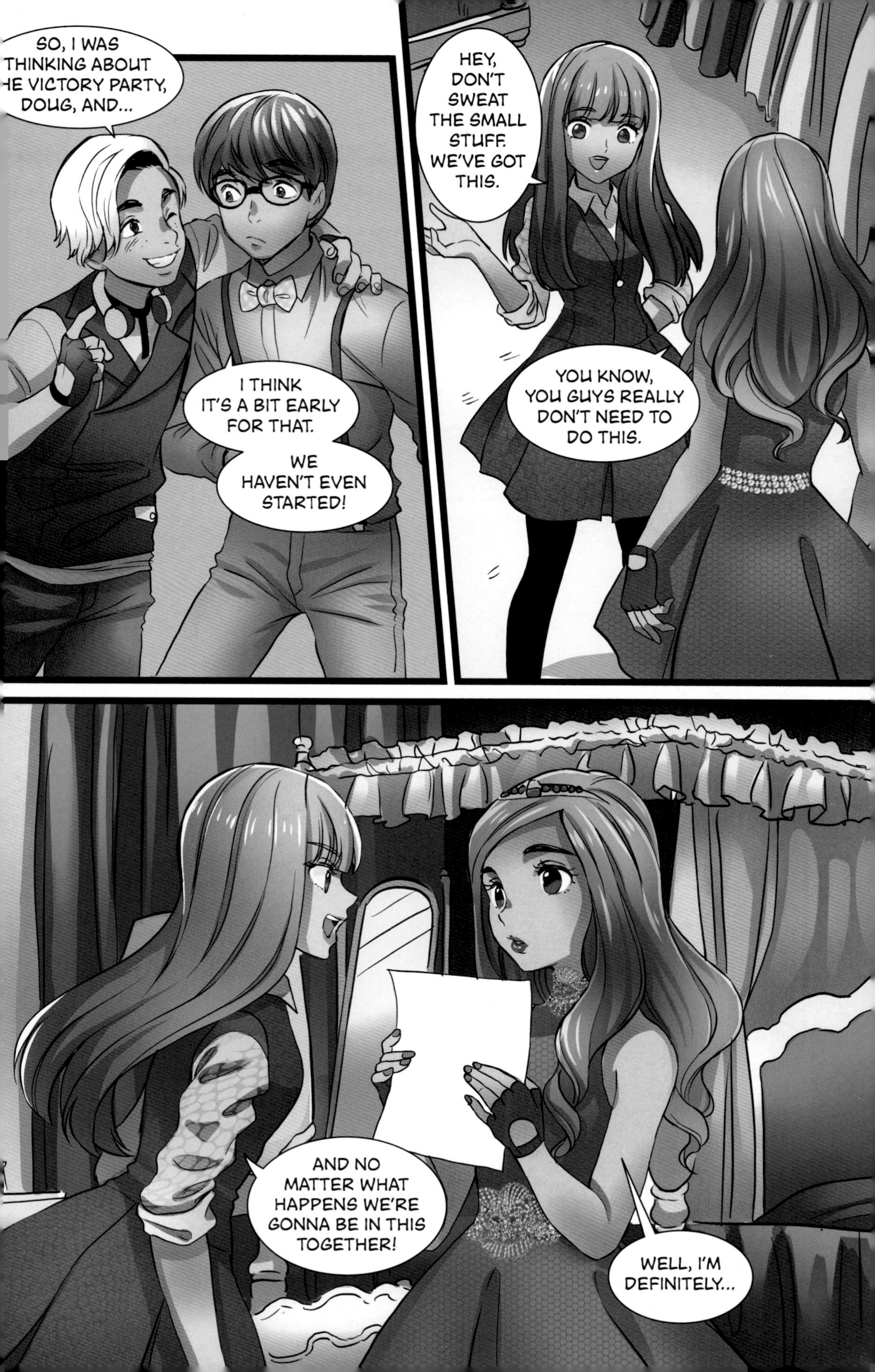
SO, I WAS THINKING ABOUT HE VICTORY PARTY, DOUG, AND...
I THINK IT'S A BIT EARLY FOR THAT.
WE HAVEN'T EVEN STARTED!
HEY, DON'T SWEAT THE SMALL STUFF. WE'VE GOT THIS.
YOU KNOW, YOU GUYS REALLY DON'T NEED TO DO THIS.
AND NO MATTER WHAT HAPPENS WE'RE GONNA BE IN THIS TOGETHER!
WELL, I'M DEFINITELY...

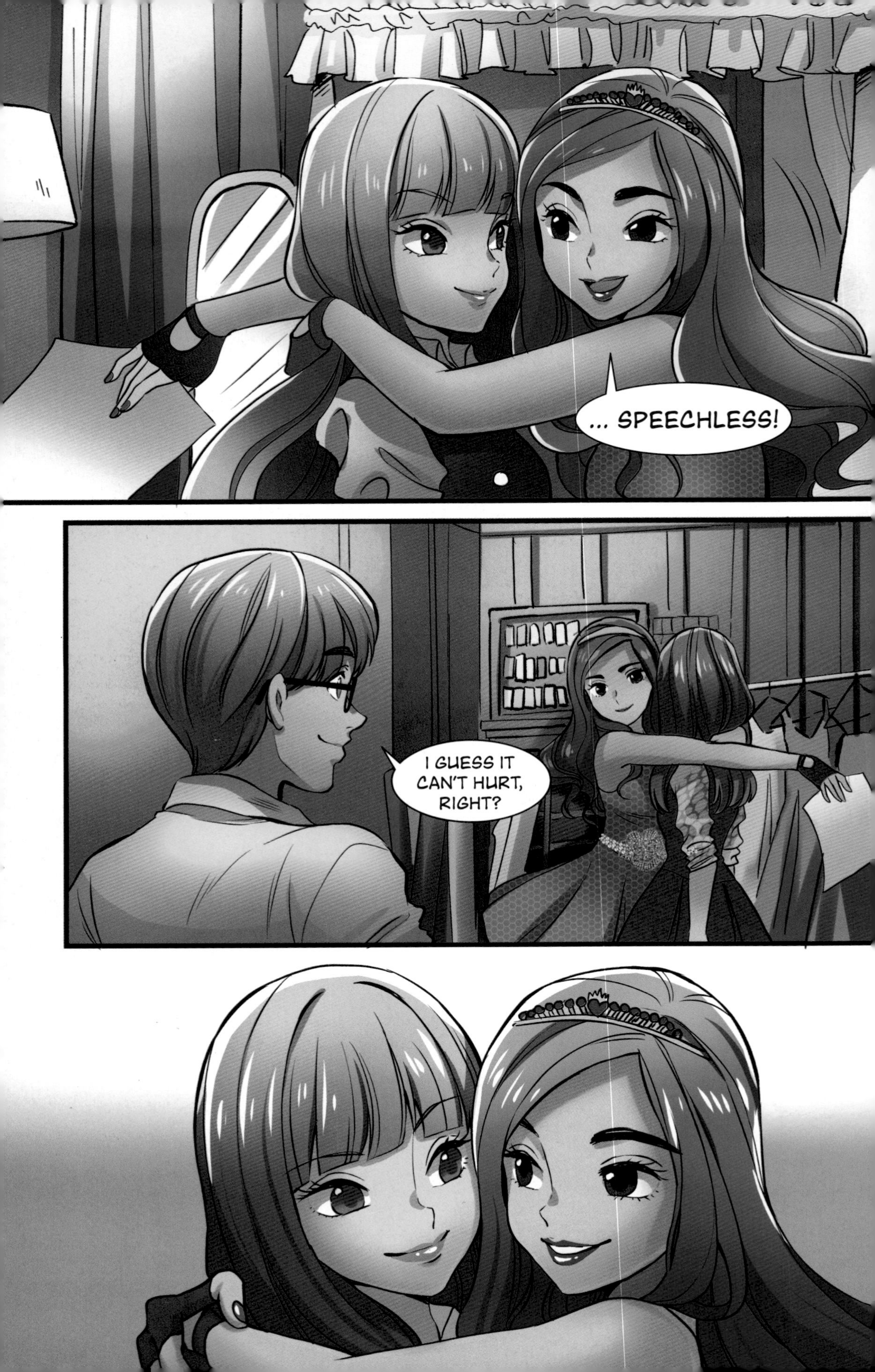
... SPEECHLESS!
I GUESS IT CAN'T HURT, RIGHT?

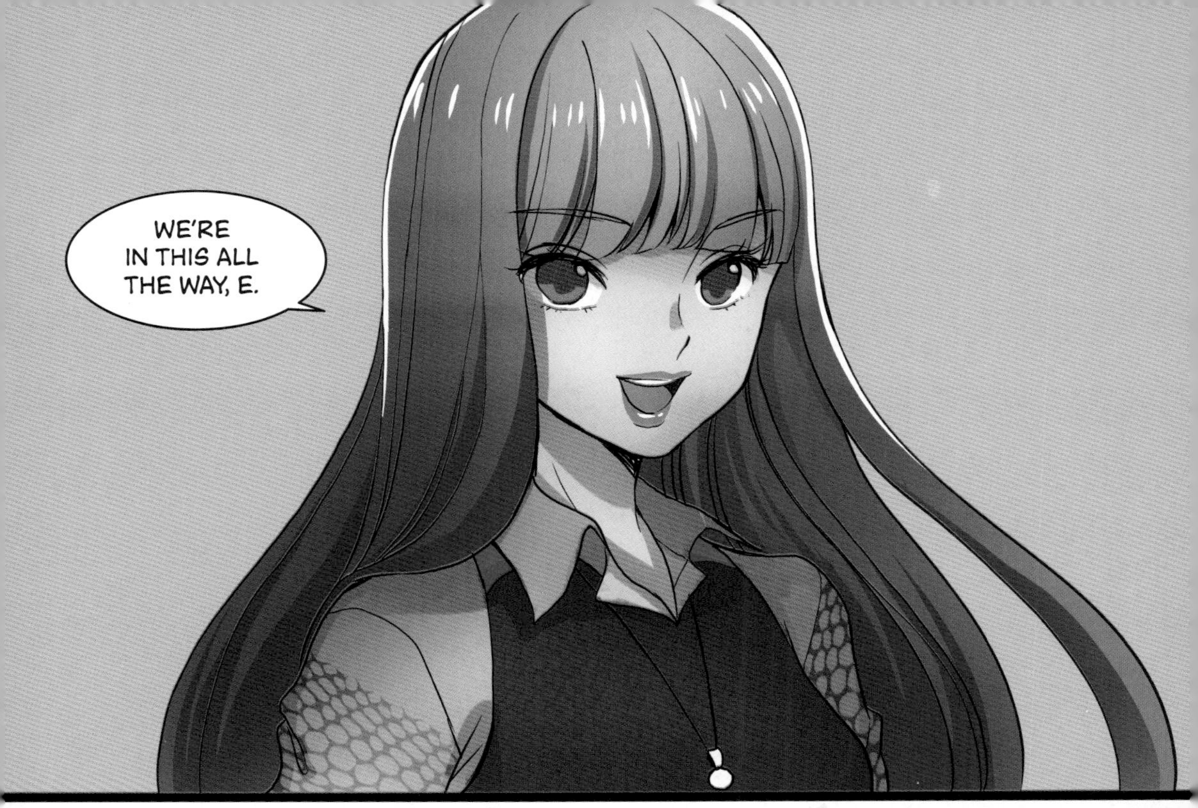
WE'RE IN THIS ALL THE WAY, E.

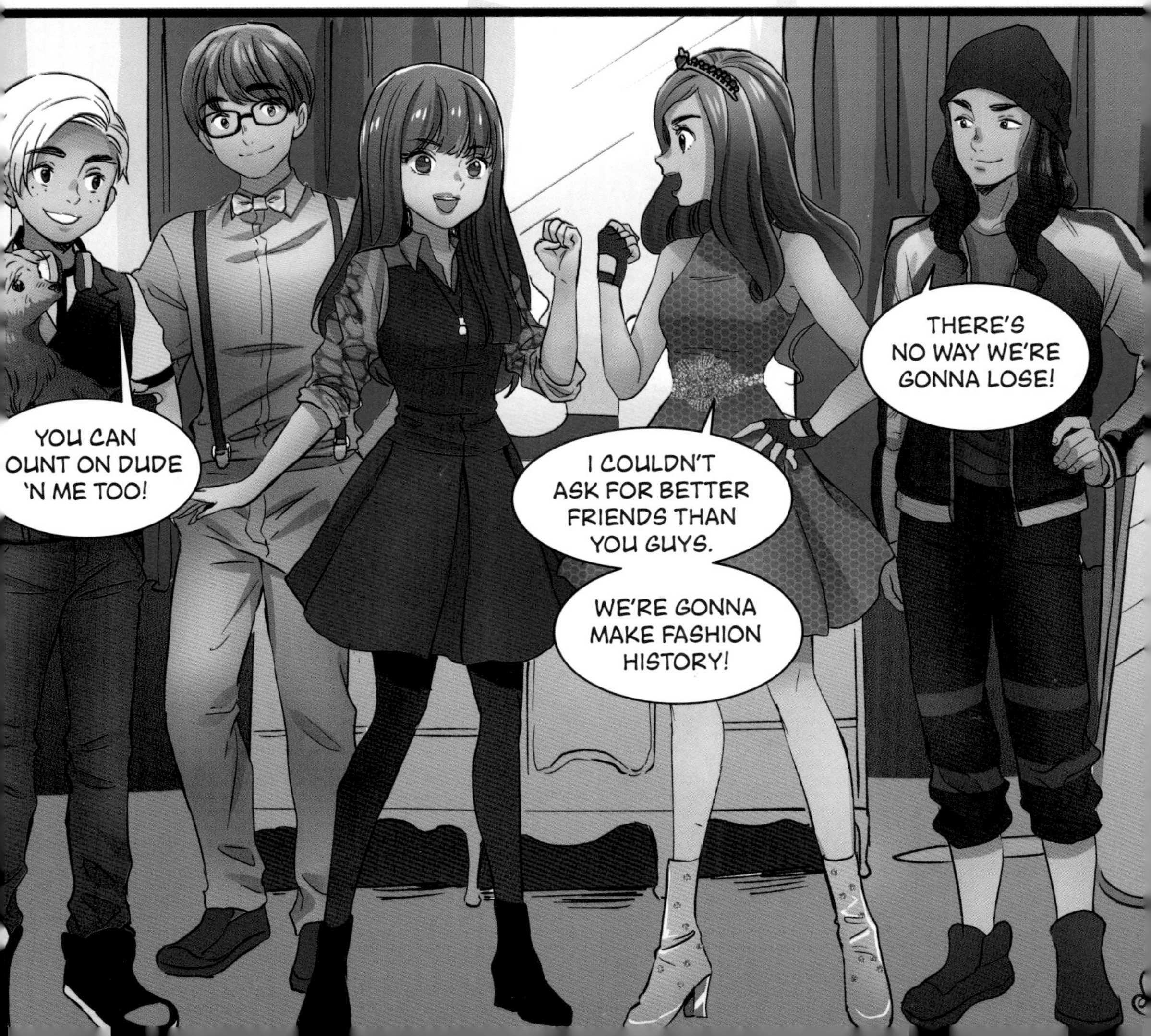
YOU CAN OUNT ON DUDE 'N ME TOO!
THERE'S NO WAY WE'RE GONNA LOSE!
I COULDN'T ASK FOR BETTER FRIENDS THAN YOU GUYS.
WE'RE GONNA MAKE FASHION HISTORY!

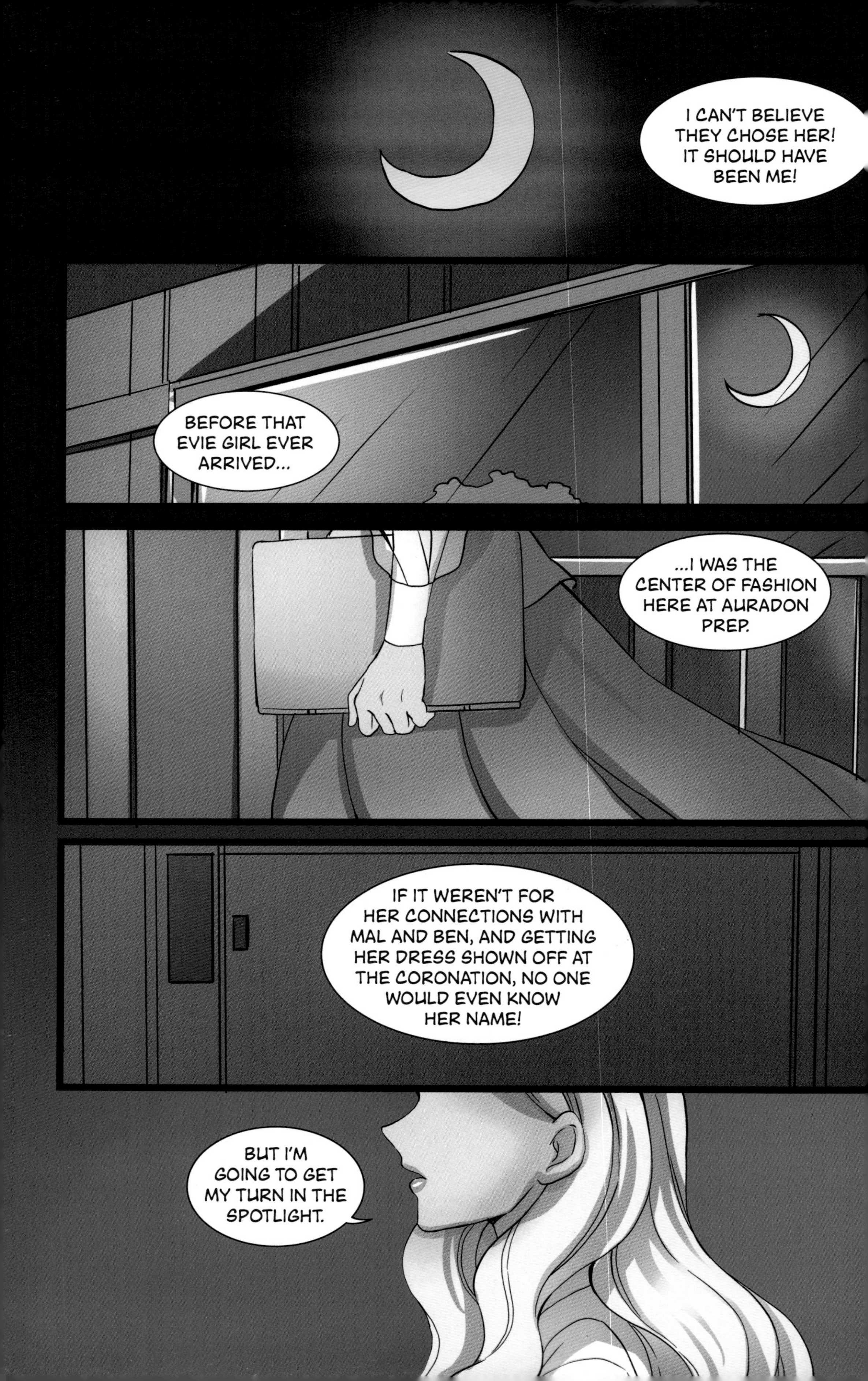
I CAN'T BELIEVE THEY CHOSE HER! IT SHOULD HAVE BEEN ME!
BEFORE THAT EVIE GIRL EVER ARRIVED...
...I WAS THE CENTER OF FASHION HERE AT AURADON PREP.
IF IT WEREN'T FOR HER CONNECTIONS WITH MAL AND BEN, AND GETTING HER DRESS SHOWN OFF AT THE CORONATION, NO ONE WOULD EVEN KNOW HER NAME!
BUT I'M GOING TO GET MY TURN IN THE SPOTLIGHT.

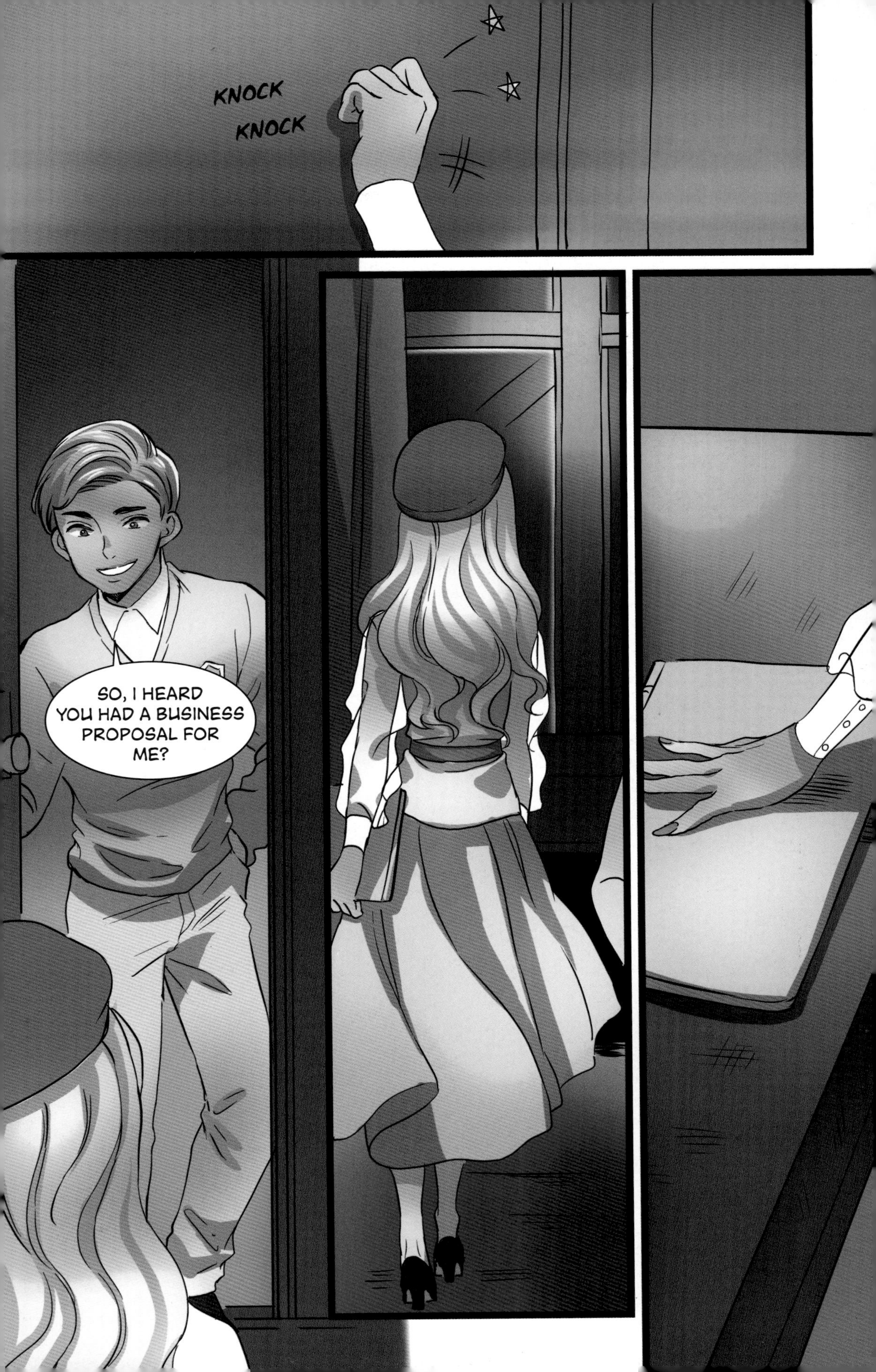
KNOCK
KNOCK
SO, I HEARD YOU HAD A BUSINESS PROPOSAL FOR ME?

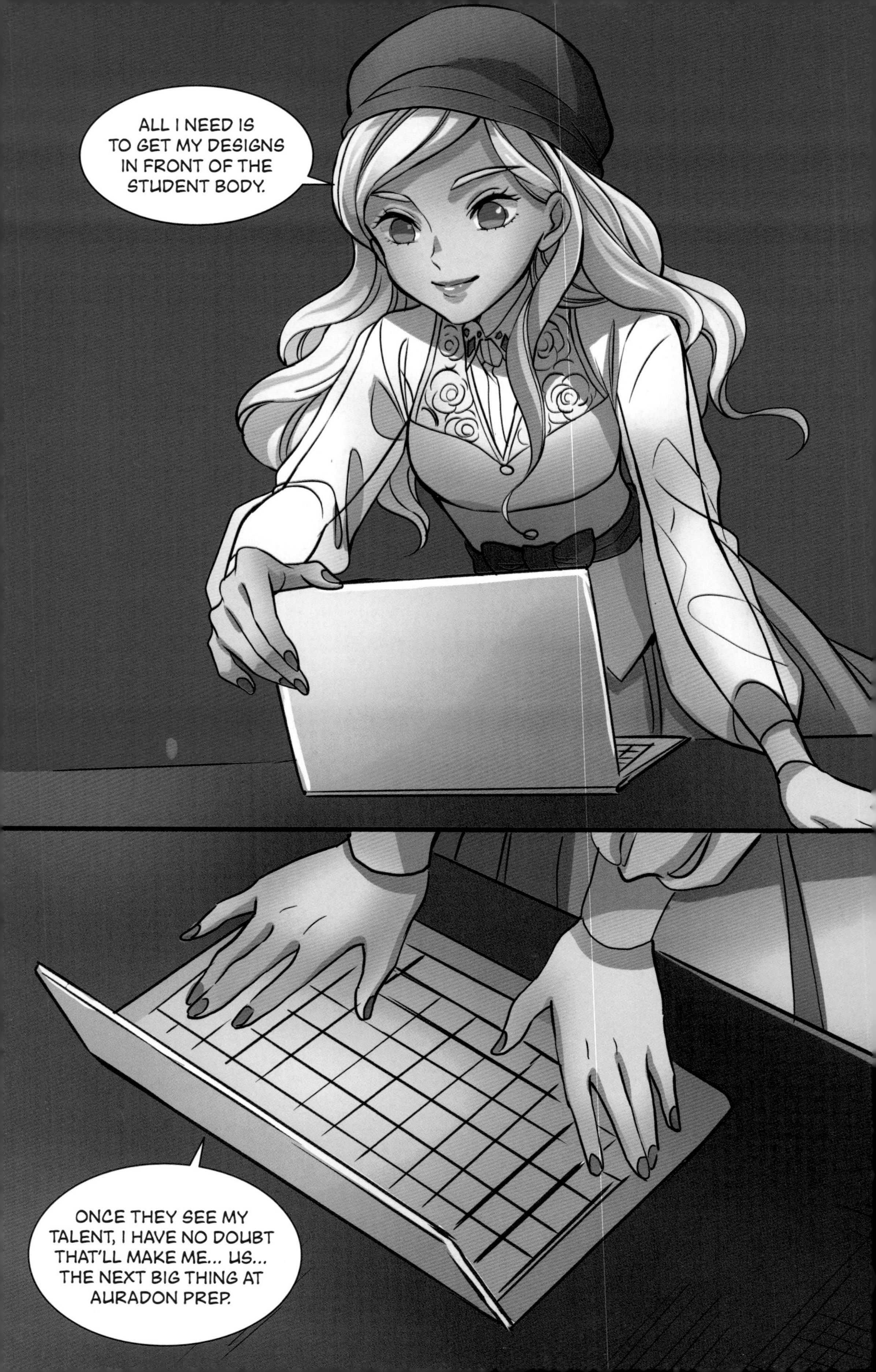
ALL I NEED IS TO GET MY DESIGNS IN FRONT OF THE STUDENT BODY.
ONCE THEY SEE MY TALENT, I HAVE NO DOUBT THAT'LL MAKE ME... US... THE NEXT BIG THING AT AURADON PREP.

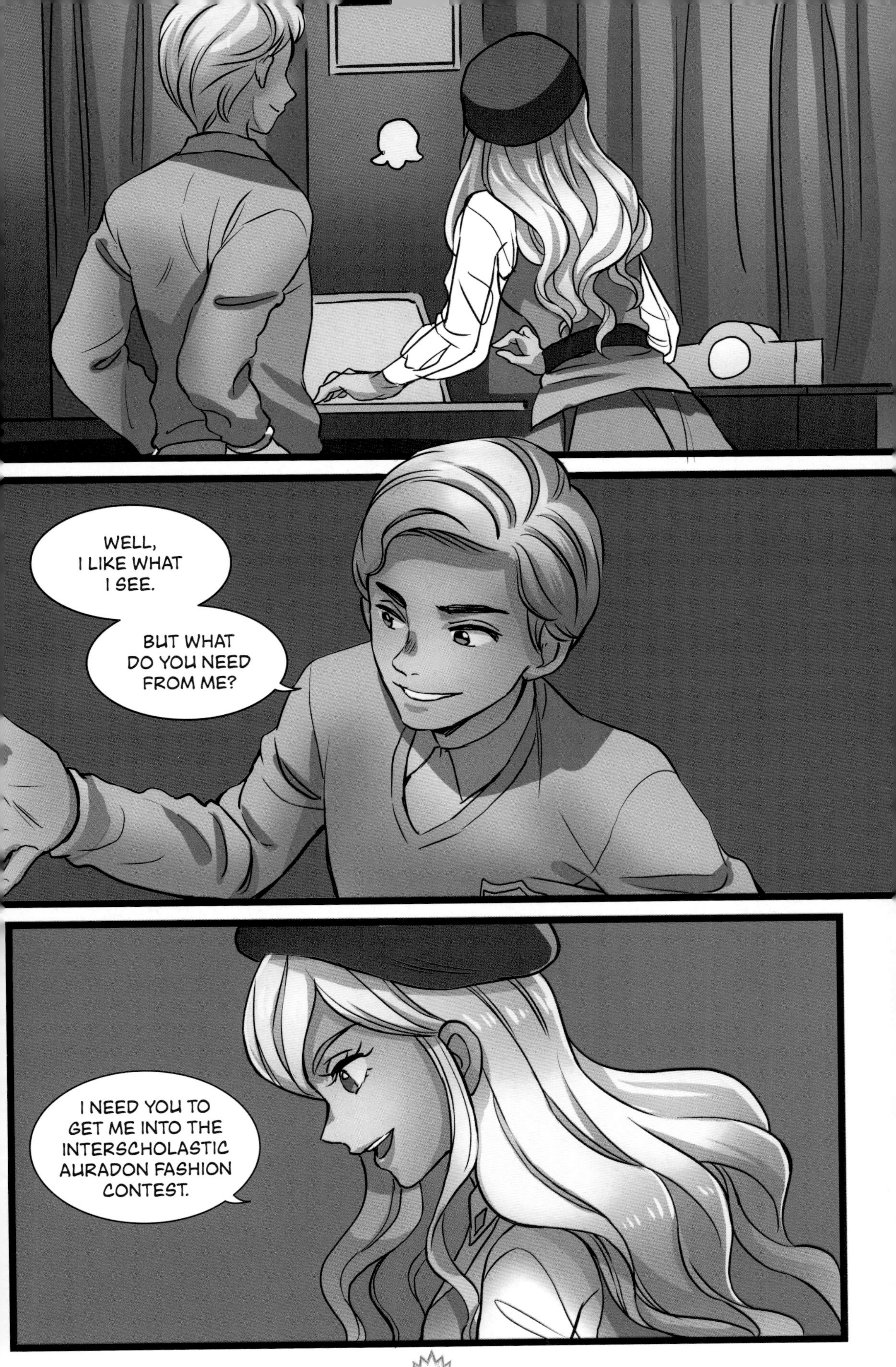
WELL, I LIKE WHAT I SEE.
BUT WHAT DO YOU NEED FROM ME?
I NEED YOU TO GET ME INTO THE INTERSCHOLASTIC AURADON FASHION CONTEST.

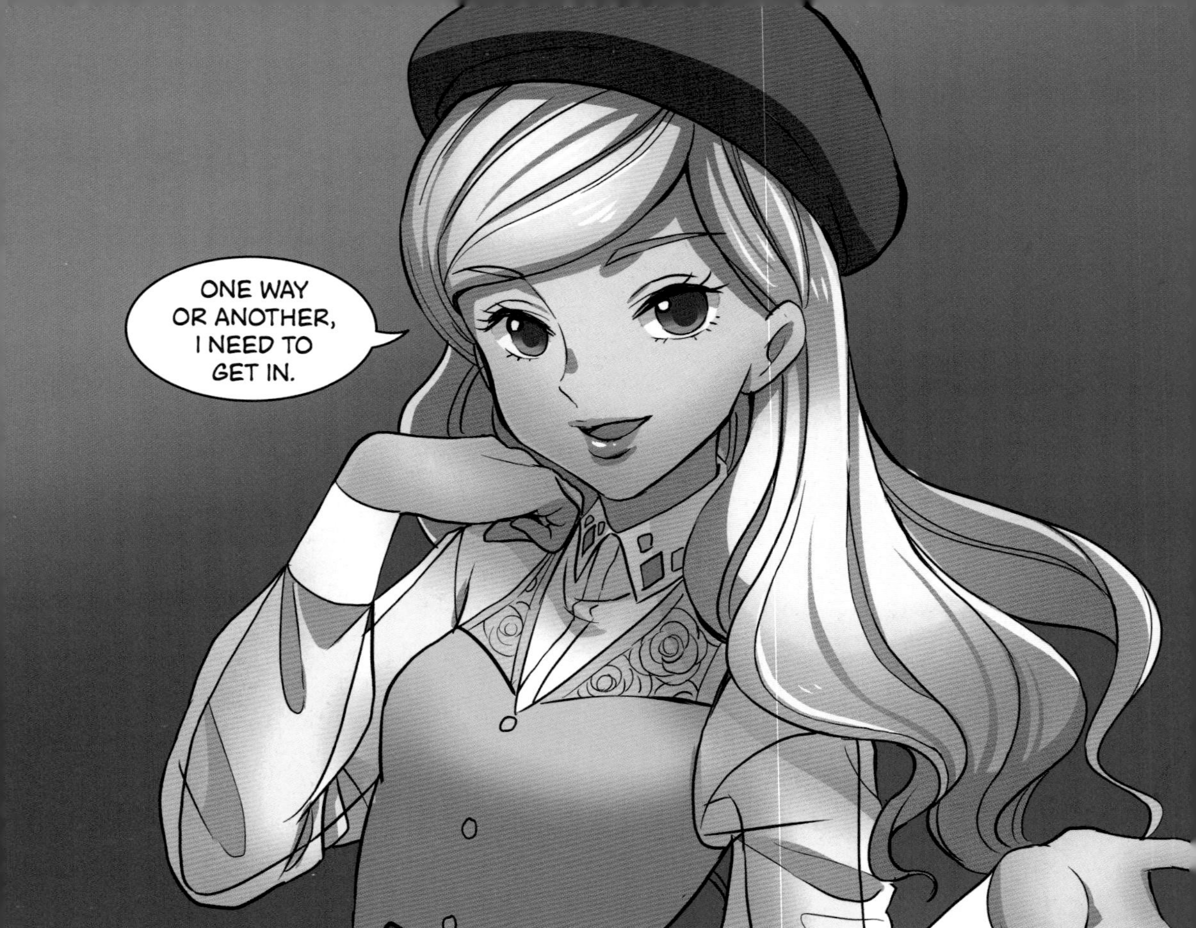
ONE WAY OR ANOTHER, I NEED TO GET IN.

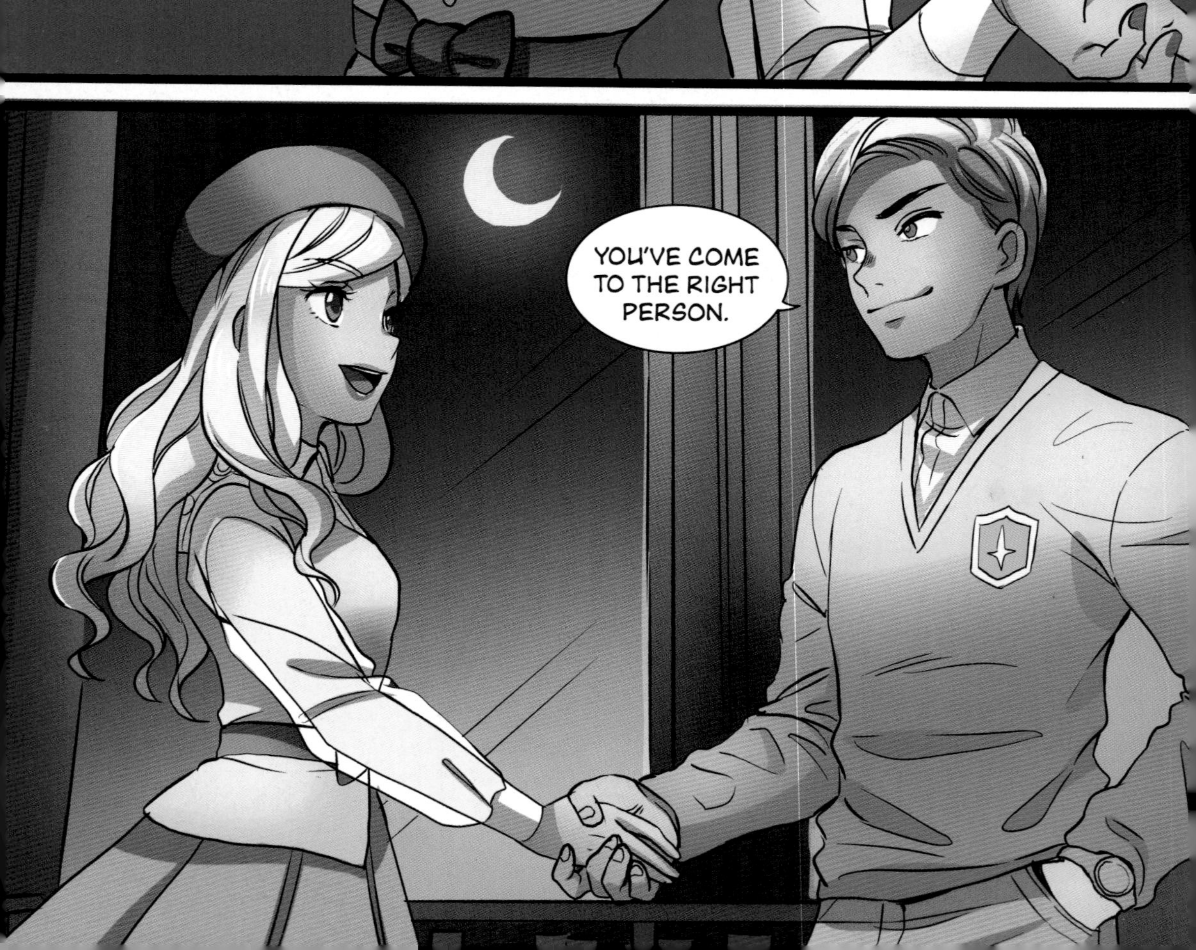
YOU'VE COME TO THE RIGHT PERSON.

EVIE'S WICKED RUNWAY

BOOK 1

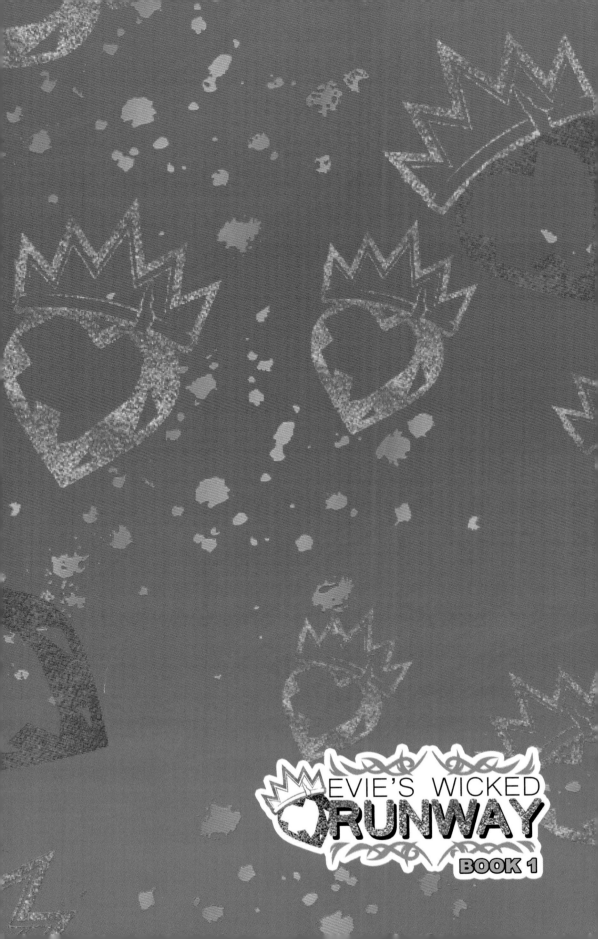

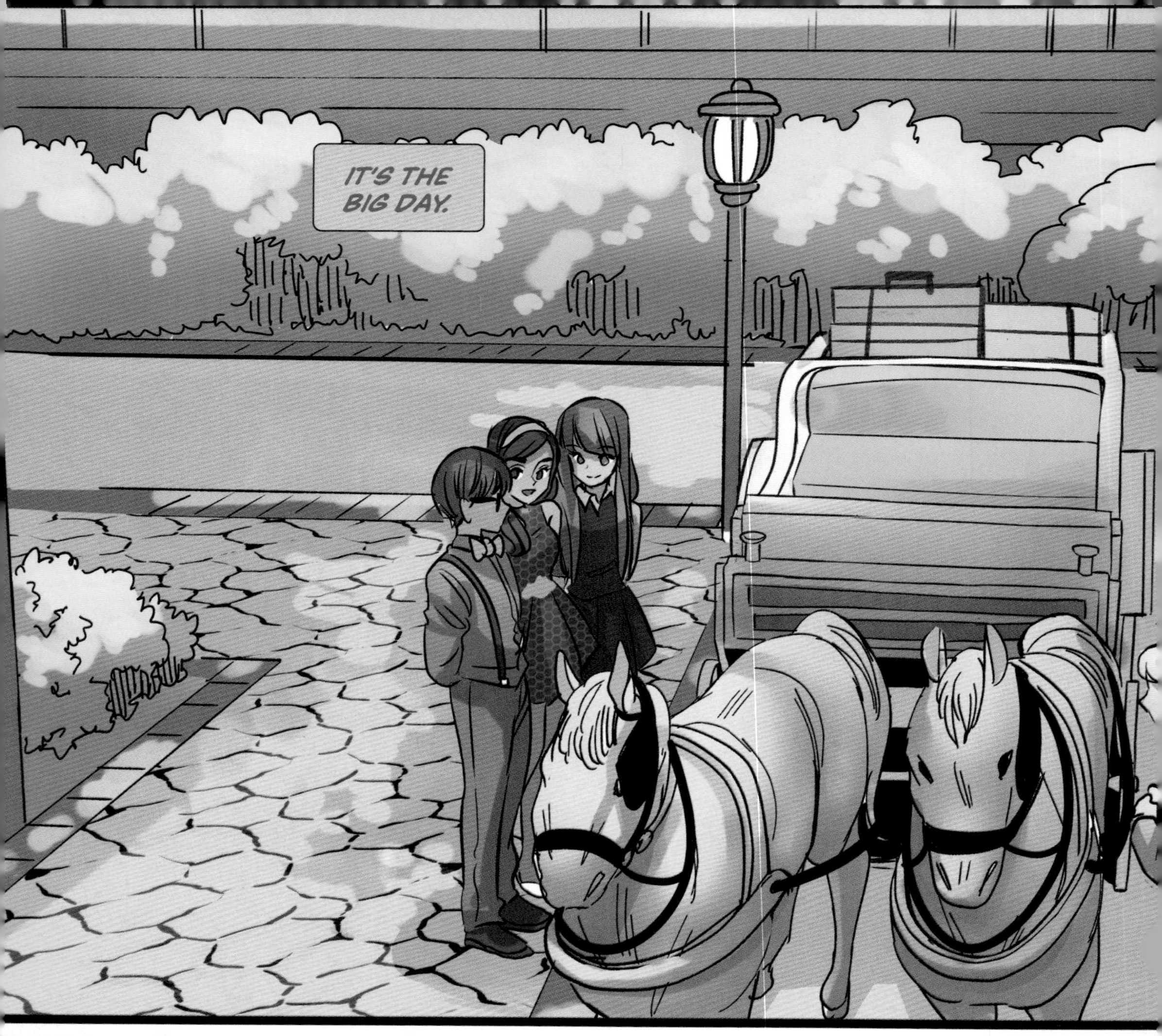
IT'S THE BIG DAY.

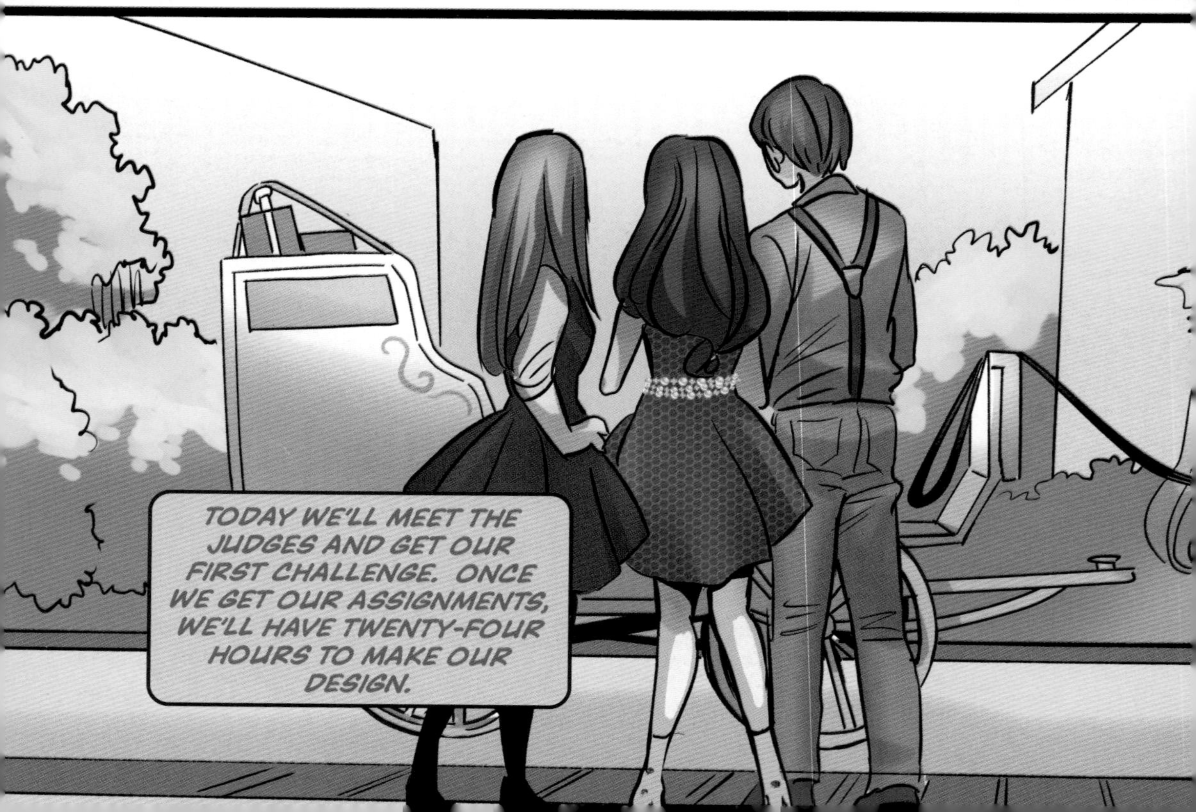
TODAY WE'LL MEET THE JUDGES AND GET OUR FIRST CHALLENGE. ONCE WE GET OUR ASSIGNMENTS, WE'LL HAVE TWENTY-FOUR HOURS TO MAKE OUR DESIGN.

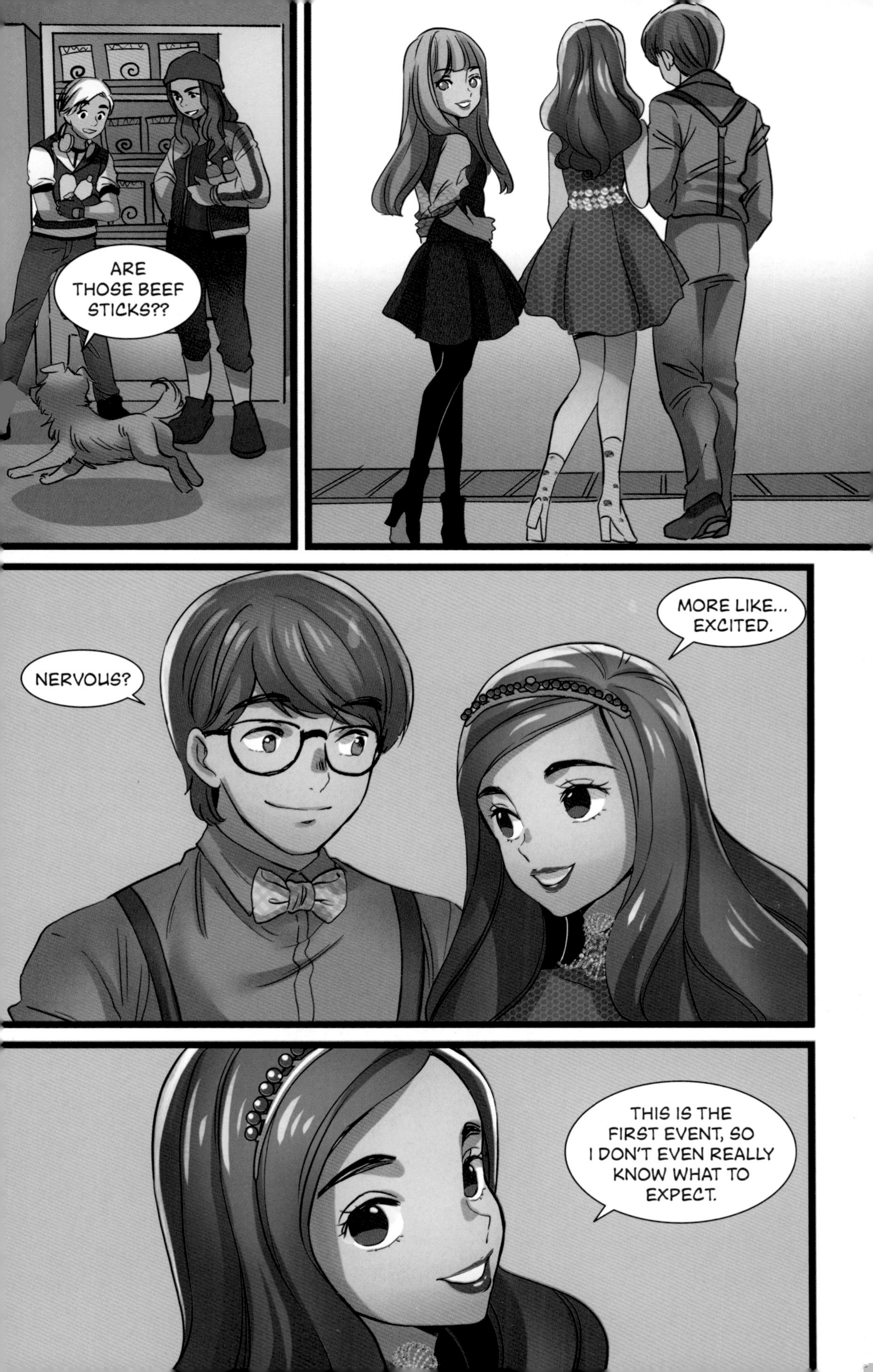
ARE THOSE BEEF STICKS??
NERVOUS?
MORE LIKE... EXCITED.
THIS IS THE FIRST EVENT, SO I DON'T EVEN REALLY KNOW WHAT TO EXPECT.

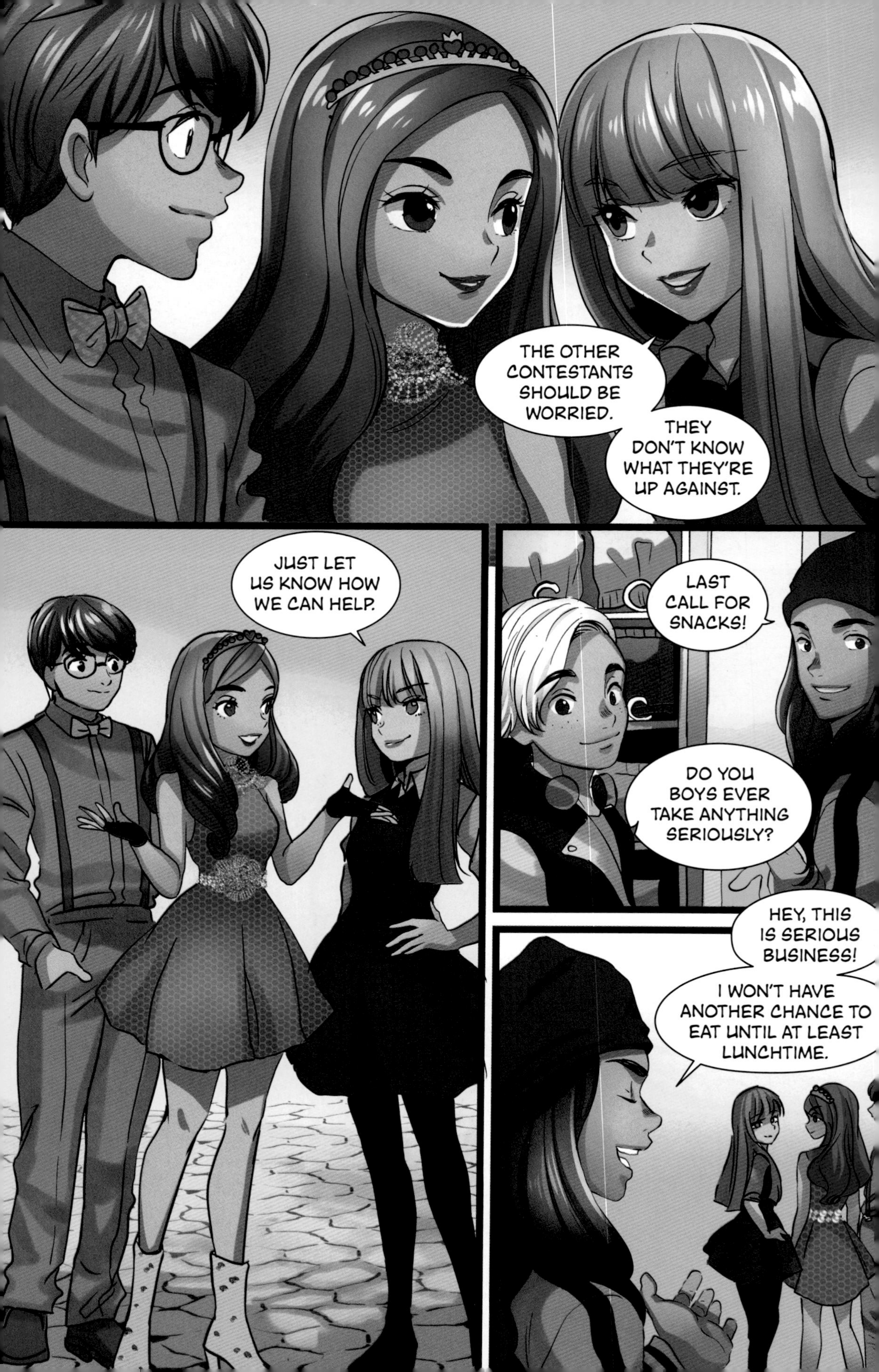
THE OTHER CONTESTANTS SHOULD BE WORRIED.
THEY DON'T KNOW WHAT THEY'RE UP AGAINST.
JUST LET US KNOW HOW WE CAN HELP.
LAST CALL FOR SNACKS!
DO YOU BOYS EVER TAKE ANYTHING SERIOUSLY?
HEY, THIS IS SERIOUS BUSINESS!
I WON'T HAVE ANOTHER CHANCE TO EAT UNTIL AT LEAST LUNCHTIME.

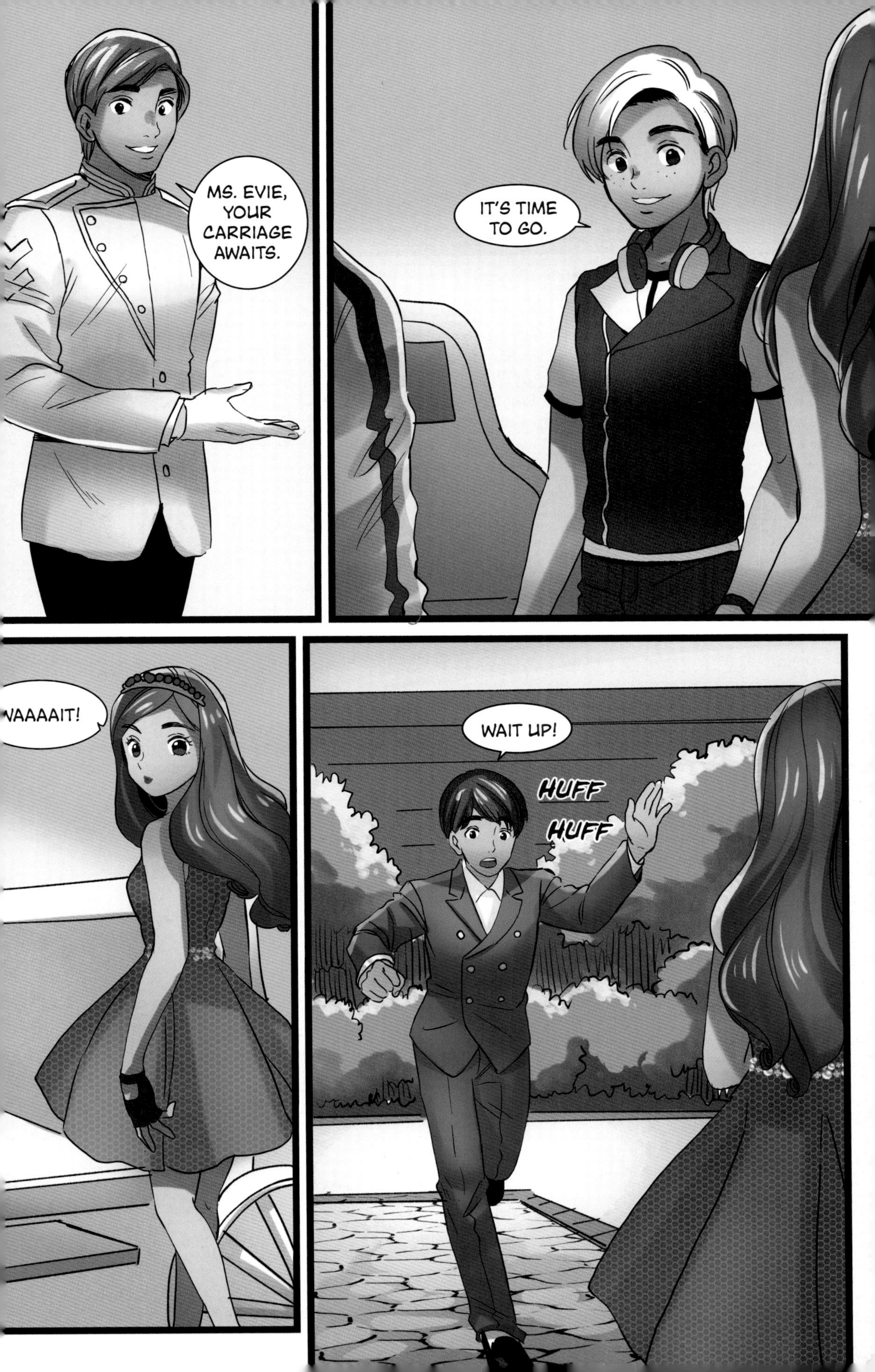
MS. EVIE, YOUR CARRIAGE AWAITS.
IT'S TIME TO GO.
WAAAAIT!
WAIT UP!
HUFF
HUFF

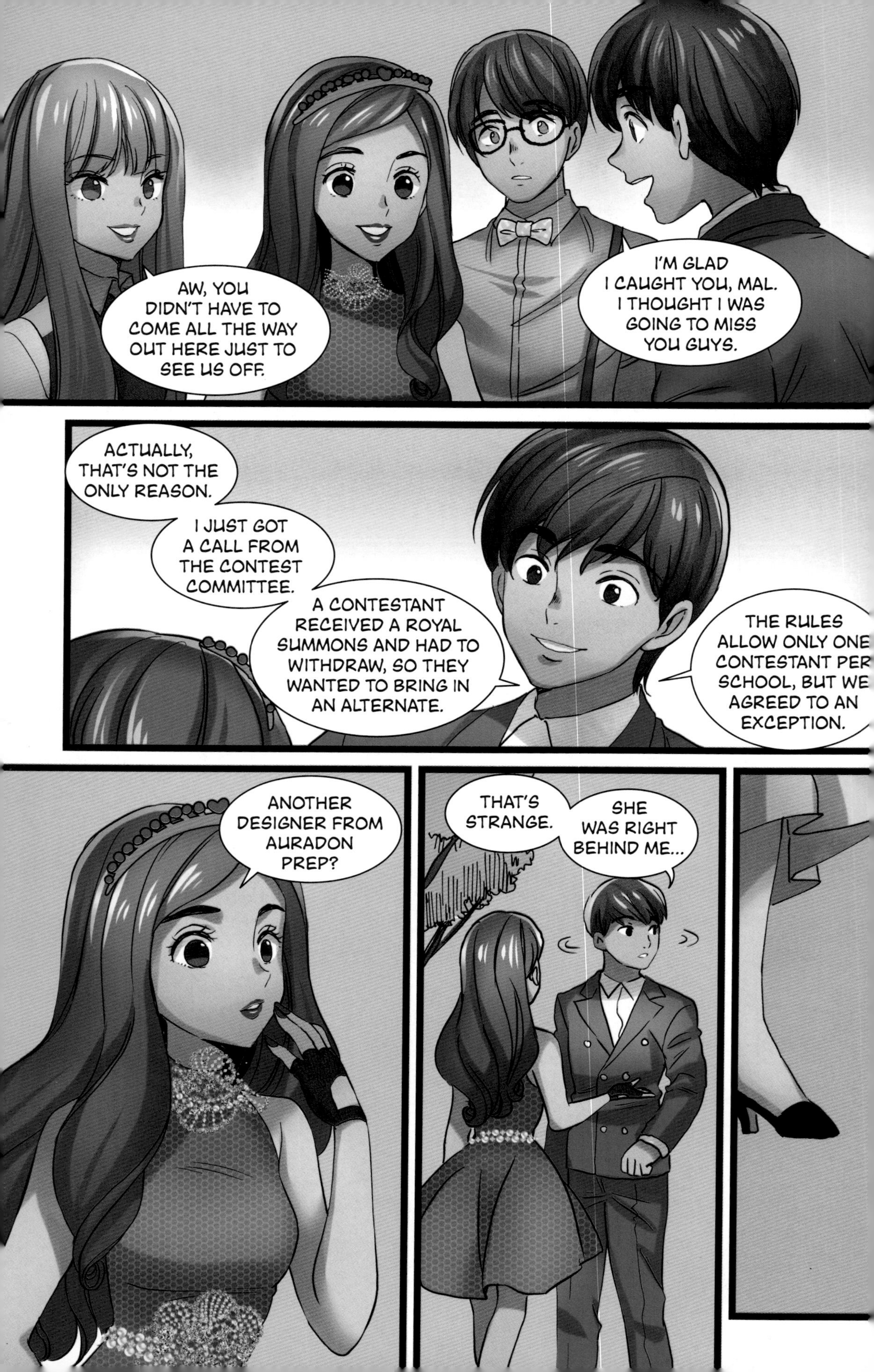
AW, YOU DIDN'T HAVE TO COME ALL THE WAY OUT HERE JUST TO SEE US OFF.
I'M GLAD I CAUGHT YOU, MAL. I THOUGHT I WAS GOING TO MISS YOU GUYS.
ACTUALLY, THAT'S NOT THE ONLY REASON.
I JUST GOT A CALL FROM THE CONTEST COMMITTEE.
A CONTESTANT RECEIVED A ROYAL SUMMONS AND HAD TO WITHDRAW, SO THEY WANTED TO BRING IN AN ALTERNATE.
THE RULES ALLOW ONLY ONE CONTESTANT PER SCHOOL, BUT WE AGREED TO AN EXCEPTION.
ANOTHER DESIGNER FROM AURADON PREP?
THAT'S STRANGE.
SHE WAS RIGHT BEHIND ME...

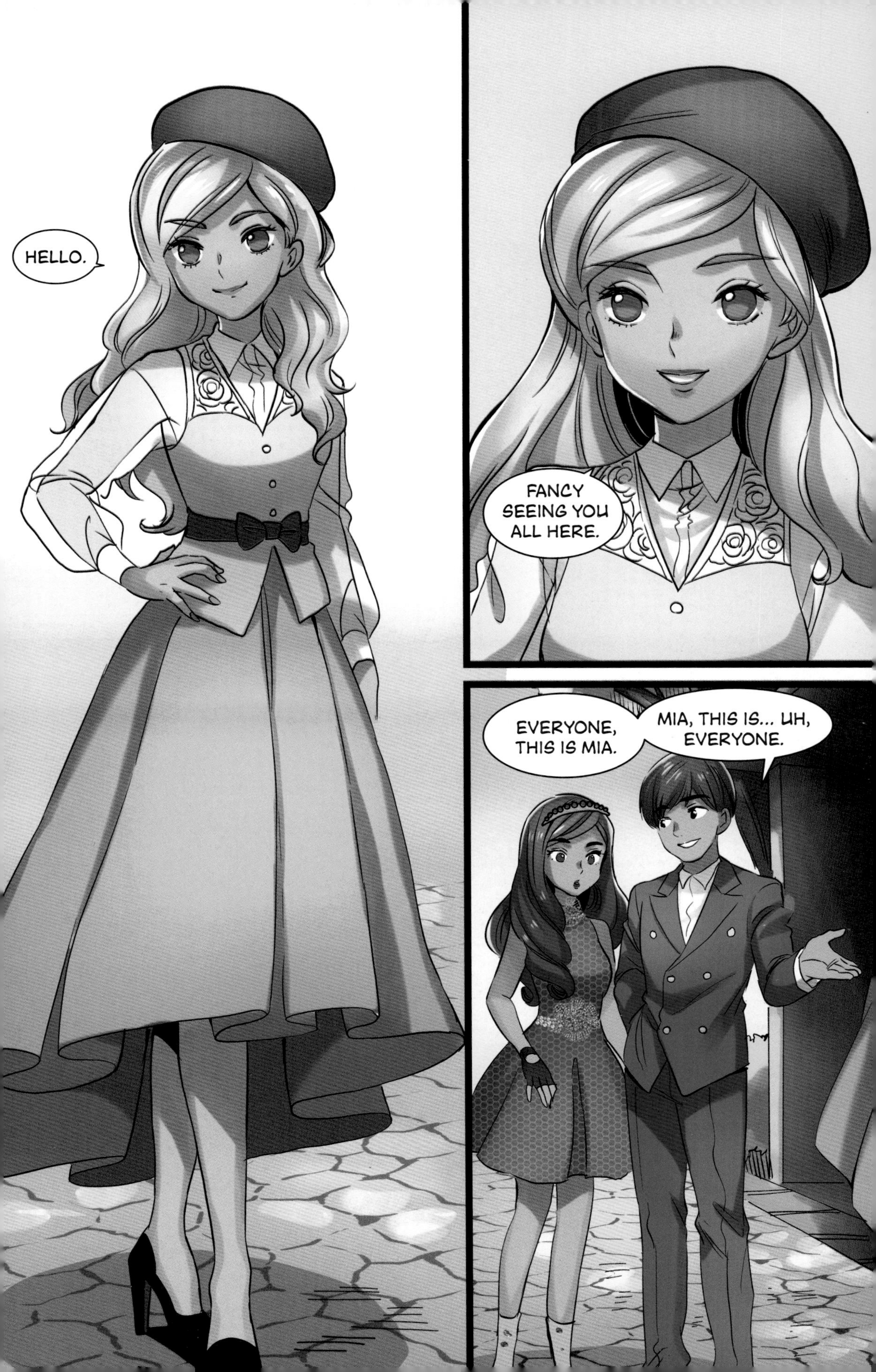
HELLO.
FANCY SEEING YOU ALL HERE.
EVERYONE, THIS IS MIA.
MIA, THIS IS... UH, EVERYONE.

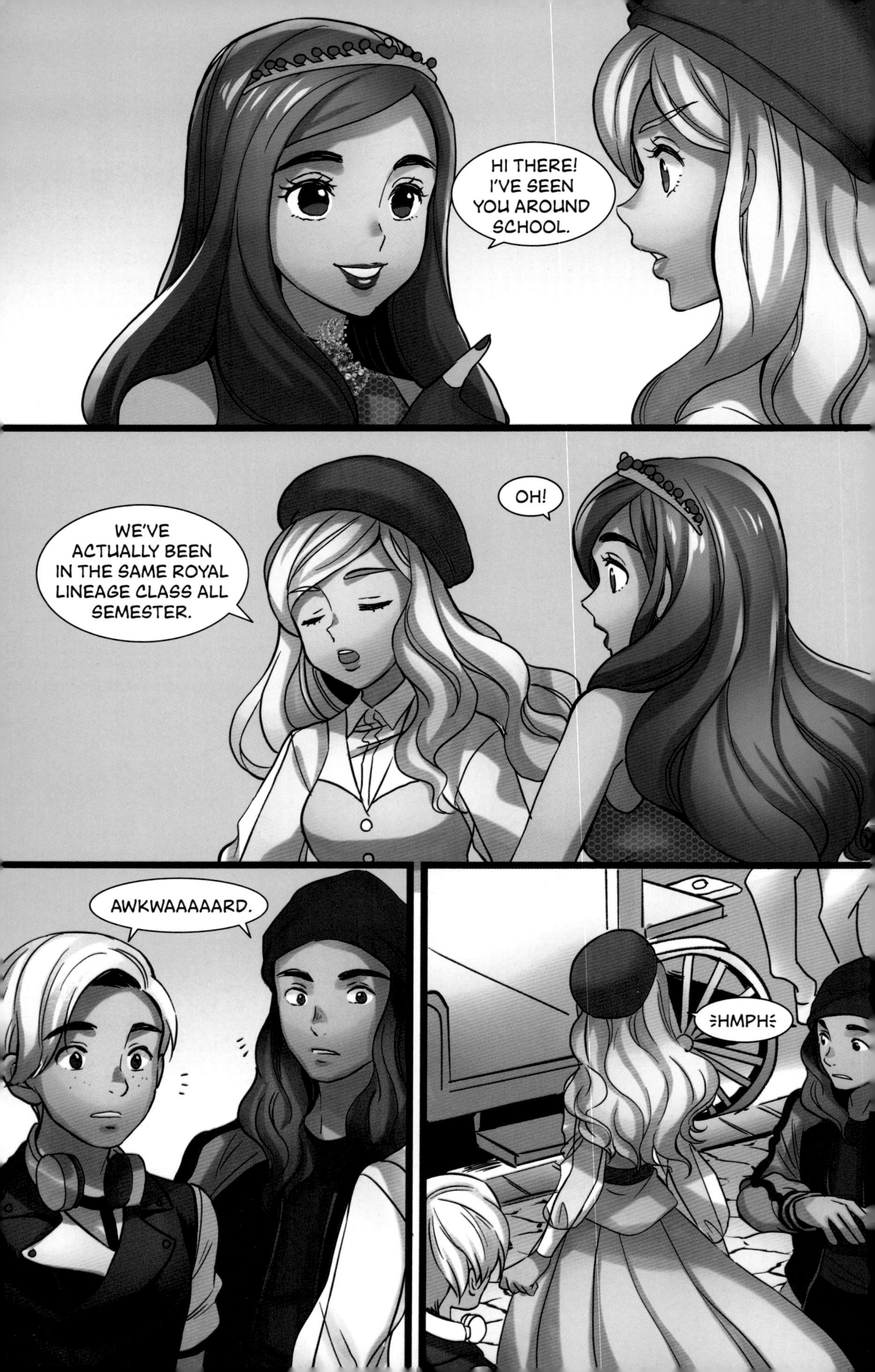
HI THERE! I'VE SEEN YOU AROUND SCHOOL.
WE'VE ACTUALLY BEEN IN THE SAME ROYAL LINEAGE CLASS ALL SEMESTER.
OH!
AWKWAAAAARD.
HMPH

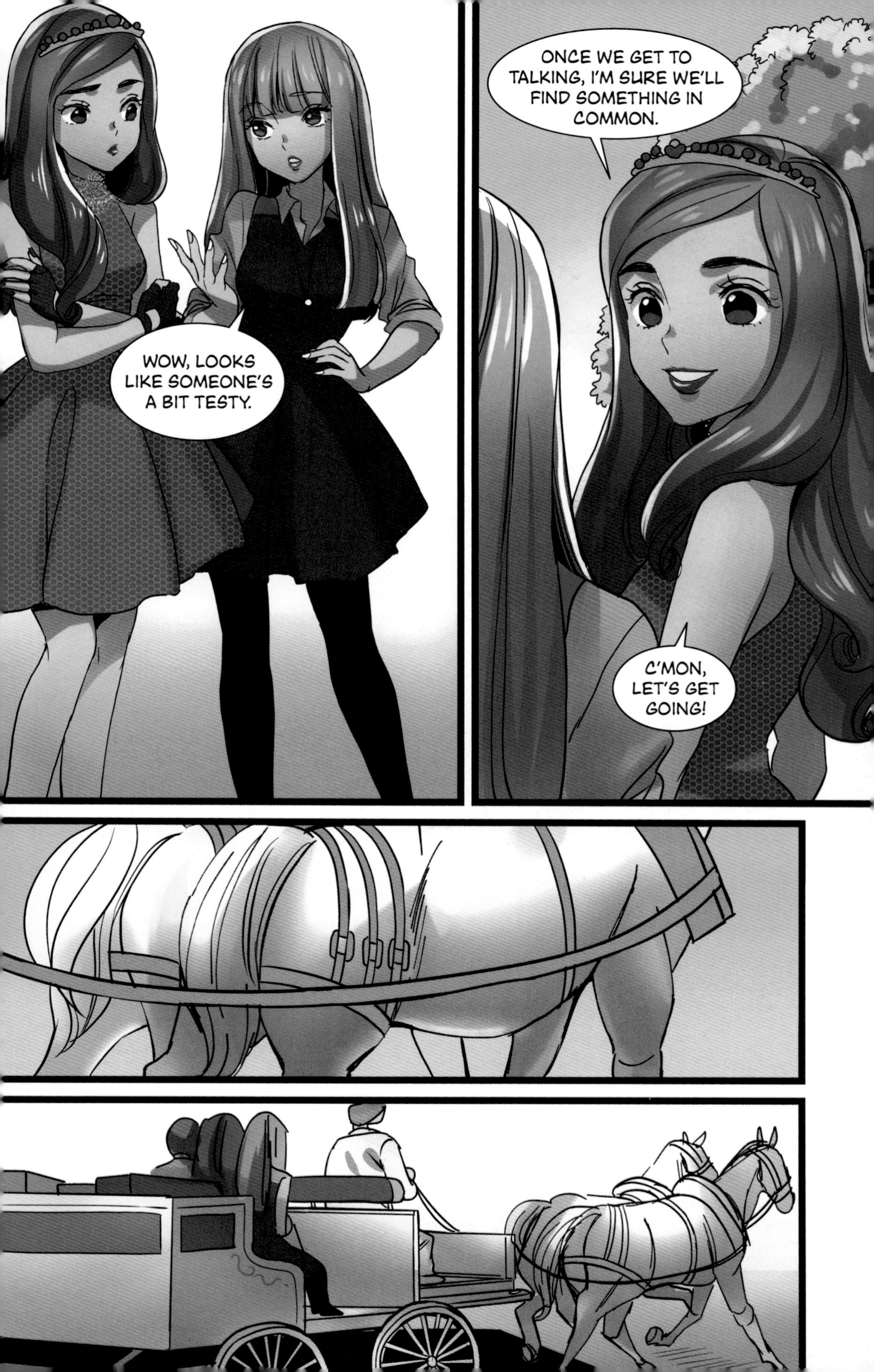
WOW, LOOKS LIKE SOMEONE'S A BIT TESTY.
ONCE WE GET TO TALKING, I'M SURE WE'LL FIND SOMETHING IN COMMON.
C'MON, LET'S GET GOING!

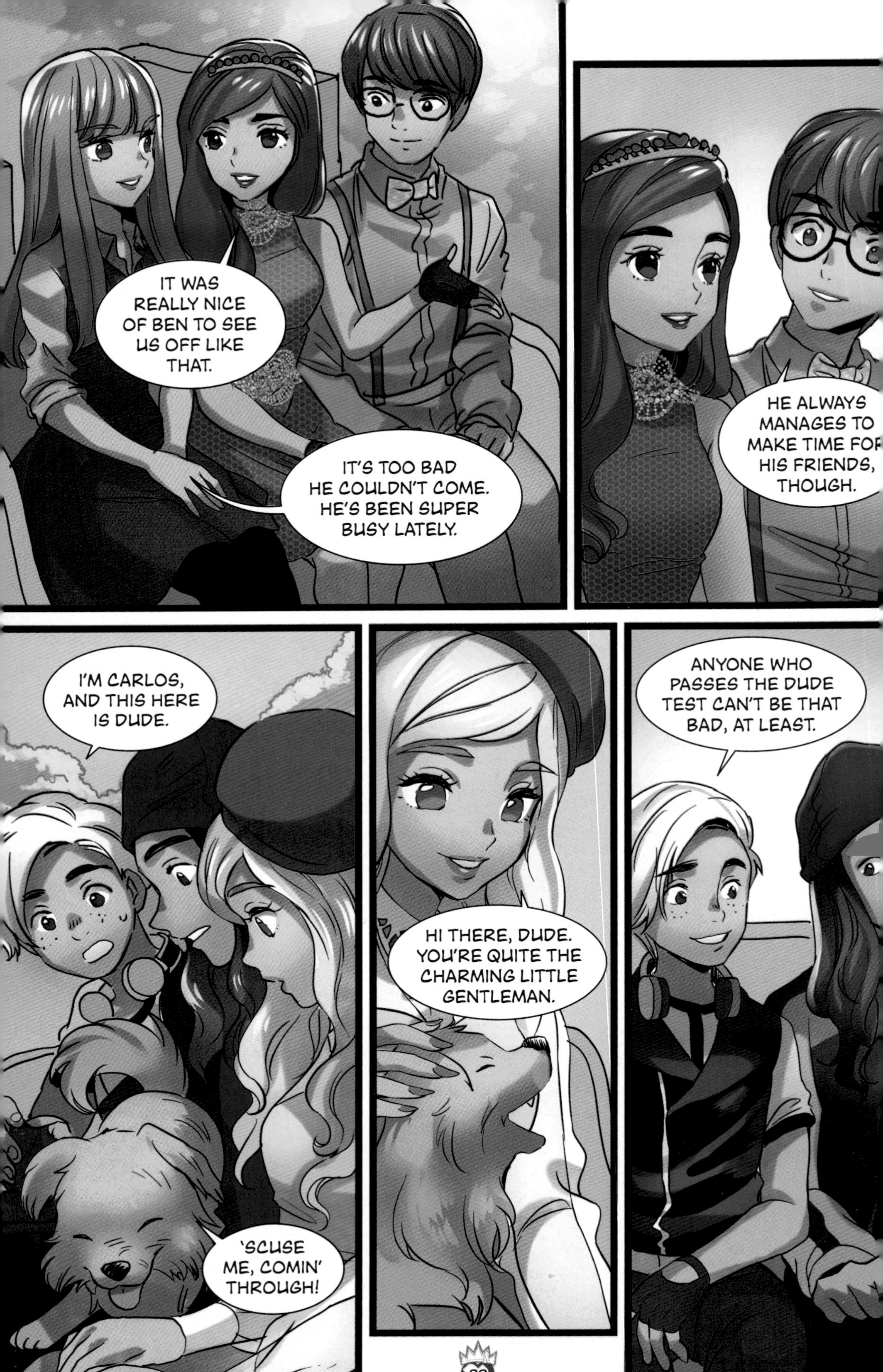
IT WAS REALLY NICE OF BEN TO SEE US OFF LIKE THAT.
IT'S TOO BAD HE COULDN'T COME. HE'S BEEN SUPER BUSY LATELY.
HE ALWAYS MANAGES TO MAKE TIME FOR HIS FRIENDS, THOUGH.
I'M CARLOS, AND THIS HERE IS DUDE.
'SCUSE ME, COMIN' THROUGH!
HI THERE, DUDE. YOU'RE QUITE THE CHARMING LITTLE GENTLEMAN.
ANYONE WHO PASSES THE DUDE TEST CAN'T BE THAT BAD, AT LEAST.

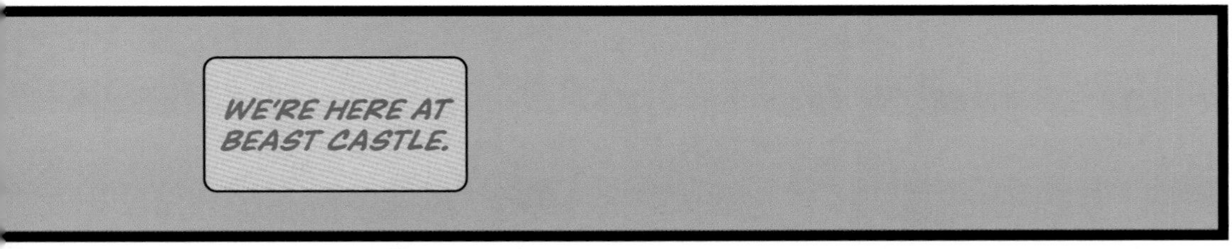
WE'RE HERE AT BEAST CASTLE.
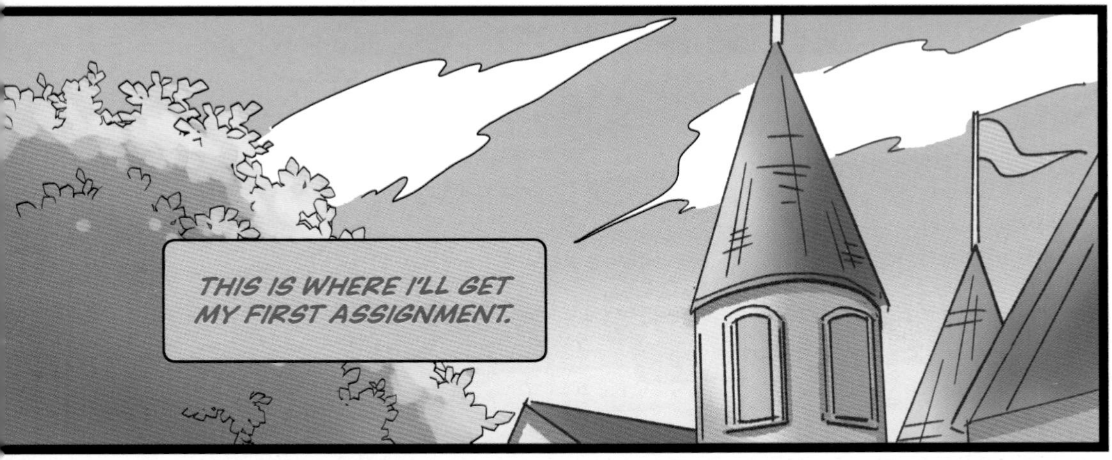
THIS IS WHERE I'LL GET MY FIRST ASSIGNMENT.
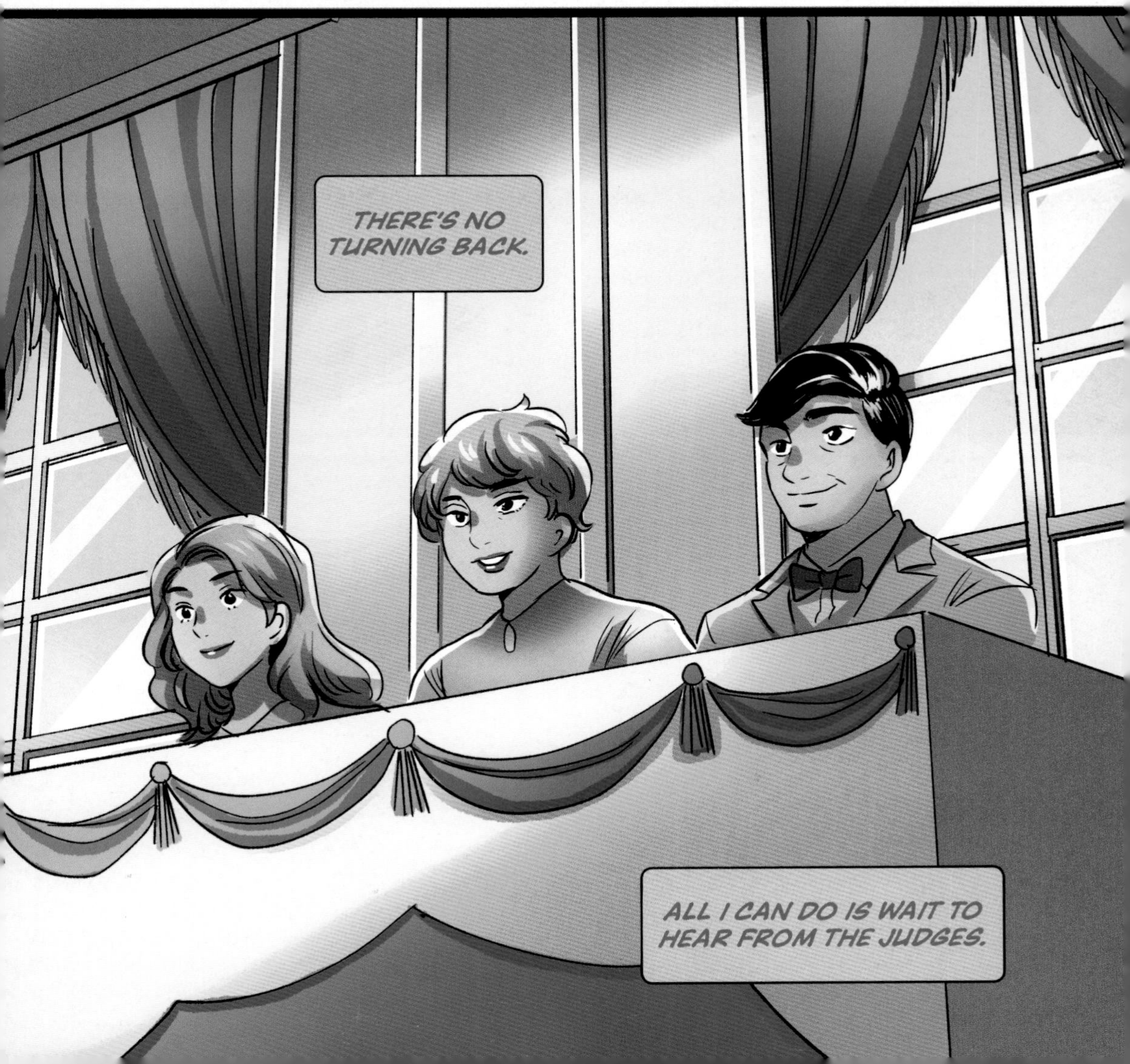
THERE'S NO TURNING BACK.
ALL I CAN DO IS WAIT TO HEAR FROM THE JUDGES.

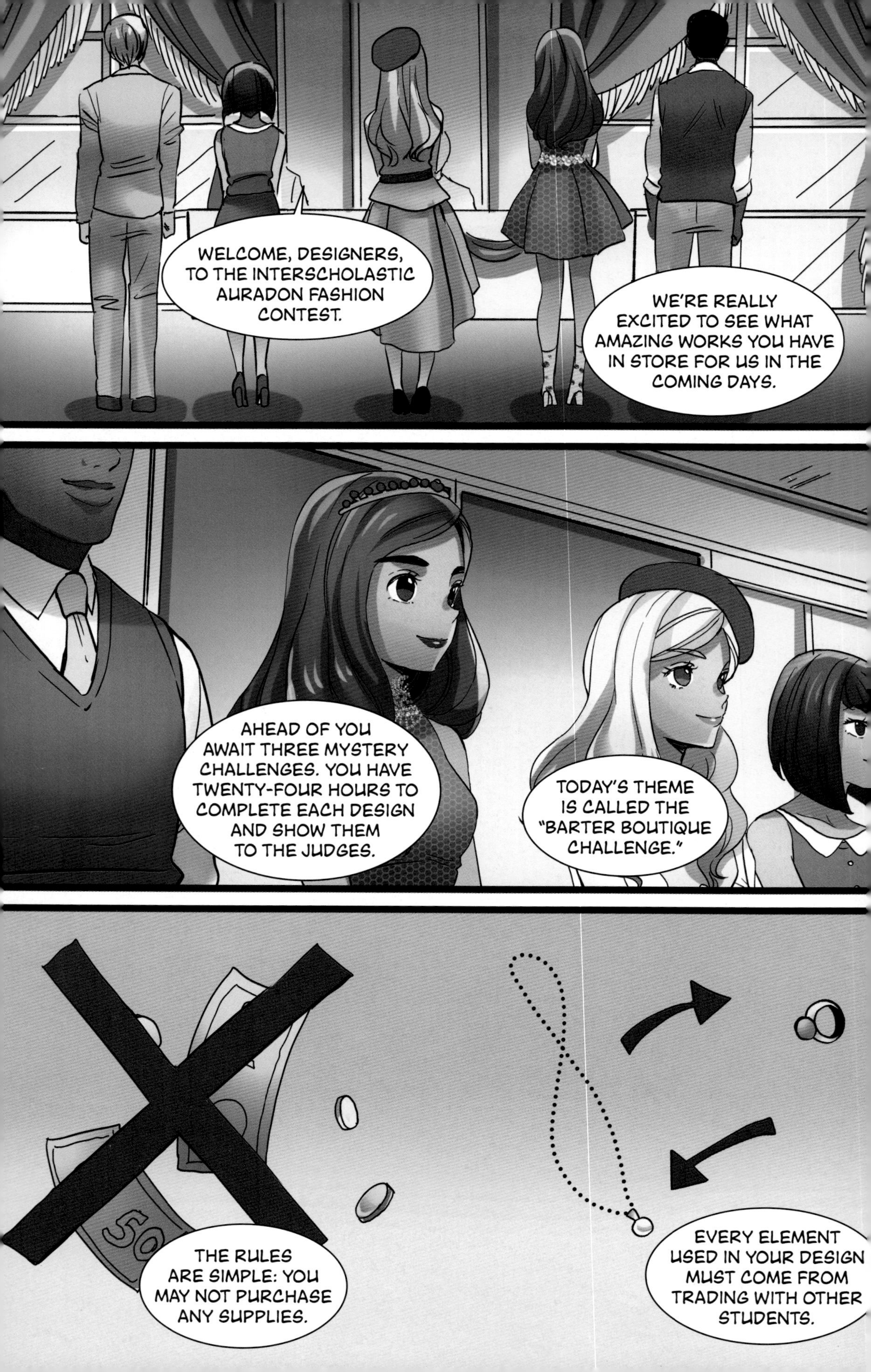
WELCOME, DESIGNERS, TO THE INTERSCHOLASTIC AURADON FASHION CONTEST.
WE'RE REALLY EXCITED TO SEE WHAT AMAZING WORKS YOU HAVE IN STORE FOR US IN THE COMING DAYS.
AHEAD OF YOU AWAIT THREE MYSTERY CHALLENGES. YOU HAVE TWENTY-FOUR HOURS TO COMPLETE EACH DESIGN AND SHOW THEM TO THE JUDGES.
TODAY'S THEME IS CALLED THE "BARTER BOUTIQUE CHALLENGE."
50
THE RULES ARE SIMPLE: YOU MAY NOT PURCHASE ANY SUPPLIES.
EVERY ELEMENT USED IN YOUR DESIGN MUST COME FROM TRADING WITH OTHER STUDENTS.

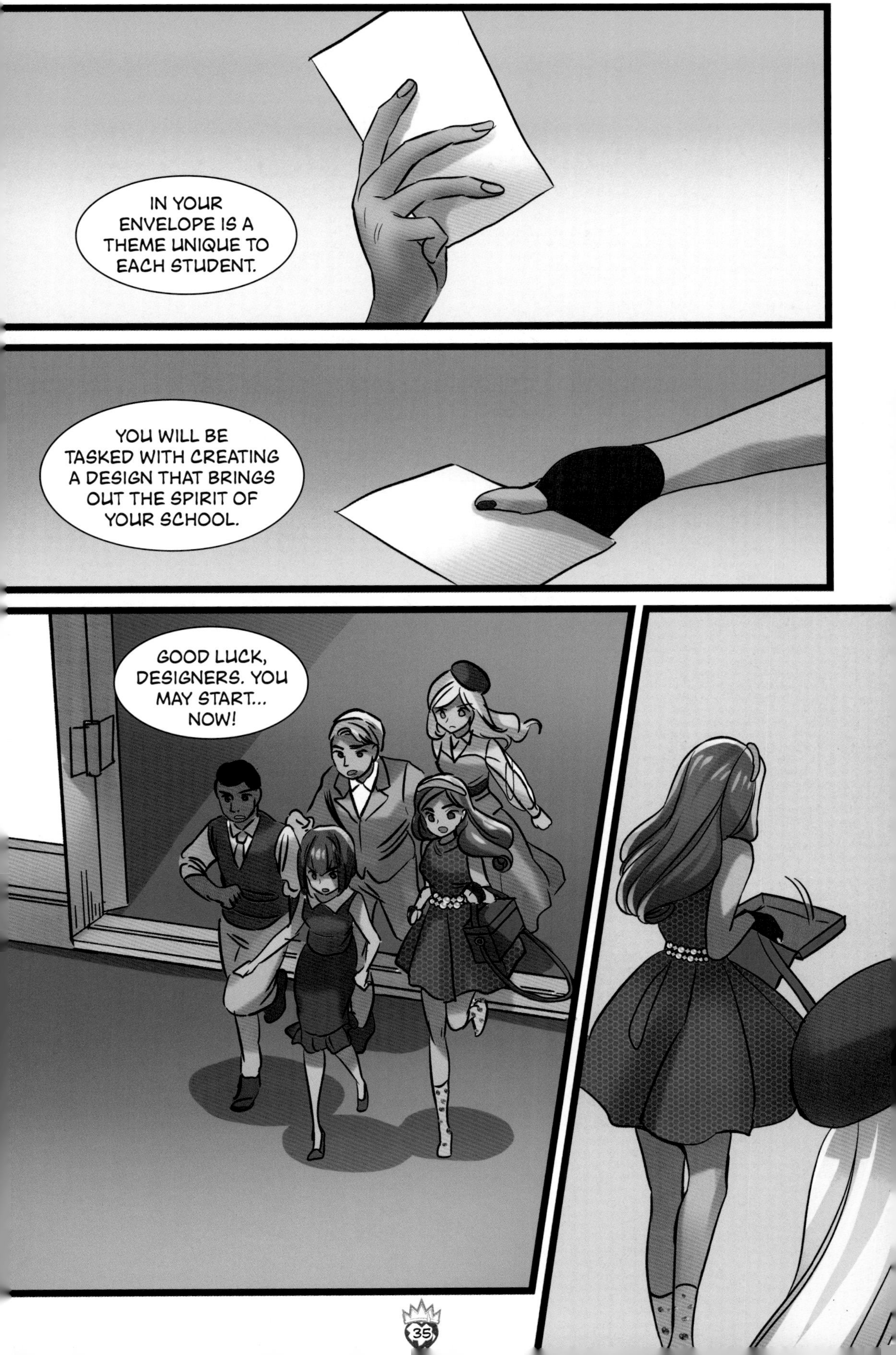
IN YOUR ENVELOPE IS A THEME UNIQUE TO EACH STUDENT.
YOU WILL BE TASKED WITH CREATING A DESIGN THAT BRINGS OUT THE SPIRIT OF YOUR SCHOOL.
GOOD LUCK, DESIGNERS. YOU MAY START... NOW!

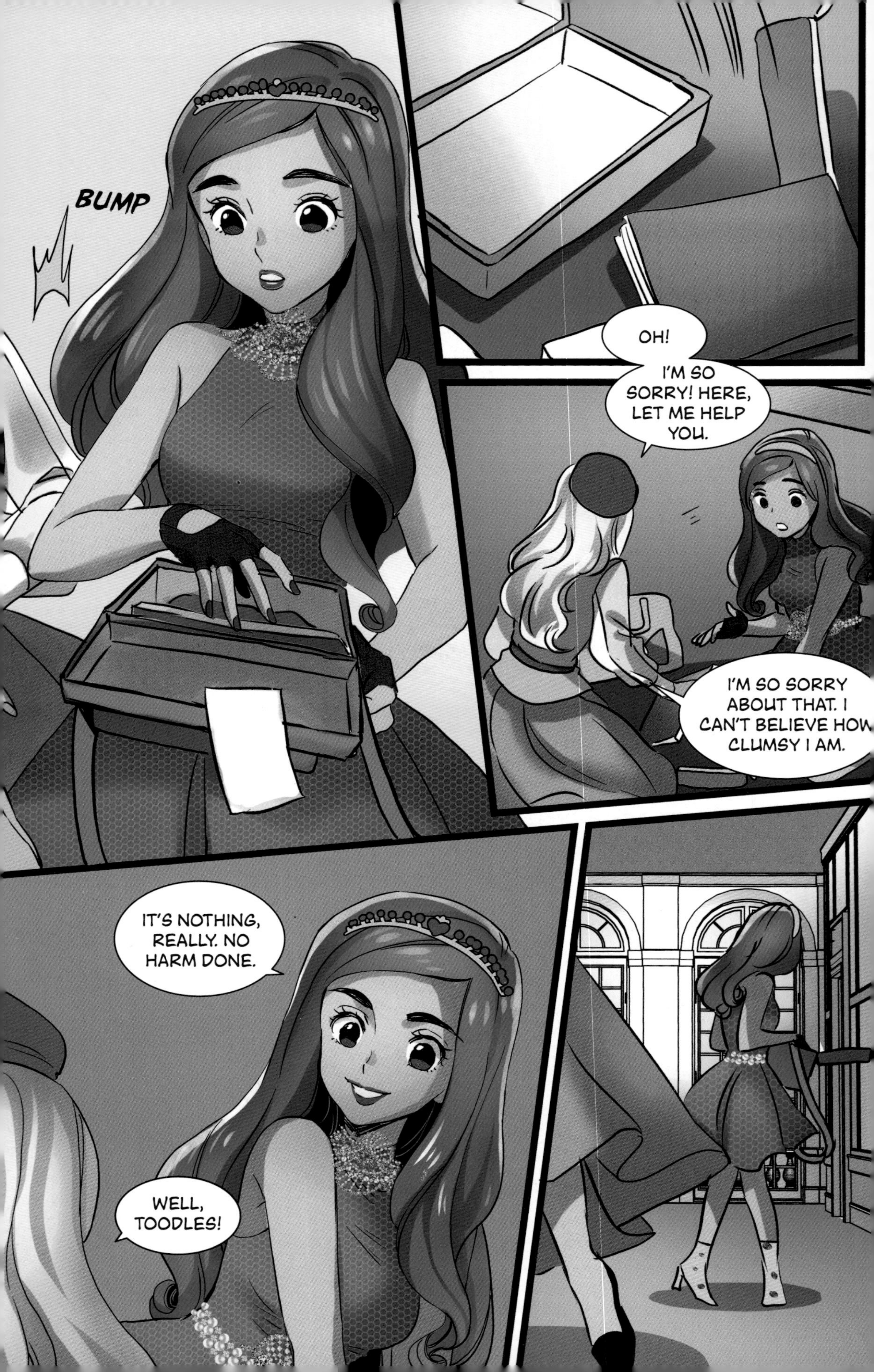
BUMP
OH!
I'M SO SORRY! HERE, LET ME HELP YOU.
I'M SO SORRY ABOUT THAT. I CAN'T BELIEVE HOW CLUMSY I AM.
IT'S NOTHING, REALLY. NO HARM DONE.
WELL, TOODLES!

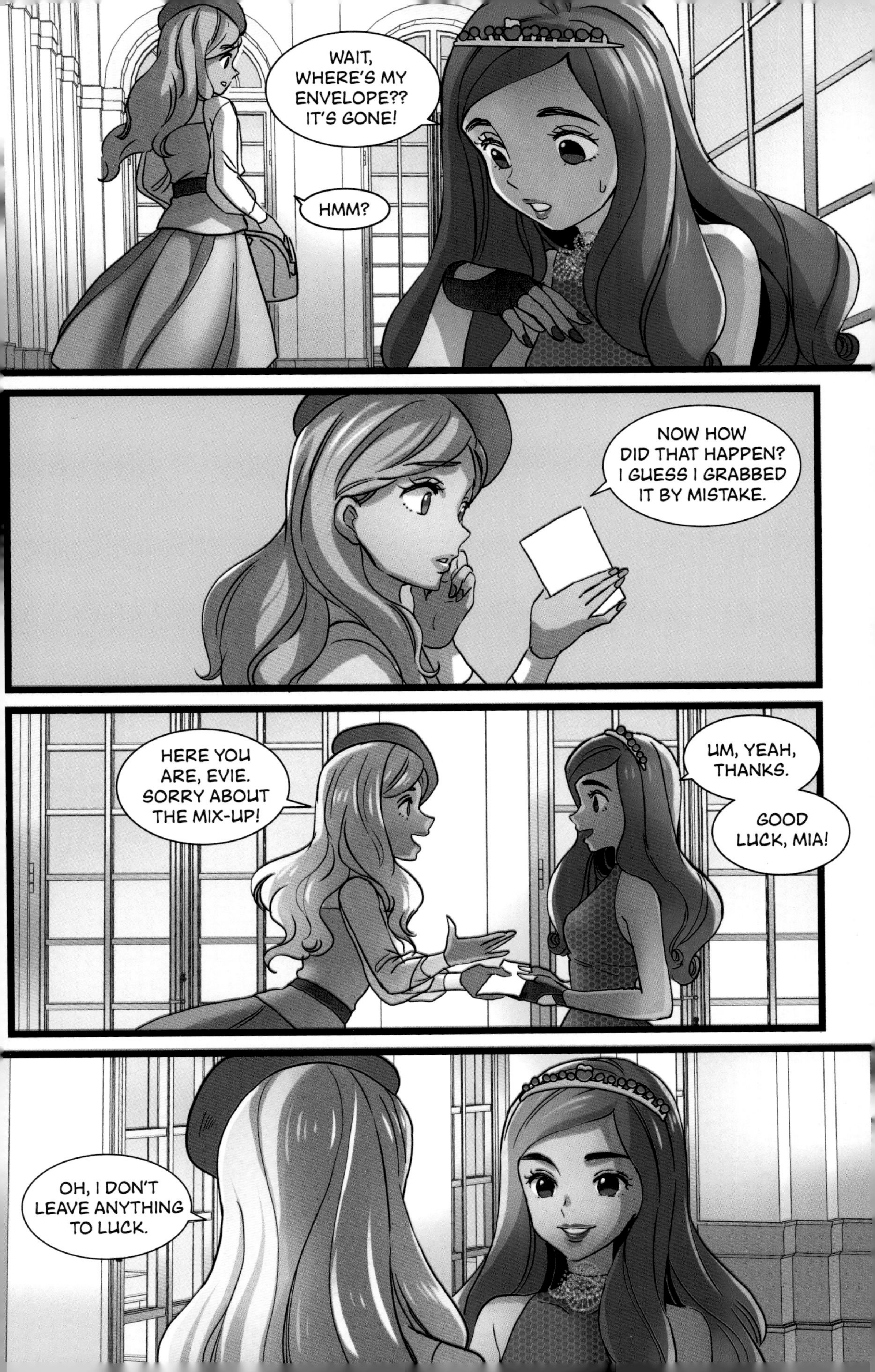
WAIT, WHERE'S MY ENVELOPE?? IT'S GONE!
HMM?
NOW HOW DID THAT HAPPEN? I GUESS I GRABBED IT BY MISTAKE.
HERE YOU ARE, EVIE. SORRY ABOUT THE MIX-UP!
UM, YEAH, THANKS.
GOOD LUCK, MIA!
OH, I DON'T LEAVE ANYTHING TO LUCK.

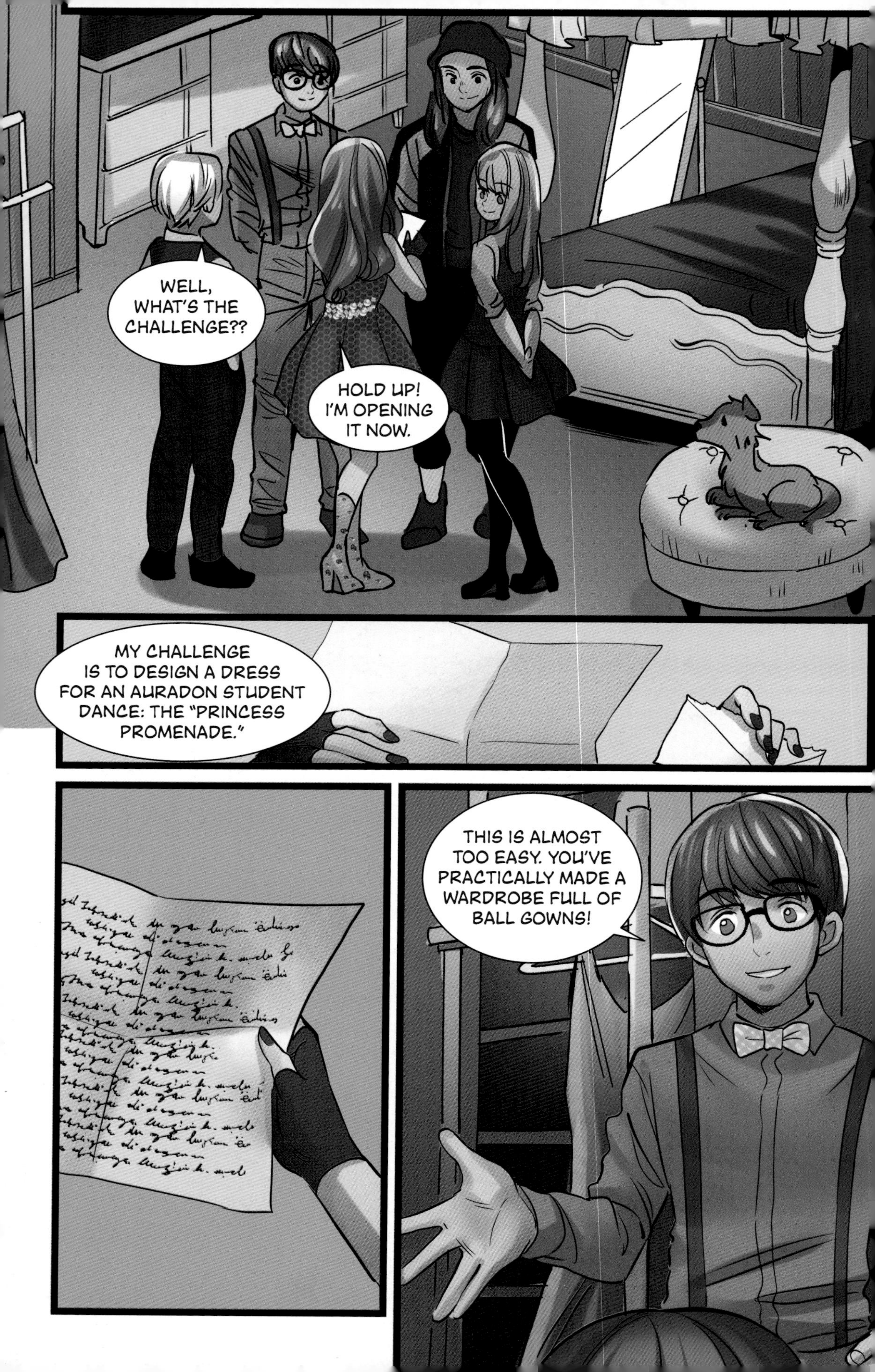
WELL, WHAT'S THE CHALLENGE??
HOLD UP! I'M OPENING IT NOW.
MY CHALLENGE IS TO DESIGN A DRESS FOR AN AURADON STUDENT DANCE: THE "PRINCESS PROMENADE."
THIS IS ALMOST TOO EASY. YOU'VE PRACTICALLY MADE A WARDROBE FULL OF BALL GOWNS!

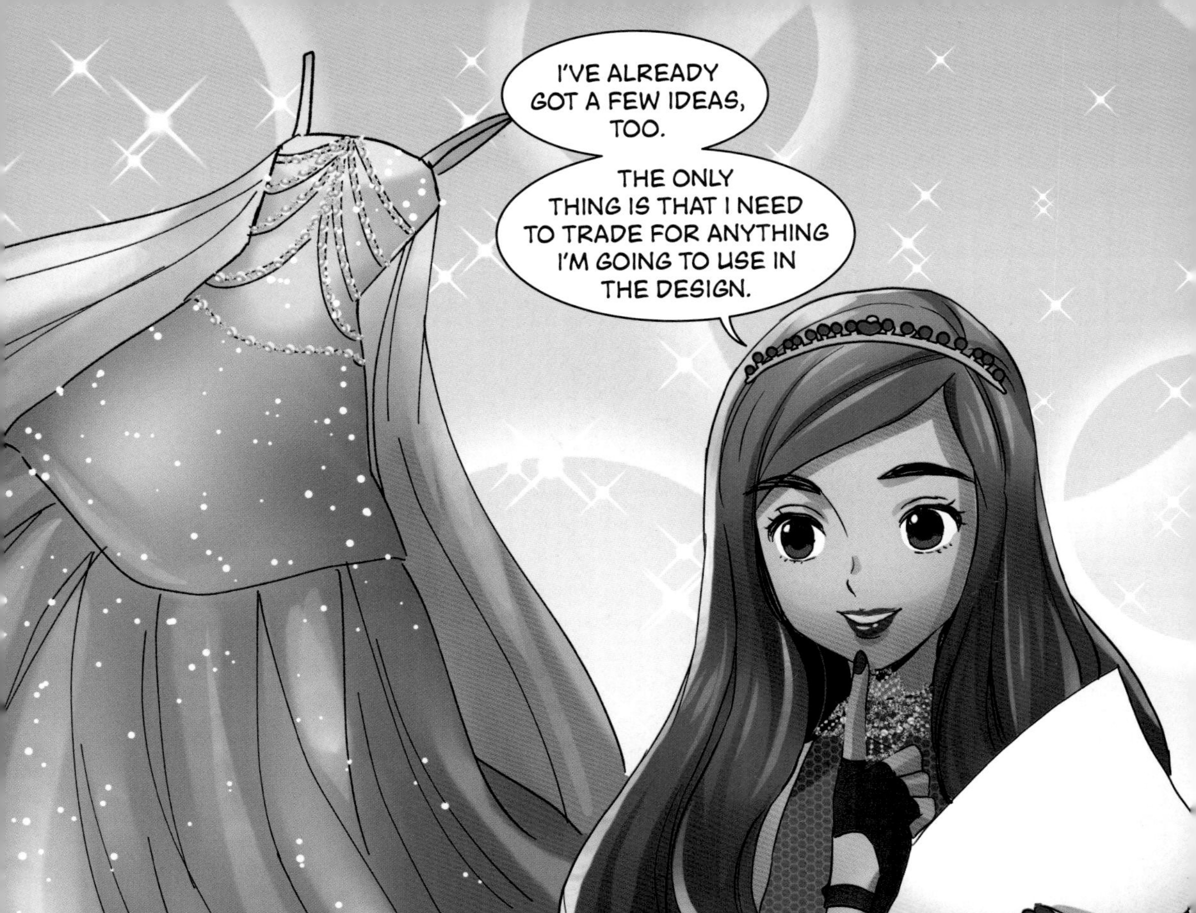
I'VE ALREADY GOT A FEW IDEAS, TOO.
THE ONLY THING IS THAT I NEED TO TRADE FOR ANYTHING I'M GOING TO USE IN THE DESIGN.

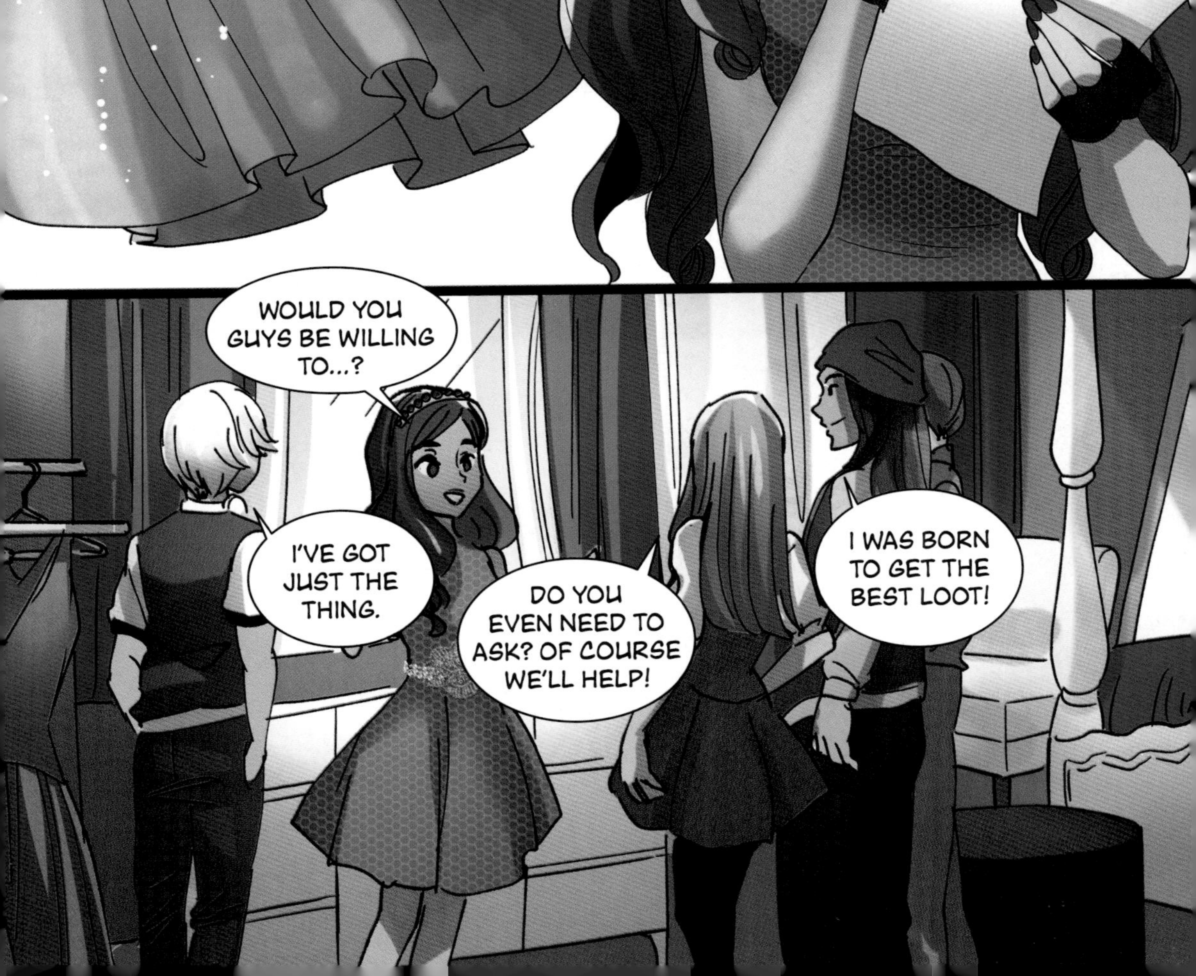
WOULD YOU GUYS BE WILLING TO...?
I'VE GOT JUST THE THING.
DO YOU EVEN NEED TO ASK? OF COURSE WE'LL HELP!
I WAS BORN TO GET THE BEST LOOT!

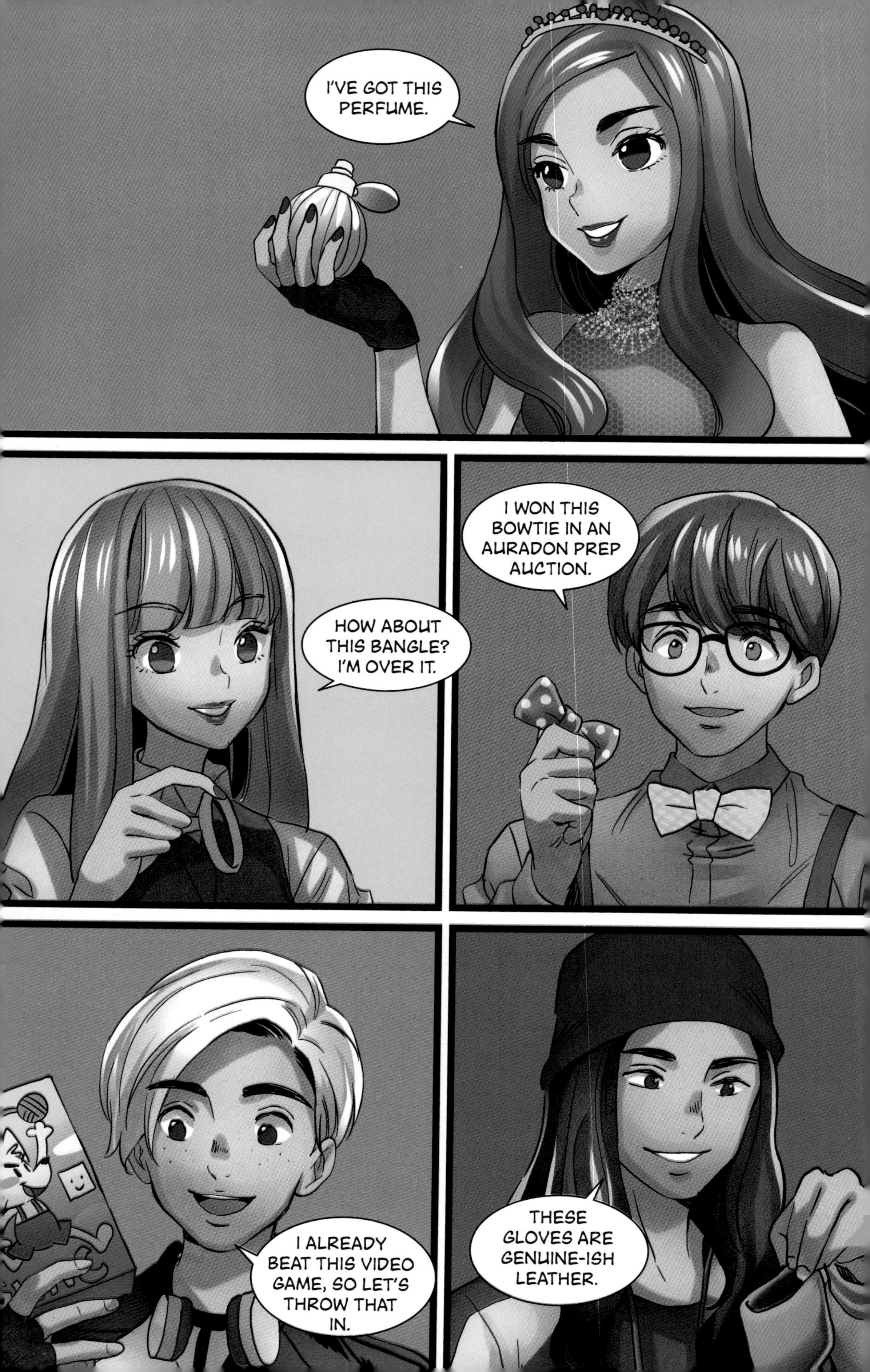
I'VE GOT THIS PERFUME.
HOW ABOUT THIS BANGLE? I'M OVER IT.
I WON THIS BOWTIE IN AN AURADON PREP AUCTION.
I ALREADY BEAT THIS VIDEO GAME, SO LET'S THROW THAT IN.
THESE GLOVES ARE GENUINE-ISH LEATHER.

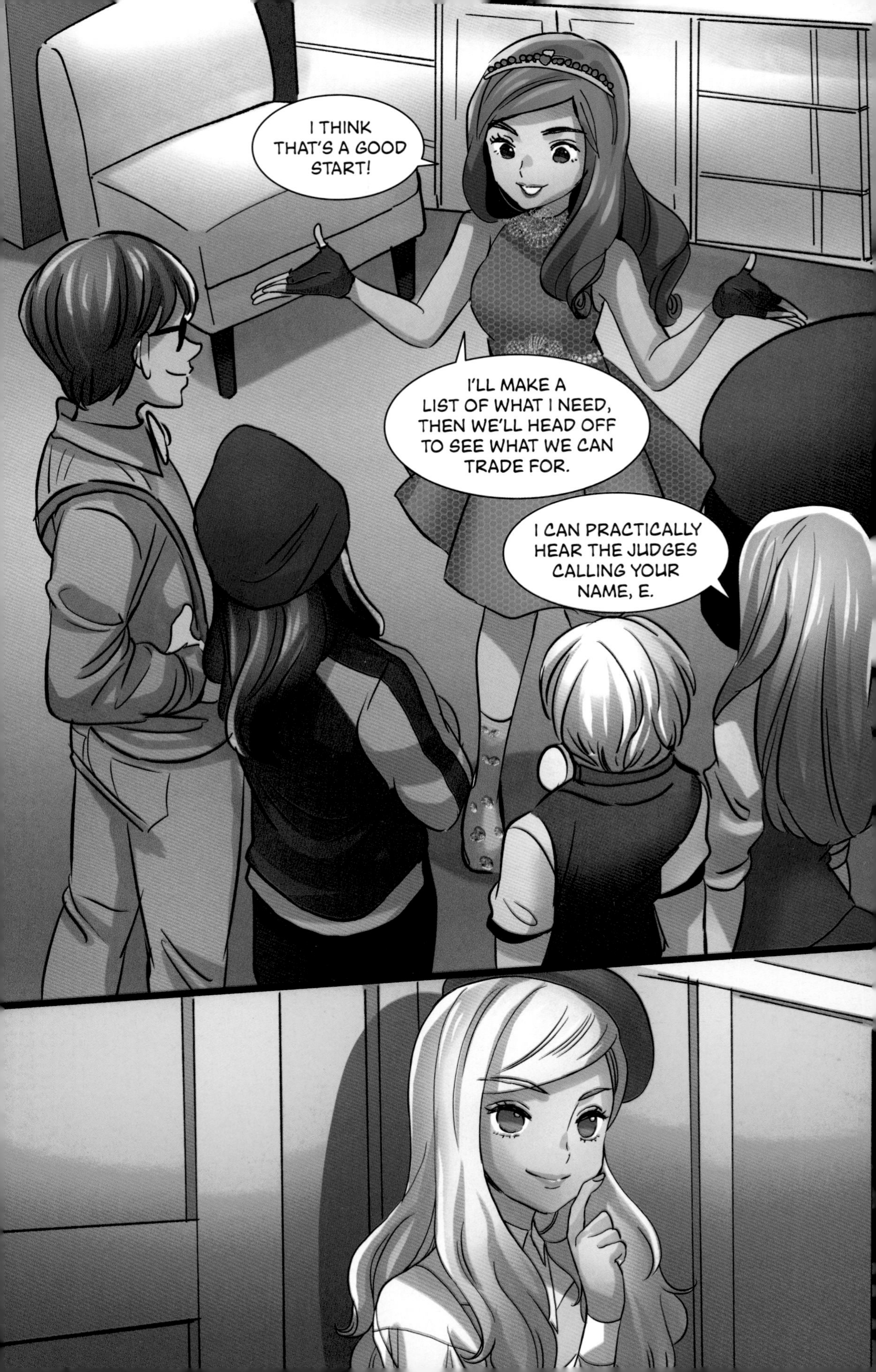
I THINK THAT'S A GOOD START!
I'LL MAKE A LIST OF WHAT I NEED, THEN WE'LL HEAD OFF TO SEE WHAT WE CAN TRADE FOR.
I CAN PRACTICALLY HEAR THE JUDGES CALLING YOUR NAME, E.

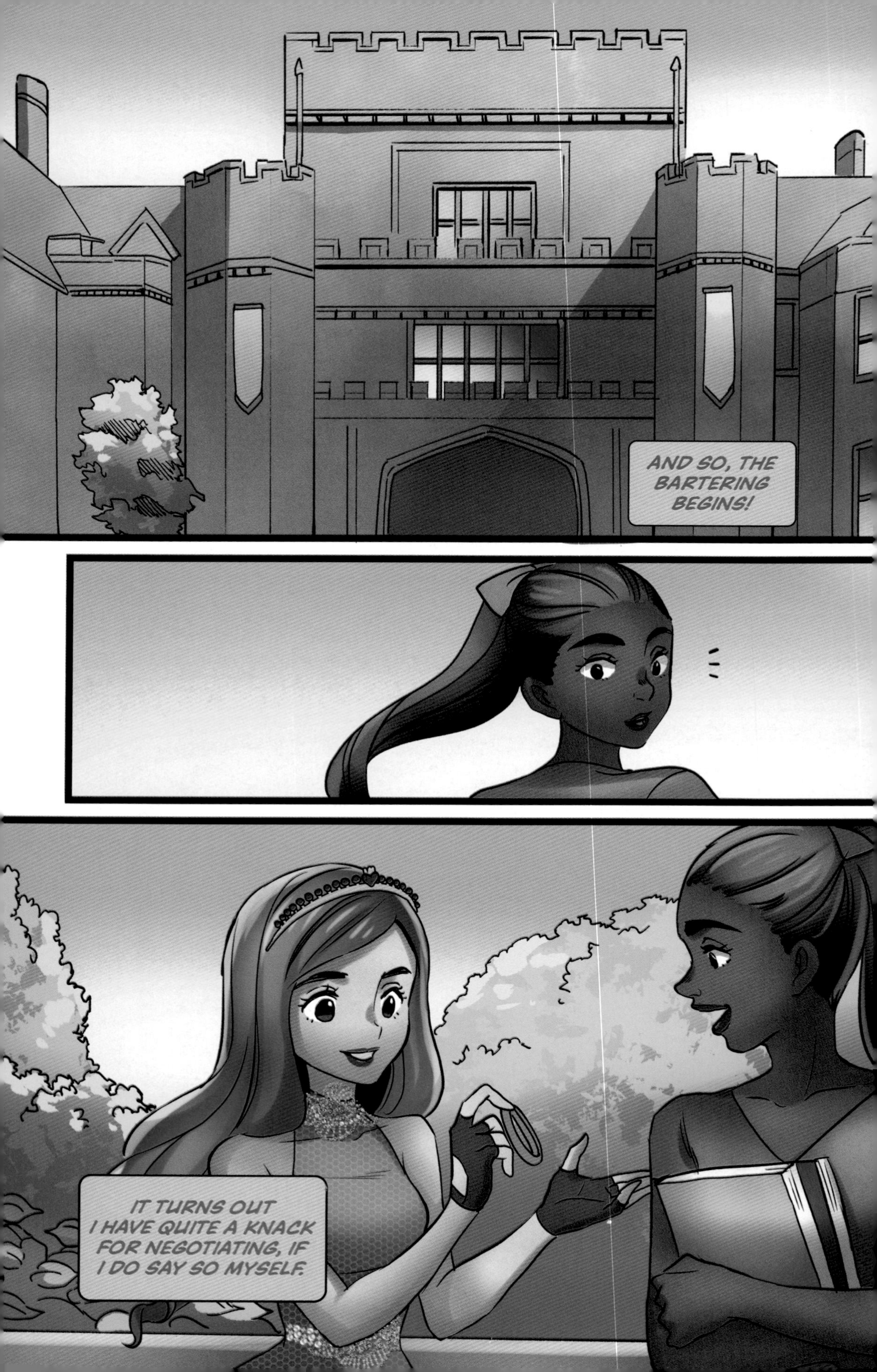
AND SO, THE BARTERING BEGINS!
IT TURNS OUT I HAVE QUITE A KNACK FOR NEGOTIATING, IF I DO SAY SO MYSELF.

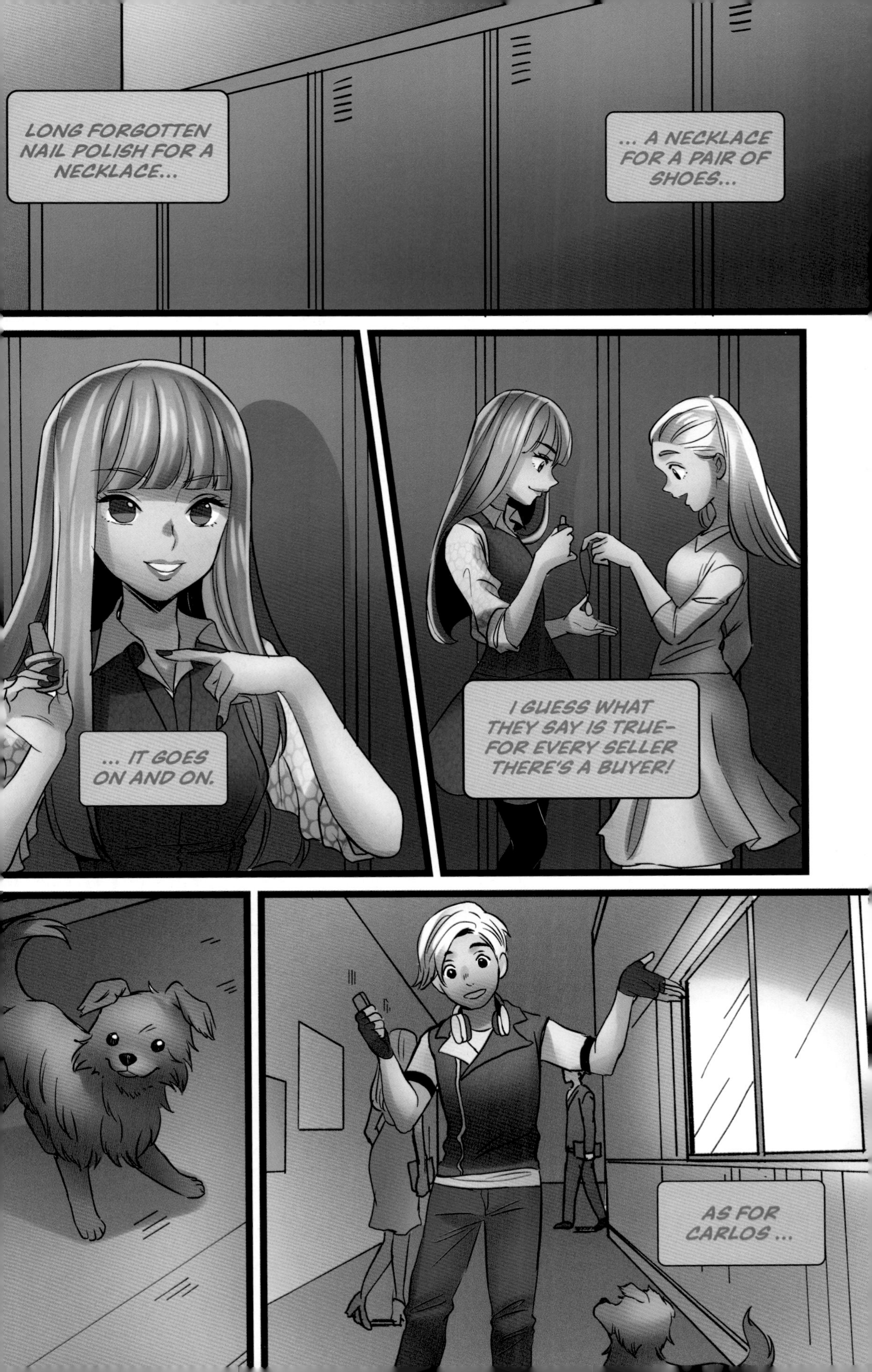
LONG FORGOTTEN NAIL POLISH FOR A NECKLACE...
... A NECKLACE FOR A PAIR OF SHOES...
... IT GOES ON AND ON.
I GUESS WHAT THEY SAY IS TRUE-FOR EVERY SELLER THERE'S A BUYER!
AS FOR CARLOS ...

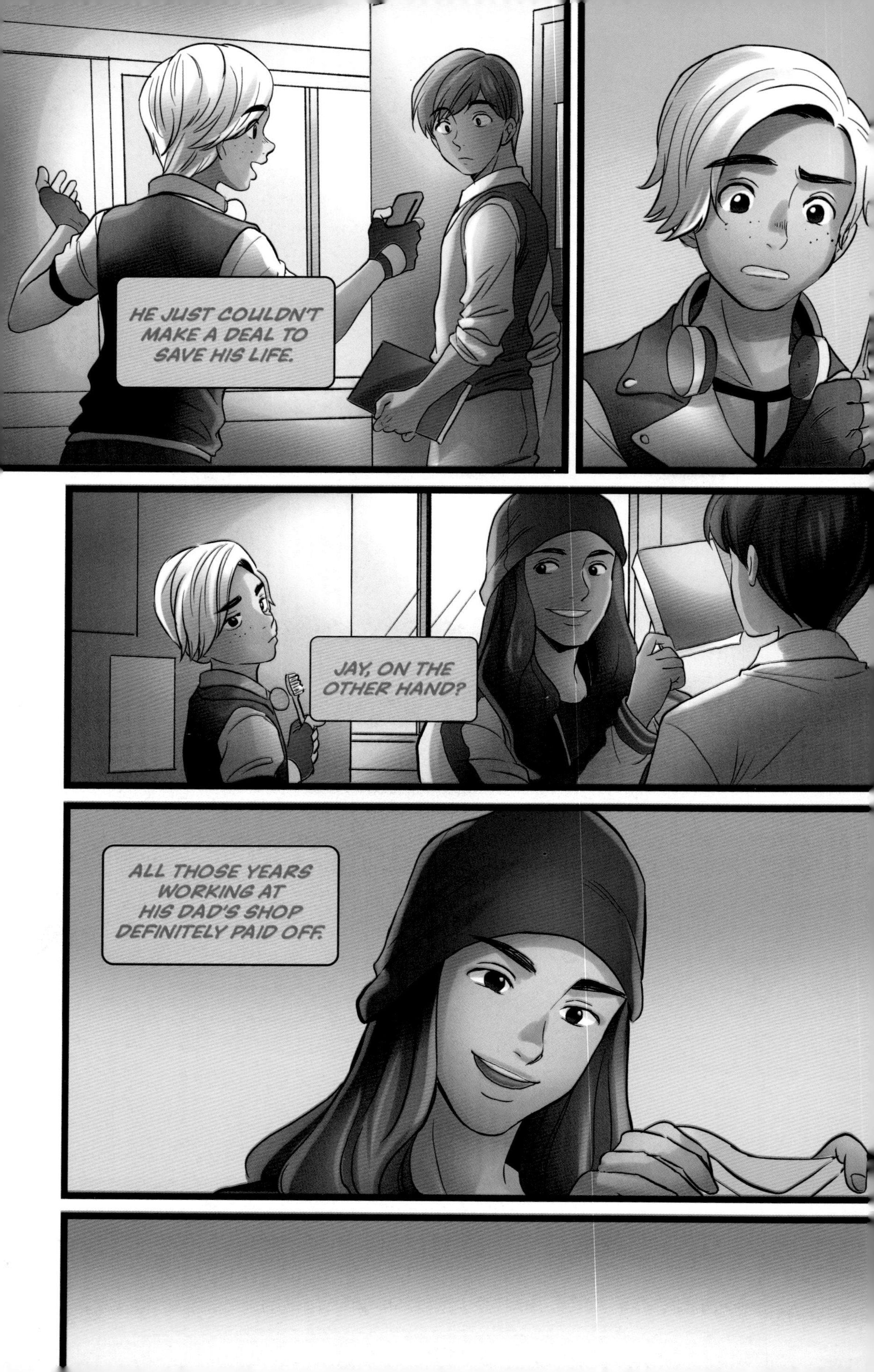
HE JUST COULDN'T MAKE A DEAL TO SAVE HIS LIFE.
JAY, ON THE OTHER HAND?
ALL THOSE YEARS WORKING AT HIS DAD'S SHOP DEFINITELY PAID OFF.

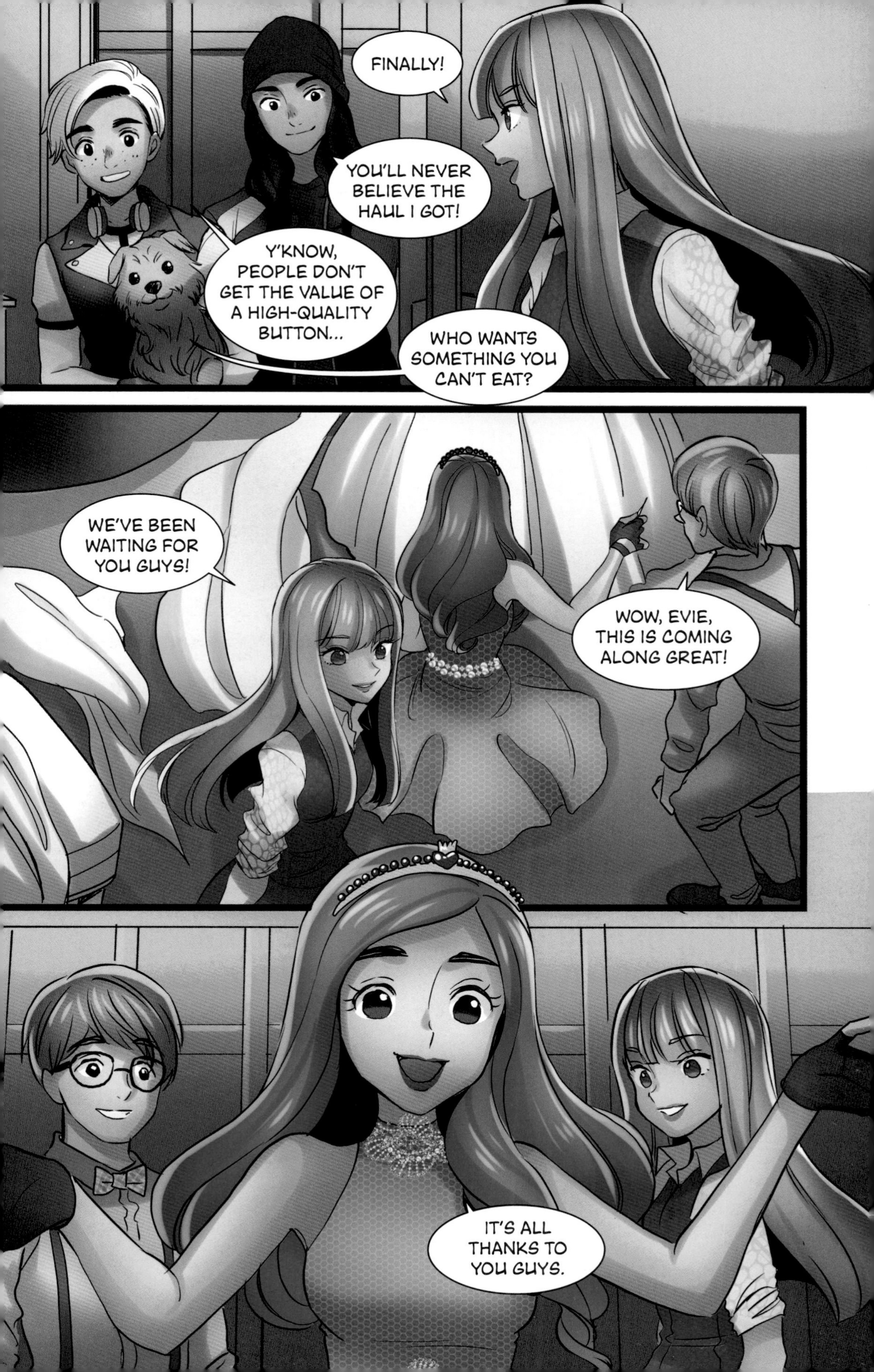
FINALLY!
YOU'LL NEVER BELIEVE THE HAUL I GOT!
Y'KNOW, PEOPLE DON'T GET THE VALUE OF A HIGH-QUALITY BUTTON...
WHO WANTS SOMETHING YOU CAN'T EAT?
WE'VE BEEN WAITING FOR YOU GUYS!
WOW, EVIE, THIS IS COMING ALONG GREAT!
IT'S ALL THANKS TO YOU GUYS.

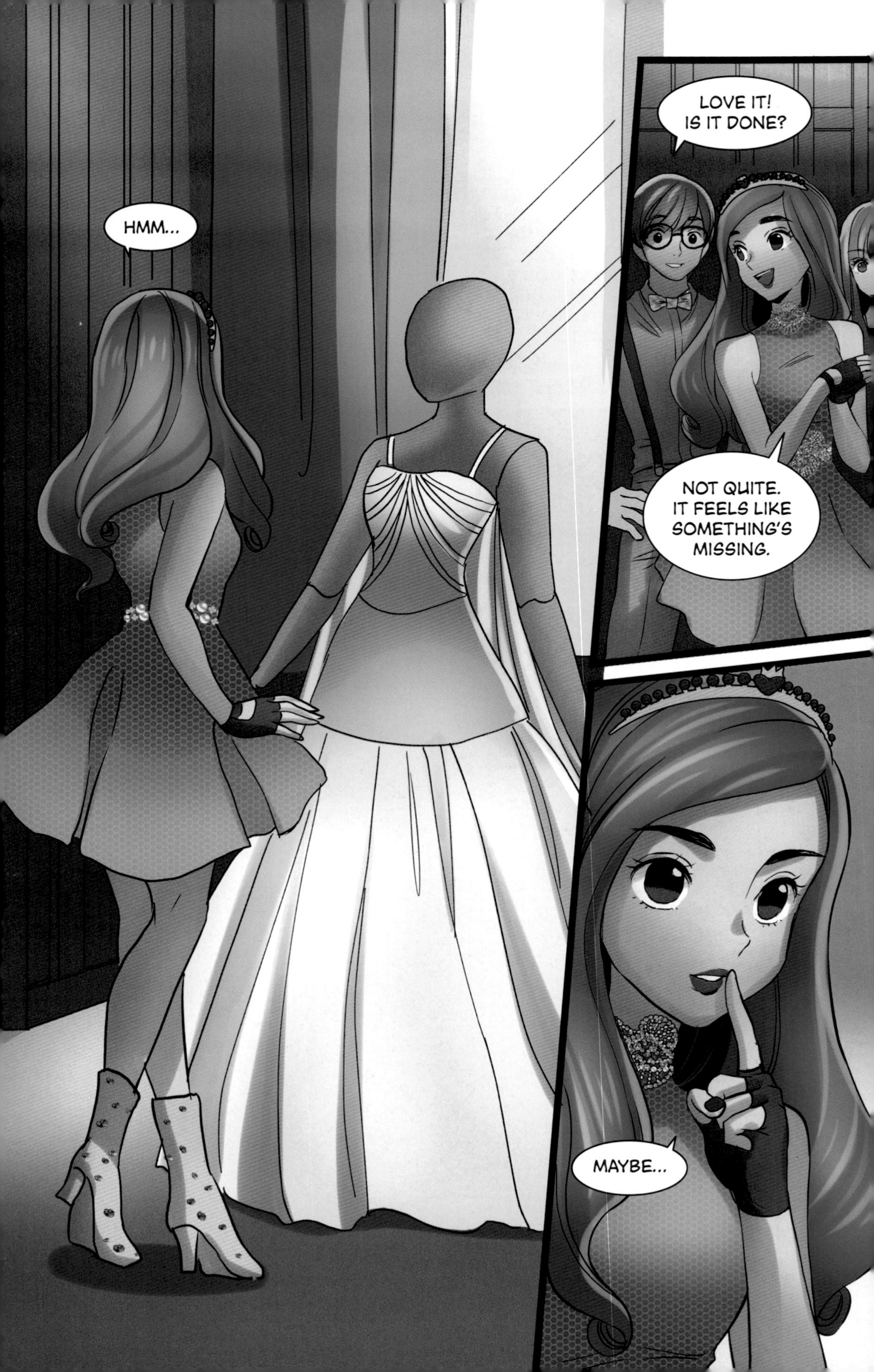
HMM...
LOVE IT! IS IT DONE?
NOT QUITE. IT FEELS LIKE SOMETHING'S MISSING.
MAYBE...

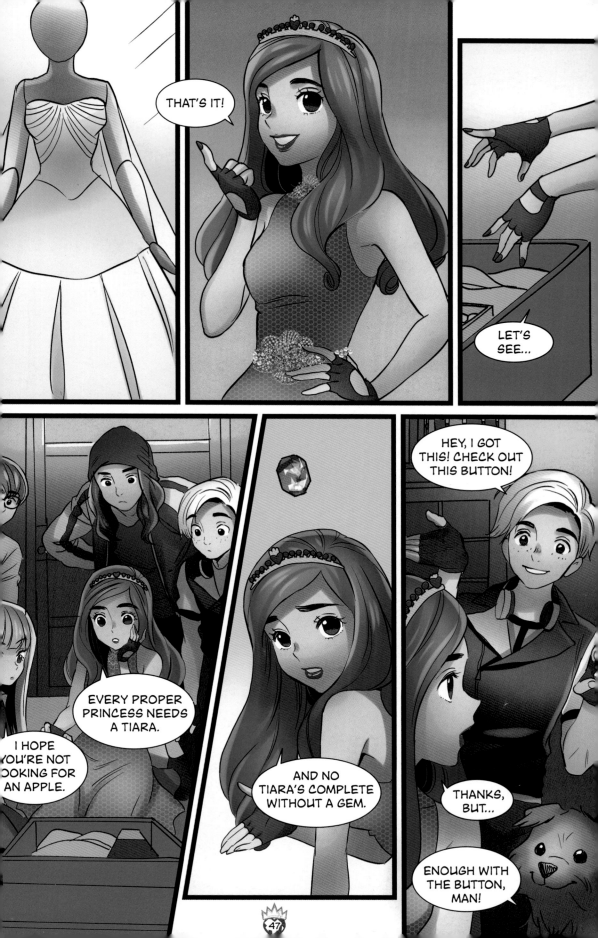

THAT'S IT!

LET'S SEE...

EVERY PROPER PRINCESS NEEDS A TIARA.

I HOPE YOU'RE NOT LOOKING FOR AN APPLE.

AND NO TIARA'S COMPLETE WITHOUT A GEM.

HEY, I GOT THIS! CHECK OUT THIS BUTTON!

THANKS, BUT...

ENOUGH WITH THE BUTTON, MAN!

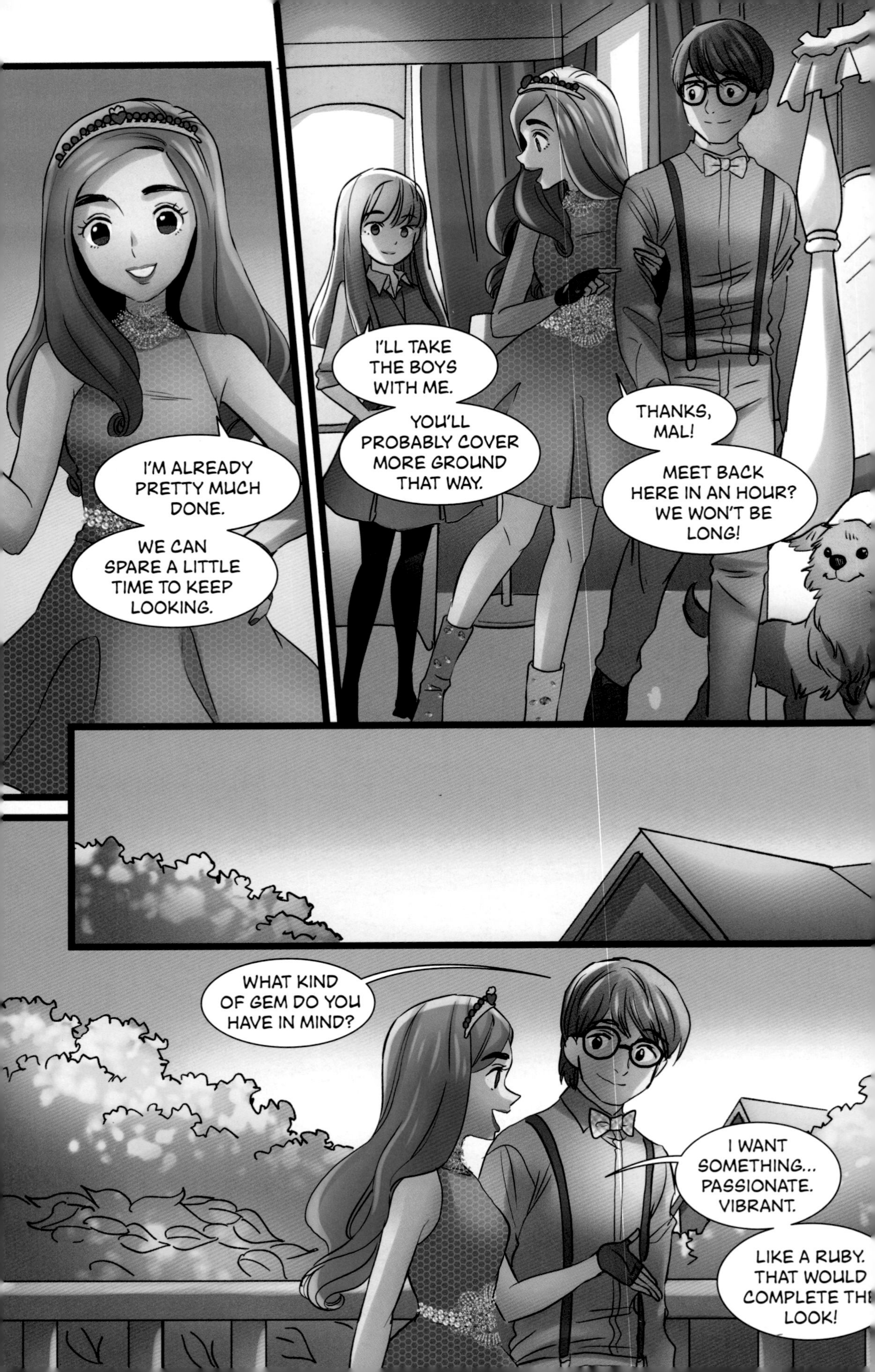
I'M ALREADY PRETTY MUCH DONE.
WE CAN SPARE A LITTLE TIME TO KEEP LOOKING.
I'LL TAKE THE BOYS WITH ME.
YOU'LL PROBABLY COVER MORE GROUND THAT WAY.
THANKS, MAL!
MEET BACK HERE IN AN HOUR? WE WON'T BE LONG!
WHAT KIND OF GEM DO YOU HAVE IN MIND?
I WANT SOMETHING... PASSIONATE. VIBRANT.
LIKE A RUBY. THAT WOULD COMPLETE TH

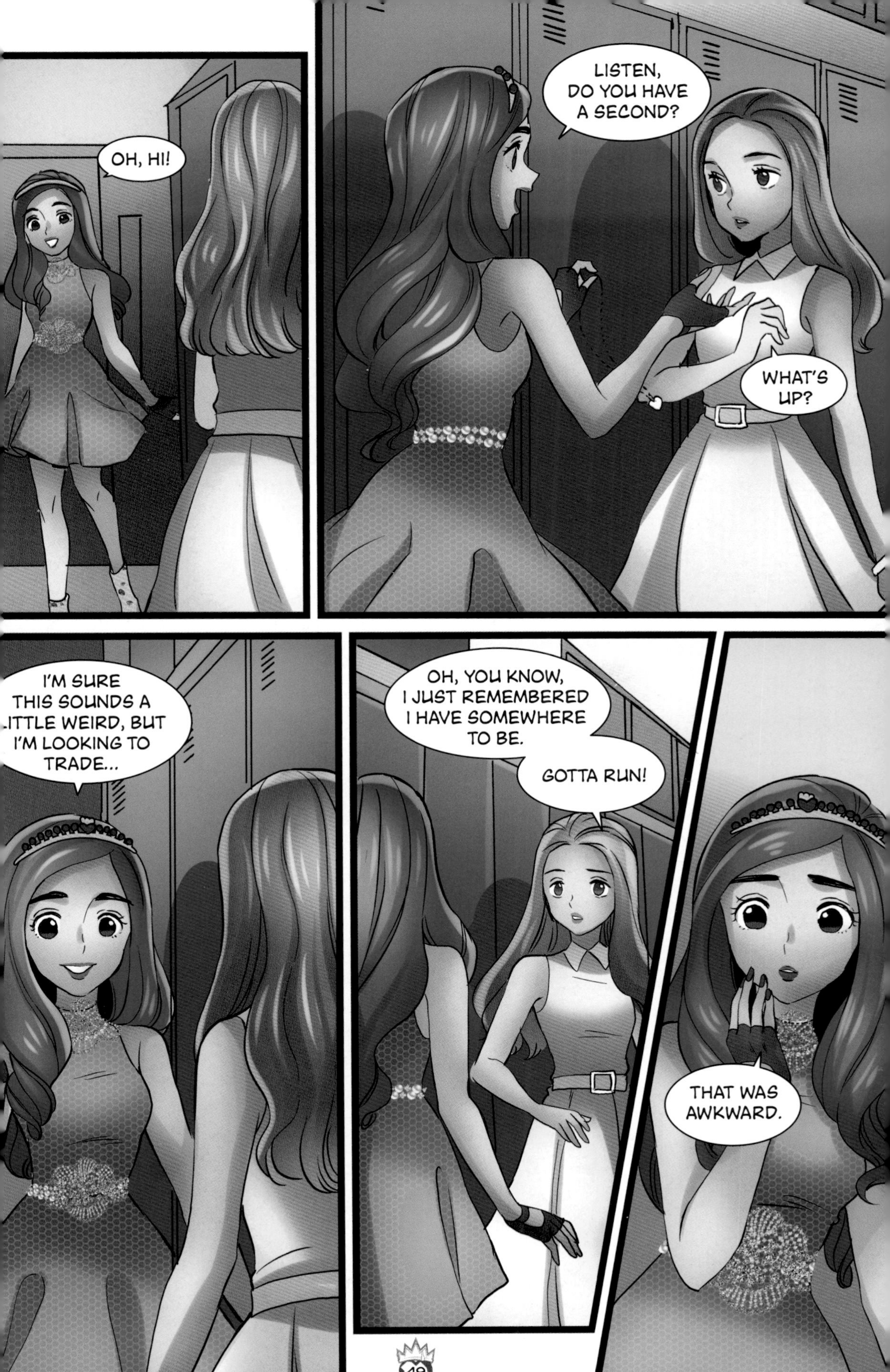
OH, HI!
LISTEN, DO YOU HAVE A SECOND?
WHAT'S UP?
I'M SURE THIS SOUNDS A LITTLE WEIRD, BUT I'M LOOKING TO TRADE...
OH, YOU KNOW, I JUST REMEMBERED I HAVE SOMEWHERE TO BE.
GOTTA RUN!
THAT WAS AWKWARD.

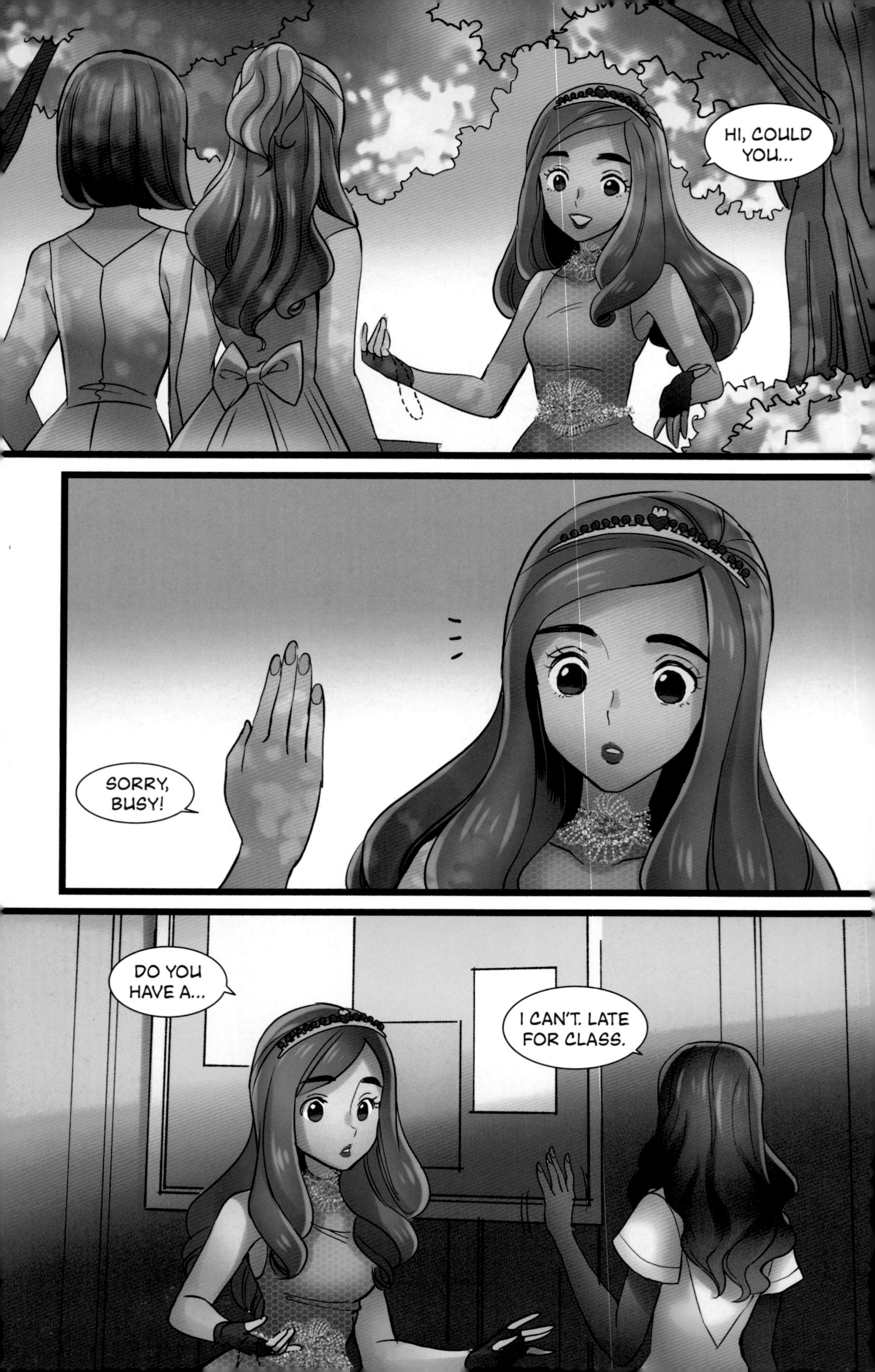
HI, COULD YOU...
SORRY, BUSY!
DO YOU HAVE A...
I CAN'T. LATE FOR CLASS.

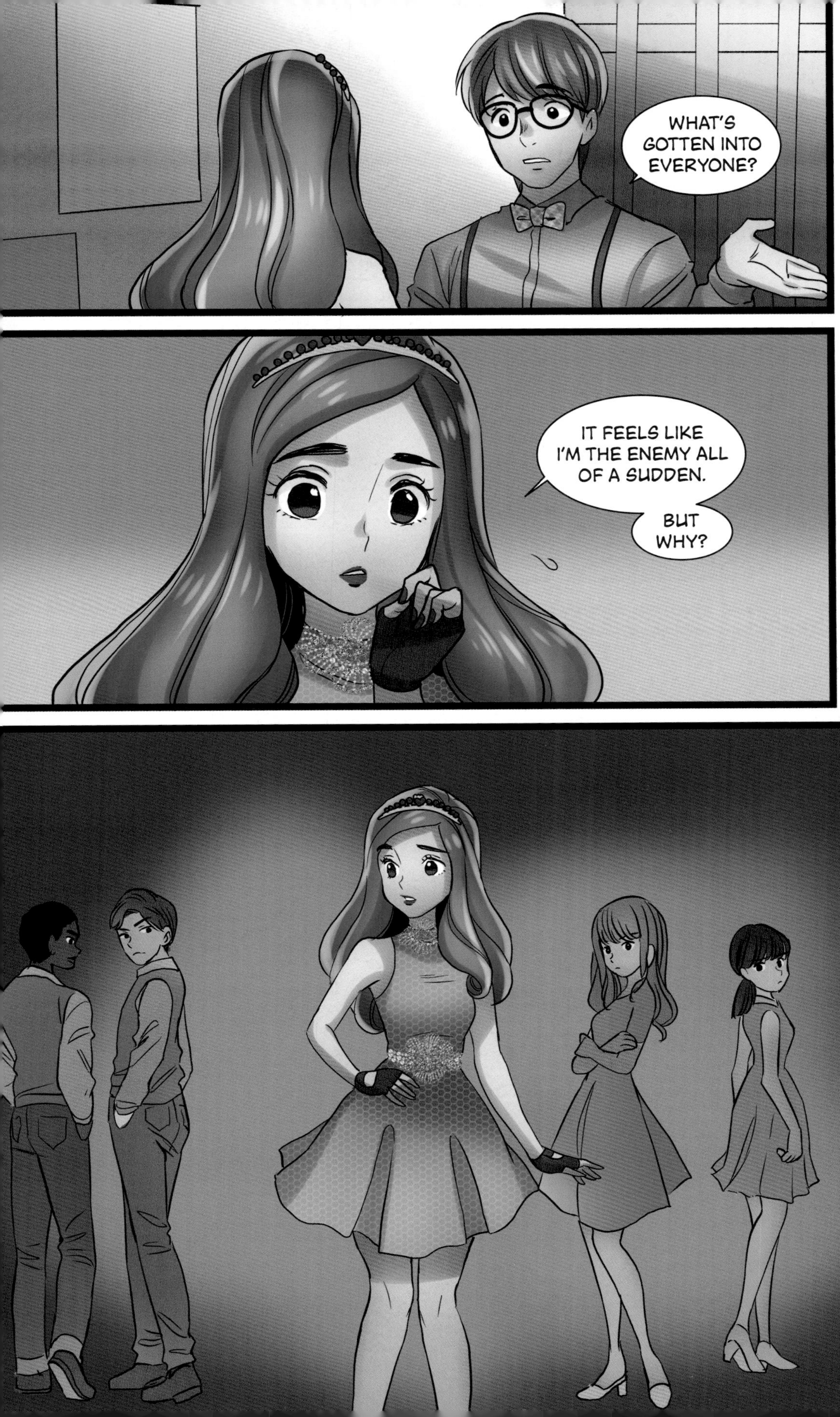
WHAT'S GOTTEN INTO EVERYONE?
IT FEELS LIKE I'M THE ENEMY ALL OF A SUDDEN.
BUT WHY?

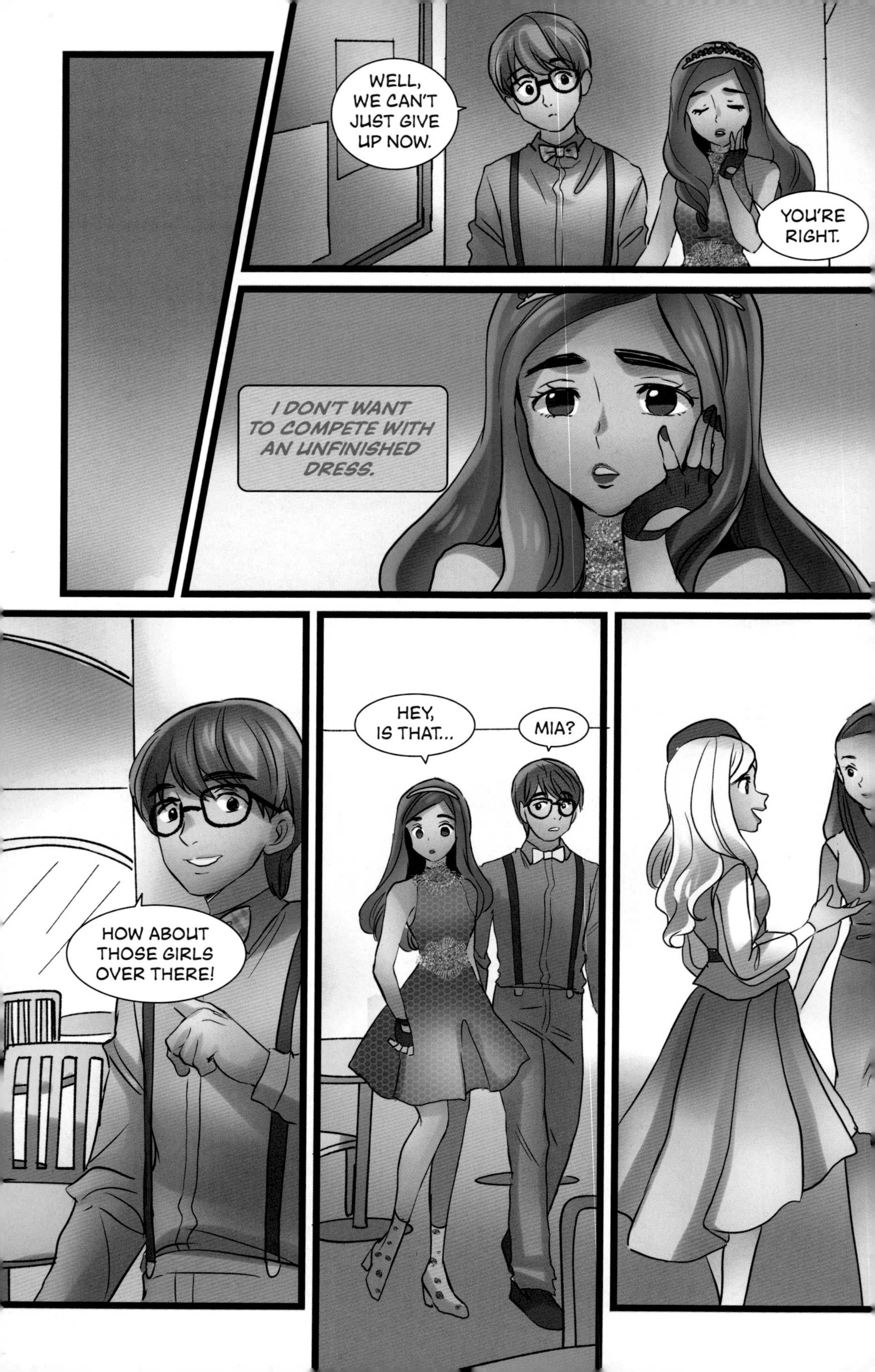
WELL, WE CAN'T JUST GIVE UP NOW.
YOU'RE RIGHT.
I DON'T WANT TO COMPETE WITH AN UNFINISHED DRESS.
HOW ABOUT THOSE GIRLS OVER THERE!
HEY, IS THAT...
MIA?

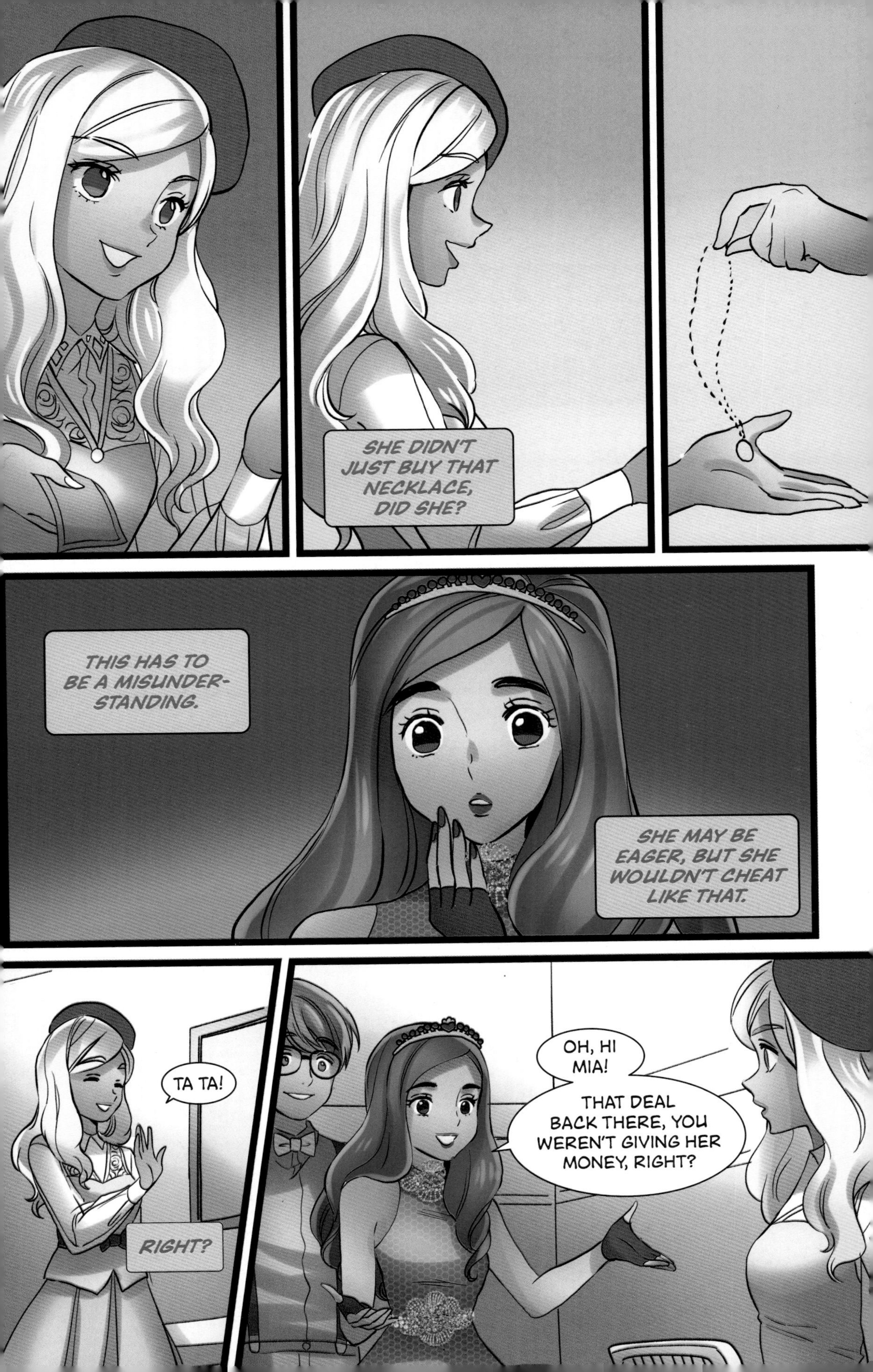
SHE DIDN'T JUST BUY THAT NECKLACE, DID SHE?
THIS HAS TO BE A MISUNDER-STANDING.
SHE MAY BE EAGER, BUT SHE WOULDN'T CHEAT LIKE THAT.
TA TA!
RIGHT?
OH, HI MIA!
THAT DEAL BACK THERE, YOU WEREN'T GIVING HER MONEY, RIGHT?

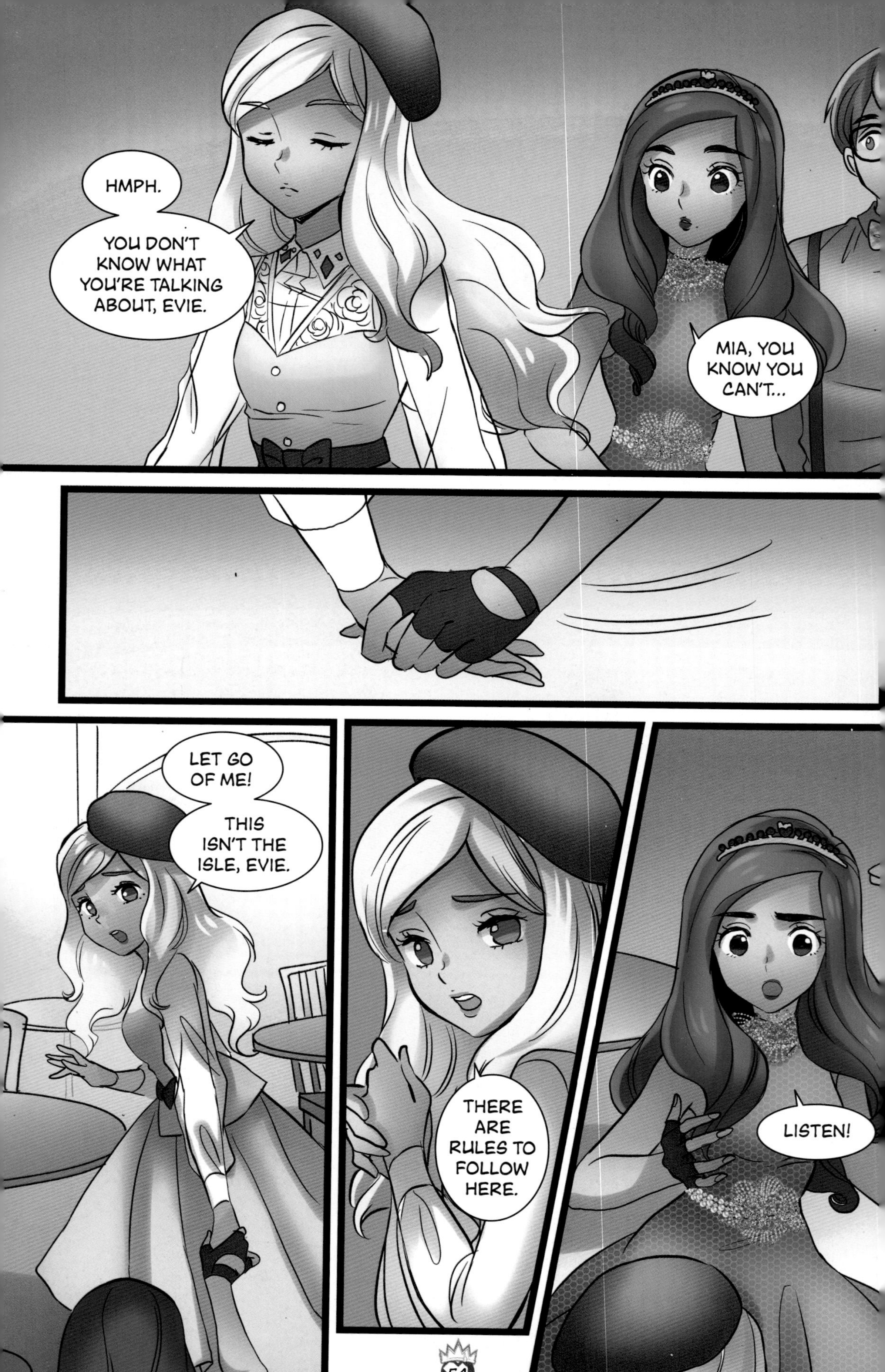
HMPH.
YOU DON'T KNOW WHAT YOU'RE TALKING ABOUT, EVIE.
MIA, YOU KNOW YOU CAN'T...
LET GO OF ME!
THIS ISN'T THE ISLE, EVIE.
THERE ARE RULES TO FOLLOW HERE.
LISTEN!

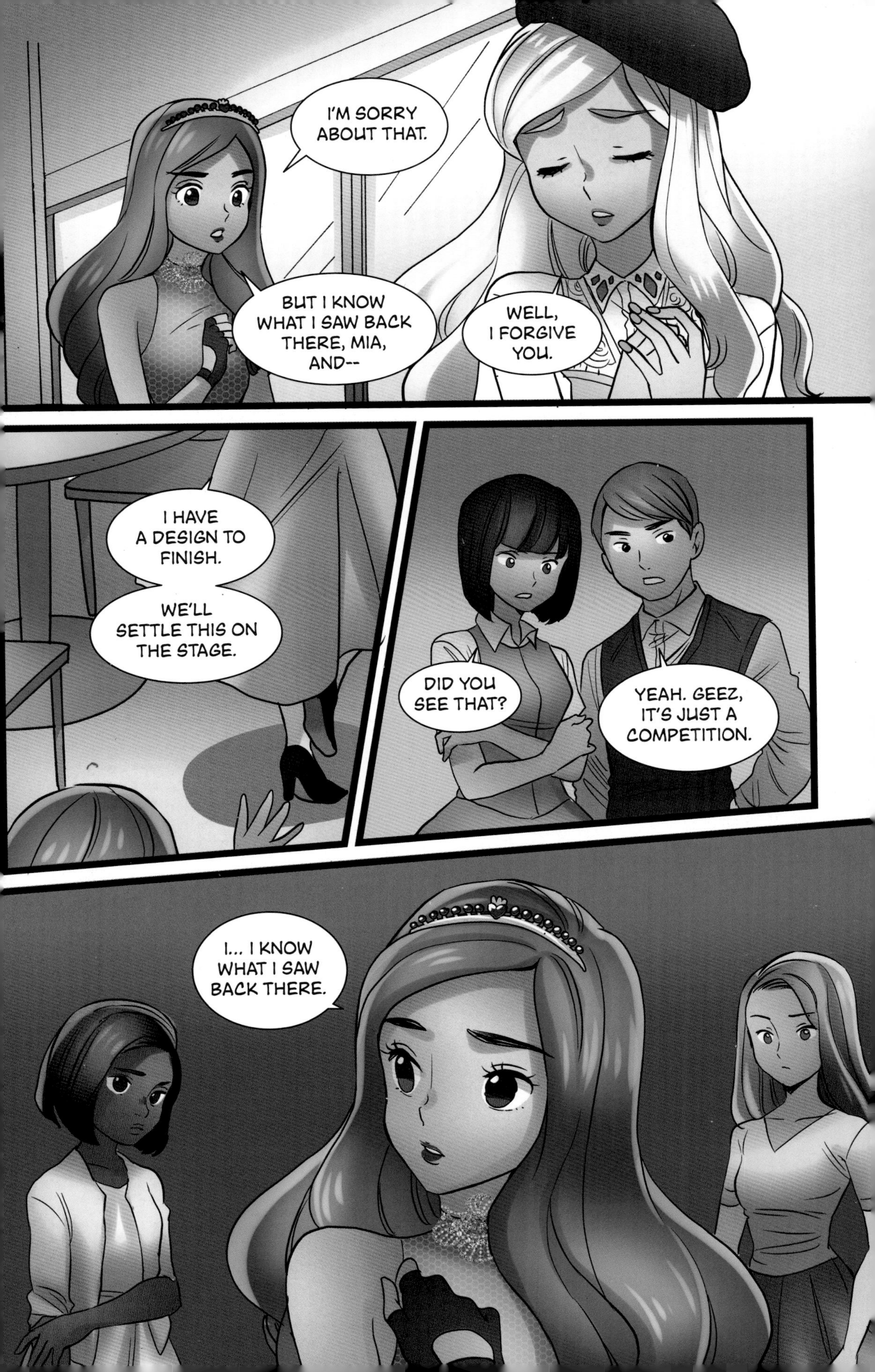
I'M SORRY ABOUT THAT.
BUT I KNOW WHAT I SAW BACK THERE, MIA, AND--
WELL, I FORGIVE YOU.
I HAVE A DESIGN TO FINISH.
WE'LL SETTLE THIS ON THE STAGE.
DID YOU SEE THAT?
YEAH. GEEZ, IT'S JUST A COMPETITION.
I... I KNOW WHAT I SAW BACK THERE.

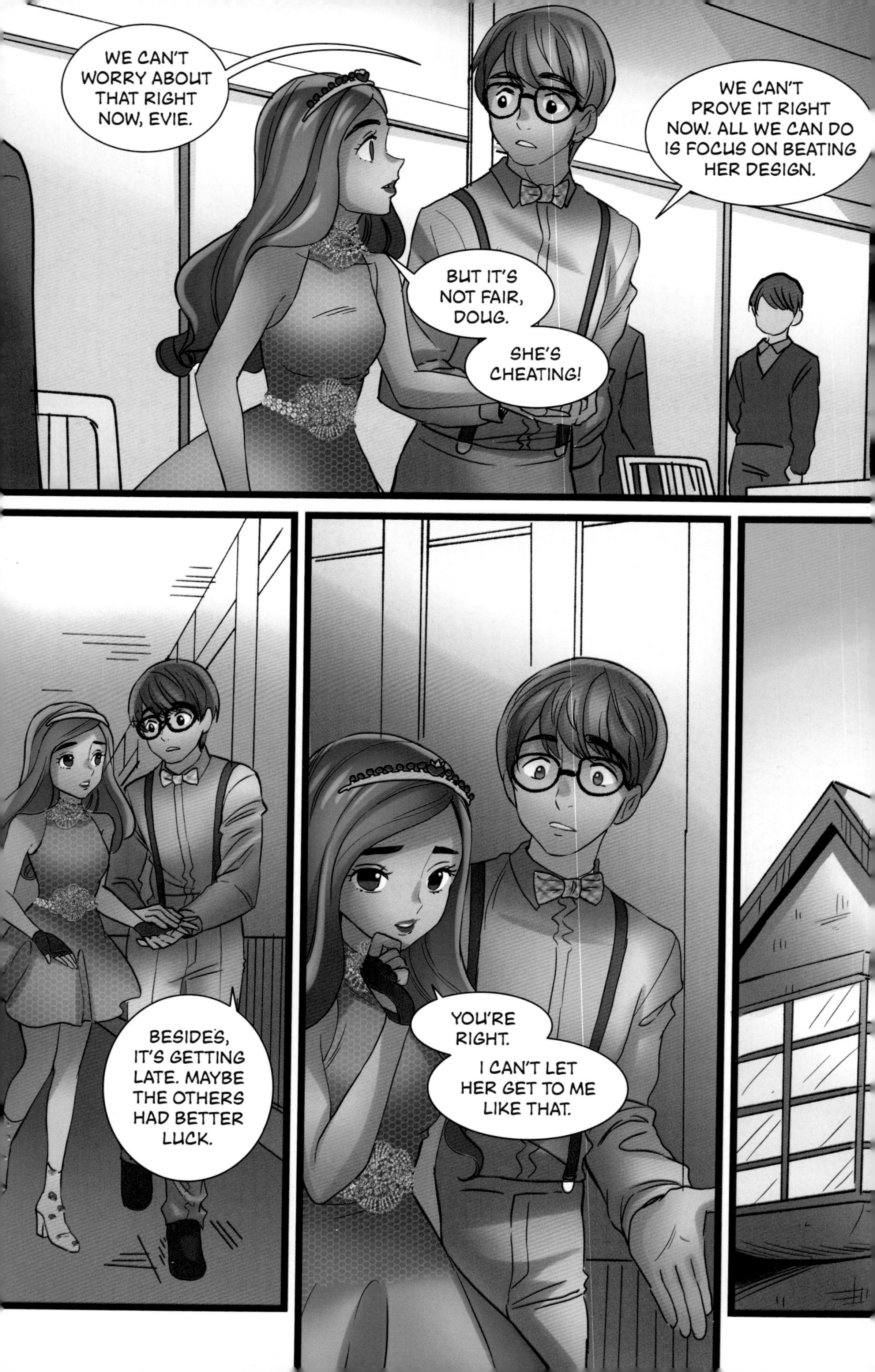
WE CAN'T WORRY ABOUT THAT RIGHT NOW, EVIE.
WE CAN'T PROVE IT RIGHT NOW. ALL WE CAN DO IS FOCUS ON BEATING HER DESIGN.
BUT IT'S NOT FAIR, DOUG.
SHE'S CHEATING!
BESIDES, IT'S GETTING LATE. MAYBE THE OTHERS HAD BETTER LUCK.
YOU'RE RIGHT.
I CAN'T LET HER GET TO ME LIKE THAT.

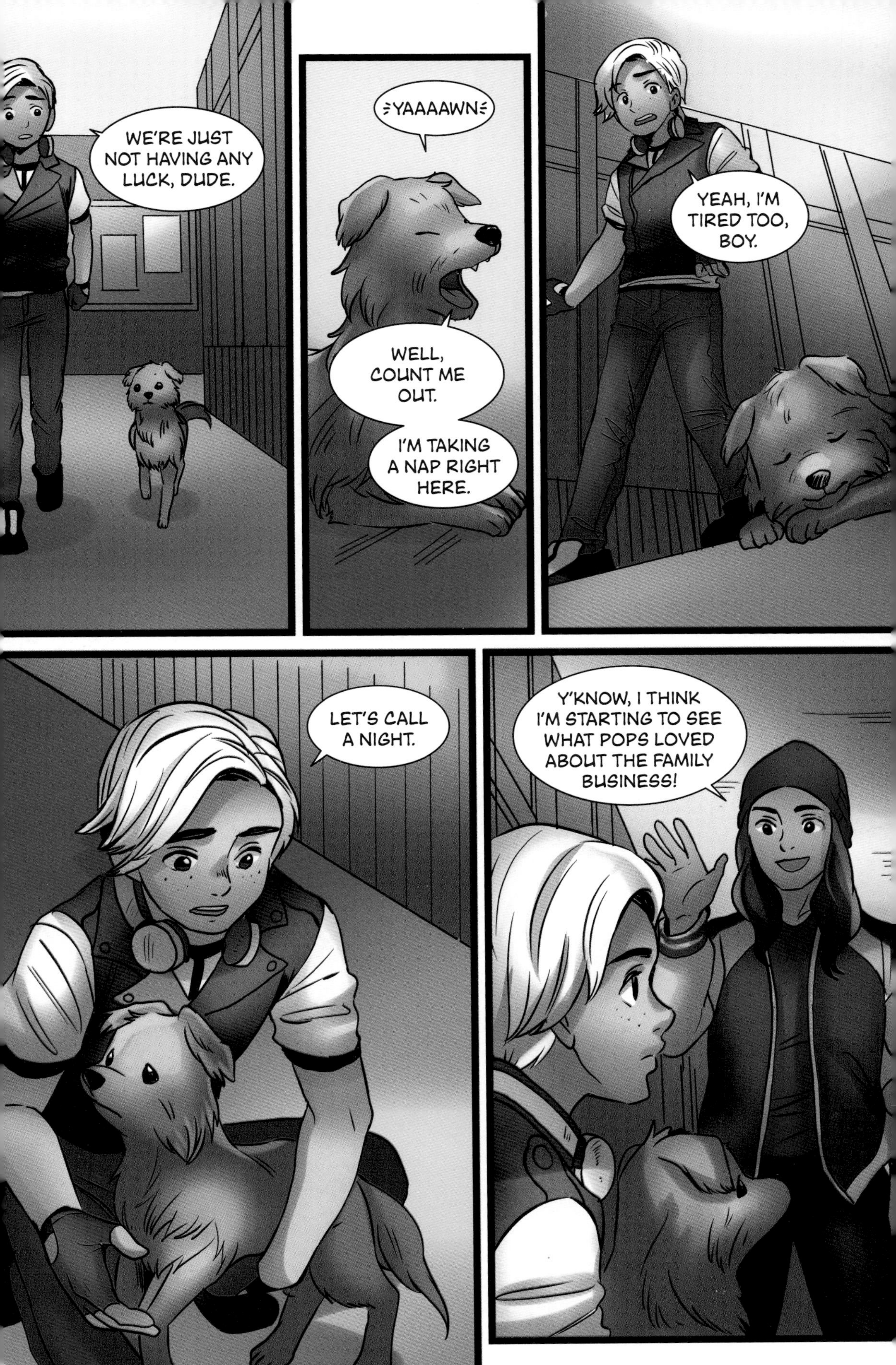
WE'RE JUST NOT HAVING ANY LUCK, DUDE.
YAAAAWN
WELL, COUNT ME OUT.
I'M TAKING A NAP RIGHT HERE.
YEAH, I'M TIRED TOO, BOY.
LET'S CALL A NIGHT.
Y'KNOW, I THINK I'M STARTING TO SEE WHAT POPS LOVED ABOUT THE FAMILY BUSINESS!

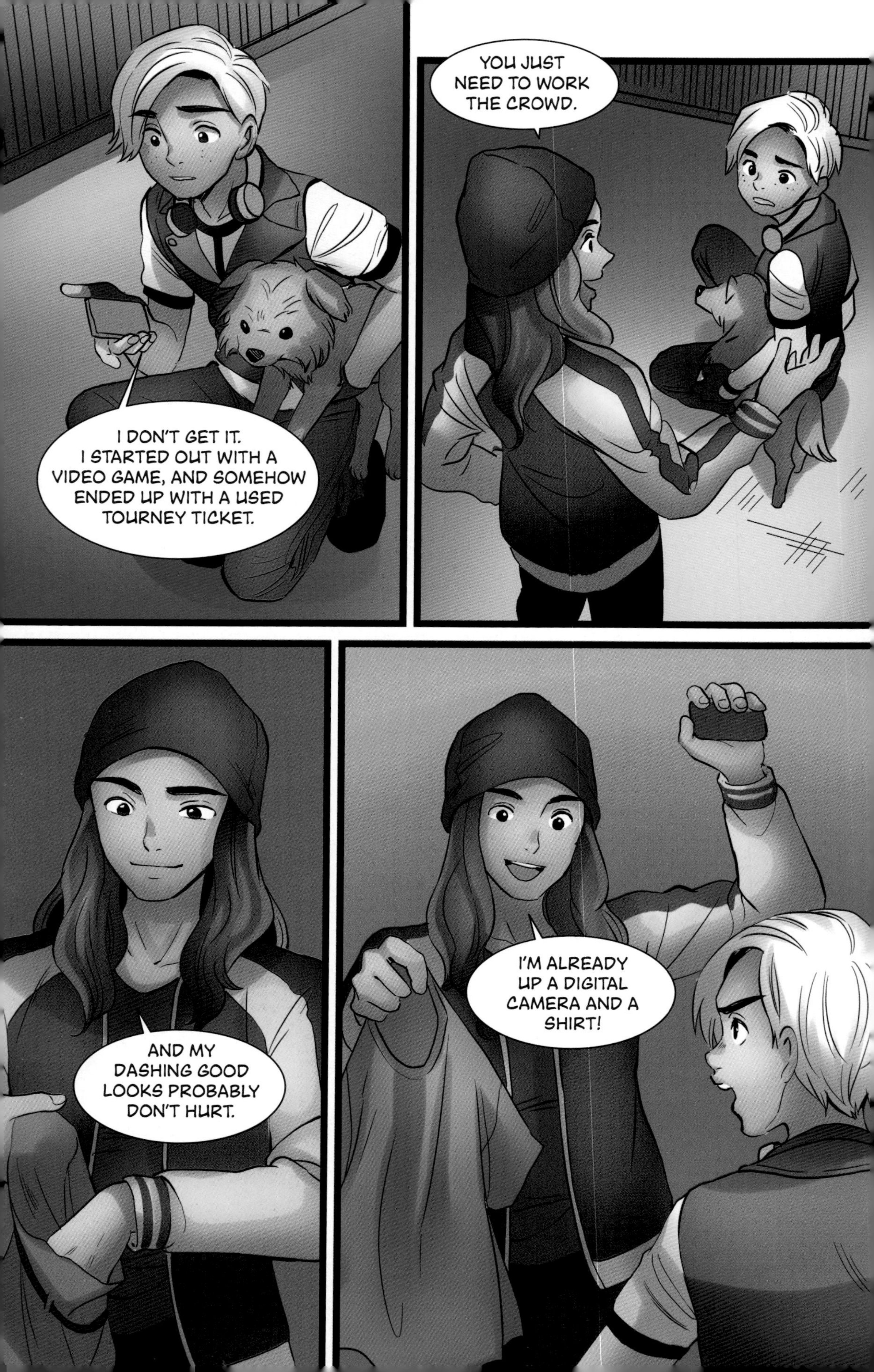
I DON'T GET IT. I STARTED OUT WITH A VIDEO GAME, AND SOMEHOW ENDED UP WITH A USED TOURNEY TICKET.
YOU JUST NEED TO WORK THE CROWD.
AND MY DASHING GOOD LOOKS PROBABLY DON'T HURT.
I'M ALREADY UP A DIGITAL CAMERA AND A SHIRT!

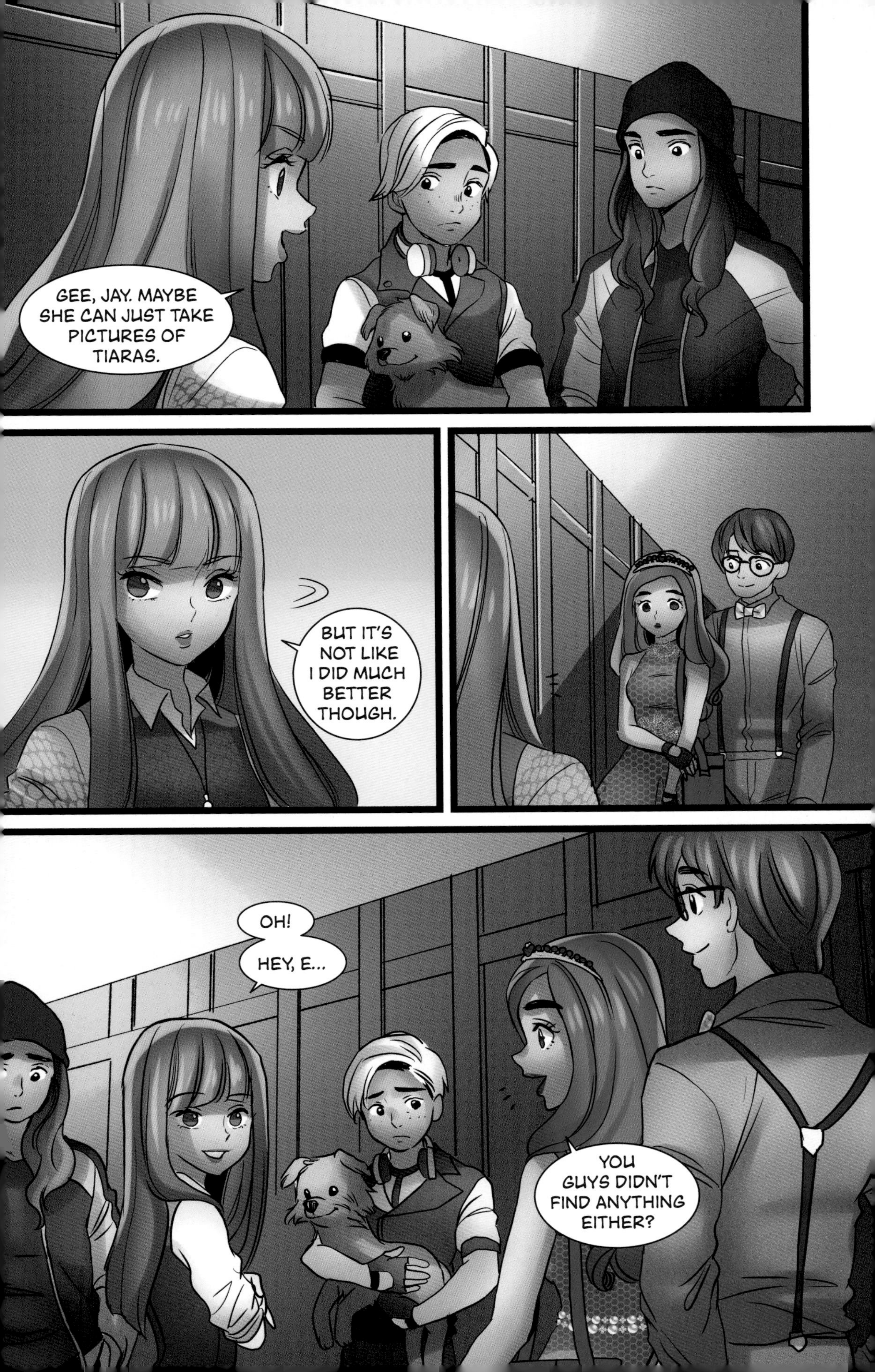
GEE, JAY. MAYBE SHE CAN JUST TAKE PICTURES OF TIARAS.
BUT IT'S NOT LIKE I DID MUCH BETTER THOUGH.
OH!
HEY, E...
YOU GUYS DIDN'T FIND ANYTHING EITHER?

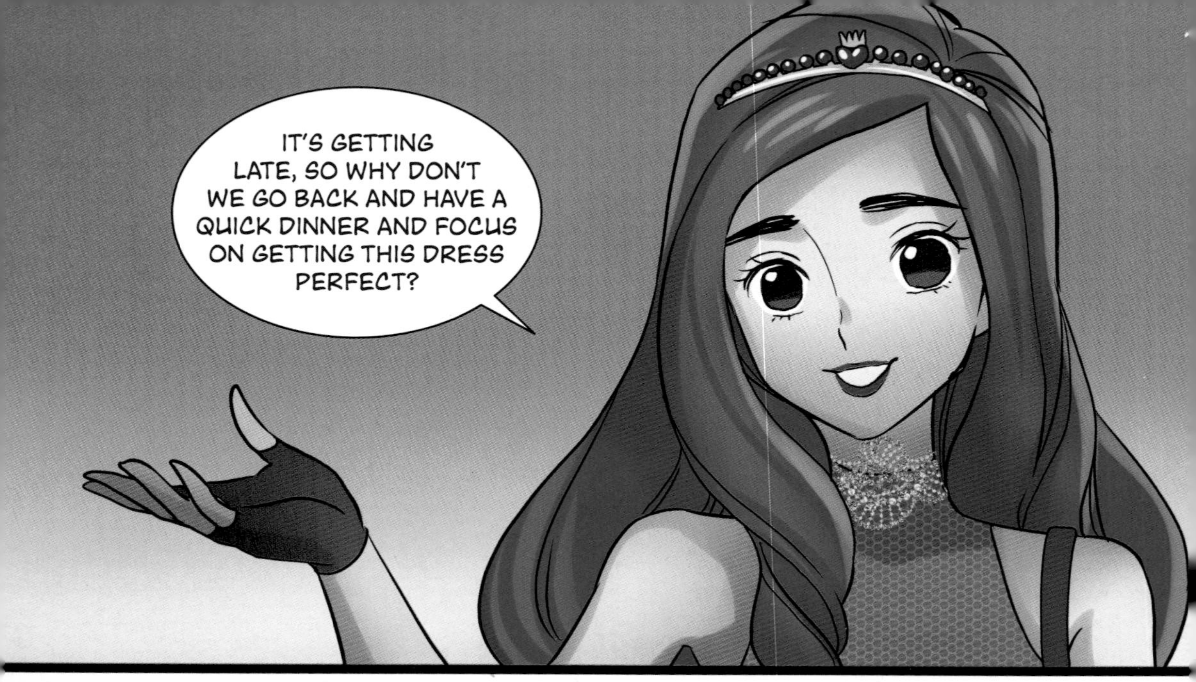
IT'S GETTING LATE, SO WHY DON'T WE GO BACK AND HAVE A QUICK DINNER AND FOCUS ON GETTING THIS DRESS PERFECT?

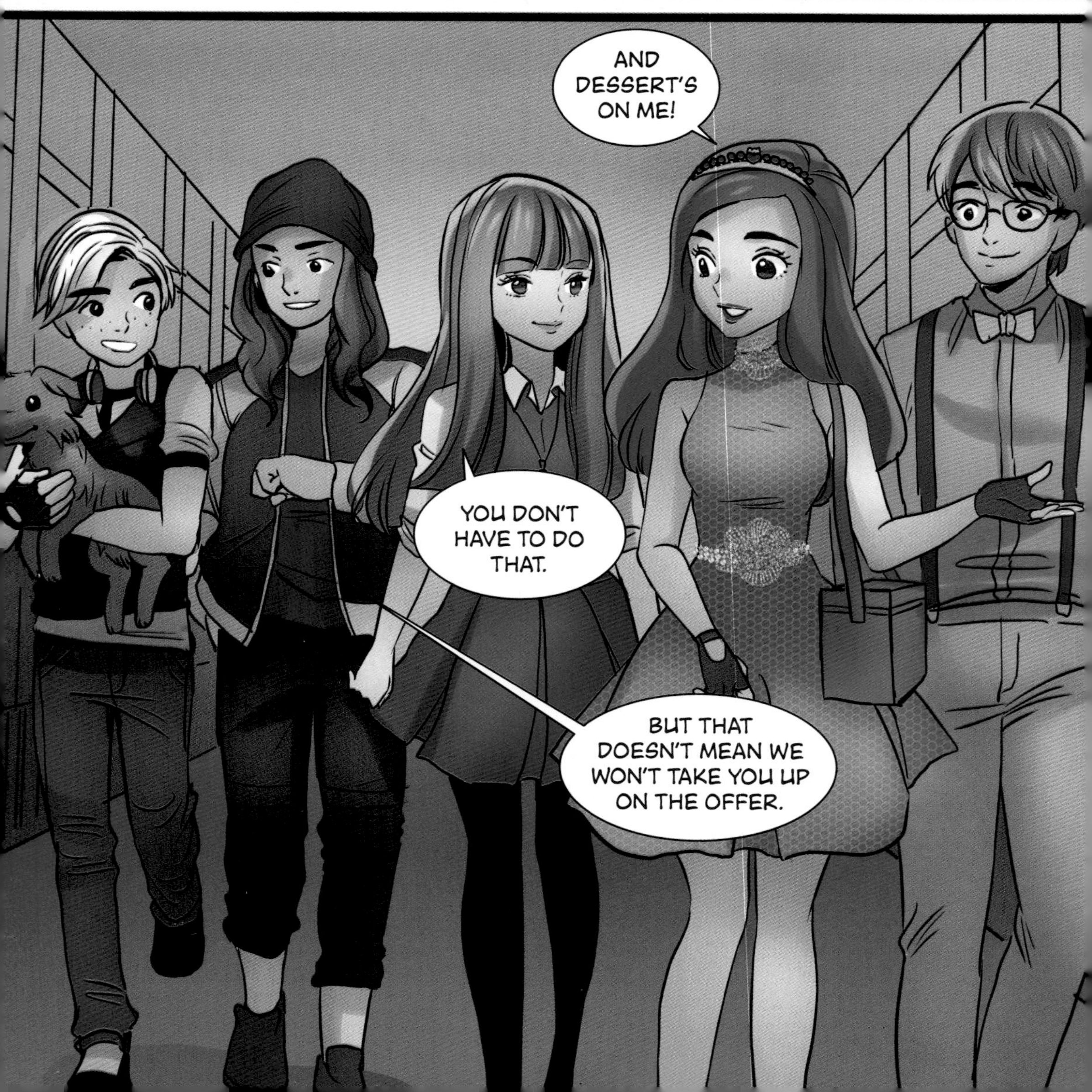
AND DESSERT'S ON ME!
YOU DON'T HAVE TO DO THAT.
BUT THAT DOESN'T MEAN WE WON'T TAKE YOU UP ON THE OFFER.

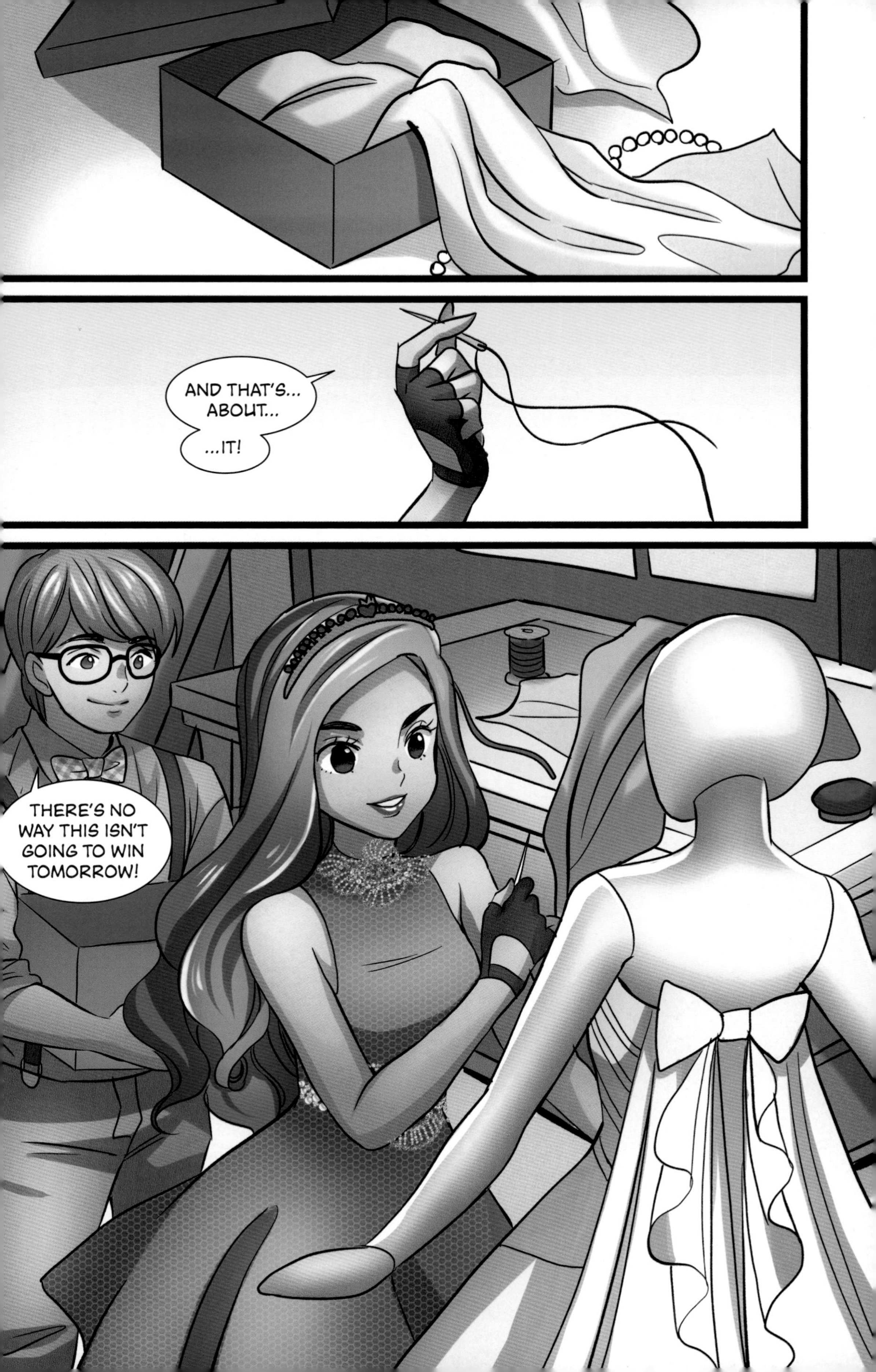
AND THAT'S... ABOUT...
...IT!
THERE'S NO WAY THIS ISN'T GOING TO WIN TOMORROW!

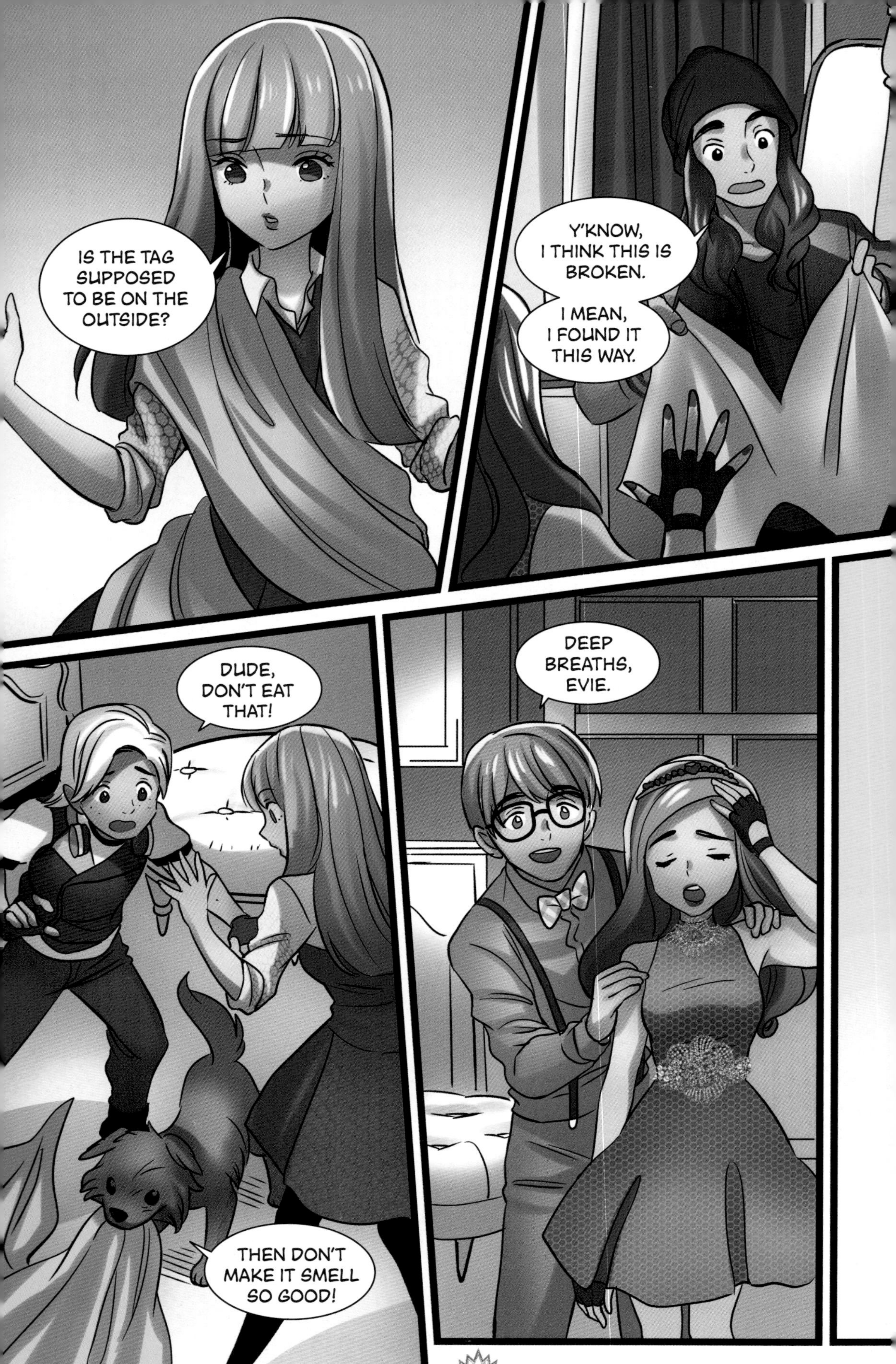
IS THE TAG SUPPOSED TO BE ON THE OUTSIDE?
Y'KNOW, I THINK THIS IS BROKEN.
I MEAN, I FOUND IT THIS WAY.
DUDE, DON'T EAT THAT!
THEN DON'T MAKE IT SMELL SO GOOD!
DEEP BREATHS, EVIE.

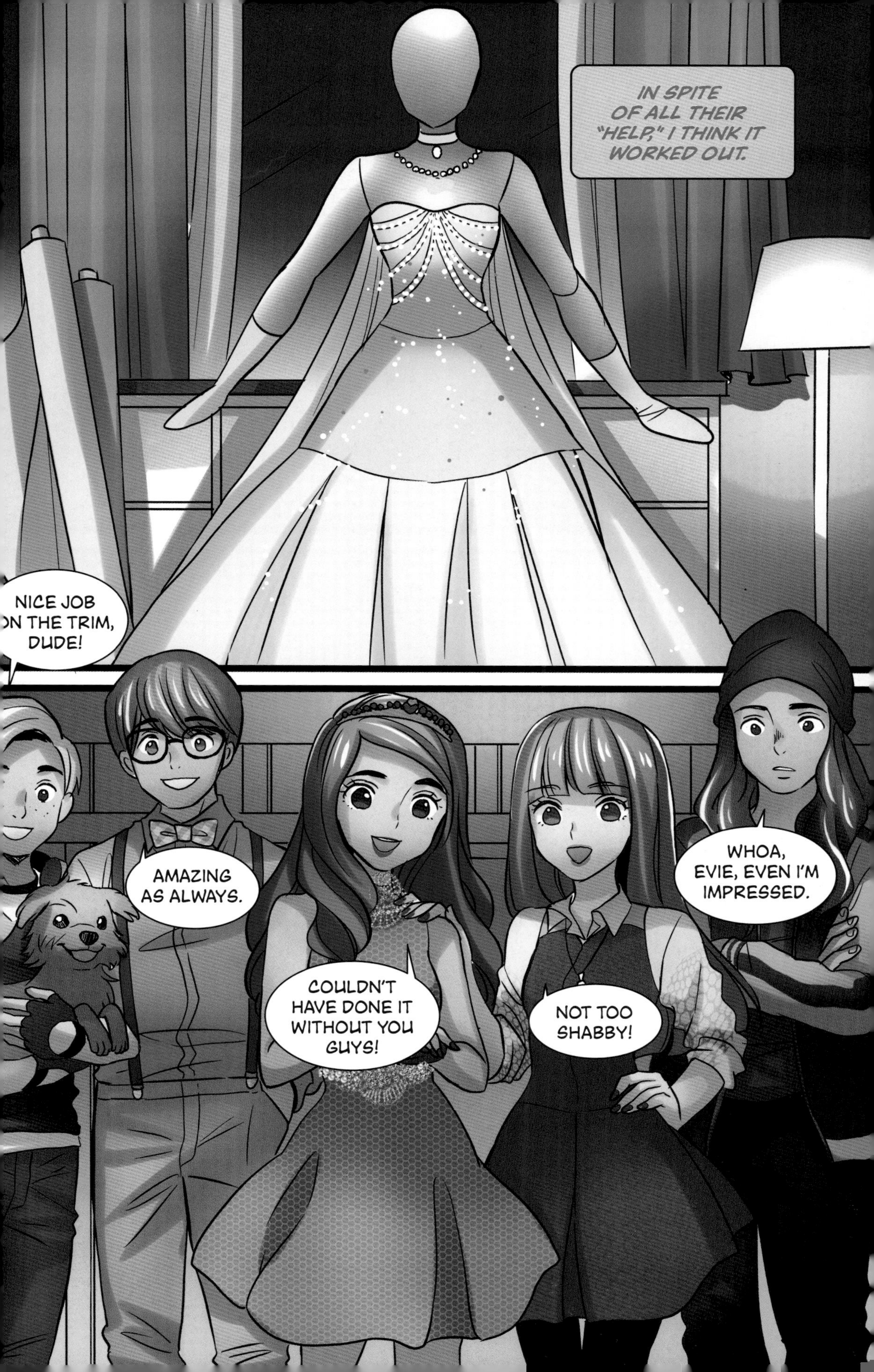
IN SPITE OF ALL THEIR "HELP," I THINK IT WORKED OUT.
NICE JOB ON THE TRIM, DUDE!
AMAZING AS ALWAYS.
COULDN'T HAVE DONE IT WITHOUT YOU GUYS!
NOT TOO SHABBY!
WHOA, EVIE, EVEN I'M IMPRESSED.

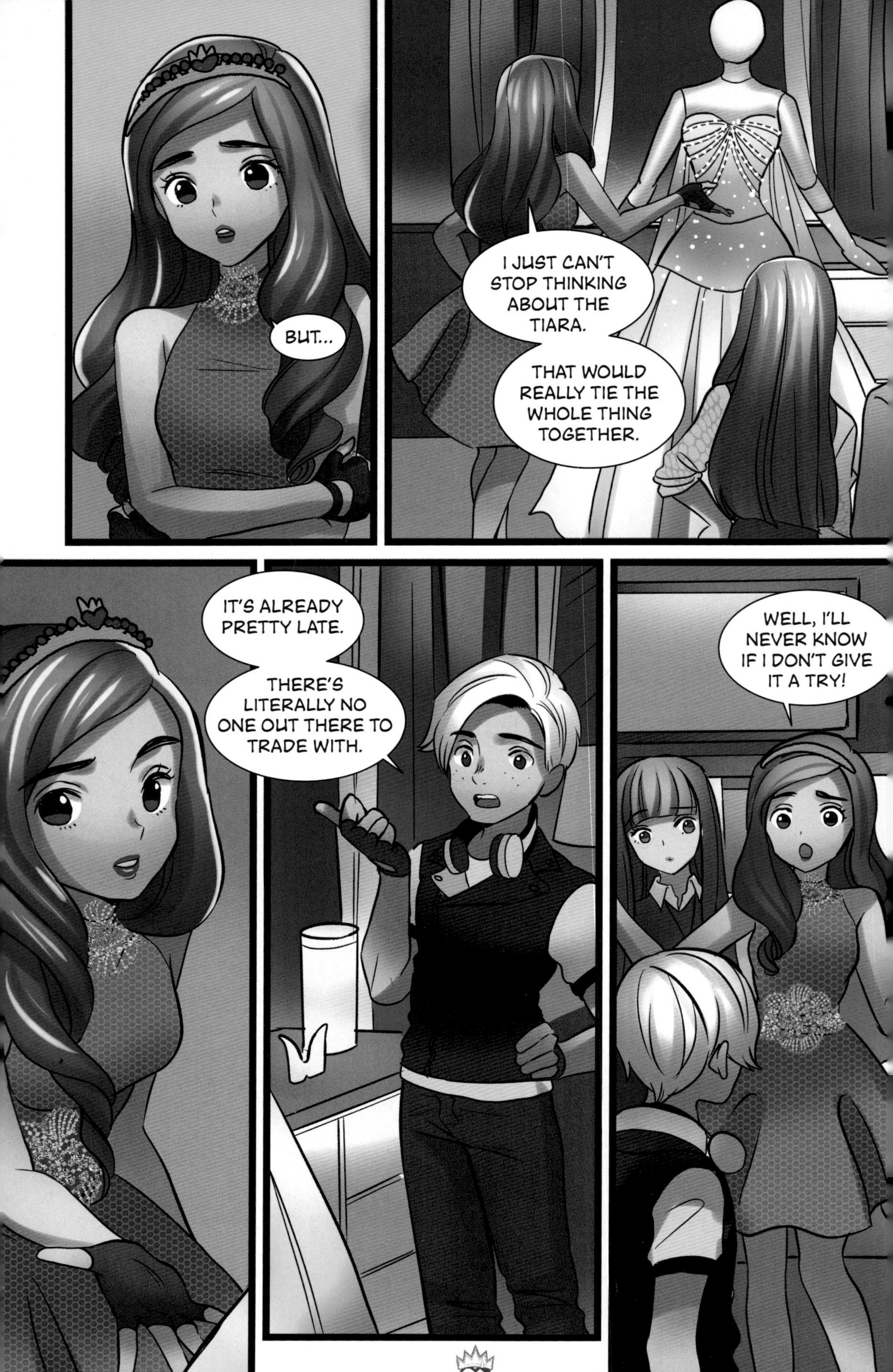
BUT...
I JUST CAN'T STOP THINKING ABOUT THE TIARA.
THAT WOULD REALLY TIE THE WHOLE THING TOGETHER.
IT'S ALREADY PRETTY LATE.
THERE'S LITERALLY NO ONE OUT THERE TO TRADE WITH.
WELL, I'LL NEVER KNOW IF I DON'T GIVE IT A TRY!

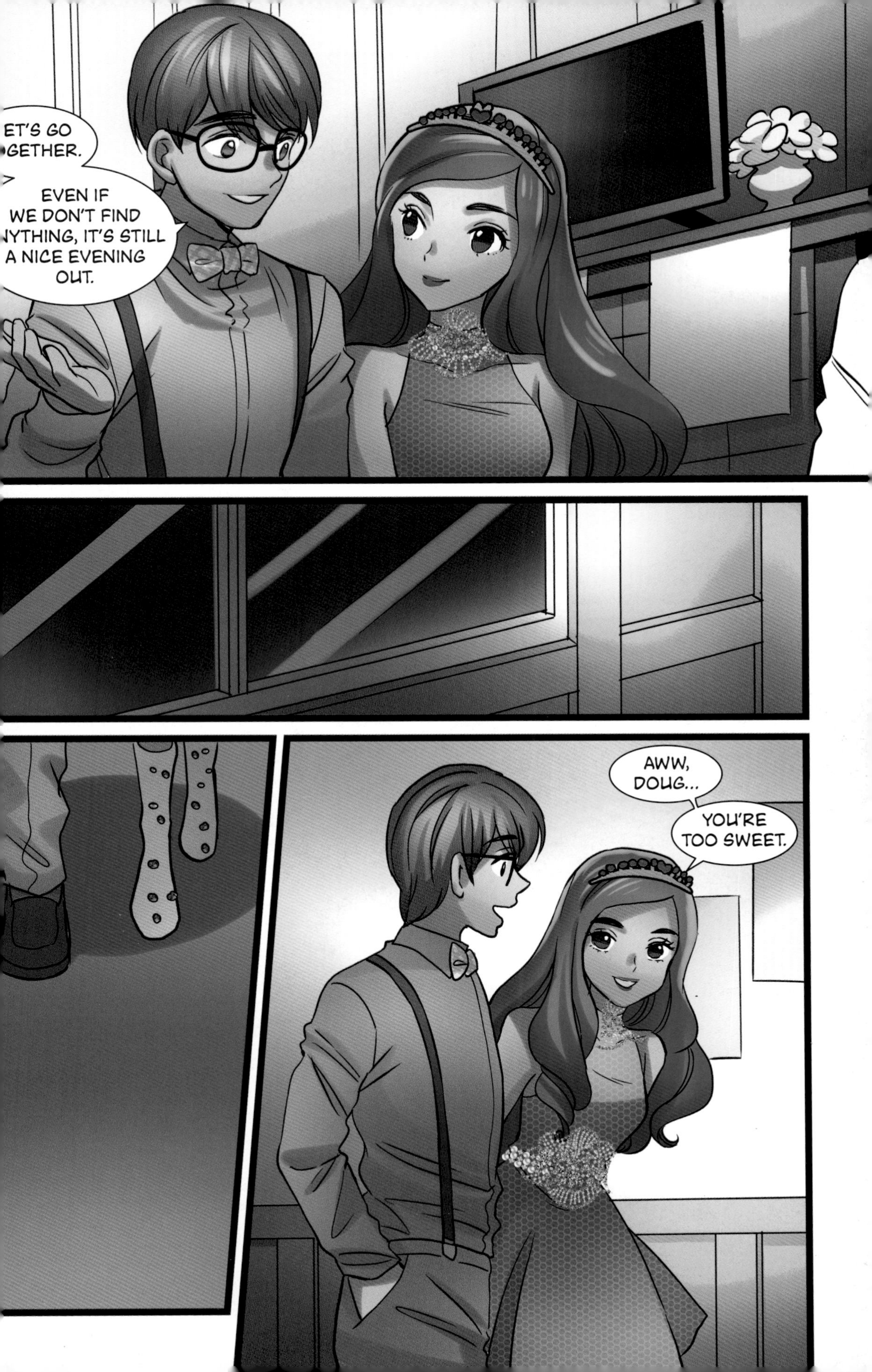
ET'S GO
GETHER.
EVEN IF WE DON'T FIND NYTHING, IT'S STILL A NICE EVENING OUT.
AWW, DOUG...
YOU'RE TOO SWEET.

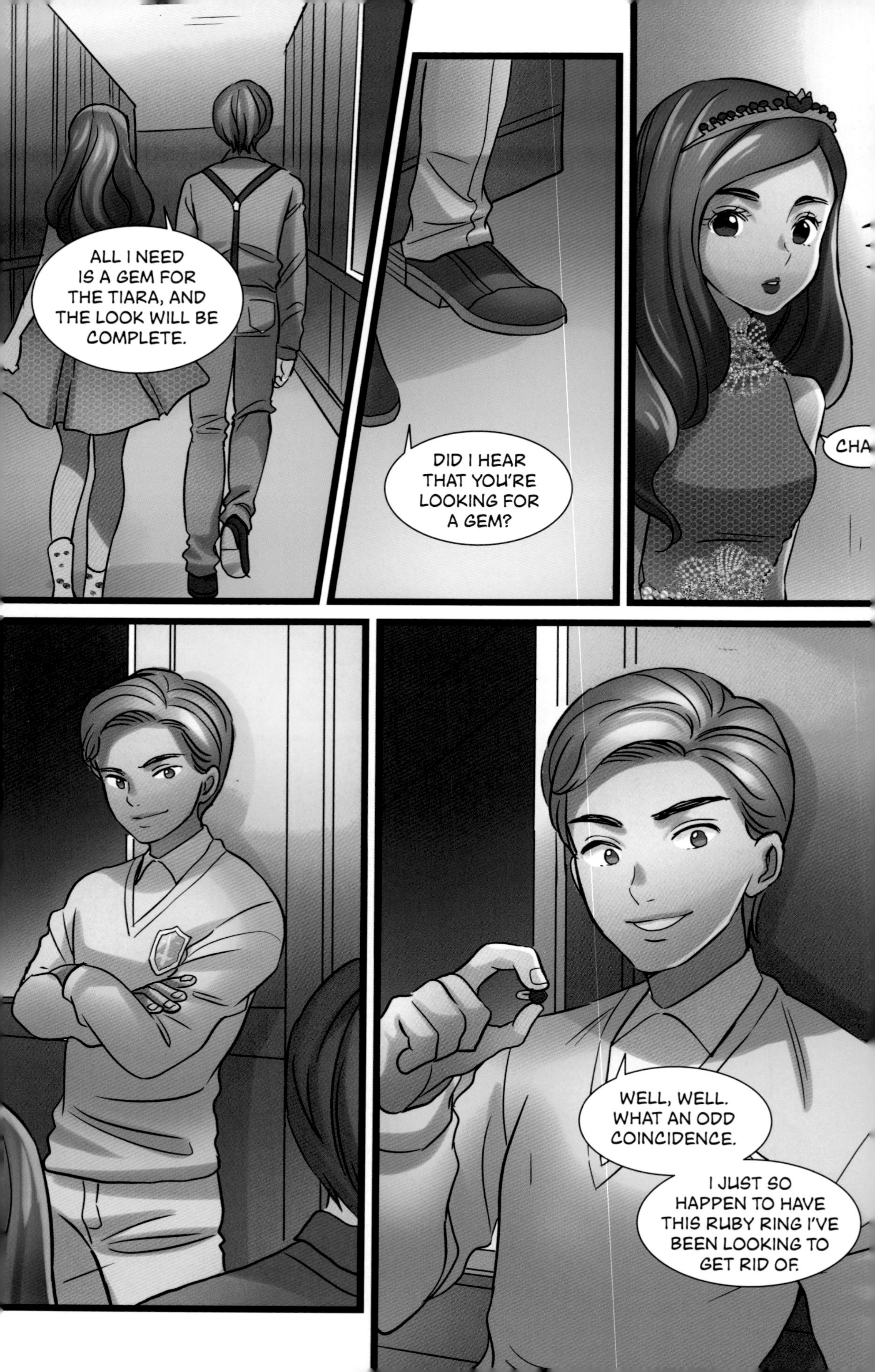
ALL I NEED IS A GEM FOR THE TIARA, AND THE LOOK WILL BE COMPLETE.
DID I HEAR THAT YOU'RE LOOKING FOR A GEM?
CHA
WELL, WELL. WHAT AN ODD COINCIDENCE.
I JUST SO HAPPEN TO HAVE THIS RUBY RING I'VE BEEN LOOKING TO GET RID OF.

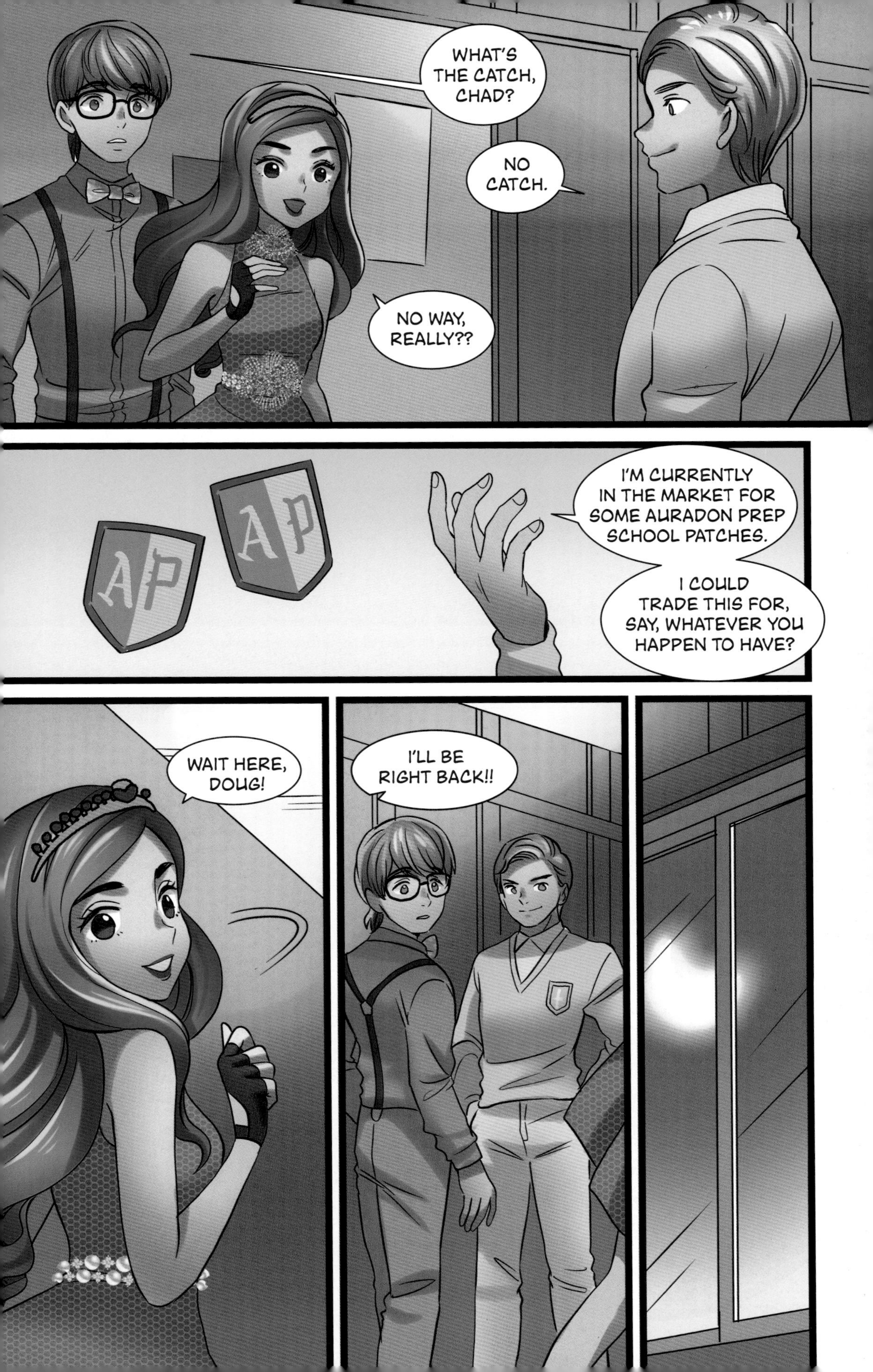
WHAT'S THE CATCH, CHAD?
NO CATCH.
NO WAY, REALLY??
I'M CURRENTLY IN THE MARKET FOR SOME AURADON PREP SCHOOL PATCHES.
I COULD TRADE THIS FOR, SAY, WHATEVER YOU HAPPEN TO HAVE?
AP
AP
WAIT HERE, DOUG!
I'LL BE RIGHT BACK!!

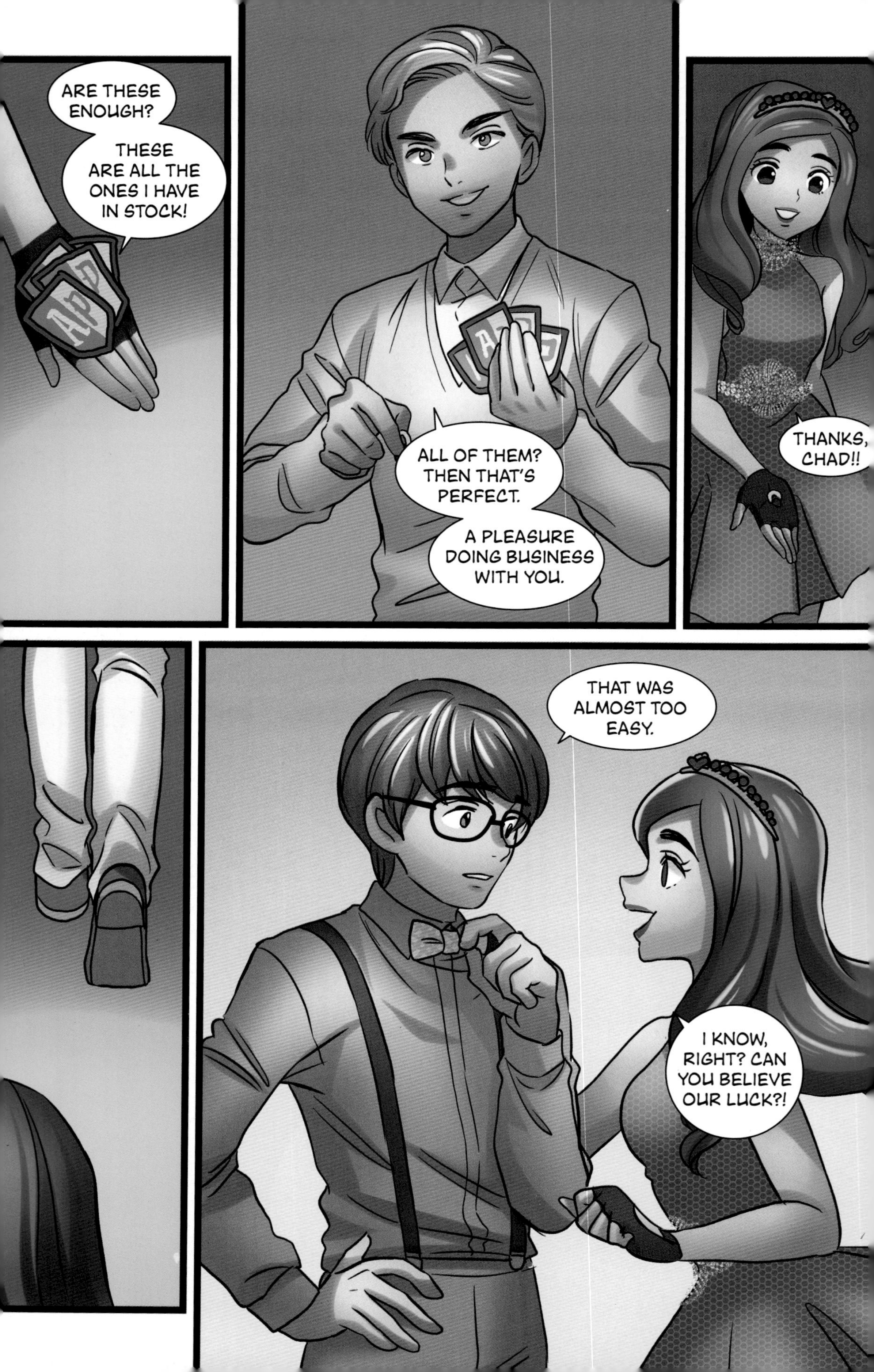
ARE THESE ENOUGH?
THESE ARE ALL THE ONES I HAVE IN STOCK!
ALL OF THEM? THEN THAT'S PERFECT.
A PLEASURE DOING BUSINESS WITH YOU.
THANKS, CHAD!!
THAT WAS ALMOST TOO EASY.
I KNOW, RIGHT? CAN YOU BELIEVE OUR LUCK?!

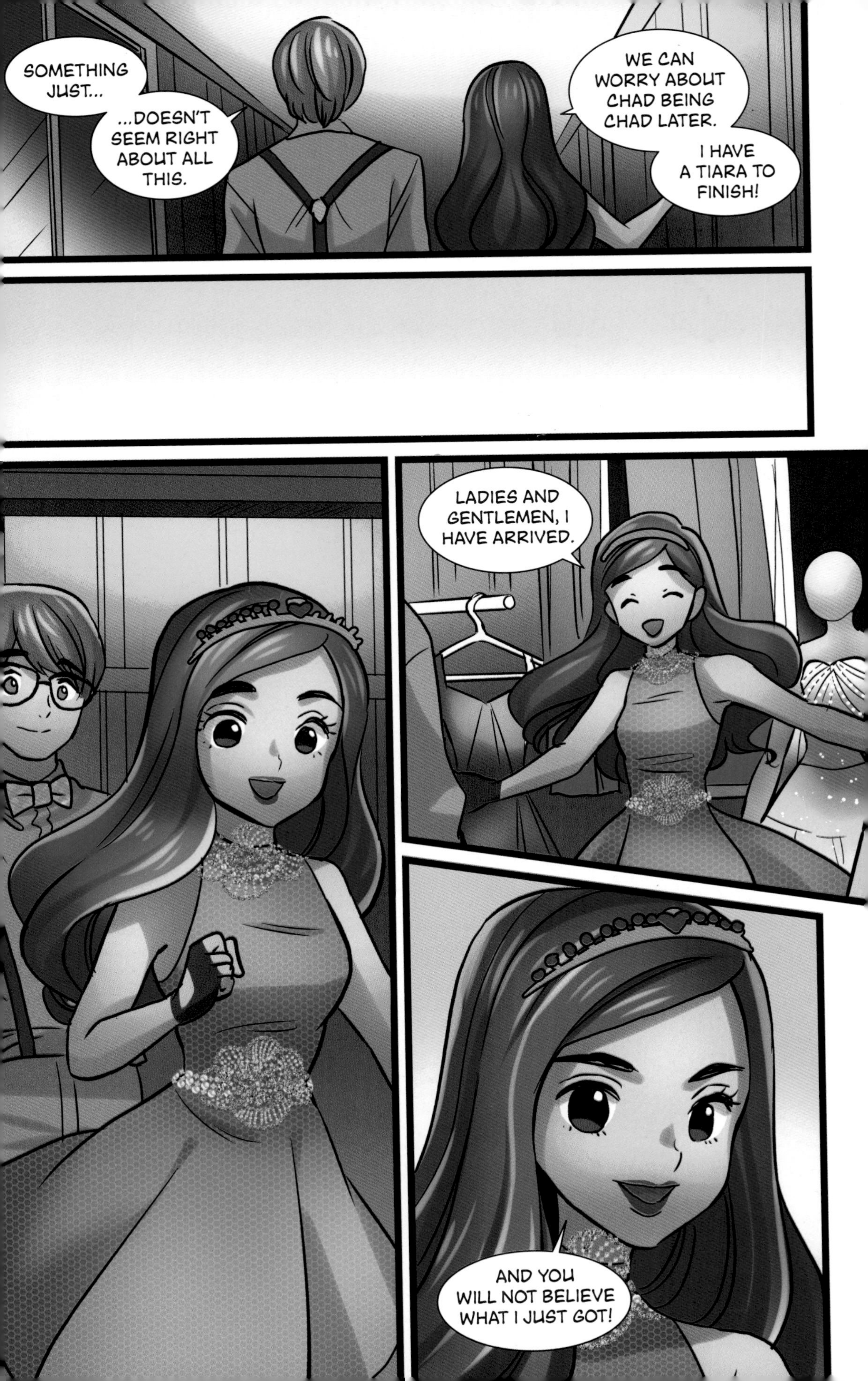
SOMETHING JUST...
...DOESN'T SEEM RIGHT ABOUT ALL THIS.
WE CAN WORRY ABOUT CHAD BEING CHAD LATER.
I HAVE A TIARA TO FINISH!
LADIES AND GENTLEMEN, I HAVE ARRIVED.
AND YOU WILL NOT BELIEVE WHAT I JUST GOT!

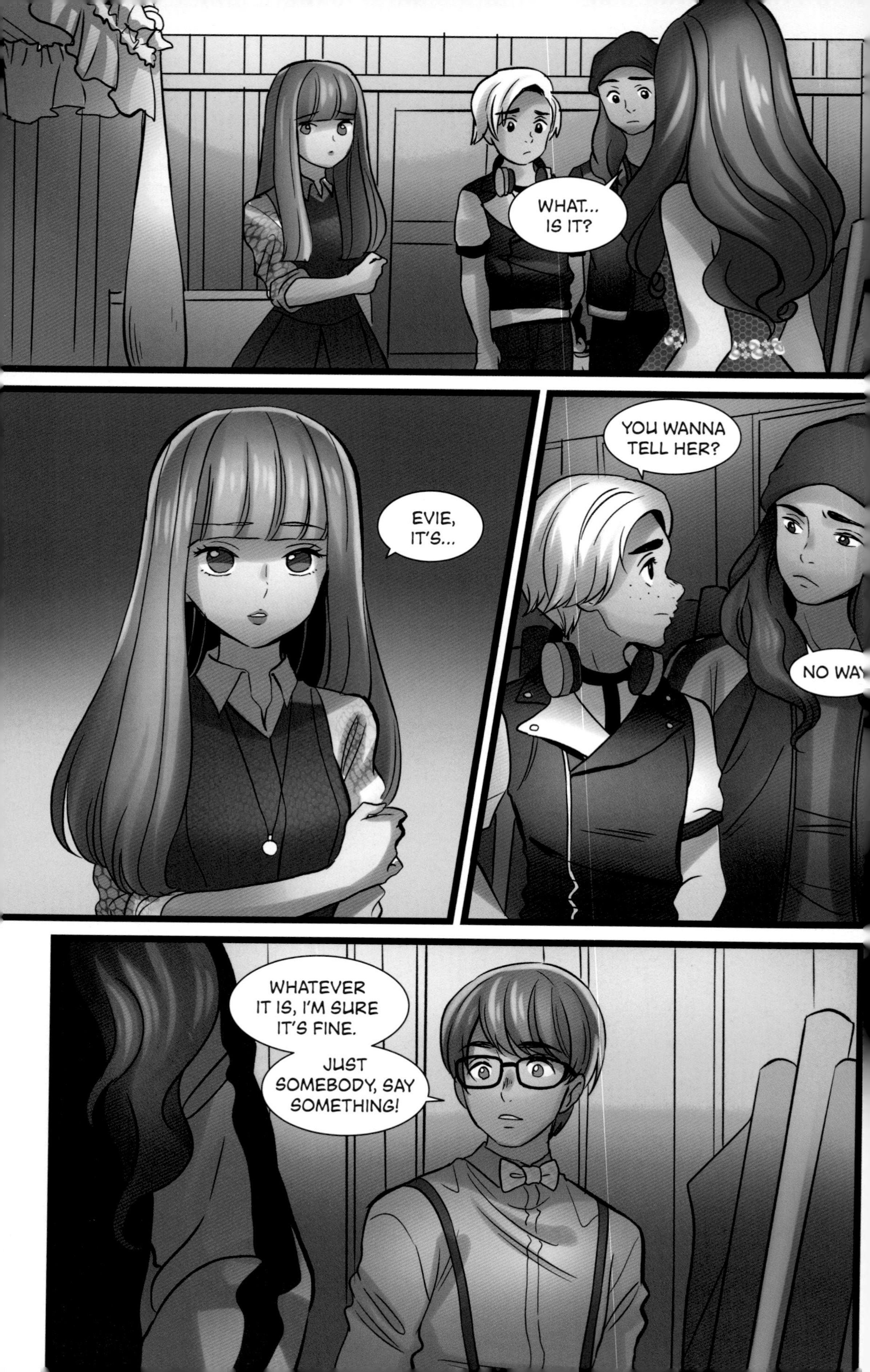
WHAT... IS IT?
EVIE, IT'S...
YOU WANNA TELL HER?
NO WAY
WHATEVER IT IS, I'M SURE IT'S FINE.
JUST SOMEBODY, SAY SOMETHING!

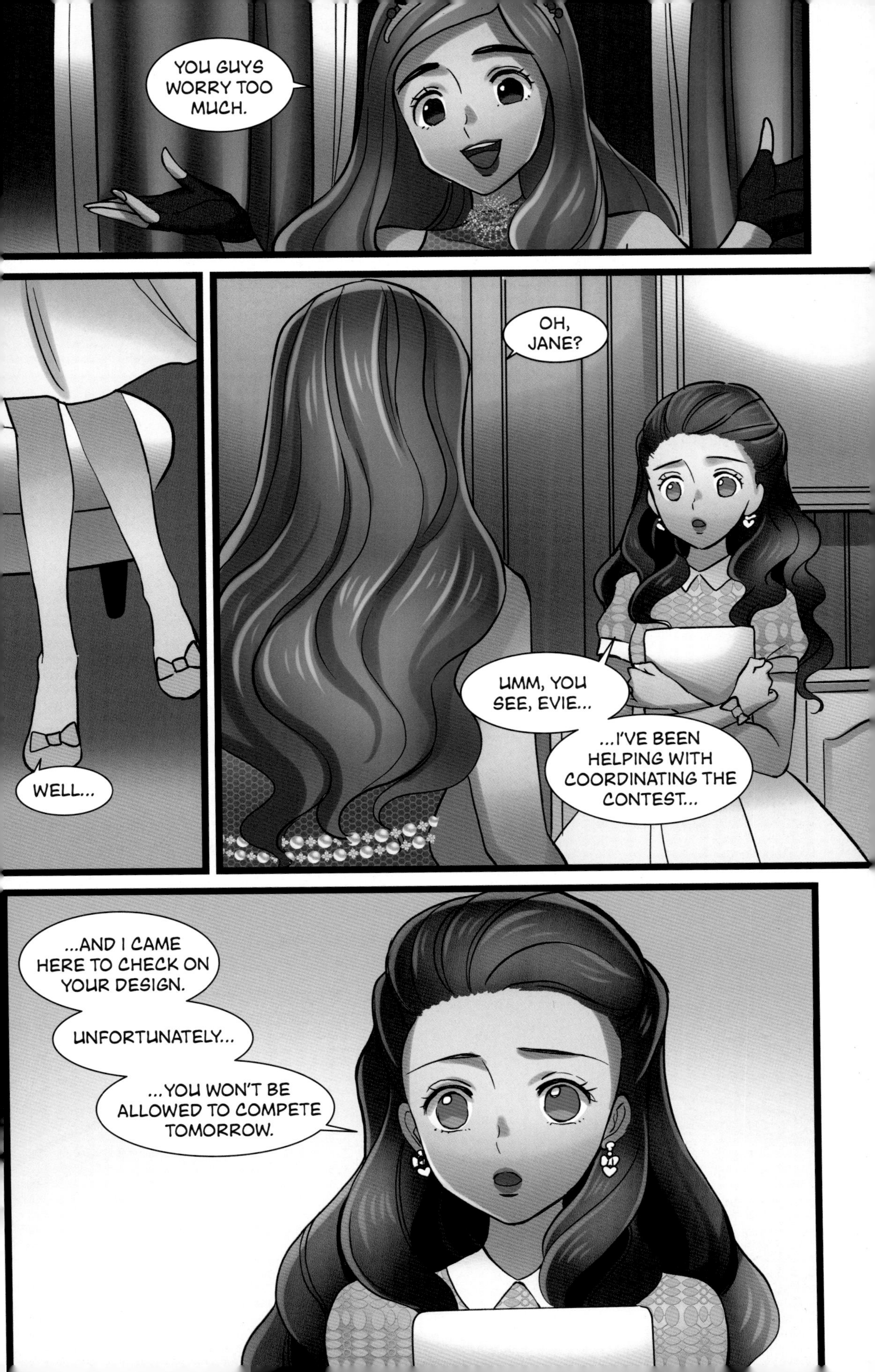
YOU GUYS WORRY TOO MUCH.
WELL...
OH, JANE?
UMM, YOU SEE, EVIE...
...I'VE BEEN HELPING WITH COORDINATING THE CONTEST...
...AND I CAME HERE TO CHECK ON YOUR DESIGN.
UNFORTUNATELY...
...YOU WON'T BE ALLOWED TO COMPETE TOMORROW.

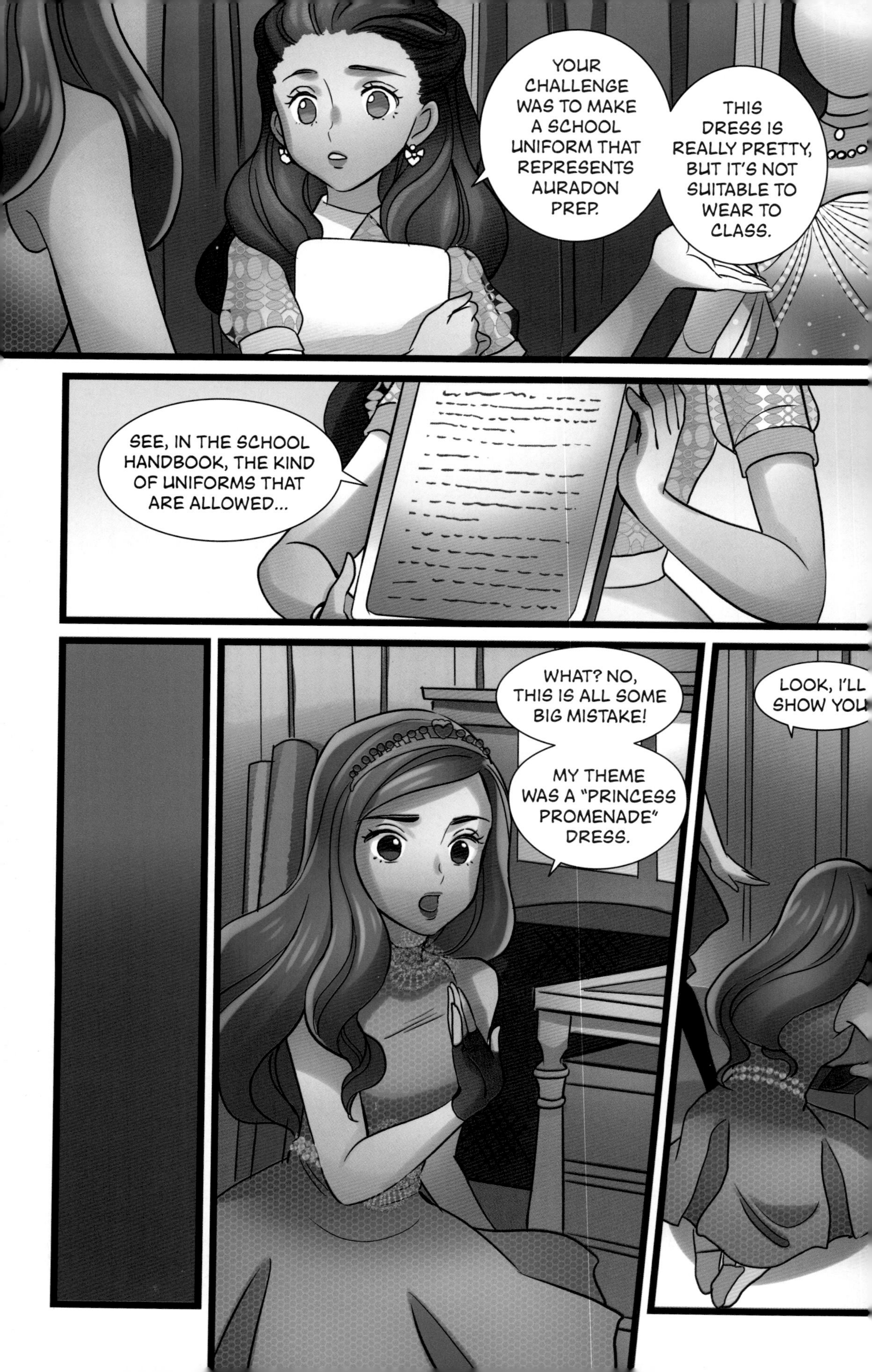
YOUR CHALLENGE WAS TO MAKE A SCHOOL UNIFORM THAT REPRESENTS AURADON PREP.
THIS DRESS IS REALLY PRETTY, BUT IT'S NOT SUITABLE TO WEAR TO CLASS.
SEE, IN THE SCHOOL HANDBOOK, THE KIND OF UNIFORMS THAT ARE ALLOWED...
WHAT? NO, THIS IS ALL SOME BIG MISTAKE!
MY THEME WAS A "PRINCESS PROMENADE" DRESS.
LOOK, I'LL SHOW YOU

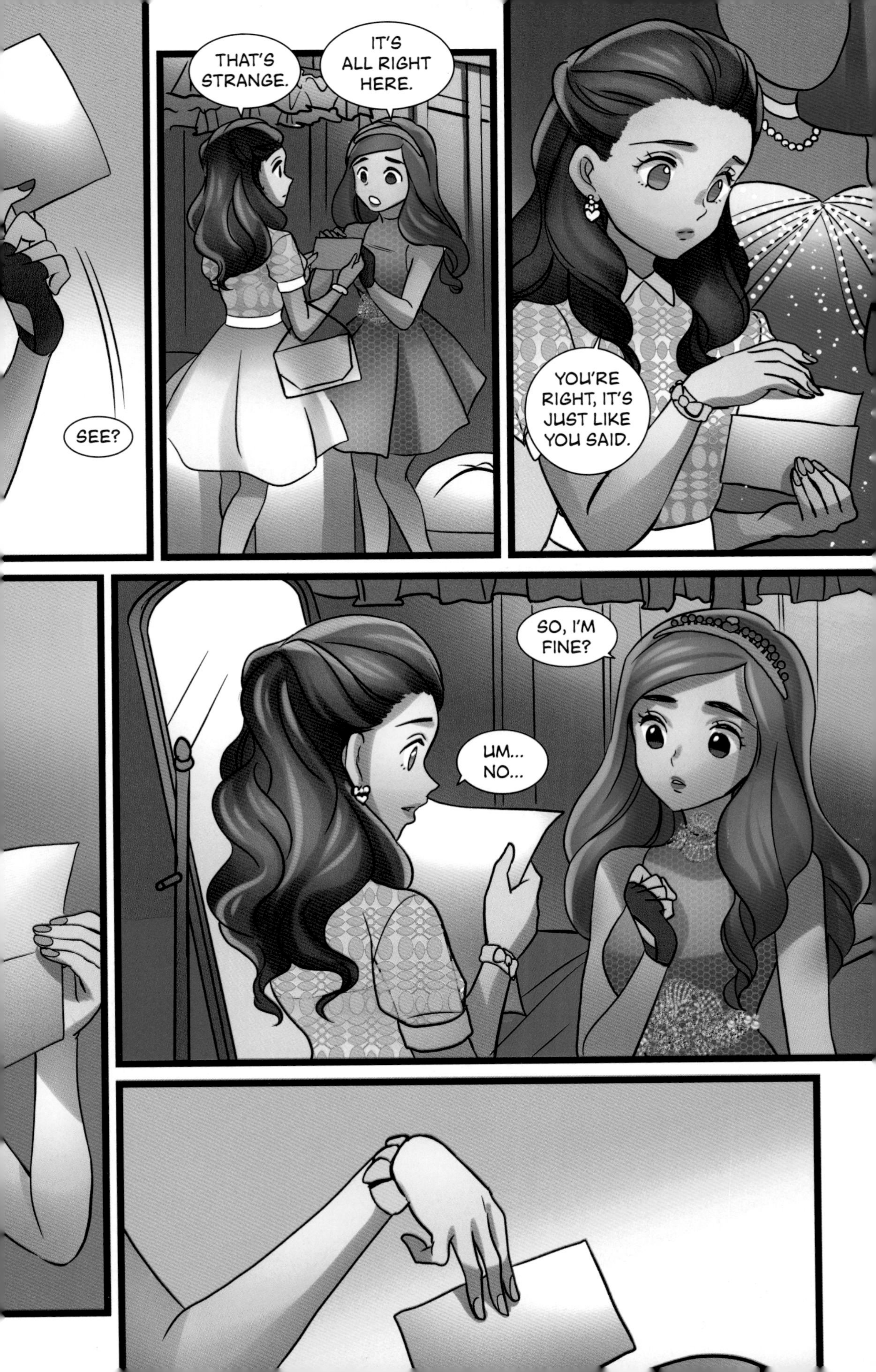
SEE?
THAT'S STRANGE.
IT'S ALL RIGHT HERE.
YOU'RE RIGHT, IT'S JUST LIKE YOU SAID.
SO, I'M FINE?
UM... NO...

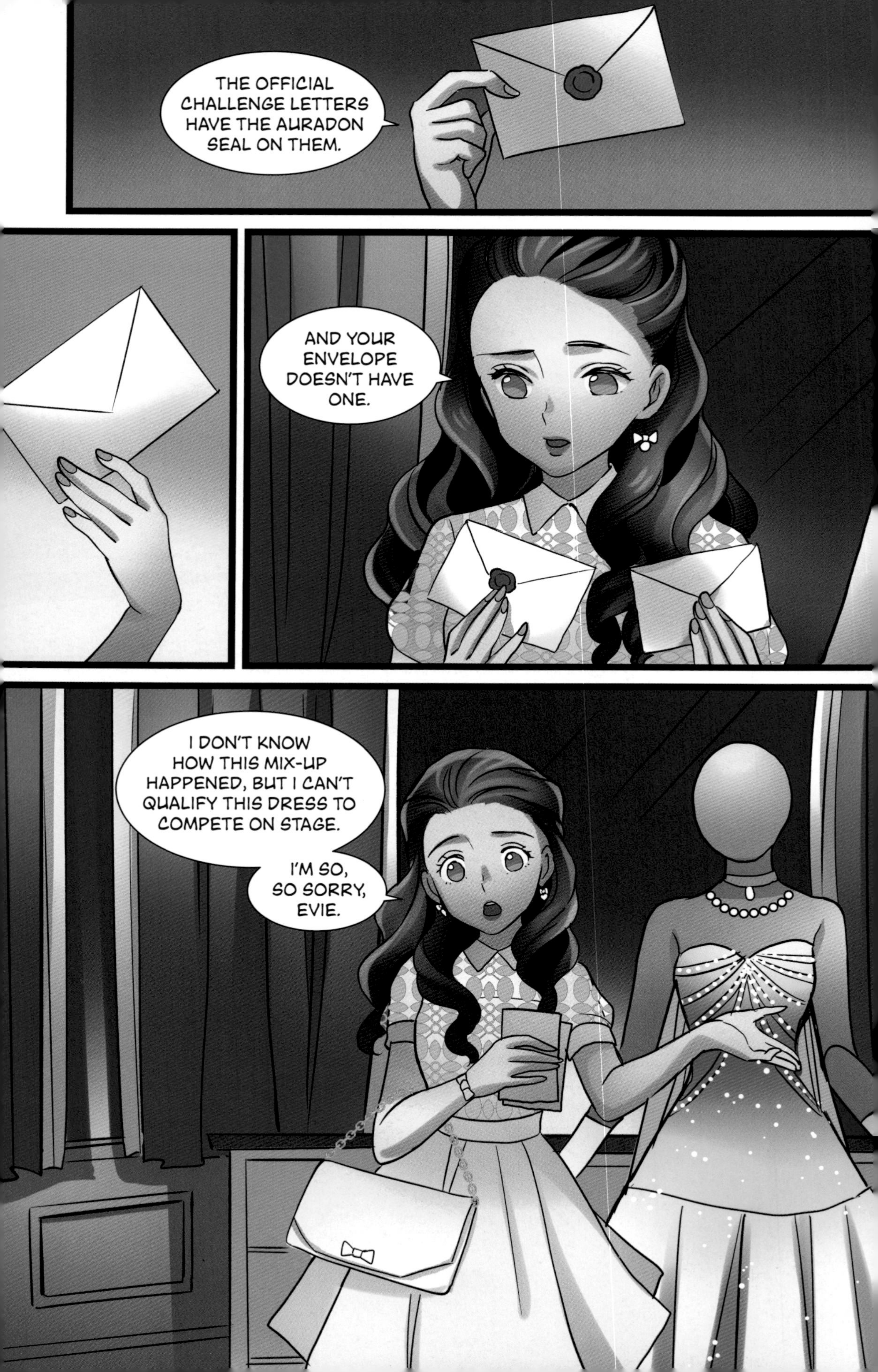
THE OFFICIAL CHALLENGE LETTERS HAVE THE AURADON SEAL ON THEM.
AND YOUR ENVELOPE DOESN'T HAVE ONE.
I DON'T KNOW HOW THIS MIX-UP HAPPENED, BUT I CAN'T QUALIFY THIS DRESS TO COMPETE ON STAGE.
I'M SO, SO SORRY, EVIE.

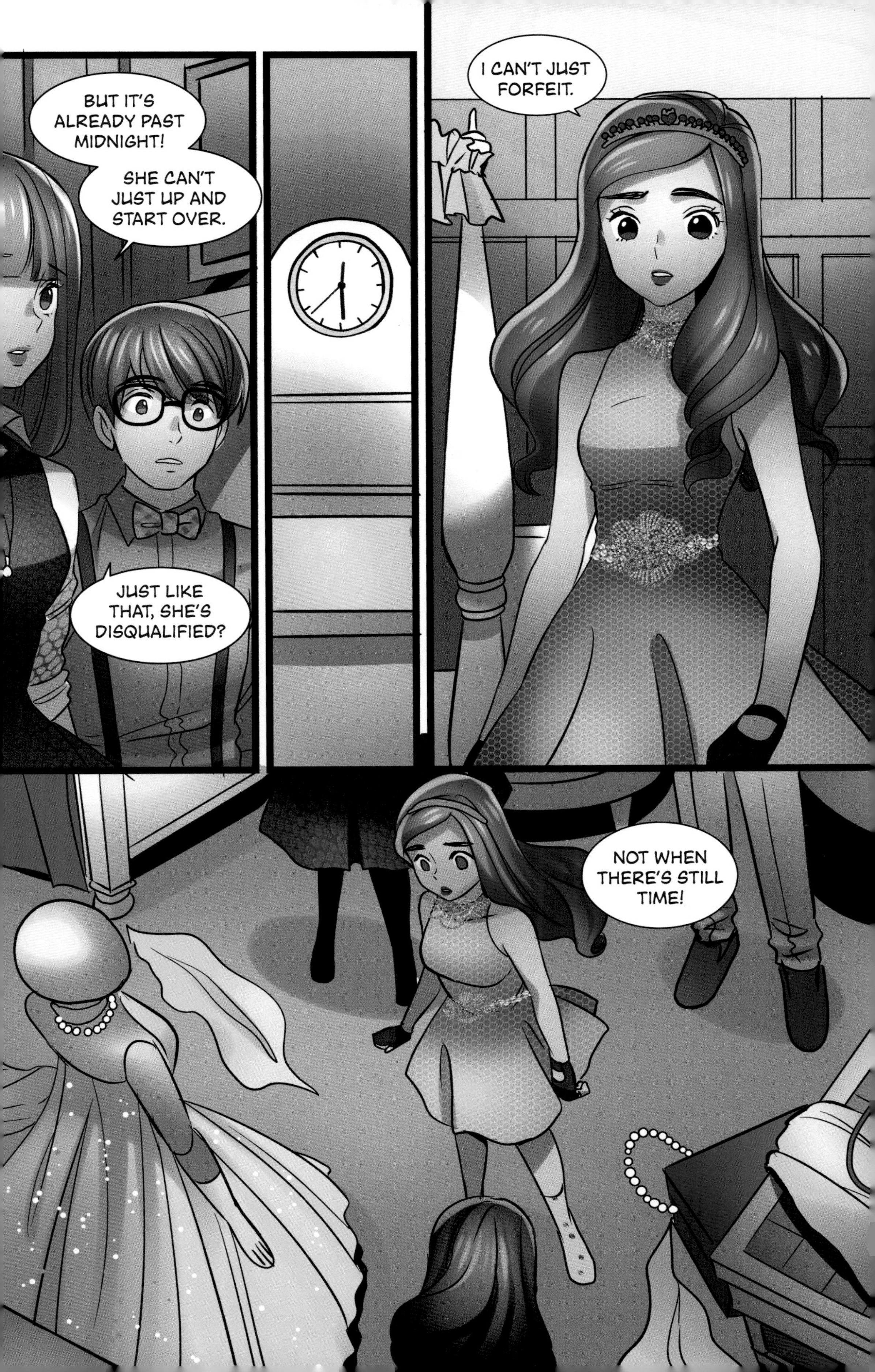
BUT IT'S ALREADY PAST MIDNIGHT!
SHE CAN'T JUST UP AND START OVER.
JUST LIKE THAT, SHE'S DISQUALIFIED?
I CAN'T JUST FORFEIT.
NOT WHEN THERE'S STILL TIME!

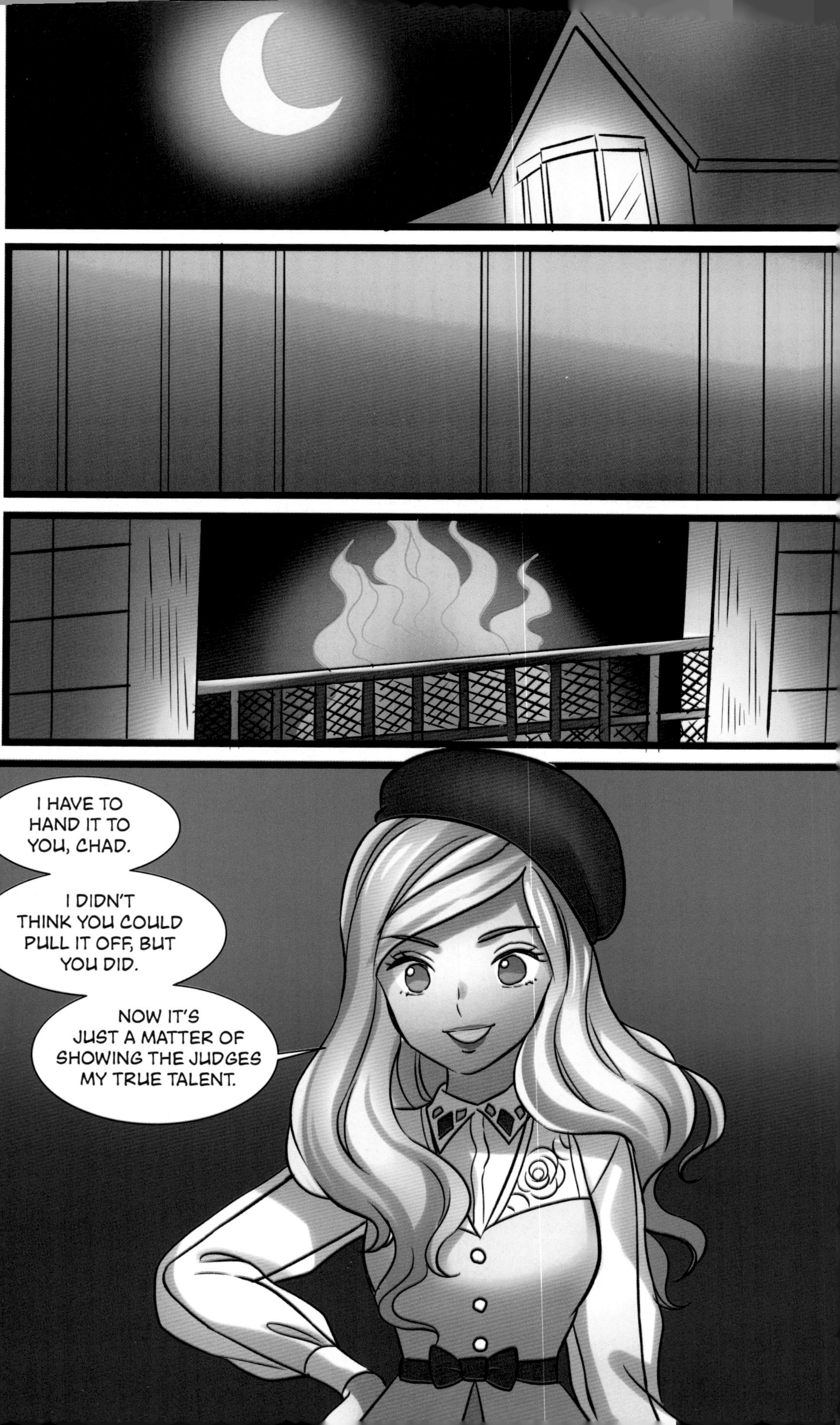
I HAVE TO HAND IT TO YOU, CHAD.
I DIDN'T THINK YOU COULD PULL IT OFF, BUT YOU DID.
NOW IT'S JUST A MATTER OF SHOWING THE JUDGES MY TRUE TALENT.

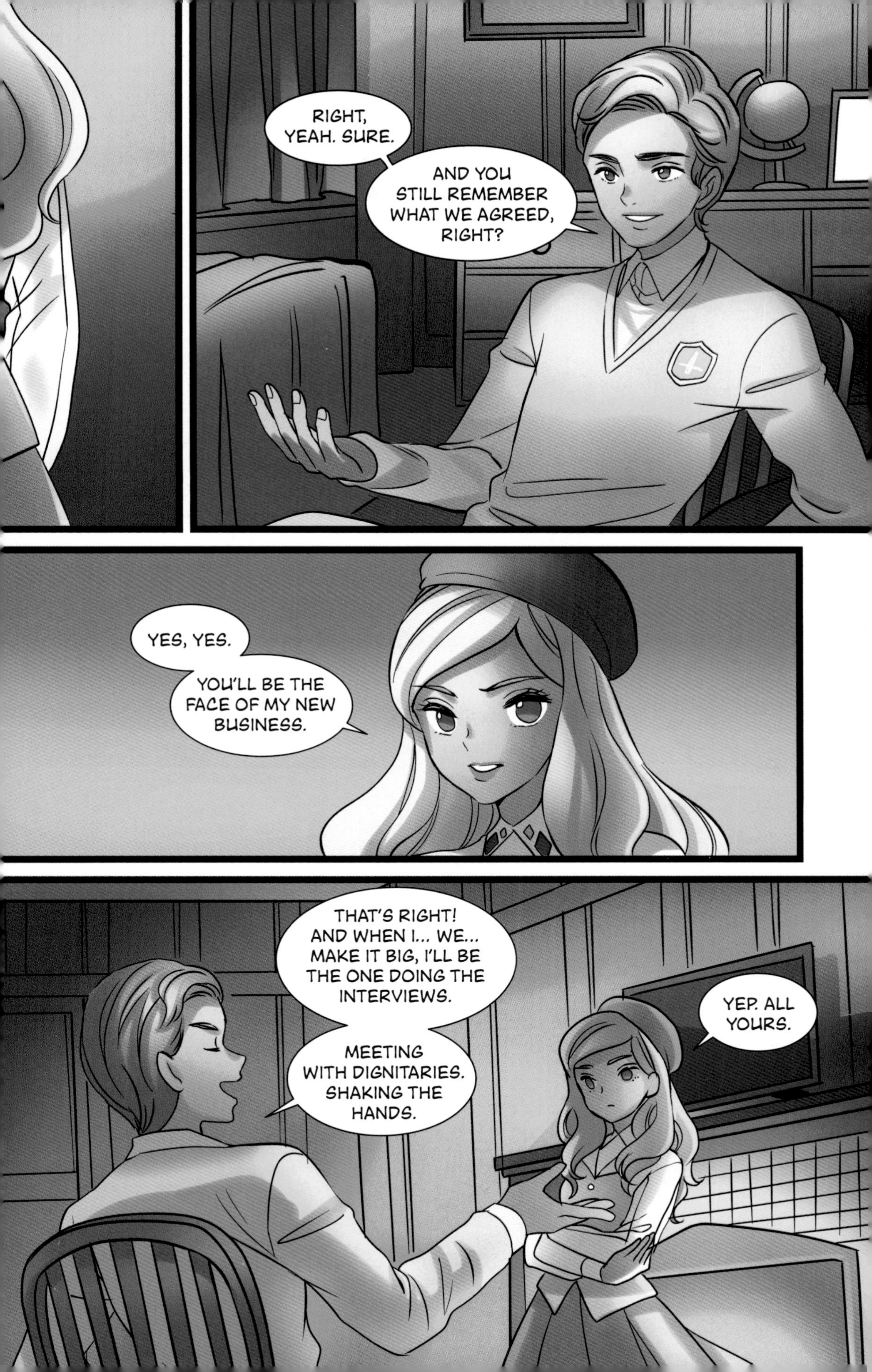
RIGHT, YEAH. SURE.
AND YOU STILL REMEMBER WHAT WE AGREED, RIGHT?
YES, YES.
YOU'LL BE THE FACE OF MY NEW BUSINESS.
THAT'S RIGHT! AND WHEN I... WE... MAKE IT BIG, I'LL BE THE ONE DOING THE INTERVIEWS.
MEETING WITH DIGNITARIES. SHAKING THE HANDS.
YEP. ALL YOURS.

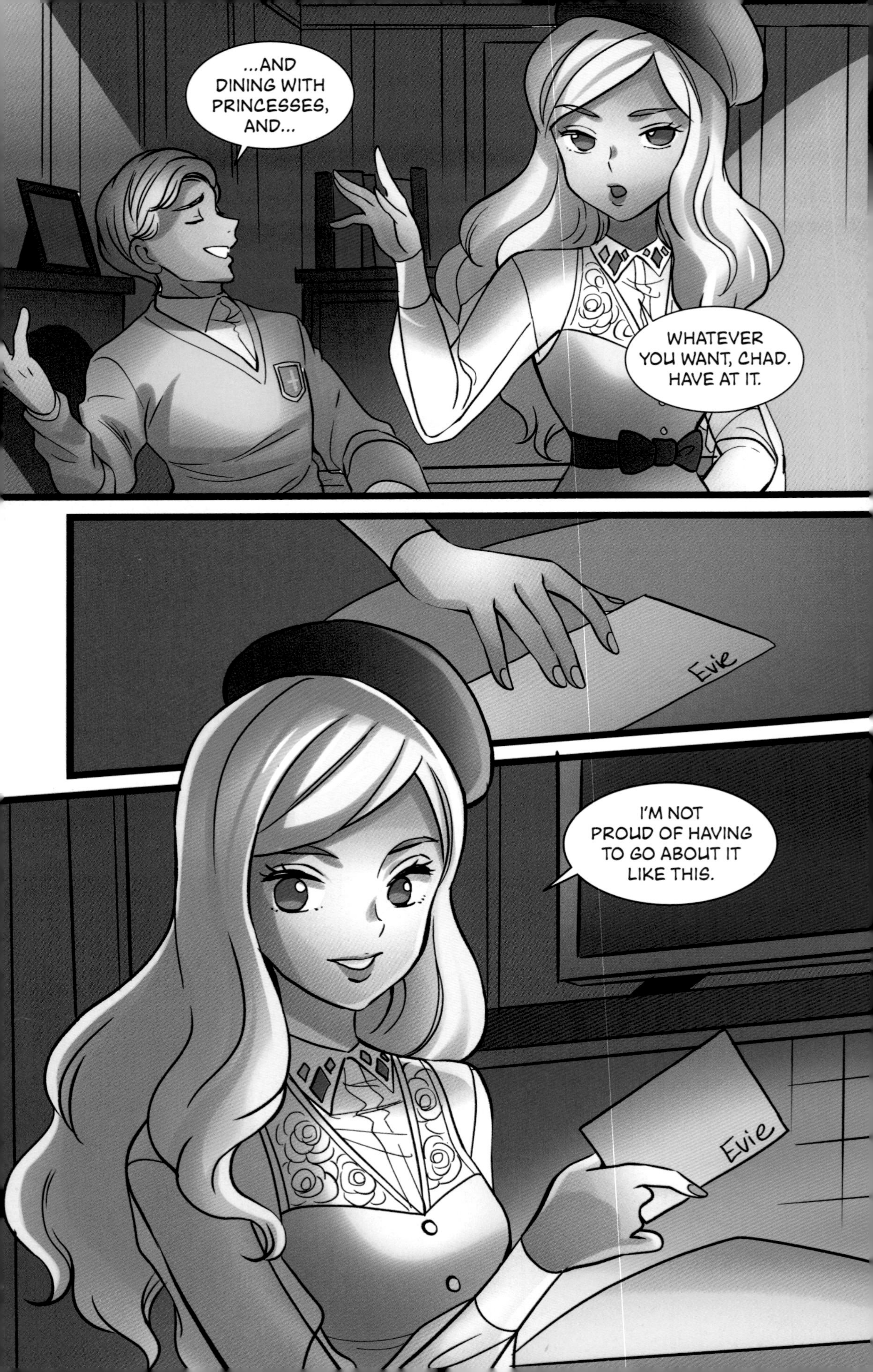
...AND DINING WITH PRINCESSES, AND...
WHATEVER YOU WANT, CHAD. HAVE AT IT.
Evie
I'M NOT PROUD OF HAVING TO GO ABOUT IT LIKE THIS.
Evie

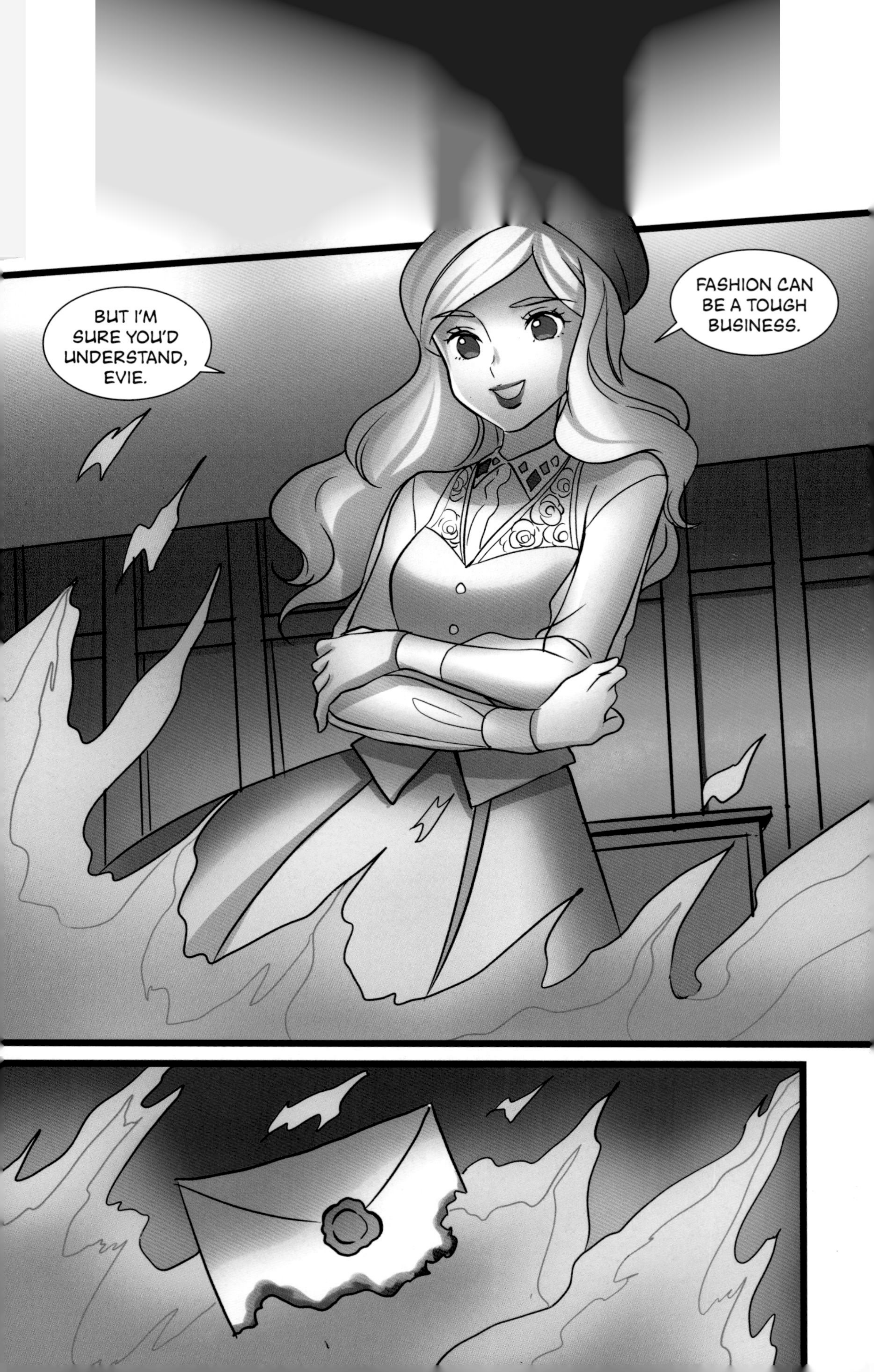
FASHION CAN BE A TOUGH BUSINESS.
BUT I'M SURE YOU'D UNDERSTAND, EVIE.

EVIE'S WICKED RUNWAY

BOOK 1

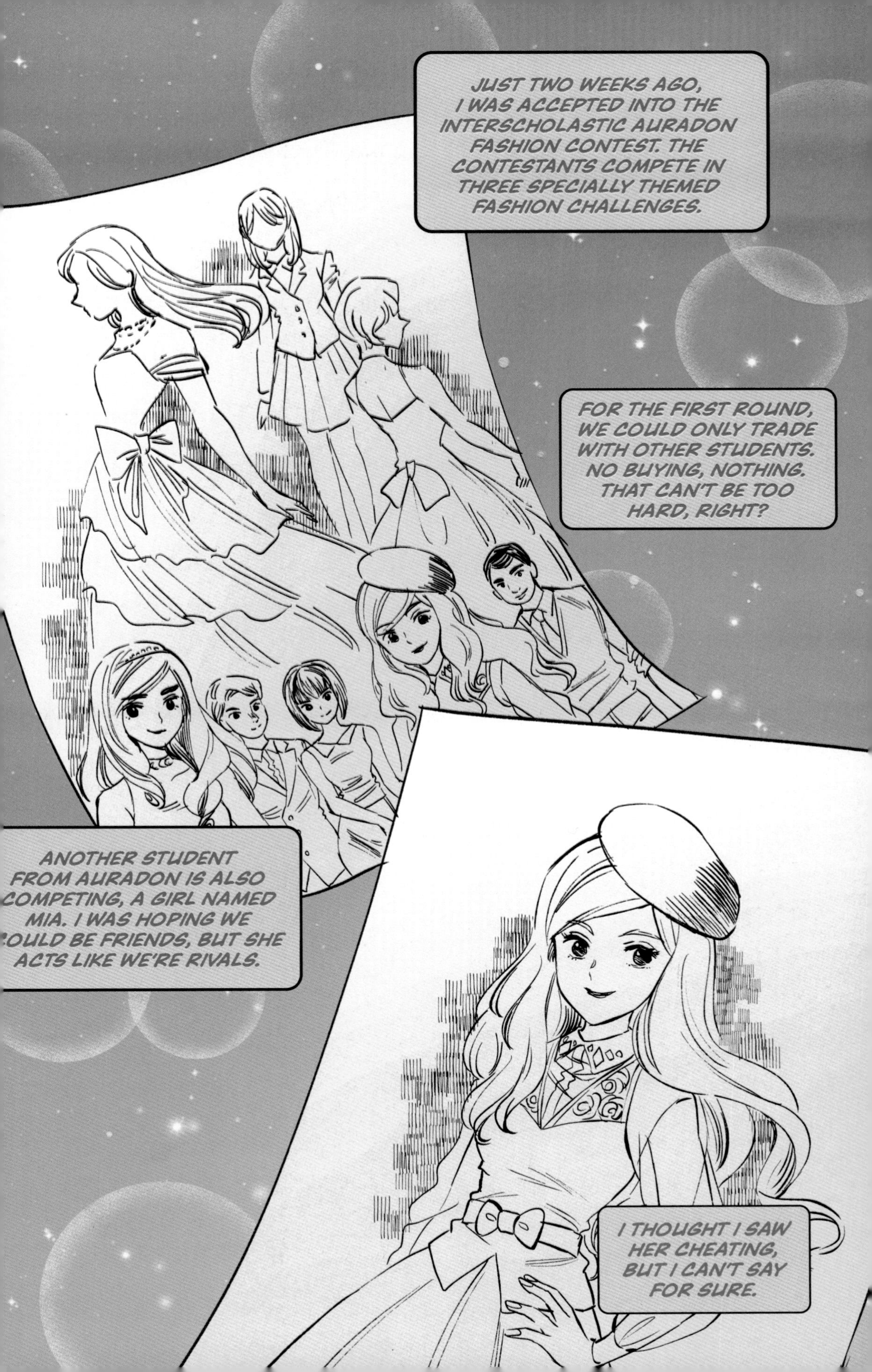

JUST TWO WEEKS AGO, I WAS ACCEPTED INTO THE INTERSCHOLASTIC AURADON FASHION CONTEST. THE CONTESTANTS COMPETE IN THREE SPECIALLY THEMED FASHION CHALLENGES.
FOR THE FIRST ROUND, WE COULD ONLY TRADE WITH OTHER STUDENTS. NO BUYING, NOTHING. THAT CAN'T BE TOO HARD, RIGHT?
ANOTHER STUDENT FROM AURADON IS ALSO COMPETING, A GIRL NAMED MIA. I WAS HOPING WE OULD BE FRIENDS, BUT SHE ACTS LIKE WE'RE RIVALS.
I THOUGHT I SAW HER CHEATING, BUT I CAN'T SAY FOR SURE.

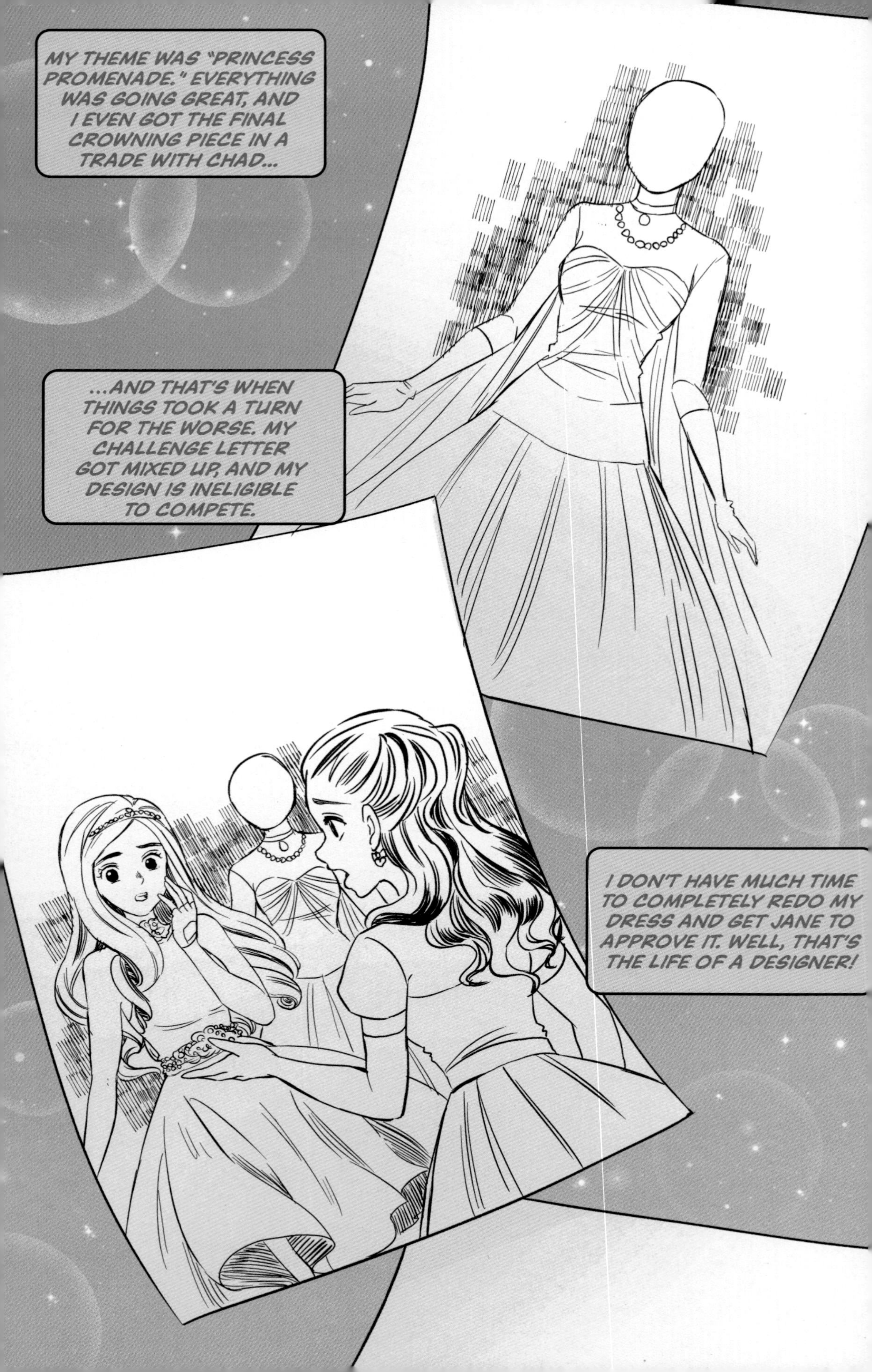
MY THEME WAS "PRINCESS PROMENADE." EVERYTHING WAS GOING GREAT, AND I EVEN GOT THE FINAL CROWNING PIECE IN A TRADE WITH CHAD...
...AND THAT'S WHEN THINGS TOOK A TURN FOR THE WORSE. MY CHALLENGE LETTER GOT MIXED UP, AND MY DESIGN IS INELIGIBLE TO COMPETE.
I DON'T HAVE MUCH TIME TO COMPLETELY REDO MY DRESS AND GET JANE TO APPROVE IT. WELL, THAT'S THE LIFE OF A DESIGNER!

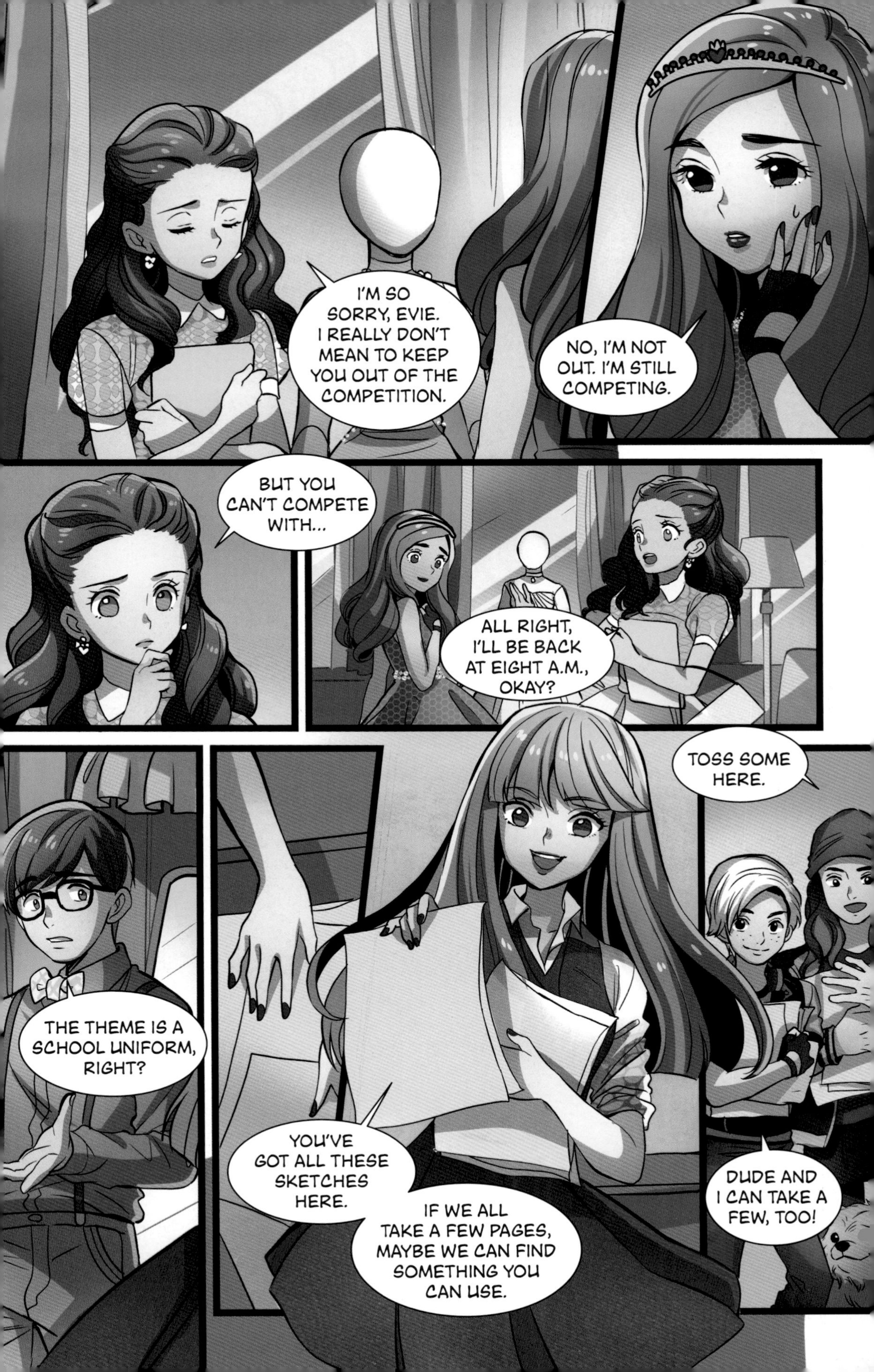
I'M SO SORRY, EVIE. I REALLY DON'T MEAN TO KEEP YOU OUT OF THE COMPETITION.
NO, I'M NOT OUT. I'M STILL COMPETING.
BUT YOU CAN'T COMPETE WITH...
ALL RIGHT, I'LL BE BACK AT EIGHT A.M., OKAY?
THE THEME IS A SCHOOL UNIFORM, RIGHT?
YOU'VE GOT ALL THESE SKETCHES HERE.
IF WE ALL TAKE A FEW PAGES, MAYBE WE CAN FIND SOMETHING YOU CAN USE.
TOSS SOME HERE.
DUDE AND I CAN TAKE A FEW, TOO!

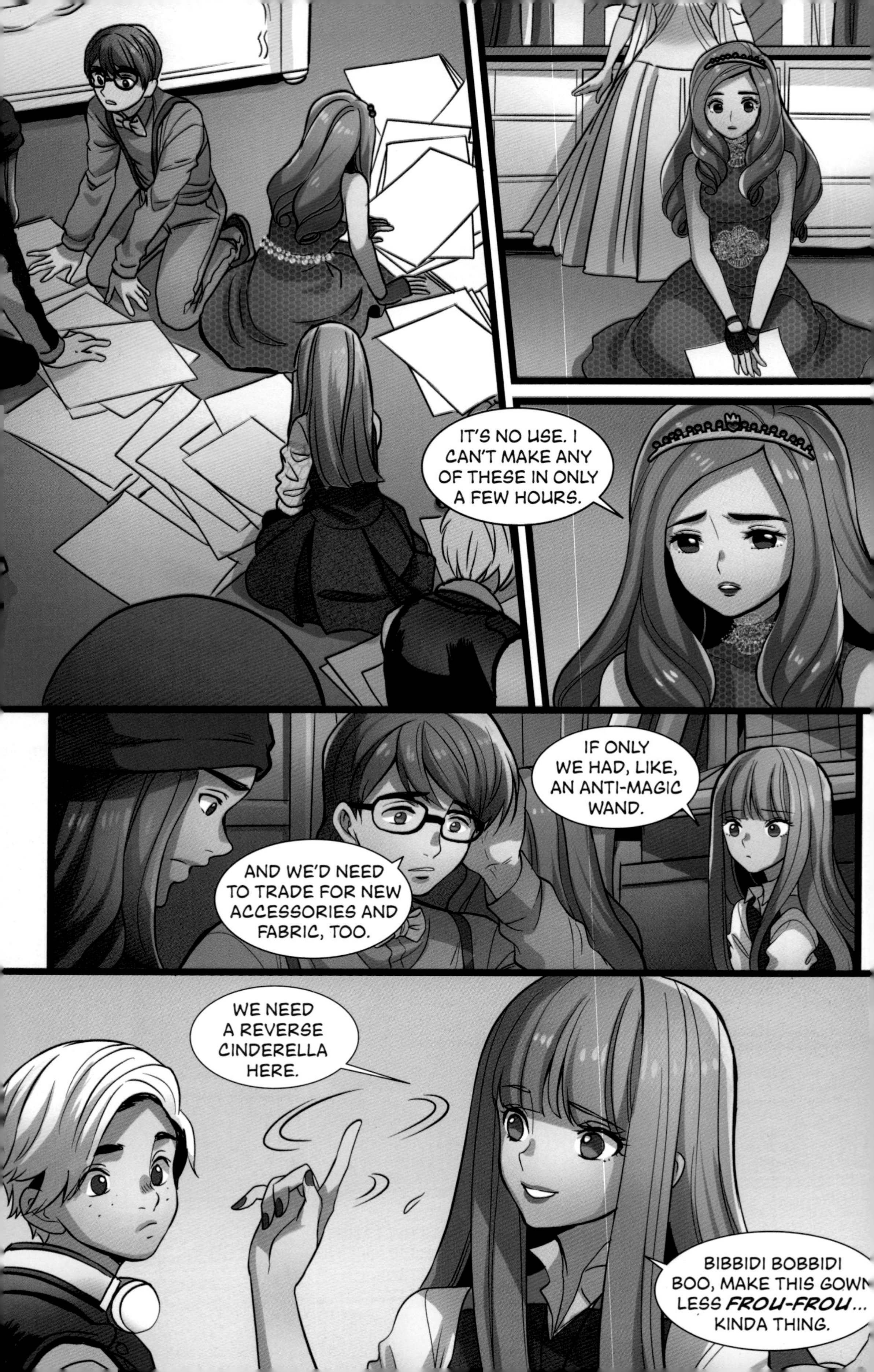
IT'S NO USE. I CAN'T MAKE ANY OF THESE IN ONLY A FEW HOURS.
IF ONLY WE HAD, LIKE, AN ANTI-MAGIC WAND.
AND WE'D NEED TO TRADE FOR NEW ACCESSORIES AND FABRIC, TOO.
WE NEED A REVERSE CINDERELLA HERE.
BIBBIDI BOBBIDI BOO, MAKE THIS GOWN LESS FROU-FROU... KINDA THING.

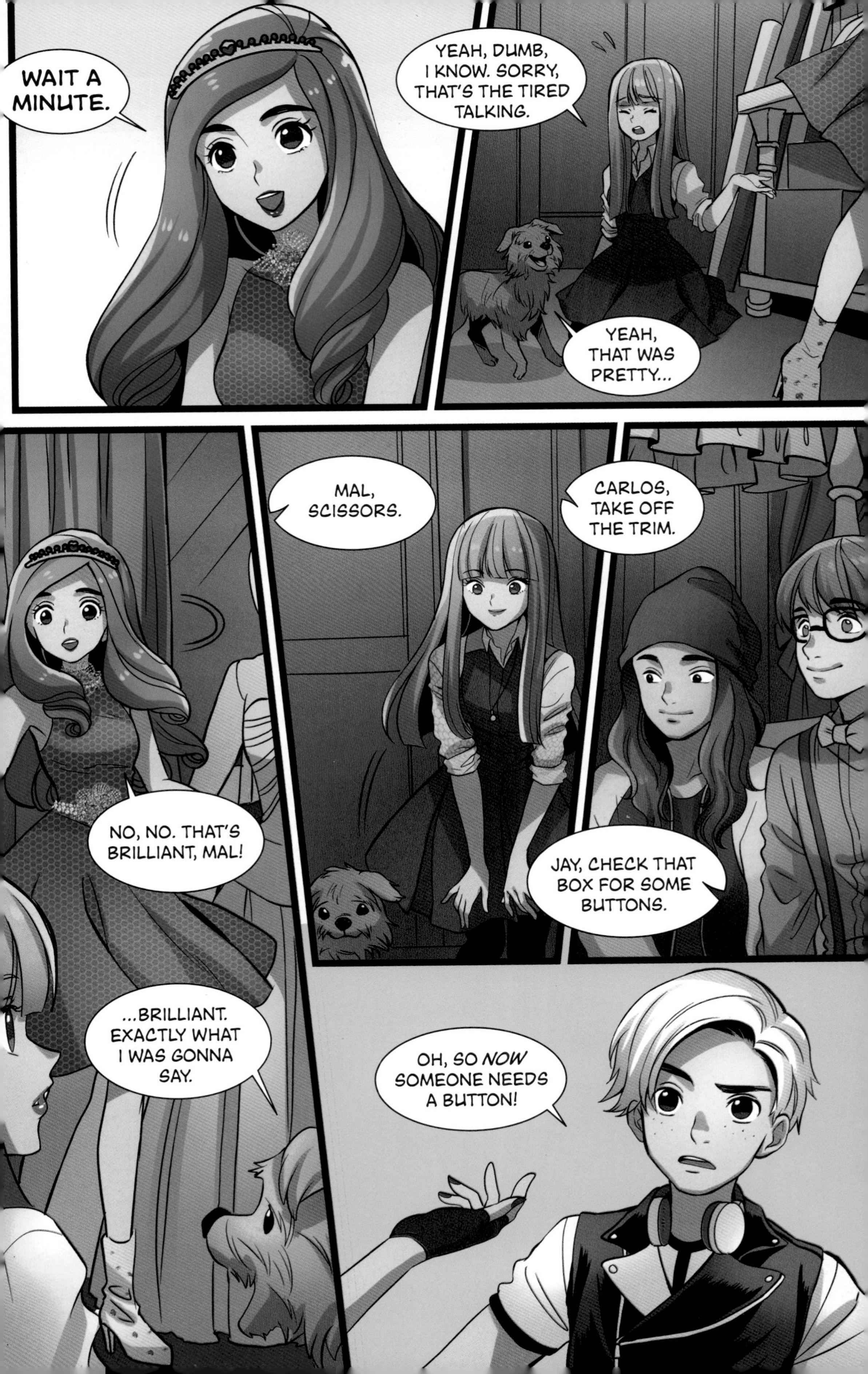
WAIT A MINUTE.
YEAH, DUMB, I KNOW. SORRY, THAT'S THE TIRED TALKING.
YEAH, THAT WAS PRETTY...
NO, NO. THAT'S BRILLIANT, MAL!
MAL, SCISSORS.
CARLOS, TAKE OFF THE TRIM.
JAY, CHECK THAT BOX FOR SOME BUTTONS.
...BRILLIANT. EXACTLY WHAT I WAS GONNA SAY.
OH, SO *NOW* SOMEONE NEEDS A BUTTON!

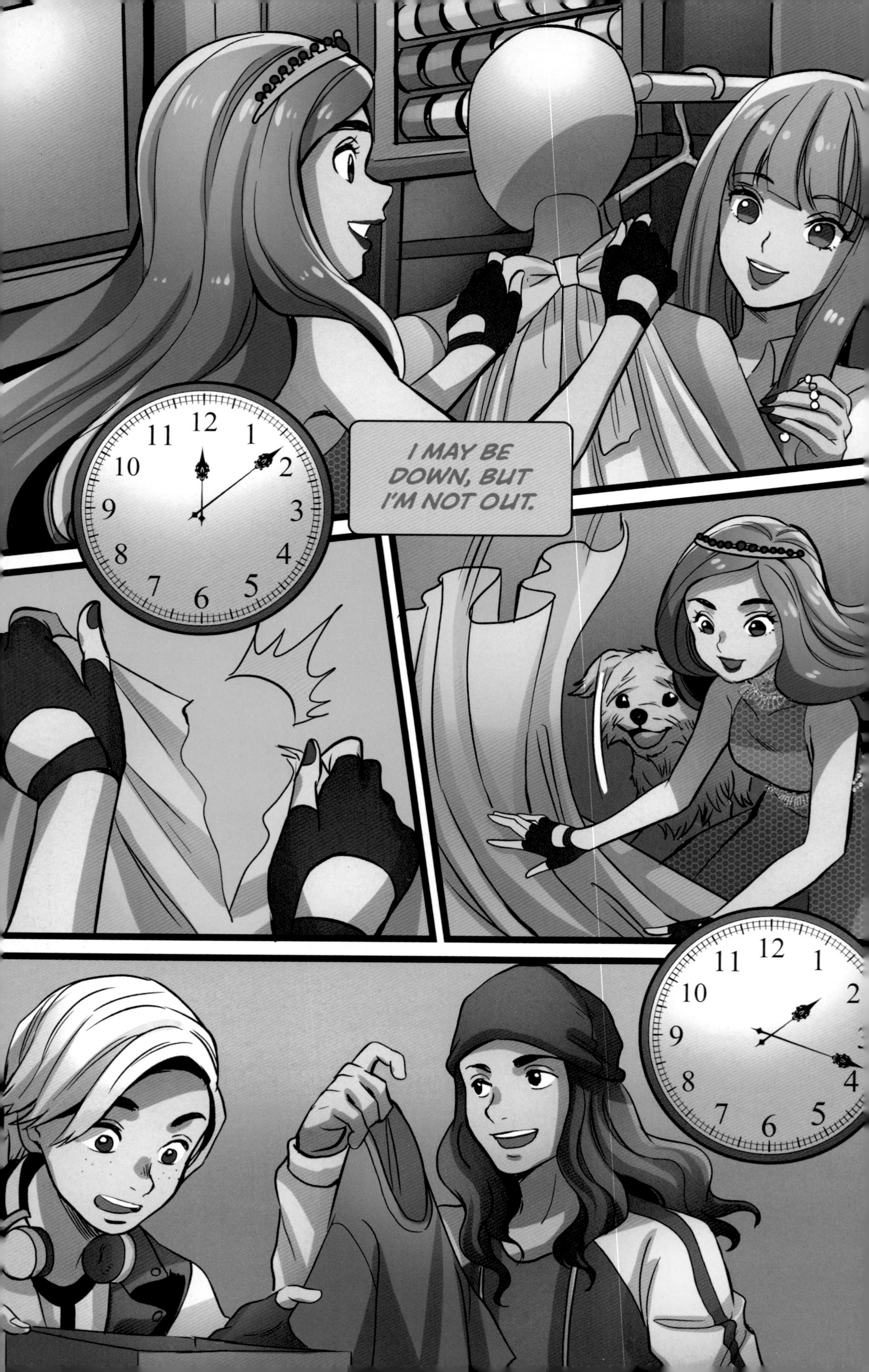
I MAY BE DOWN, BUT I'M NOT OUT.

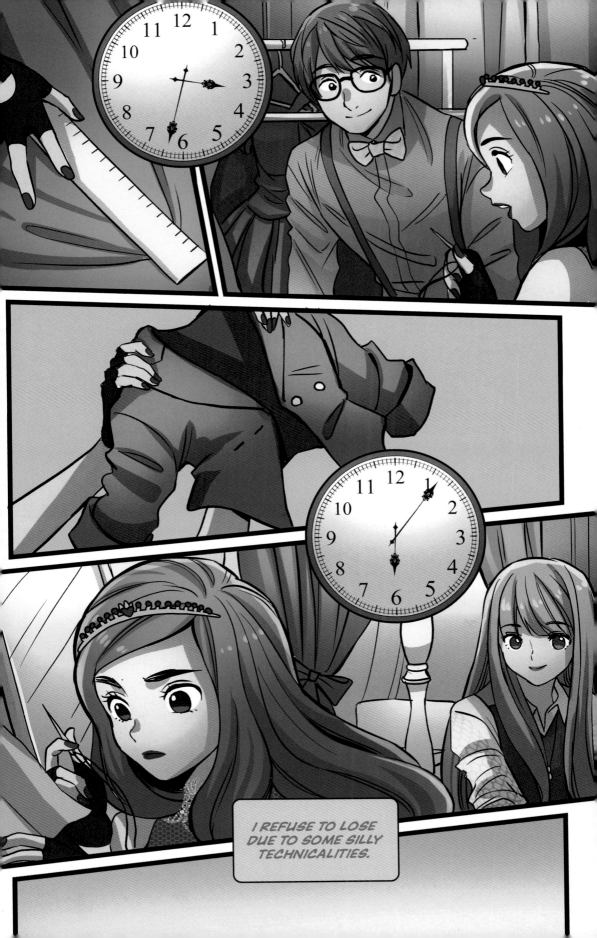

I REFUSE TO LOSE
DUE TO SOME SILLY
TECHNICALITIES.

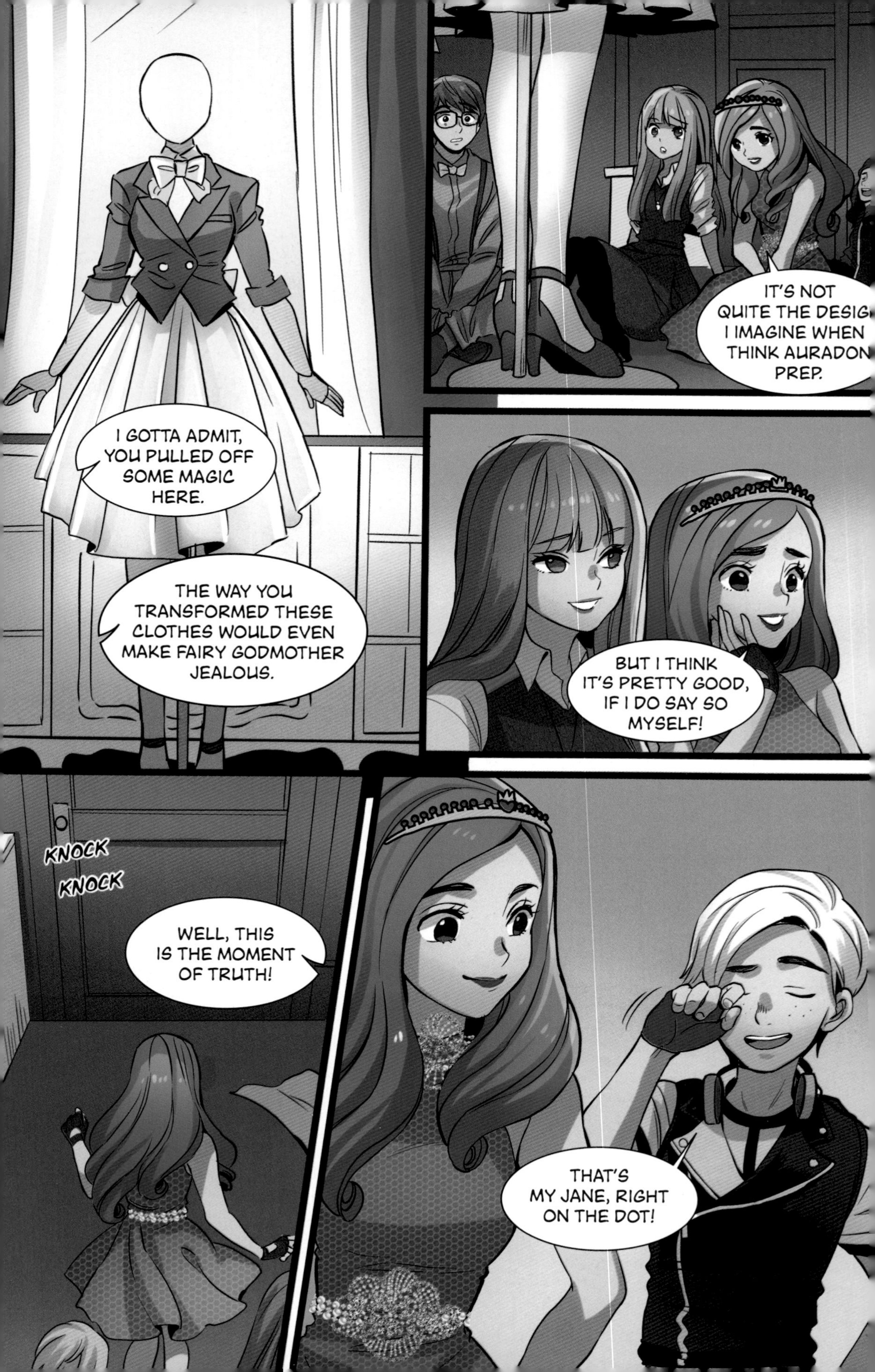
I GOTTA ADMIT, YOU PULLED OFF SOME MAGIC HERE.
THE WAY YOU TRANSFORMED THESE CLOTHES WOULD EVEN MAKE FAIRY GODMOTHER JEALOUS.
IT'S NOT QUITE THE DESIG I IMAGINE WHEN THINK AURADON PREP.
BUT I THINK IT'S PRETTY GOOD, IF I DO SAY SO MYSELF!
KNOCK
KNOCK
WELL, THIS IS THE MOMENT OF TRUTH!
THAT'S MY JANE, RIGHT ON THE DOT!

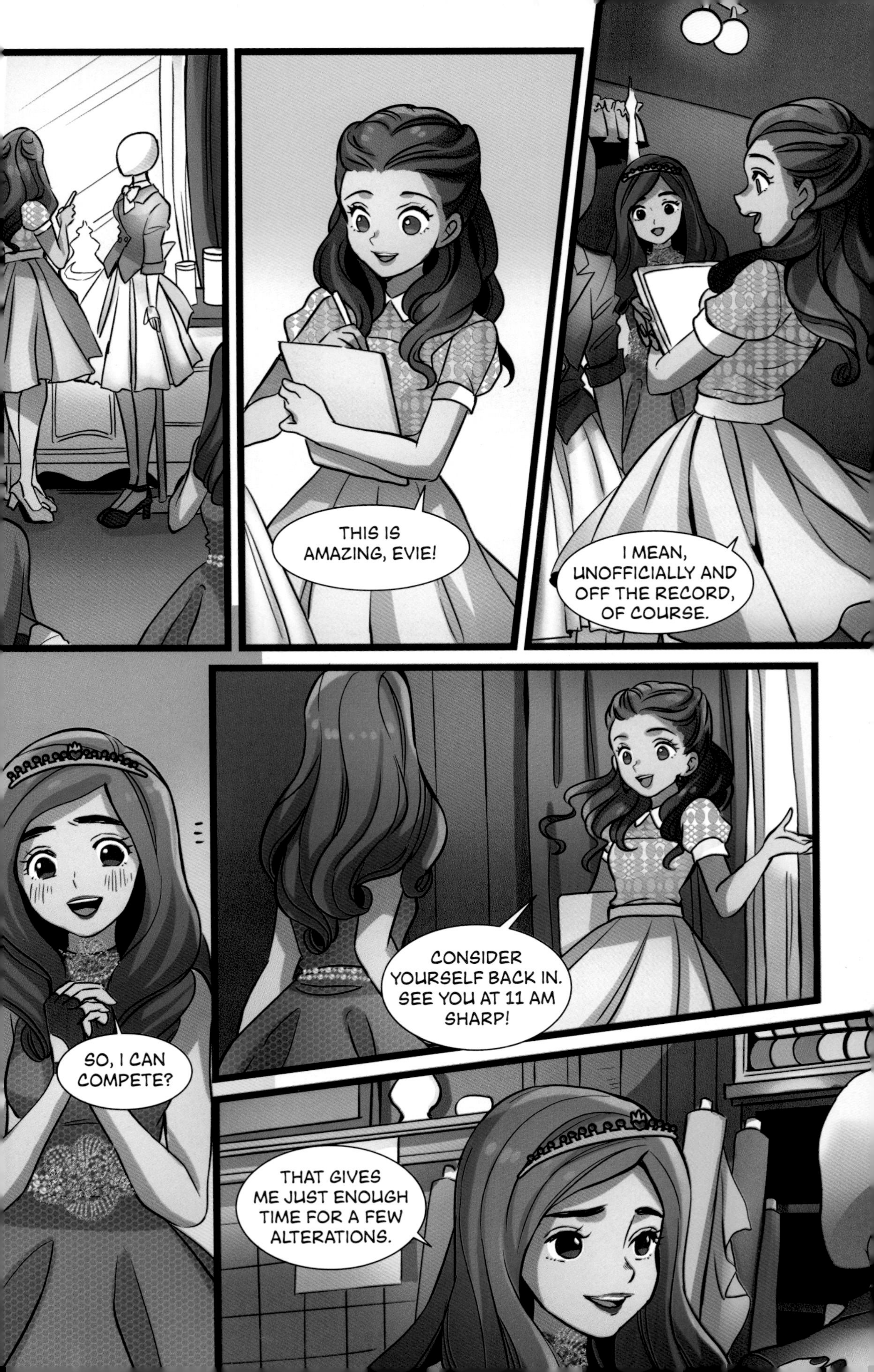
THIS IS AMAZING, EVIE!
I MEAN, UNOFFICIALLY AND OFF THE RECORD, OF COURSE.
SO, I CAN COMPETE?
CONSIDER YOURSELF BACK IN. SEE YOU AT 11 AM SHARP!
THAT GIVES ME JUST ENOUGH TIME FOR A FEW ALTERATIONS.

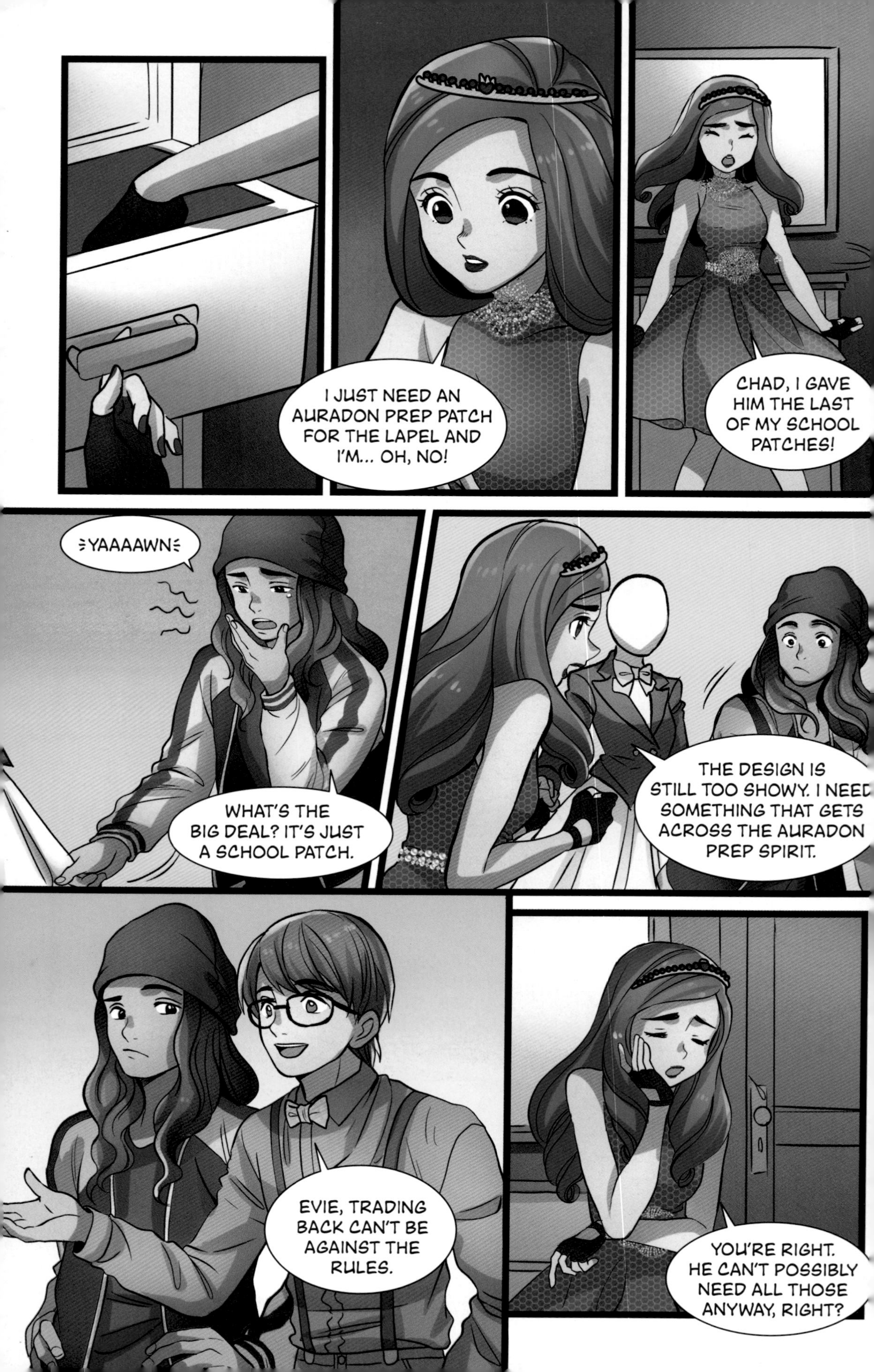
I JUST NEED AN AURADON PREP PATCH FOR THE LAPEL AND I'M... OH, NO!
CHAD, I GAVE HIM THE LAST OF MY SCHOOL PATCHES!
YAAAAWN
WHAT'S THE BIG DEAL? IT'S JUST A SCHOOL PATCH.
THE DESIGN IS STILL TOO SHOWY. I NEED SOMETHING THAT GETS ACROSS THE AURADON PREP SPIRIT.
EVIE, TRADING BACK CAN'T BE AGAINST THE RULES.
YOU'RE RIGHT. HE CAN'T POSSIBLY NEED ALL THOSE ANYWAY, RIGHT?

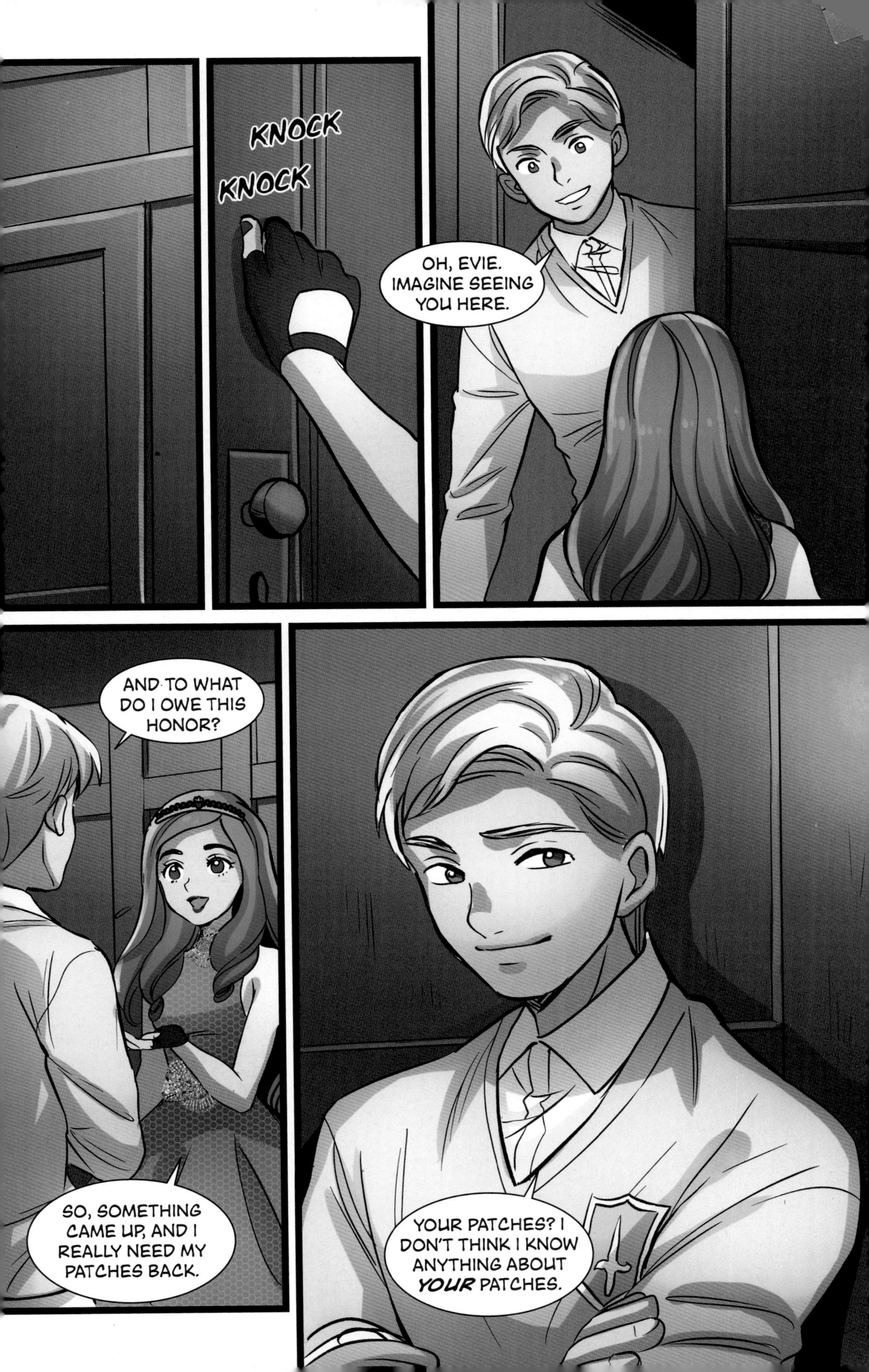
KNOCK
KNOCK
OH, EVIE. IMAGINE SEEING YOU HERE.
AND TO WHAT DO I OWE THIS HONOR?
SO, SOMETHING CAME UP, AND I REALLY NEED MY PATCHES BACK.
YOUR PATCHES? I DON'T THINK I KNOW ANYTHING ABOUT *YOUR* PATCHES.

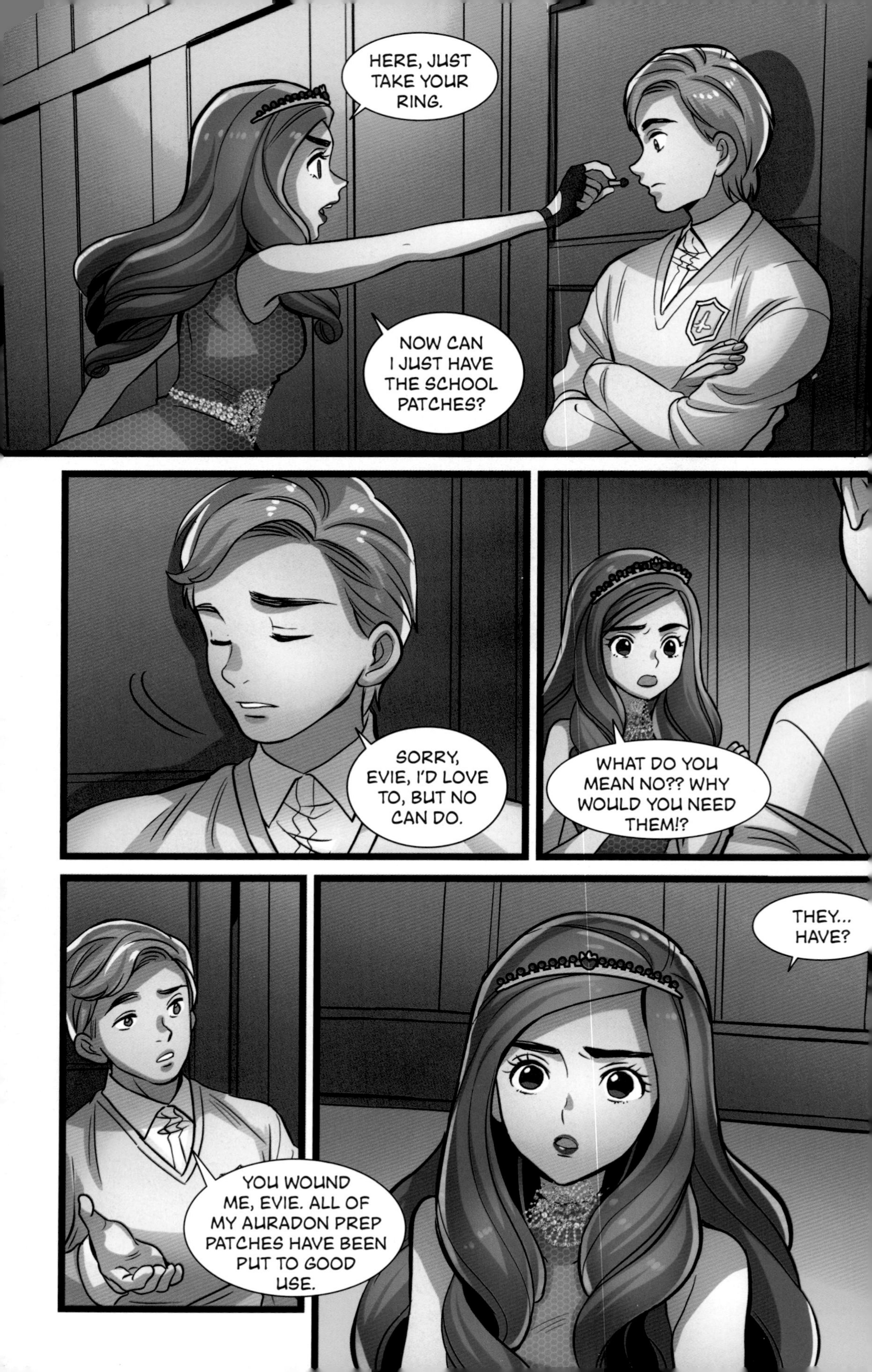
HERE, JUST TAKE YOUR RING.
NOW CAN I JUST HAVE THE SCHOOL PATCHES?
SORRY, EVIE, I'D LOVE TO, BUT NO CAN DO.
WHAT DO YOU MEAN NO?? WHY WOULD YOU NEED THEM!?
YOU WOUND ME, EVIE. ALL OF MY AURADON PREP PATCHES HAVE BEEN PUT TO GOOD USE.
THEY... HAVE?

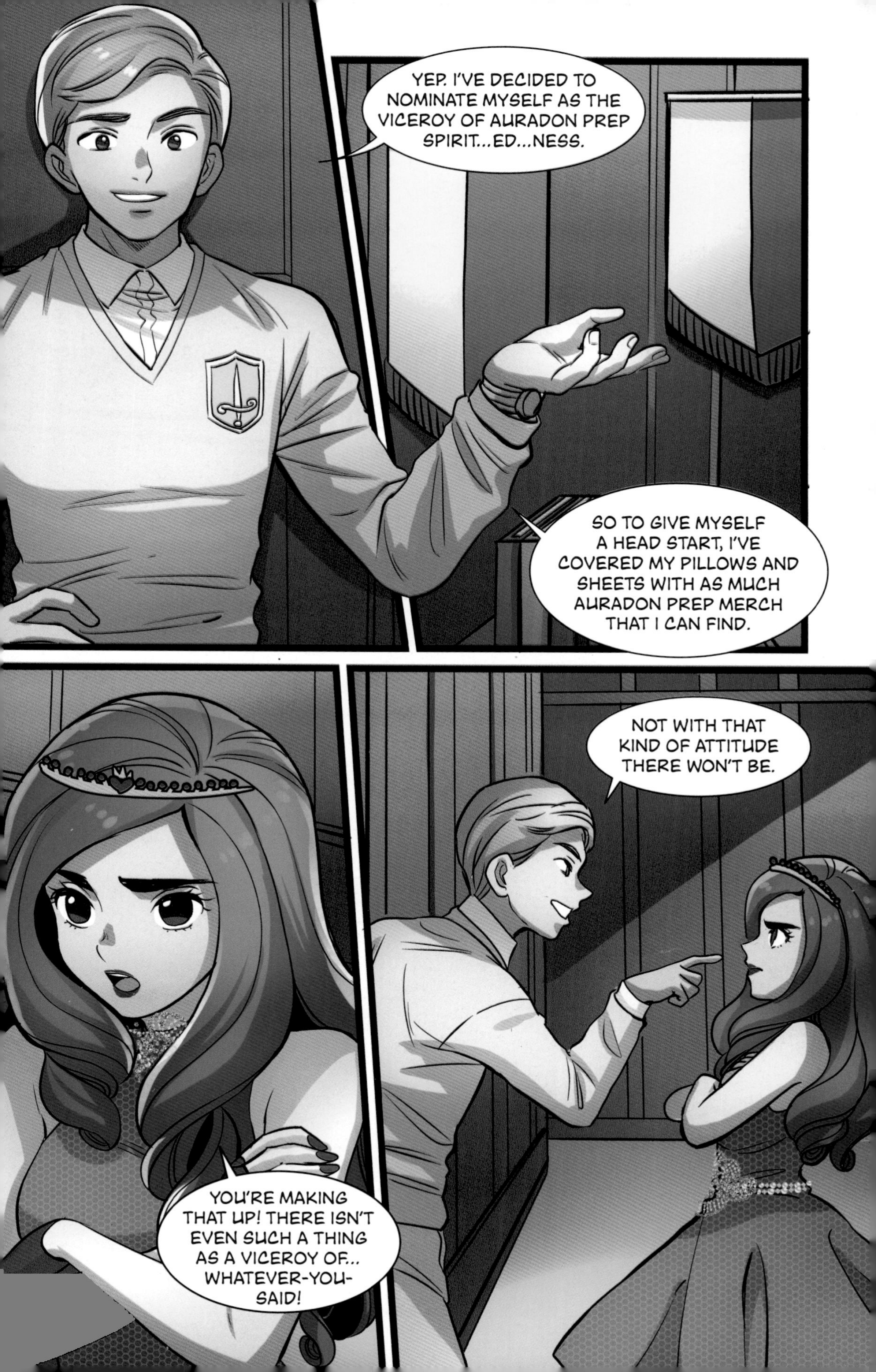
YEP. I'VE DECIDED TO NOMINATE MYSELF AS THE VICEROY OF AURADON PREP SPIRIT...ED...NESS.
SO TO GIVE MYSELF A HEAD START, I'VE COVERED MY PILLOWS AND SHEETS WITH AS MUCH AURADON PREP MERCH THAT I CAN FIND.
YOU'RE MAKING THAT UP! THERE ISN'T EVEN SUCH A THING AS A VICEROY OF... WHATEVER-YOU-SAID!
NOT WITH THAT KIND OF ATTITUDE THERE WON'T BE.

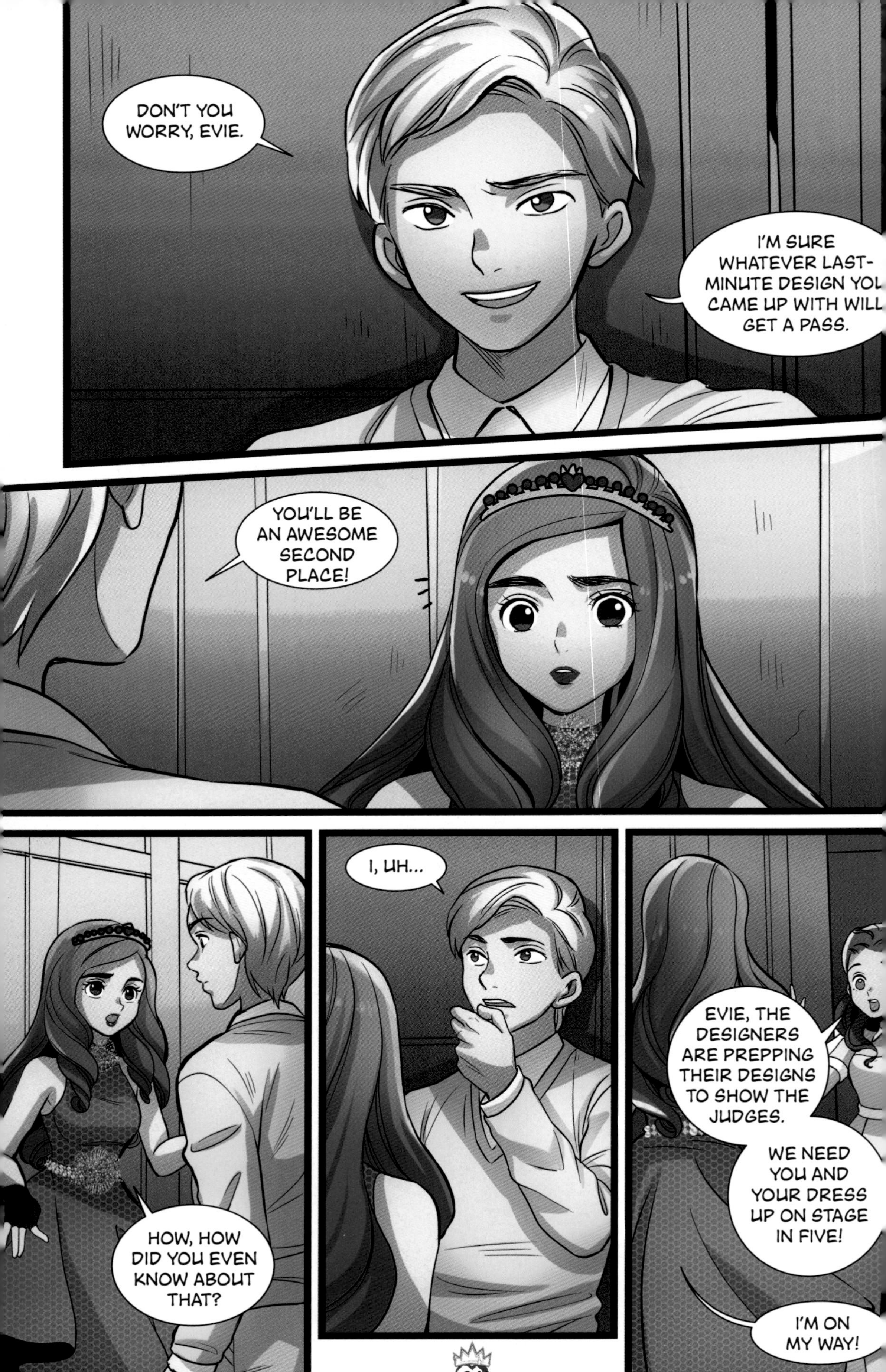
DON'T YOU WORRY, EVIE.
I'M SURE WHATEVER LAST-MINUTE DESIGN YOU CAME UP WITH WILL GET A PASS.
YOU'LL BE AN AWESOME SECOND PLACE!
HOW, HOW DID YOU EVEN KNOW ABOUT THAT?
I, UH...
EVIE, THE DESIGNERS ARE PREPPING THEIR DESIGNS TO SHOW THE JUDGES.
WE NEED YOU AND YOUR DRESS UP ON STAGE IN FIVE!
I'M ON MY WAY!

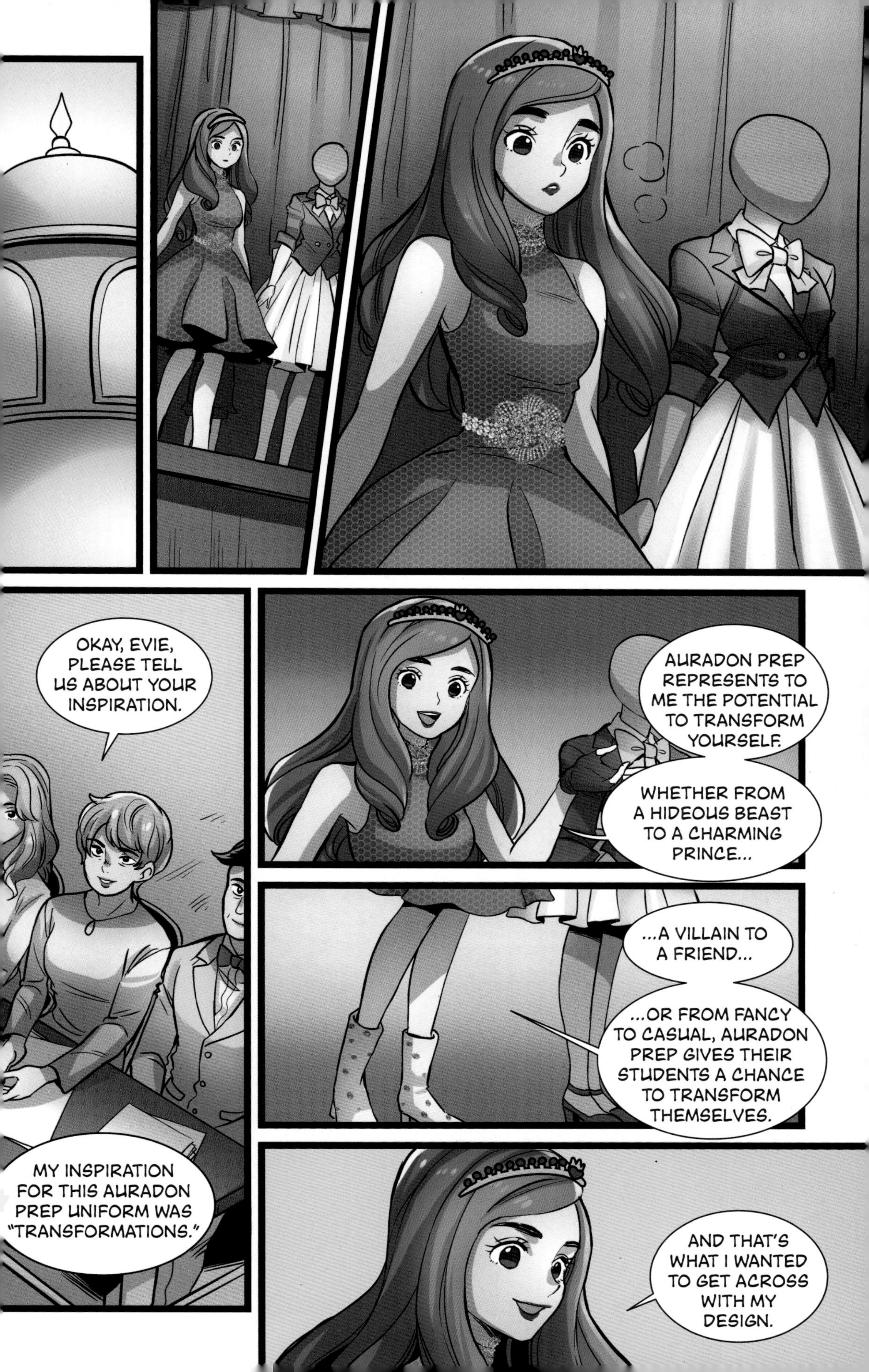
OKAY, EVIE, PLEASE TELL US ABOUT YOUR INSPIRATION.
MY INSPIRATION FOR THIS AURADON PREP UNIFORM WAS "TRANSFORMATIONS."
AURADON PREP REPRESENTS TO ME THE POTENTIAL TO TRANSFORM YOURSELF.
WHETHER FROM A HIDEOUS BEAST TO A CHARMING PRINCE...
...A VILLAIN TO A FRIEND...
...OR FROM FANCY TO CASUAL, AURADON PREP GIVES THEIR STUDENTS A CHANCE TO TRANSFORM THEMSELVES.
AND THAT'S WHAT I WANTED TO GET ACROSS WITH MY DESIGN.

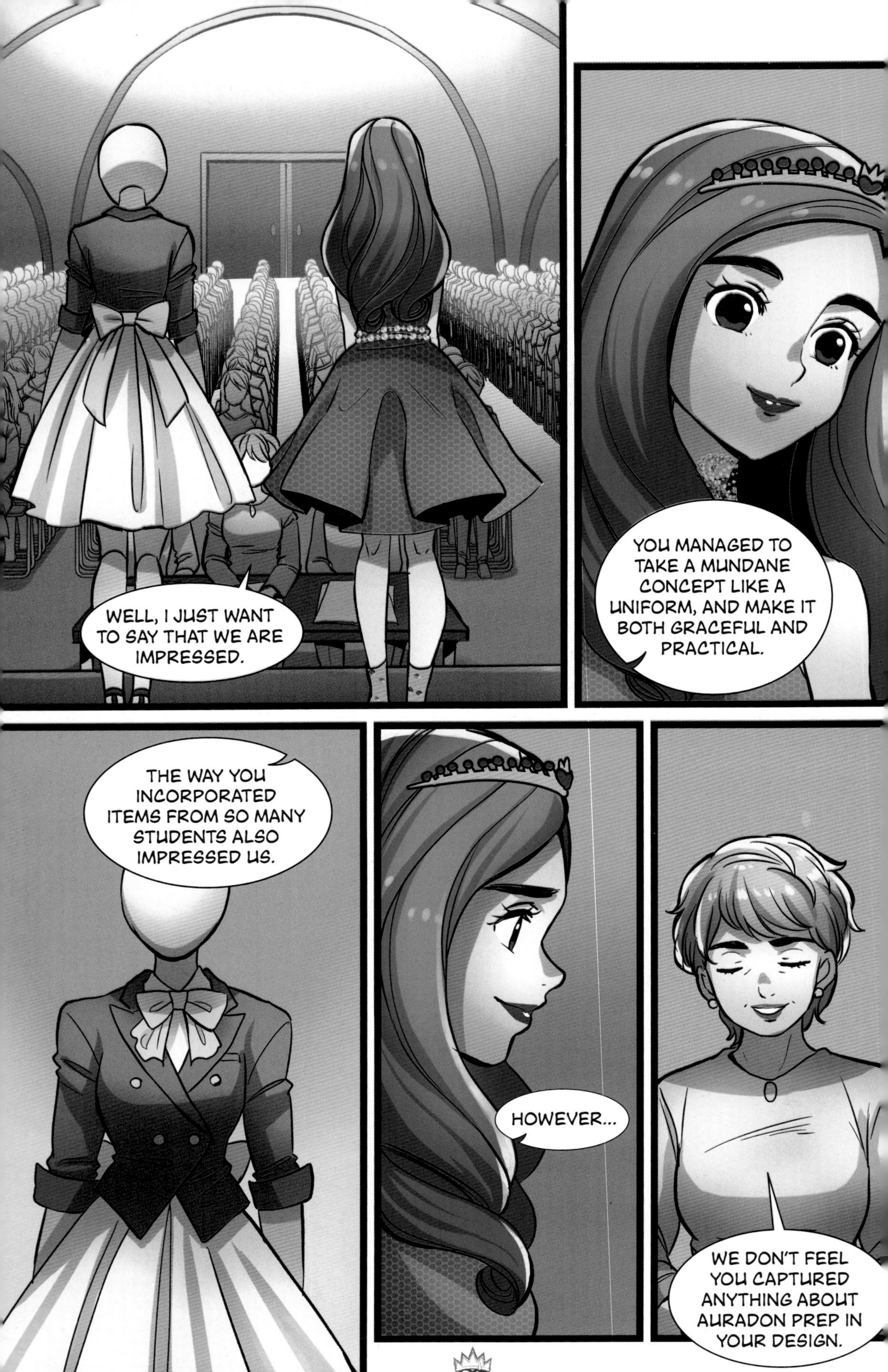
WELL, I JUST WANT TO SAY THAT WE ARE IMPRESSED.
YOU MANAGED TO TAKE A MUNDANE CONCEPT LIKE A UNIFORM, AND MAKE IT BOTH GRACEFUL AND PRACTICAL.
THE WAY YOU INCORPORATED ITEMS FROM SO MANY STUDENTS ALSO IMPRESSED US.
HOWEVER...
WE DON'T FEEL YOU CAPTURED ANYTHING ABOUT AURADON PREP IN YOUR DESIGN.

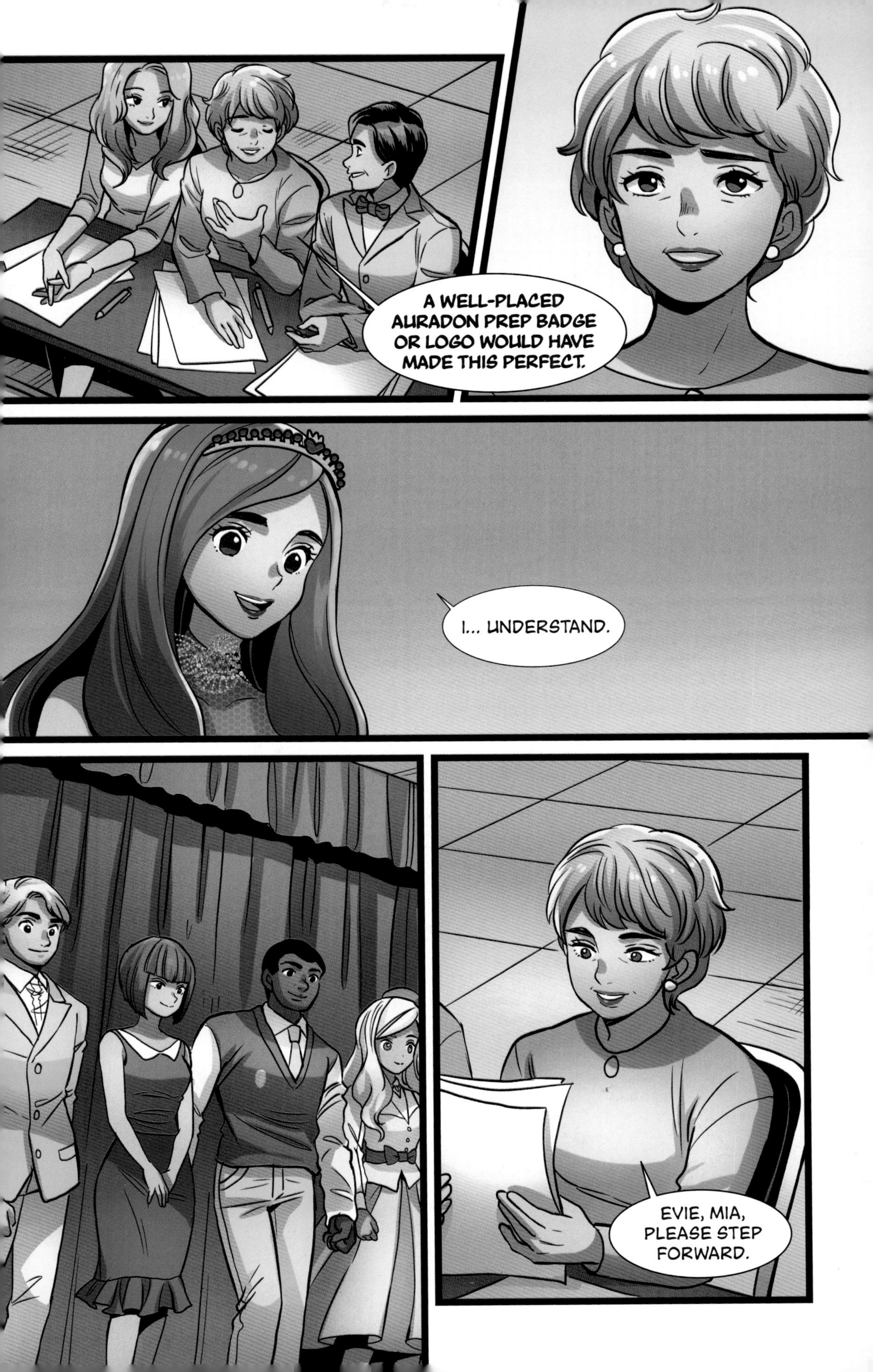
A WELL-PLACED AURADON PREP BADGE OR LOGO WOULD HAVE MADE THIS PERFECT.
I... UNDERSTAND.
EVIE, MIA, PLEASE STEP FORWARD.

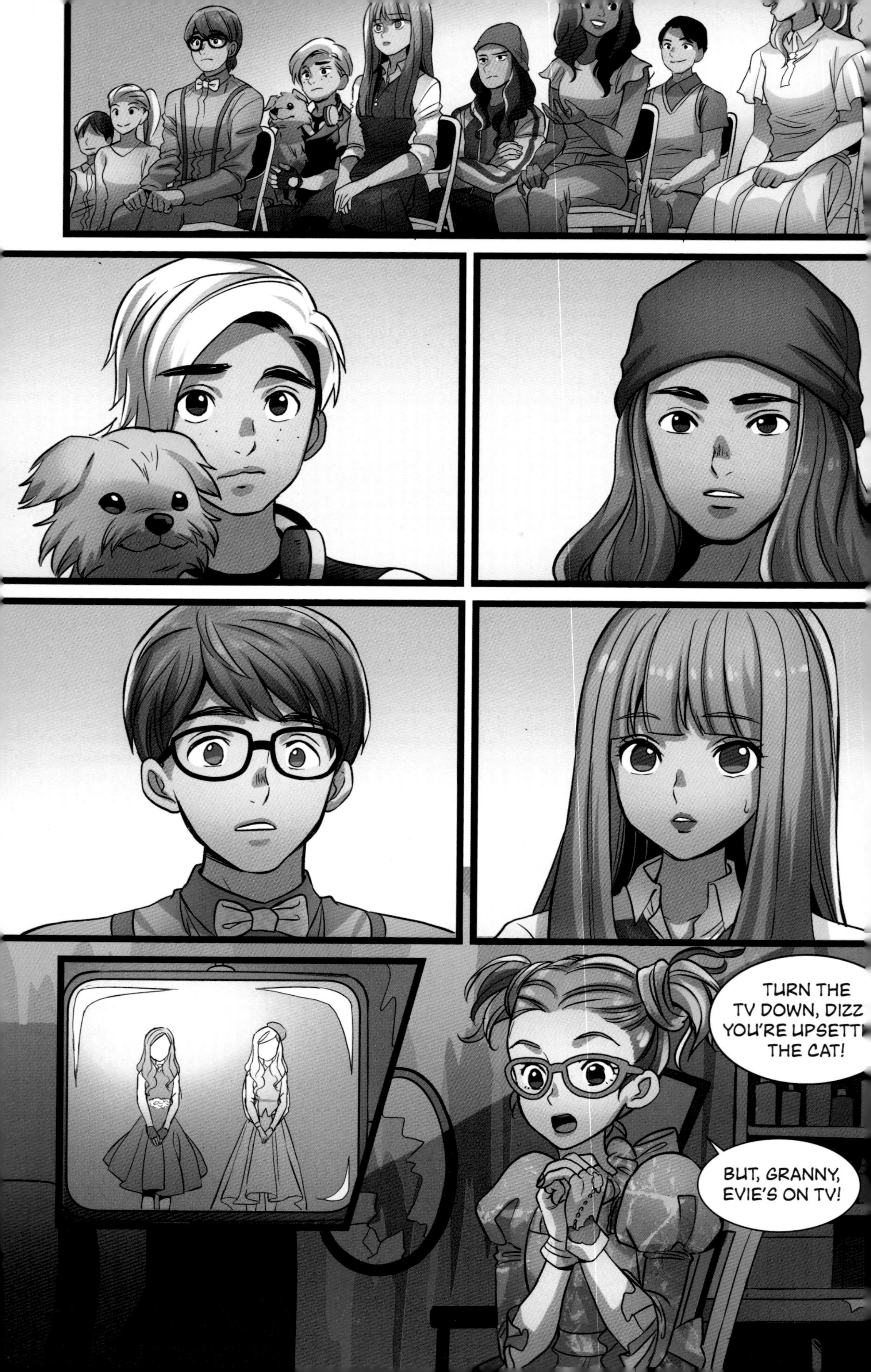
TURN THE TV DOWN, DIZZ YOU'RE UPSETT THE CAT!
BUT, GRANNY, EVIE'S ON TV!

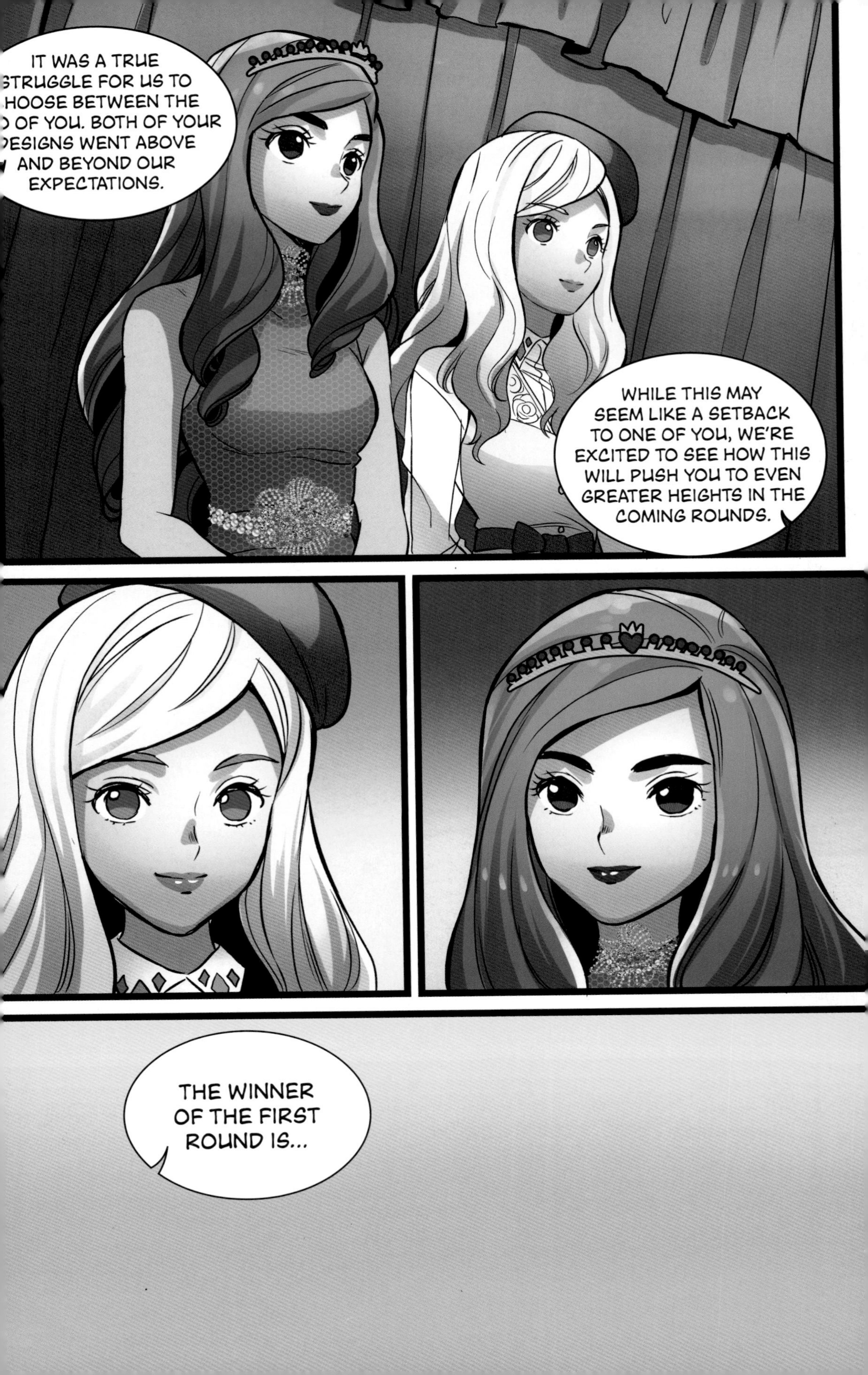
IT WAS A TRUE STRUGGLE FOR US TO HOOSE BETWEEN THE OF YOU. BOTH OF YOUR ESIGNS WENT ABOVE AND BEYOND OUR EXPECTATIONS.
WHILE THIS MAY SEEM LIKE A SETBACK TO ONE OF YOU, WE'RE EXCITED TO SEE HOW THIS WILL PUSH YOU TO EVEN GREATER HEIGHTS IN THE COMING ROUNDS.
THE WINNER OF THE FIRST ROUND IS...

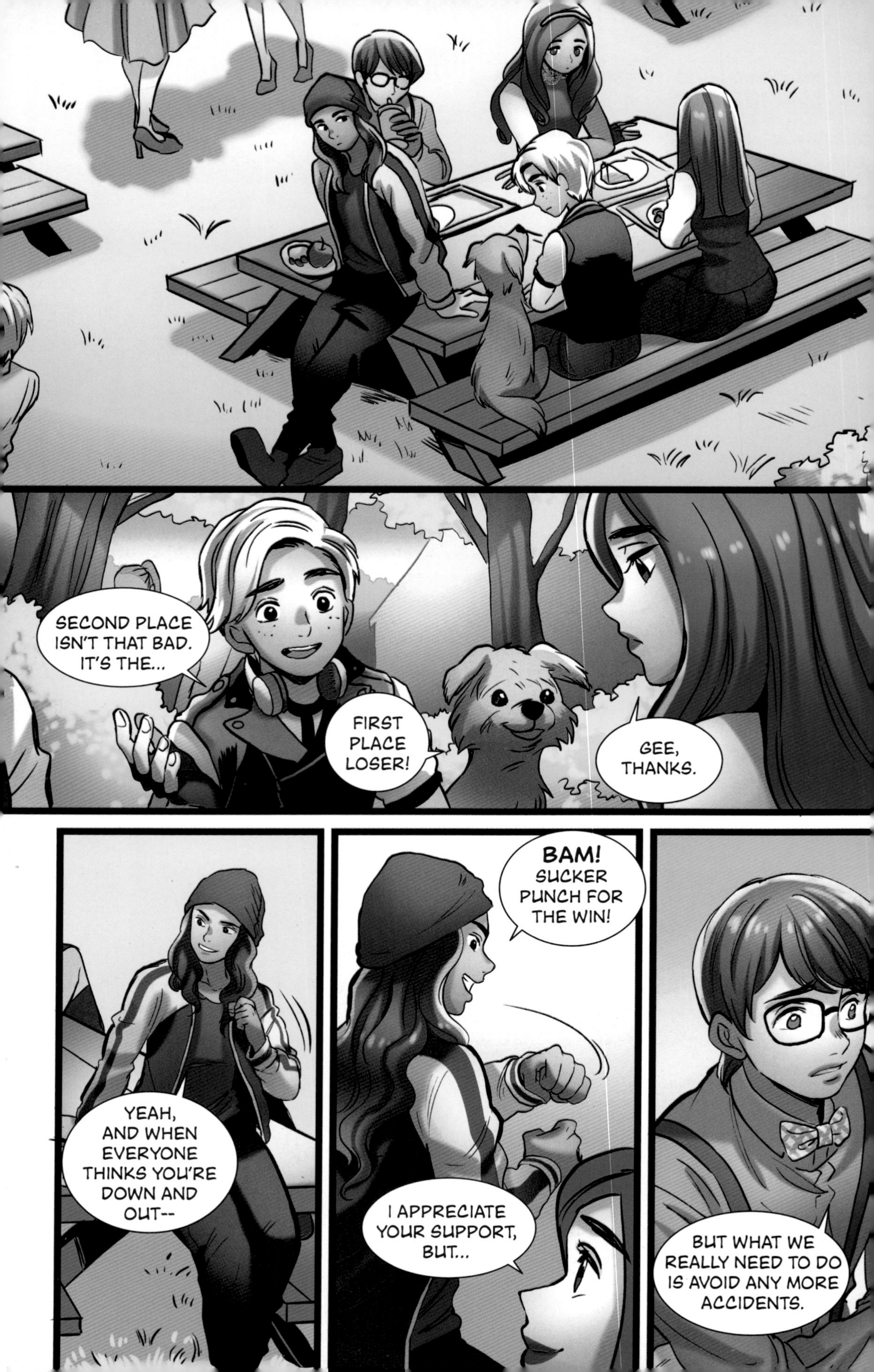
SECOND PLACE ISN'T THAT BAD. IT'S THE...
FIRST PLACE LOSER!
GEE, THANKS.
YEAH, AND WHEN EVERYONE THINKS YOU'RE DOWN AND OUT--
BAM! SUCKER PUNCH FOR THE WIN!
I APPRECIATE YOUR SUPPORT, BUT...
BUT WHAT WE REALLY NEED TO DO IS AVOID ANY MORE ACCIDENTS.

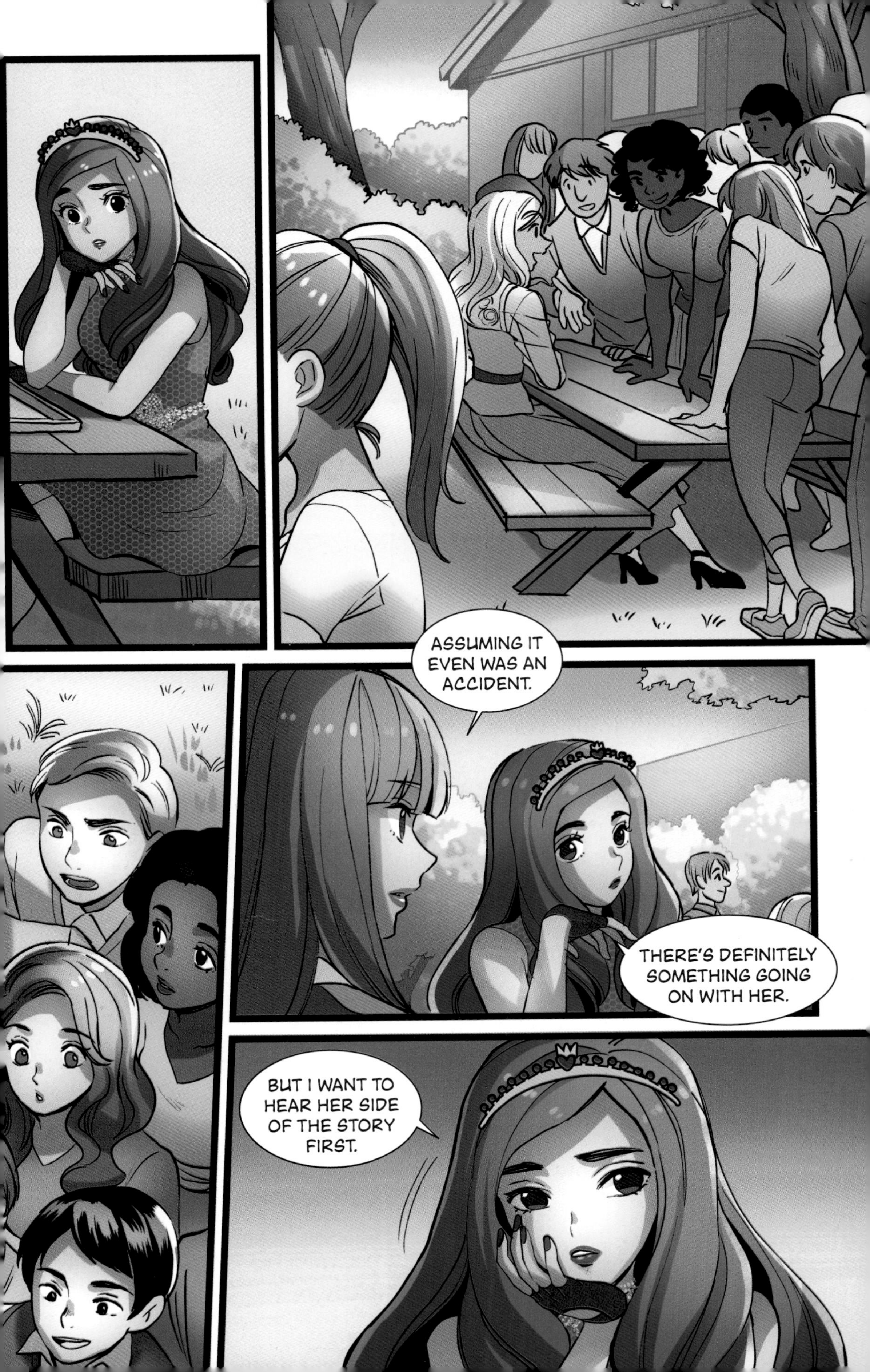
ASSUMING IT EVEN WAS AN ACCIDENT.
THERE'S DEFINITELY SOMETHING GOING ON WITH HER.
BUT I WANT TO HEAR HER SIDE OF THE STORY FIRST.

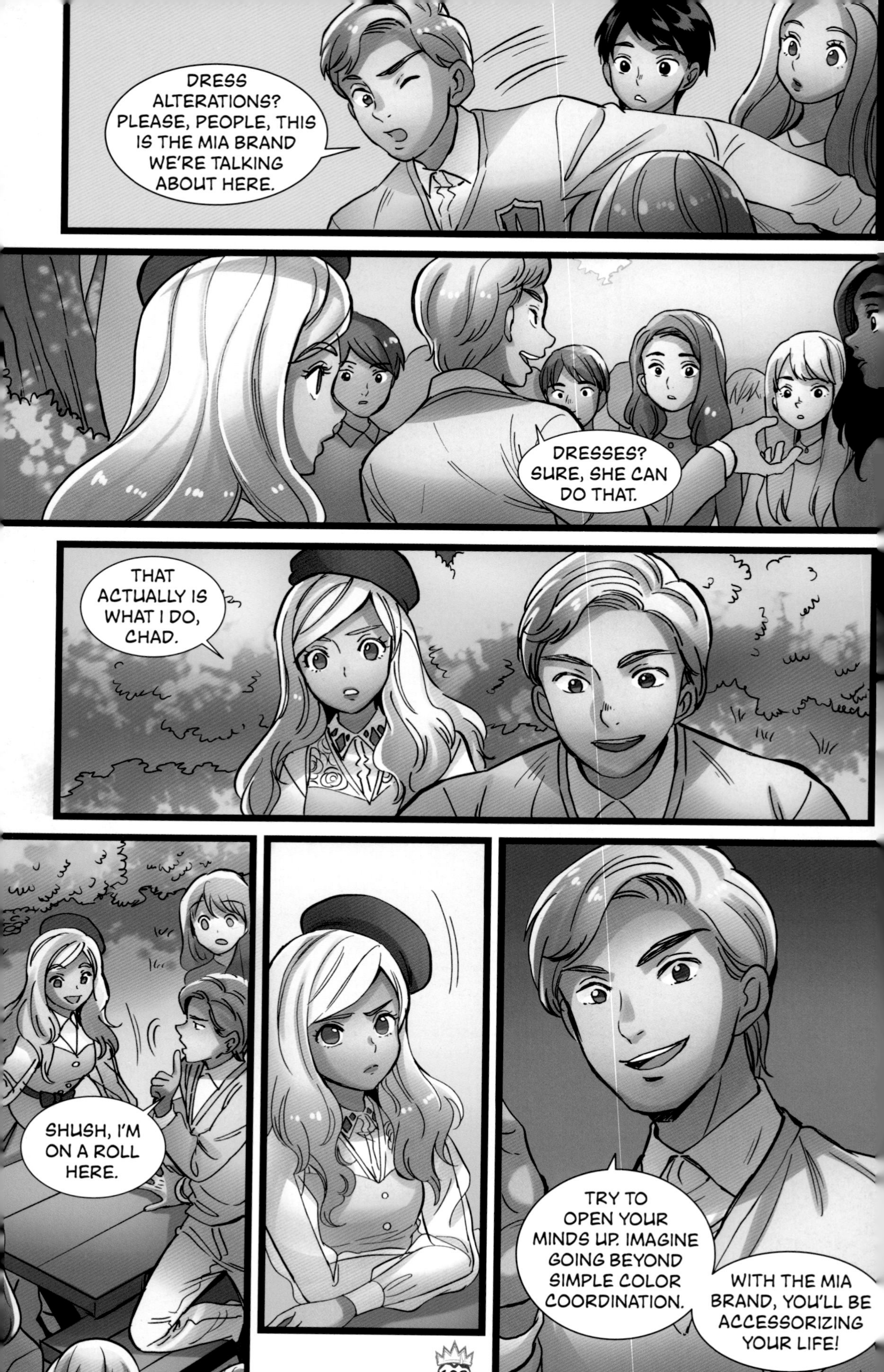

DRESS ALTERATIONS? PLEASE, PEOPLE, THIS IS THE MIA BRAND WE'RE TALKING ABOUT HERE.
DRESSES? SURE, SHE CAN DO THAT.
THAT ACTUALLY IS WHAT I DO, CHAD.
SHUSH, I'M ON A ROLL HERE.
TRY TO OPEN YOUR MINDS UP. IMAGINE GOING BEYOND SIMPLE COLOR COORDINATION.
WITH THE MIA BRAND, YOU'LL BE ACCESSORIZING YOUR LIFE!

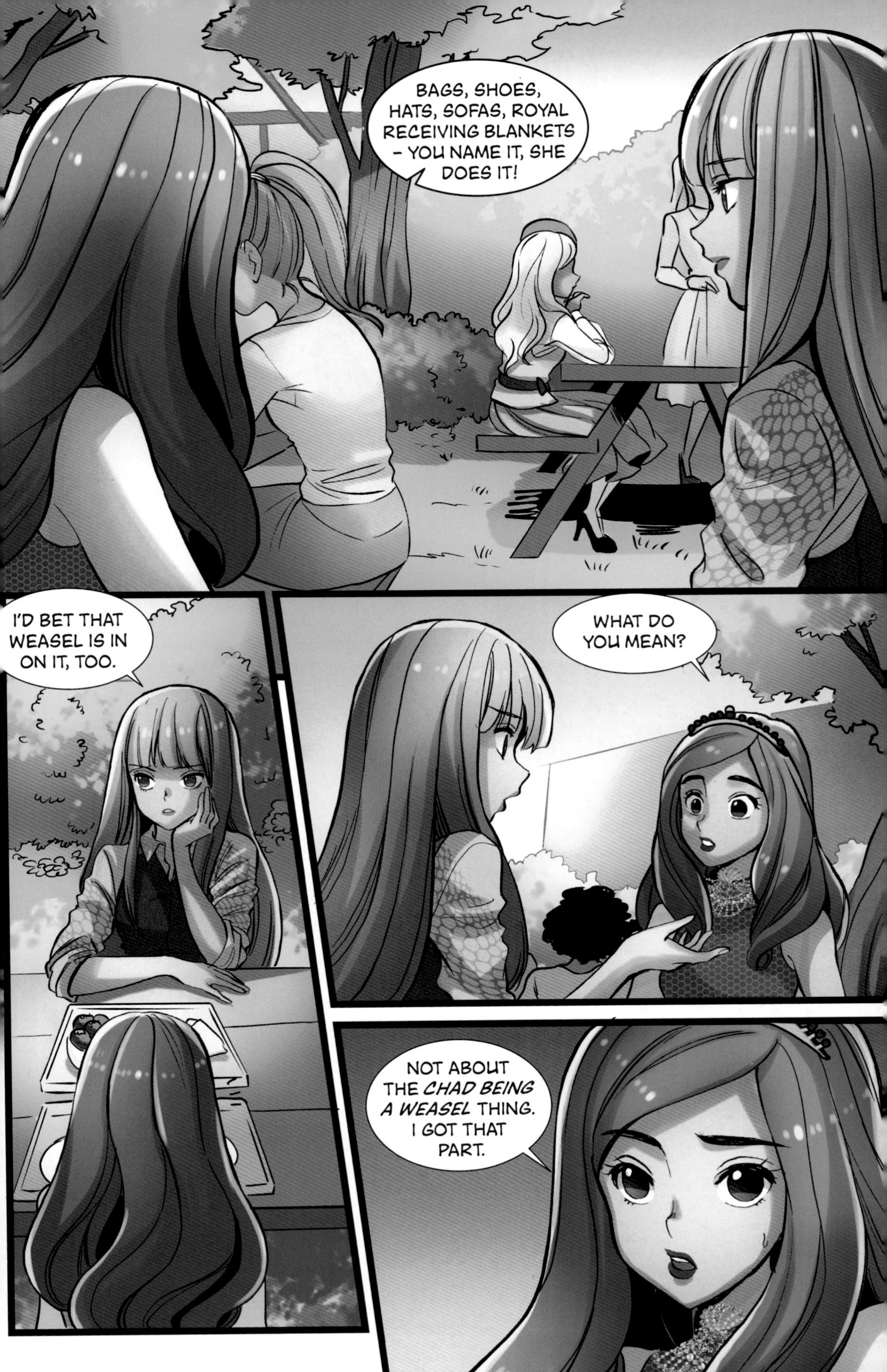
BAGS, SHOES, HATS, SOFAS, ROYAL RECEIVING BLANKETS – YOU NAME IT, SHE DOES IT!
I'D BET THAT WEASEL IS IN ON IT, TOO.
WHAT DO YOU MEAN?
NOT ABOUT THE *CHAD BEING A WEASEL* THING. I GOT THAT PART.

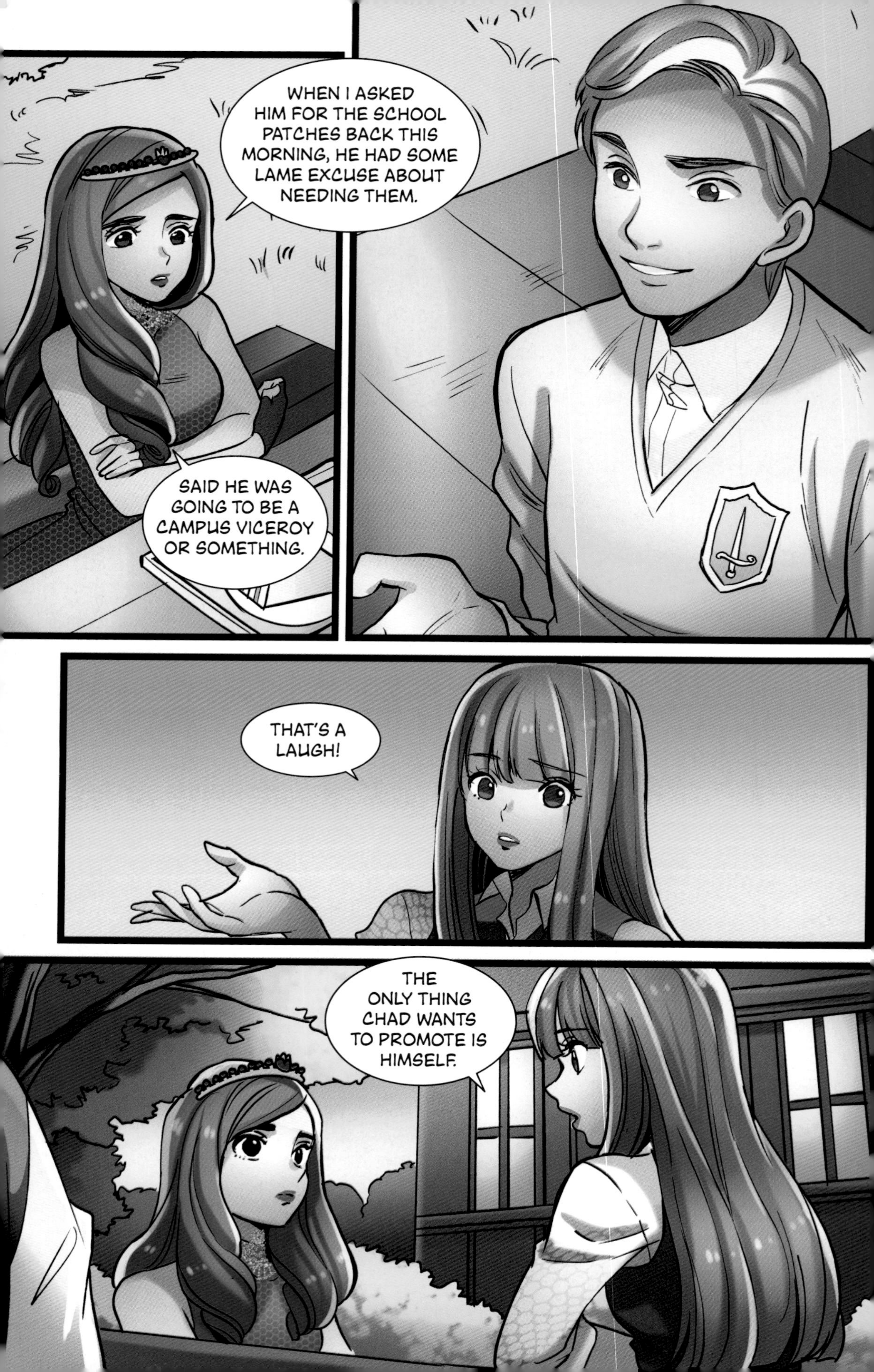
WHEN I ASKED HIM FOR THE SCHOOL PATCHES BACK THIS MORNING, HE HAD SOME LAME EXCUSE ABOUT NEEDING THEM.
SAID HE WAS GOING TO BE A CAMPUS VICEROY OR SOMETHING.
THAT'S A LAUGH!
THE ONLY THING CHAD WANTS TO PROMOTE IS HIMSELF.

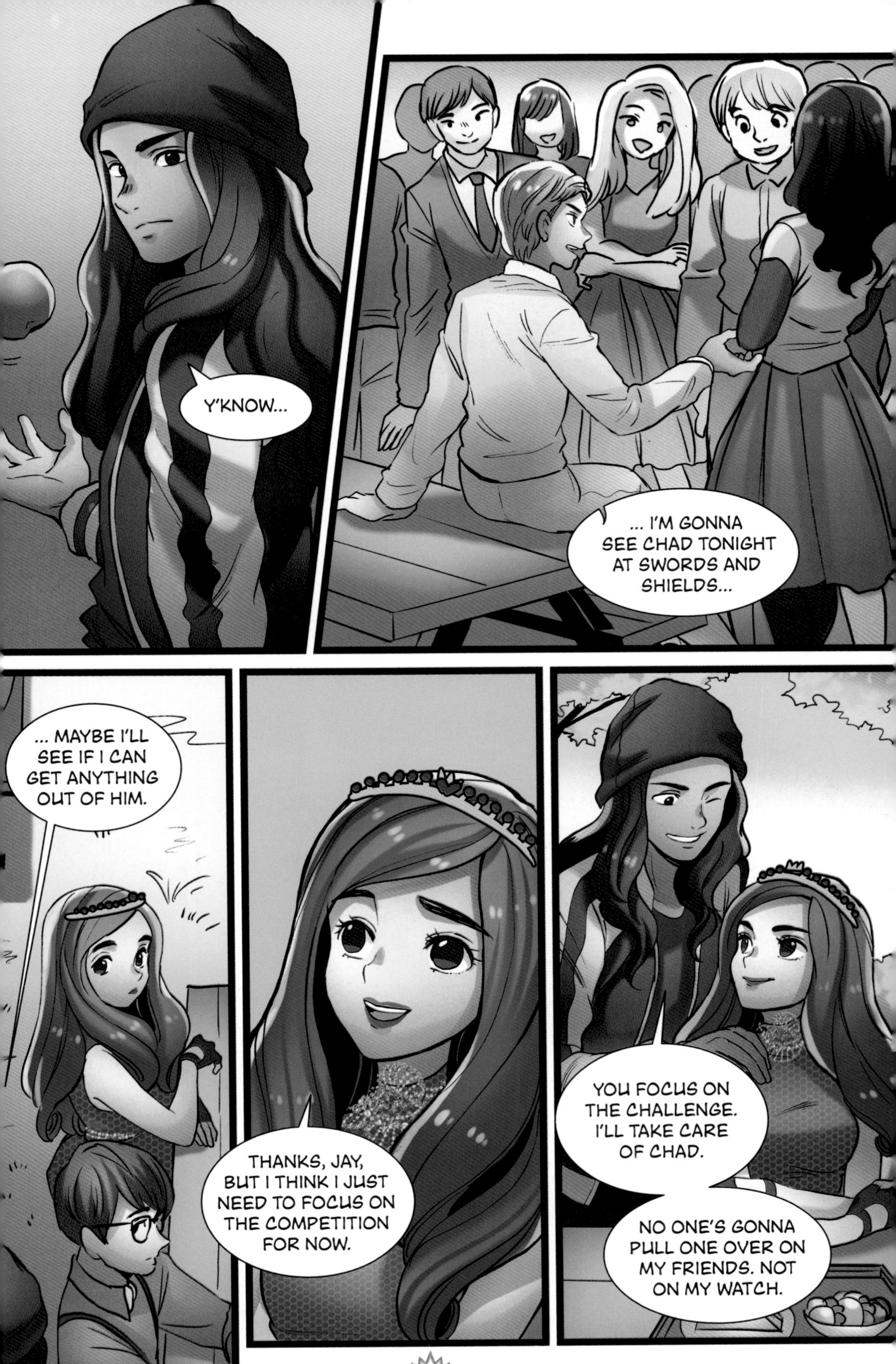
Y'KNOW...
... I'M GONNA SEE CHAD TONIGHT AT SWORDS AND SHIELDS...
... MAYBE I'LL SEE IF I CAN GET ANYTHING OUT OF HIM.
THANKS, JAY, BUT I THINK I JUST NEED TO FOCUS ON THE COMPETITION FOR NOW.
YOU FOCUS ON THE CHALLENGE. I'LL TAKE CARE OF CHAD.
NO ONE'S GONNA PULL ONE OVER ON MY FRIENDS. NOT ON MY WATCH.

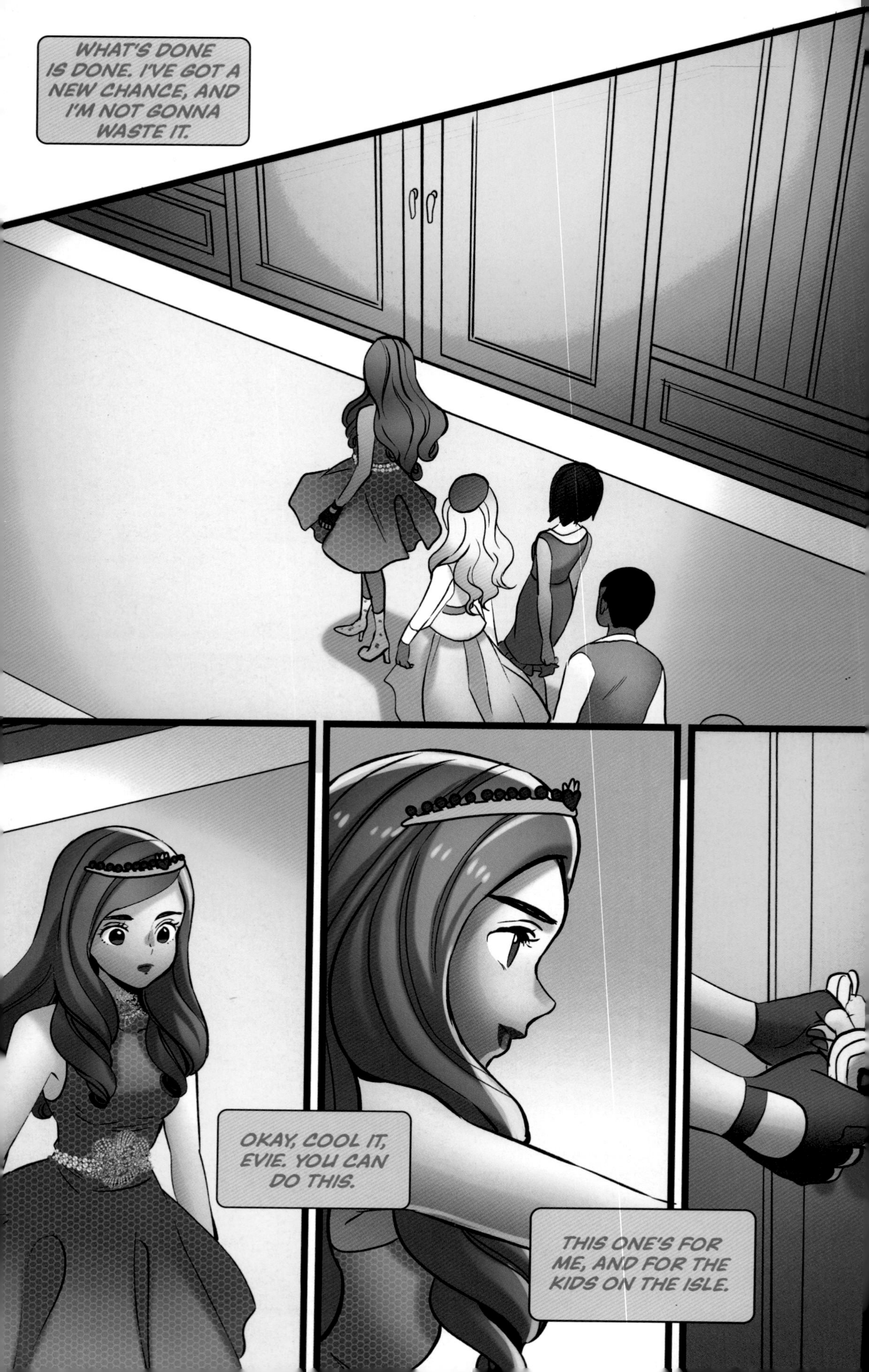
WHAT'S DONE IS DONE. I'VE GOT A NEW CHANCE, AND I'M NOT GONNA WASTE IT.
OKAY, COOL IT, EVIE. YOU CAN DO THIS.
THIS ONE'S FOR ME, AND FOR THE KIDS ON THE ISLE.

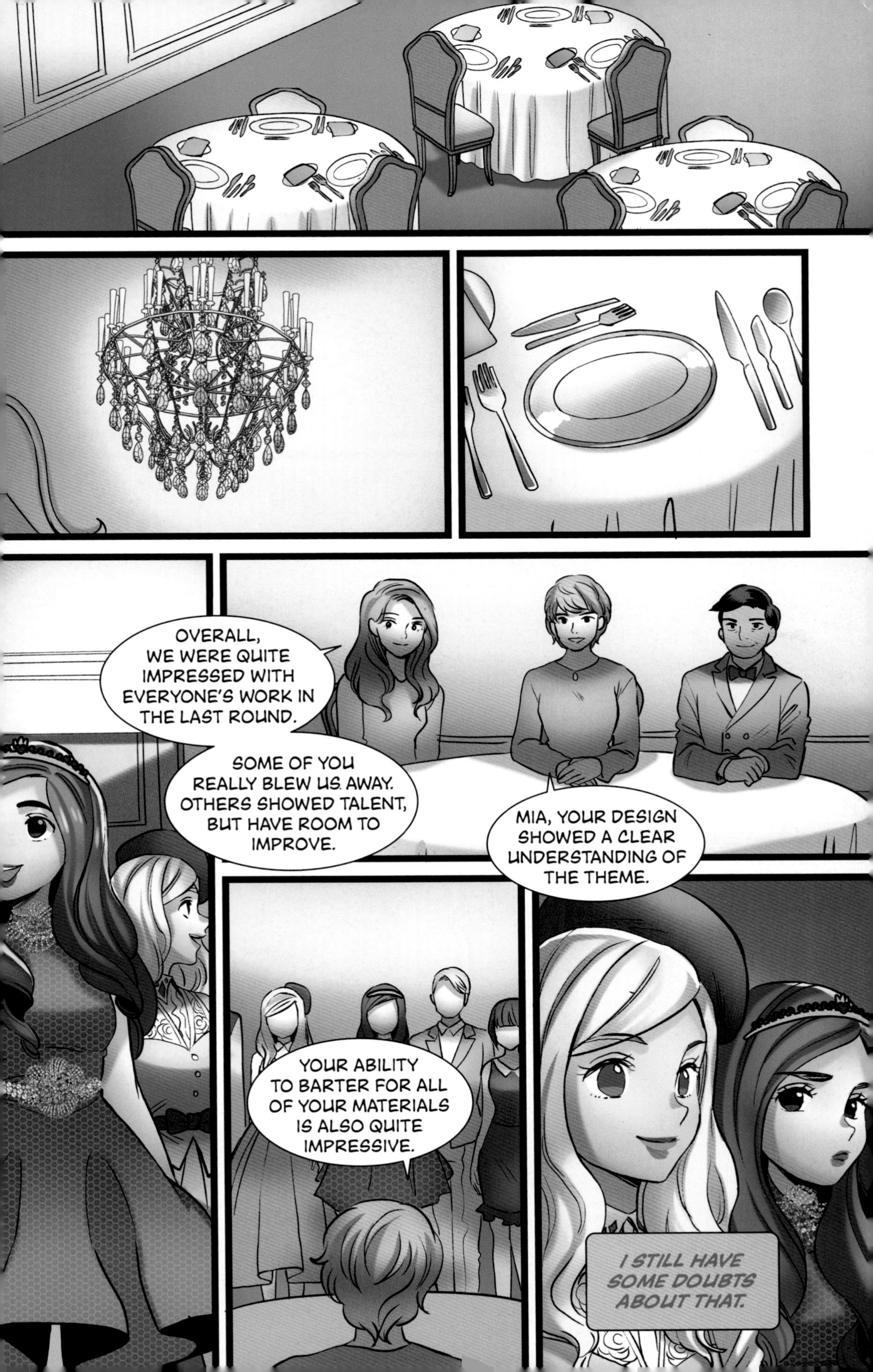
OVERALL, WE WERE QUITE IMPRESSED WITH EVERYONE'S WORK IN THE LAST ROUND.
SOME OF YOU REALLY BLEW US AWAY. OTHERS SHOWED TALENT, BUT HAVE ROOM TO IMPROVE.
MIA, YOUR DESIGN SHOWED A CLEAR UNDERSTANDING OF THE THEME.
YOUR ABILITY TO BARTER FOR ALL OF YOUR MATERIALS IS ALSO QUITE IMPRESSIVE.
I STILL HAVE SOME DOUBTS ABOUT THAT.

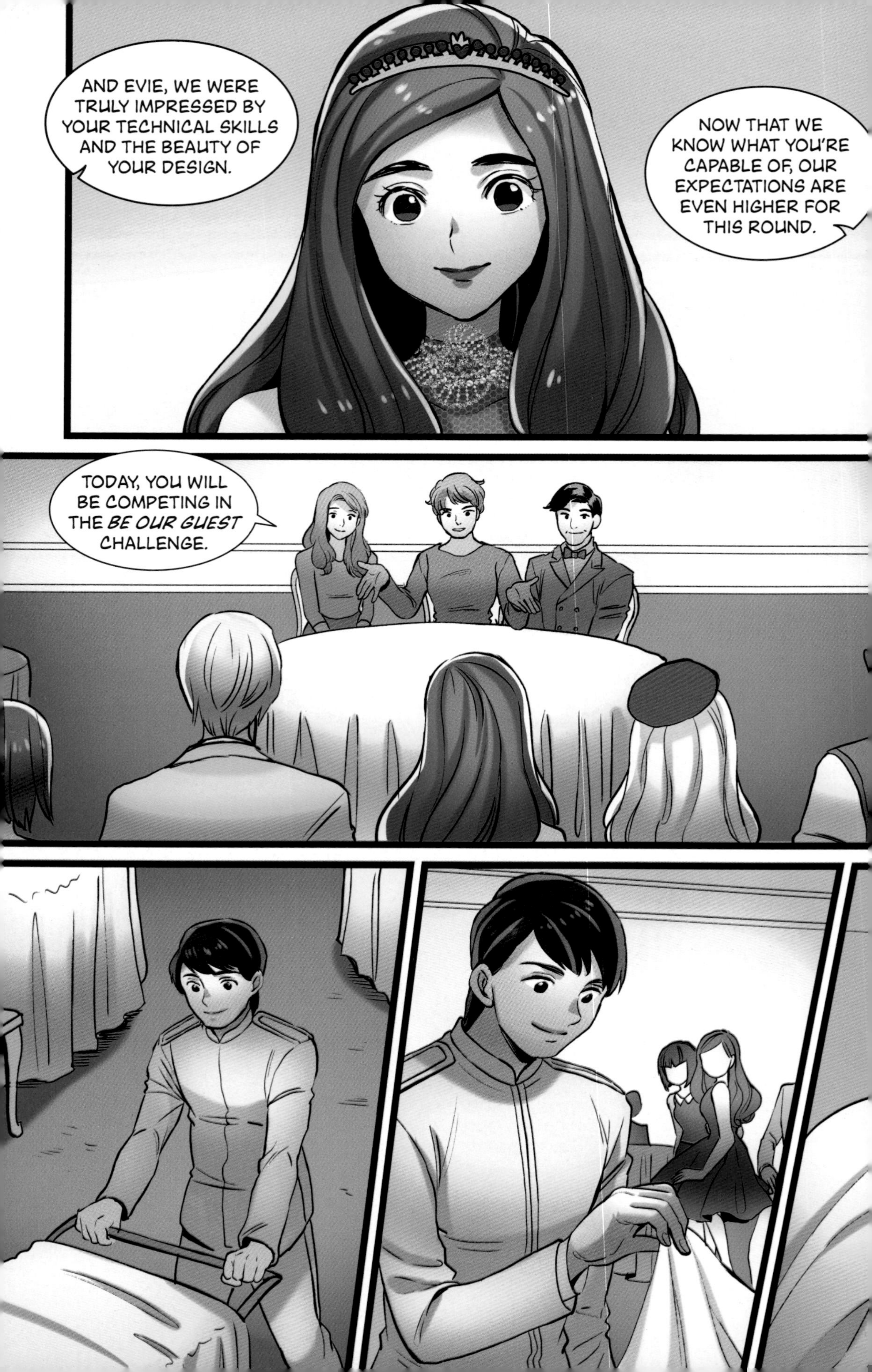
AND EVIE, WE WERE TRULY IMPRESSED BY YOUR TECHNICAL SKILLS AND THE BEAUTY OF YOUR DESIGN.
NOW THAT WE KNOW WHAT YOU'RE CAPABLE OF, OUR EXPECTATIONS ARE EVEN HIGHER FOR THIS ROUND.
TODAY, YOU WILL BE COMPETING IN THE *BE OUR GUEST* CHALLENGE.

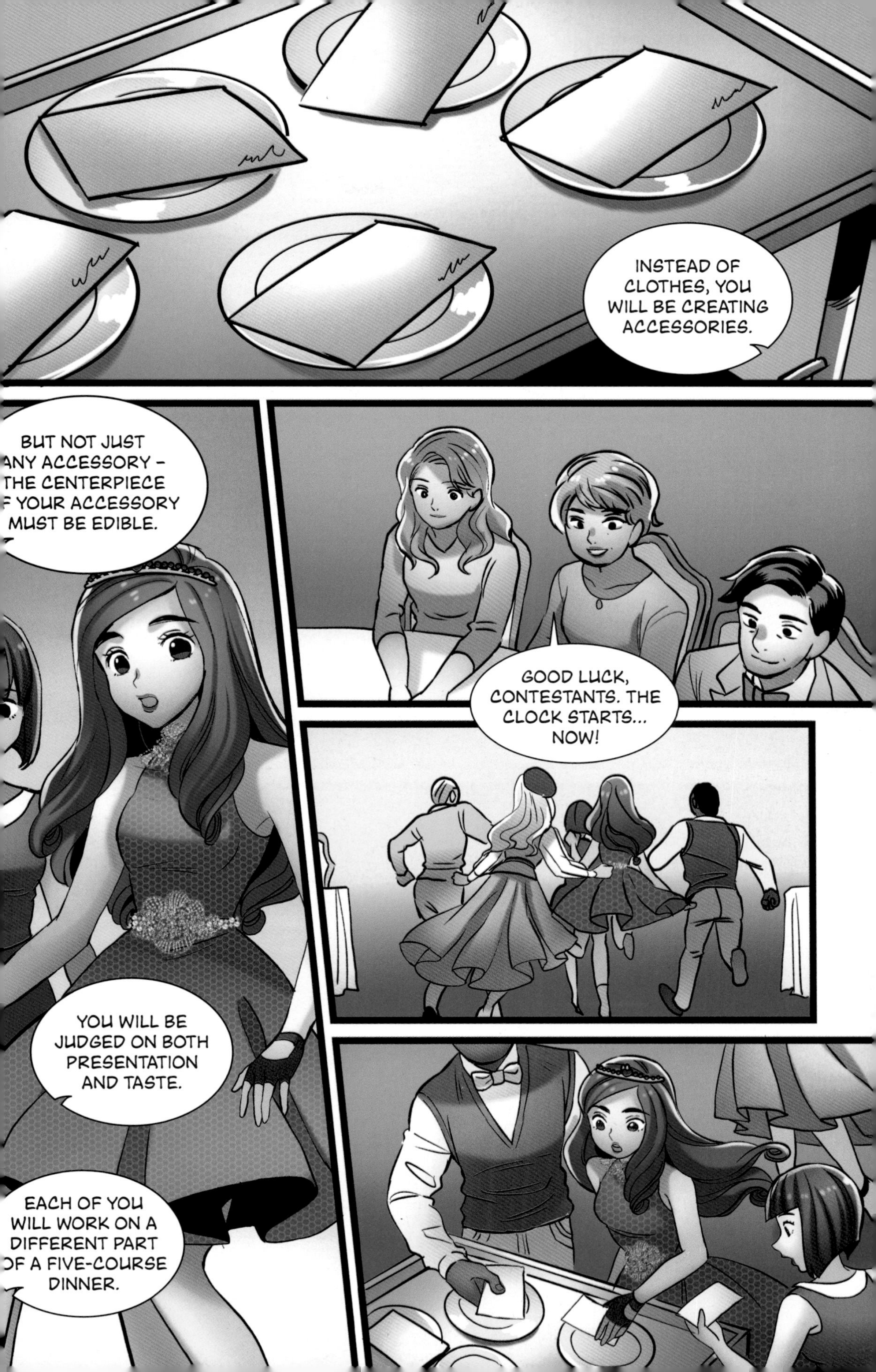
INSTEAD OF CLOTHES, YOU WILL BE CREATING ACCESSORIES.
BUT NOT JUST ANY ACCESSORY – THE CENTERPIECE F YOUR ACCESSORY MUST BE EDIBLE.
YOU WILL BE JUDGED ON BOTH PRESENTATION AND TASTE.
EACH OF YOU WILL WORK ON A DIFFERENT PART OF A FIVE-COURSE DINNER.
GOOD LUCK, CONTESTANTS. THE CLOCK STARTS... NOW!

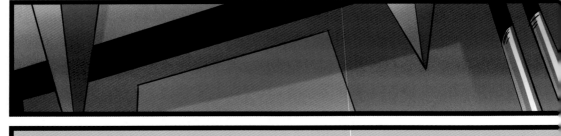

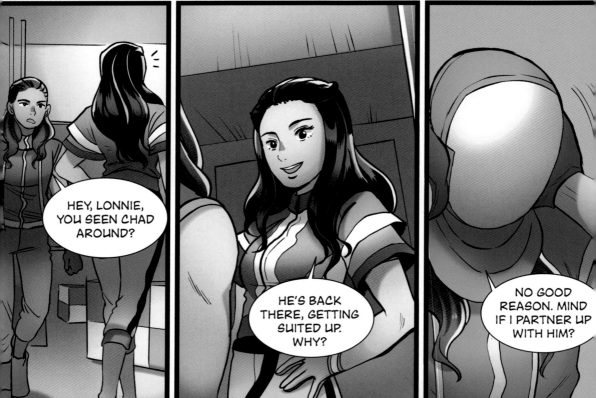

HEY, LONNIE, YOU SEEN CHAD AROUND?

HE'S BACK THERE, GETTING SUITED UP. WHY?

NO GOOD REASON. MIND IF I PARTNER UP WITH HIM?

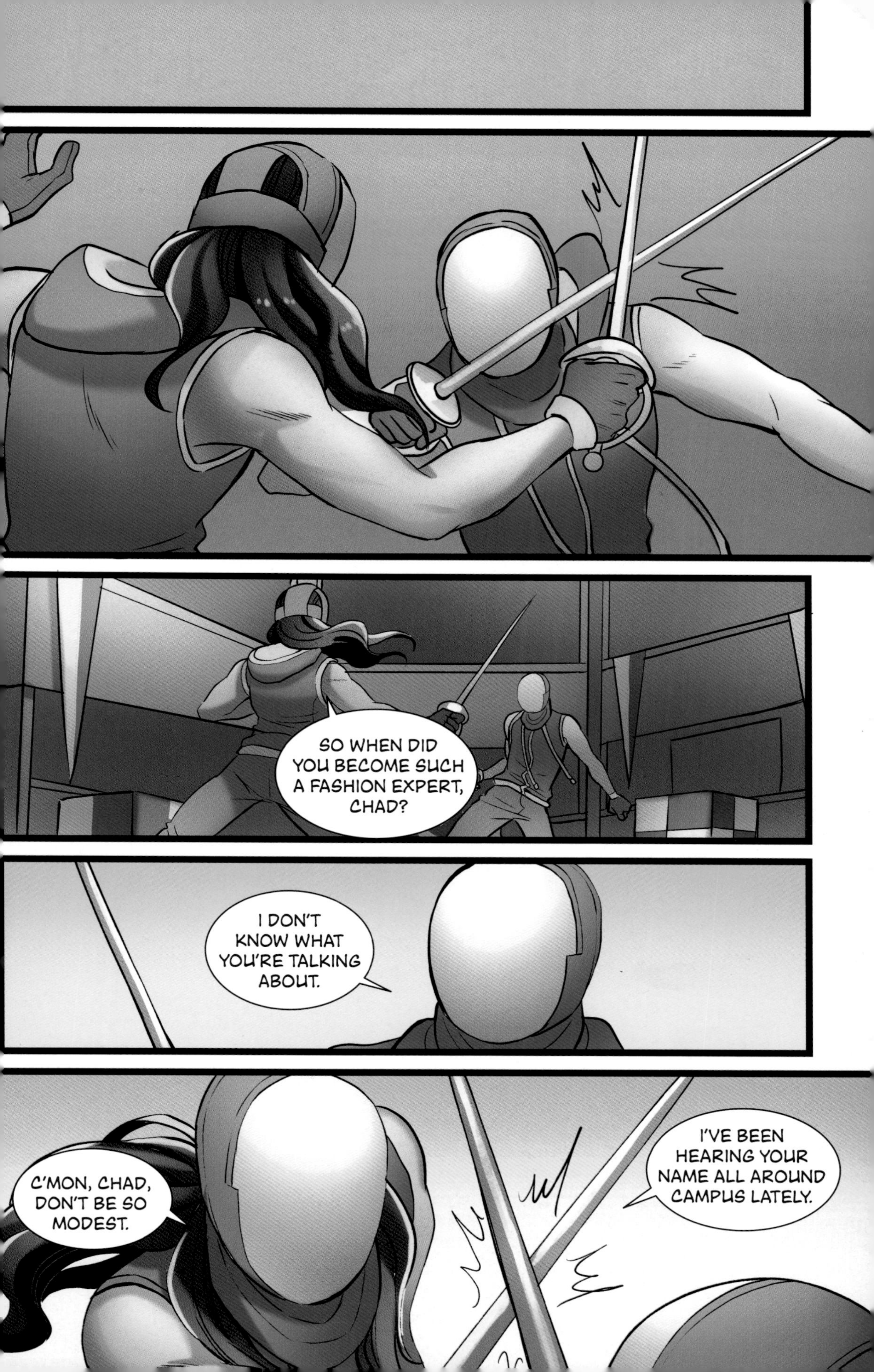
SO WHEN DID YOU BECOME SUCH A FASHION EXPERT, CHAD?
I DON'T KNOW WHAT YOU'RE TALKING ABOUT.
C'MON, CHAD, DON'T BE SO MODEST.
I'VE BEEN HEARING YOUR NAME ALL AROUND CAMPUS LATELY.

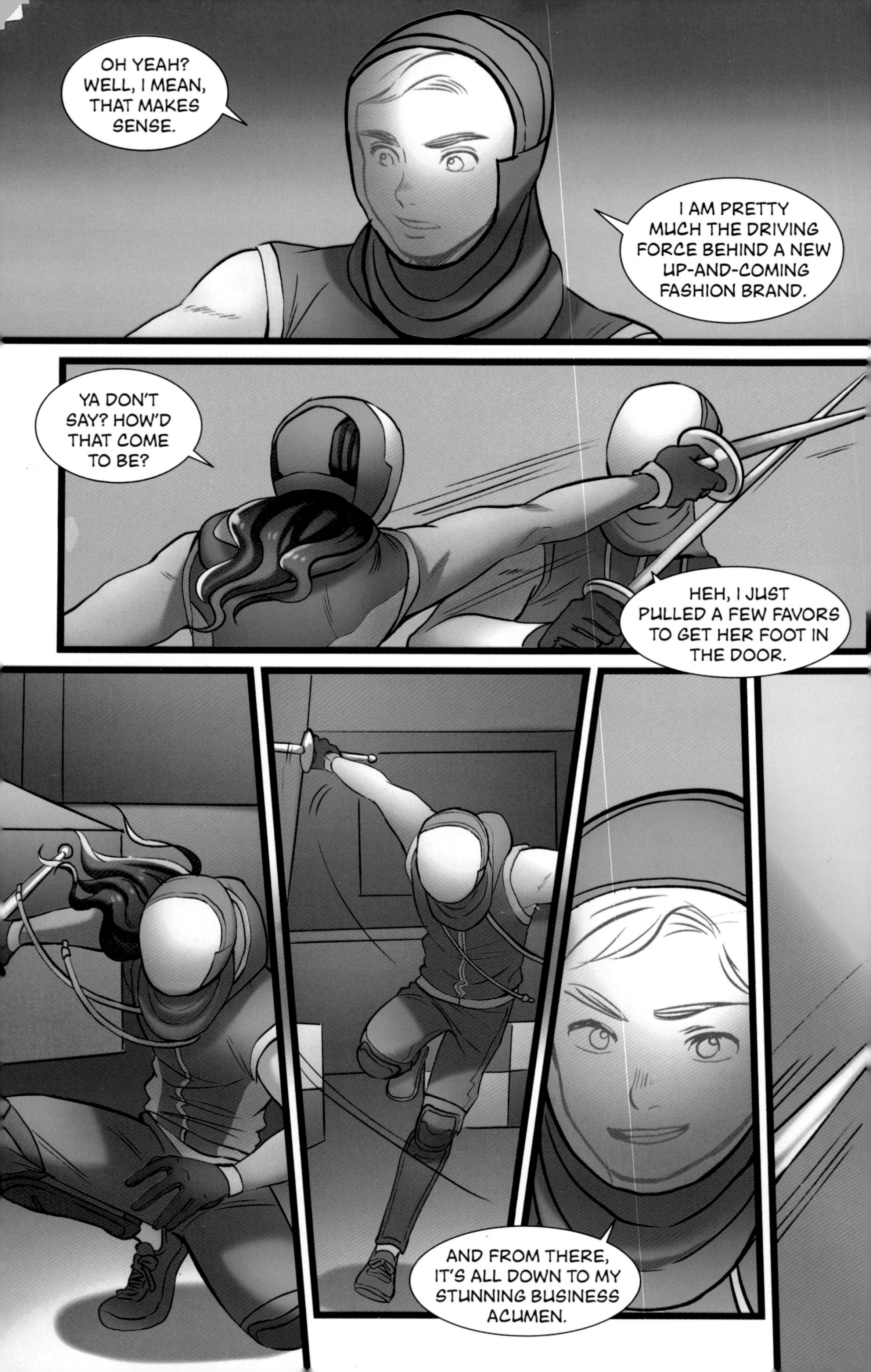
OH YEAH? WELL, I MEAN, THAT MAKES SENSE.
I AM PRETTY MUCH THE DRIVING FORCE BEHIND A NEW UP-AND-COMING FASHION BRAND.
YA DON'T SAY? HOW'D THAT COME TO BE?
HEH, I JUST PULLED A FEW FAVORS TO GET HER FOOT IN THE DOOR.
AND FROM THERE, IT'S ALL DOWN TO MY STUNNING BUSINESS ACUMEN.

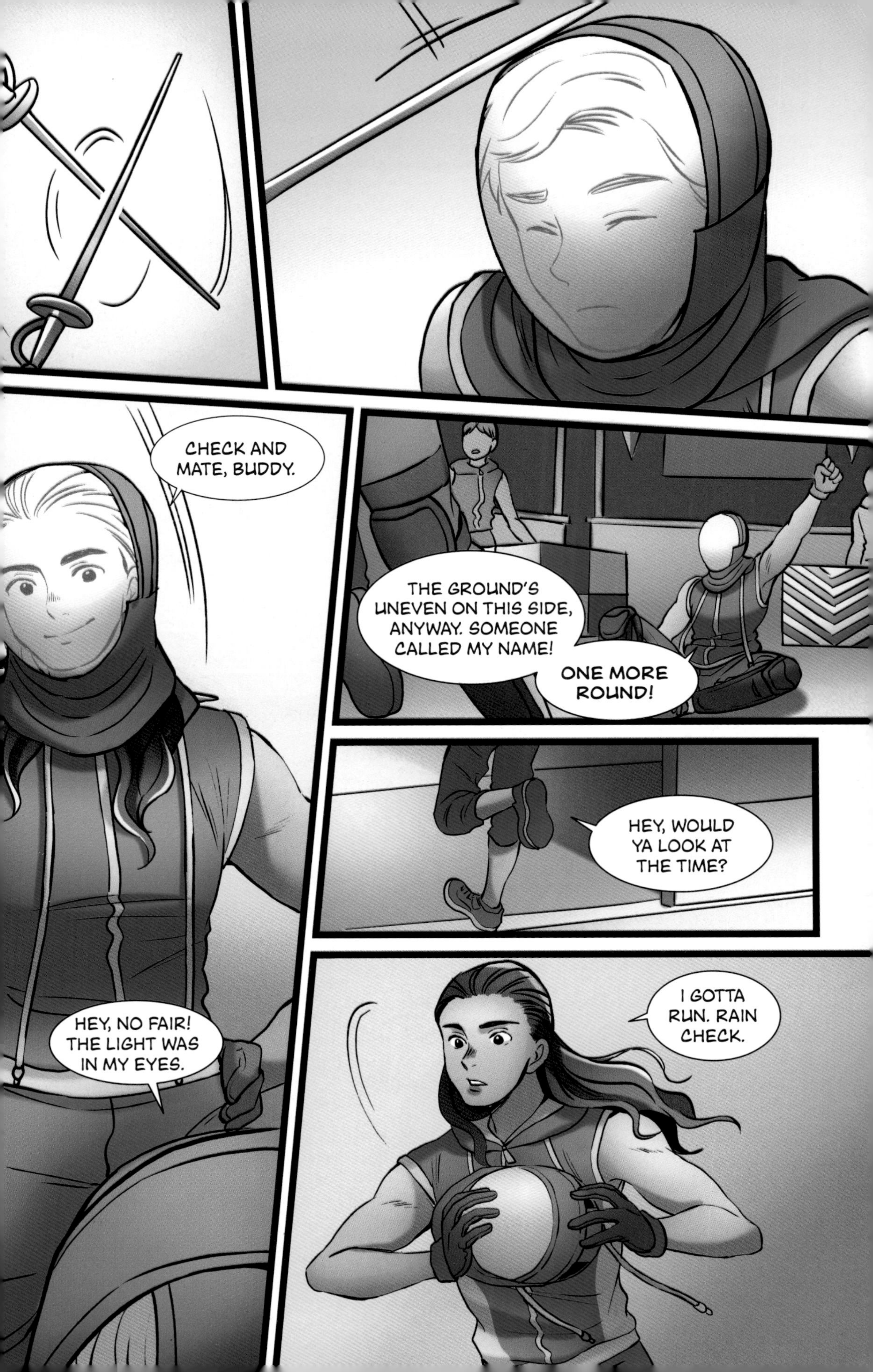
CHECK AND MATE, BUDDY.
HEY, NO FAIR! THE LIGHT WAS IN MY EYES.
THE GROUND'S UNEVEN ON THIS SIDE, ANYWAY. SOMEONE CALLED MY NAME!
ONE MORE ROUND!
HEY, WOULD YA LOOK AT THE TIME?
I GOTTA RUN. RAIN CHECK.

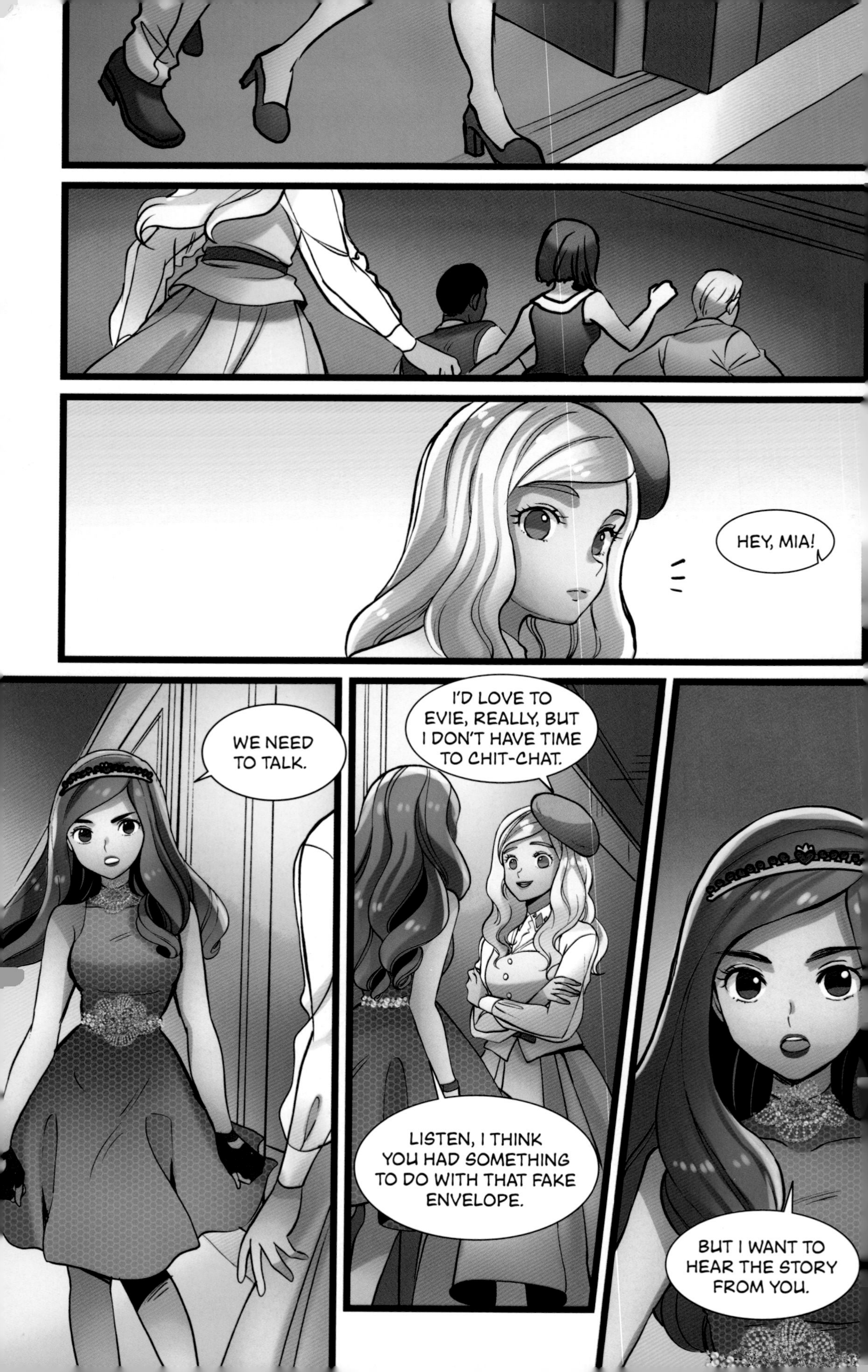
HEY, MIA!
WE NEED TO TALK.
I'D LOVE TO EVIE, REALLY, BUT I DON'T HAVE TIME TO CHIT-CHAT.
LISTEN, I THINK YOU HAD SOMETHING TO DO WITH THAT FAKE ENVELOPE.
BUT I WANT TO HEAR THE STORY FROM YOU.

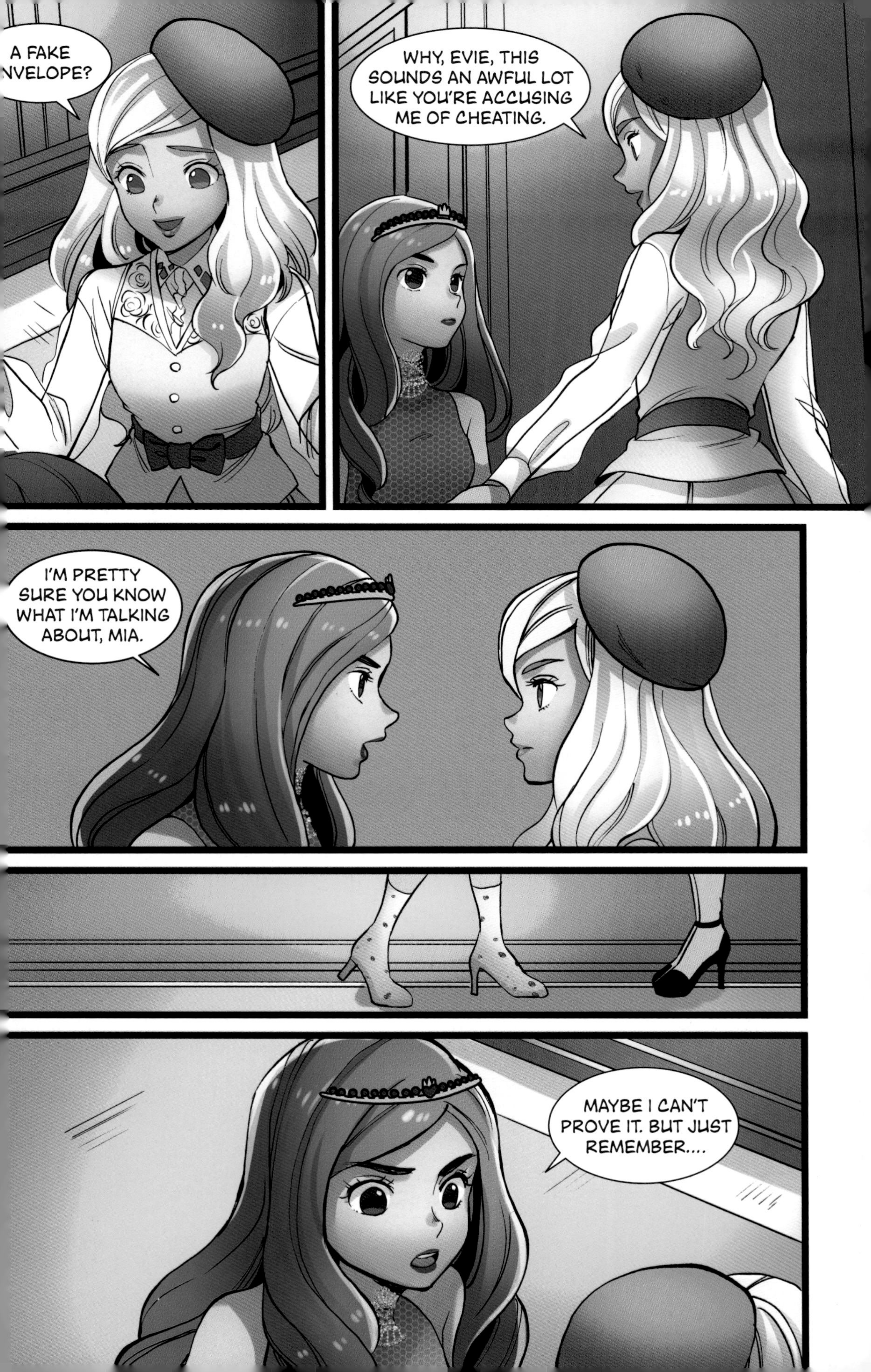
A FAKE NVELOPE?
WHY, EVIE, THIS SOUNDS AN AWFUL LOT LIKE YOU'RE ACCUSING ME OF CHEATING.
I'M PRETTY SURE YOU KNOW WHAT I'M TALKING ABOUT, MIA.
MAYBE I CAN'T PROVE IT. BUT JUST REMEMBER....

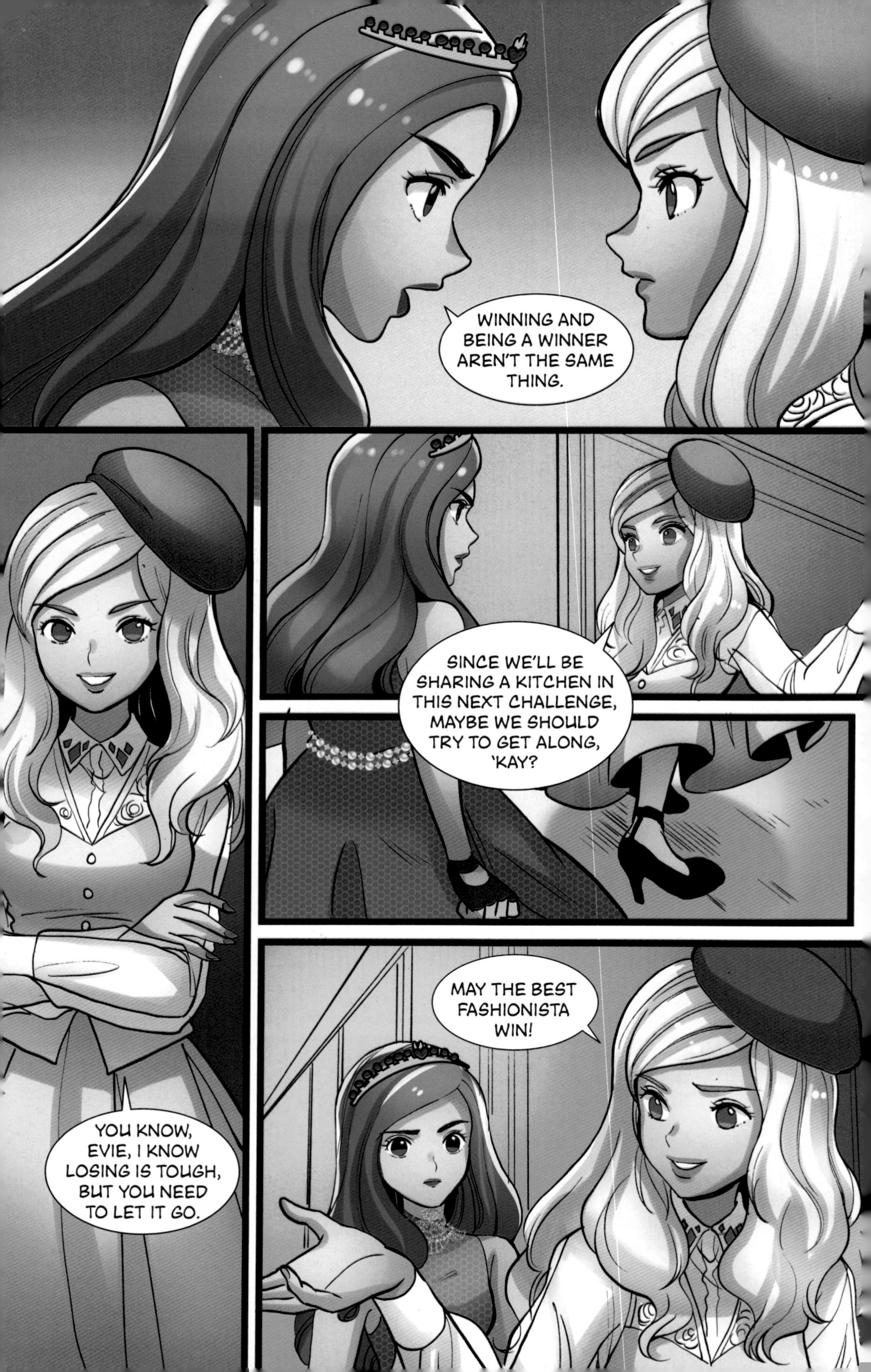
WINNING AND BEING A WINNER AREN'T THE SAME THING.
YOU KNOW, EVIE, I KNOW LOSING IS TOUGH, BUT YOU NEED TO LET IT GO.
SINCE WE'LL BE SHARING A KITCHEN IN THIS NEXT CHALLENGE, MAYBE WE SHOULD TRY TO GET ALONG, 'KAY?
MAY THE BEST FASHIONISTA WIN!

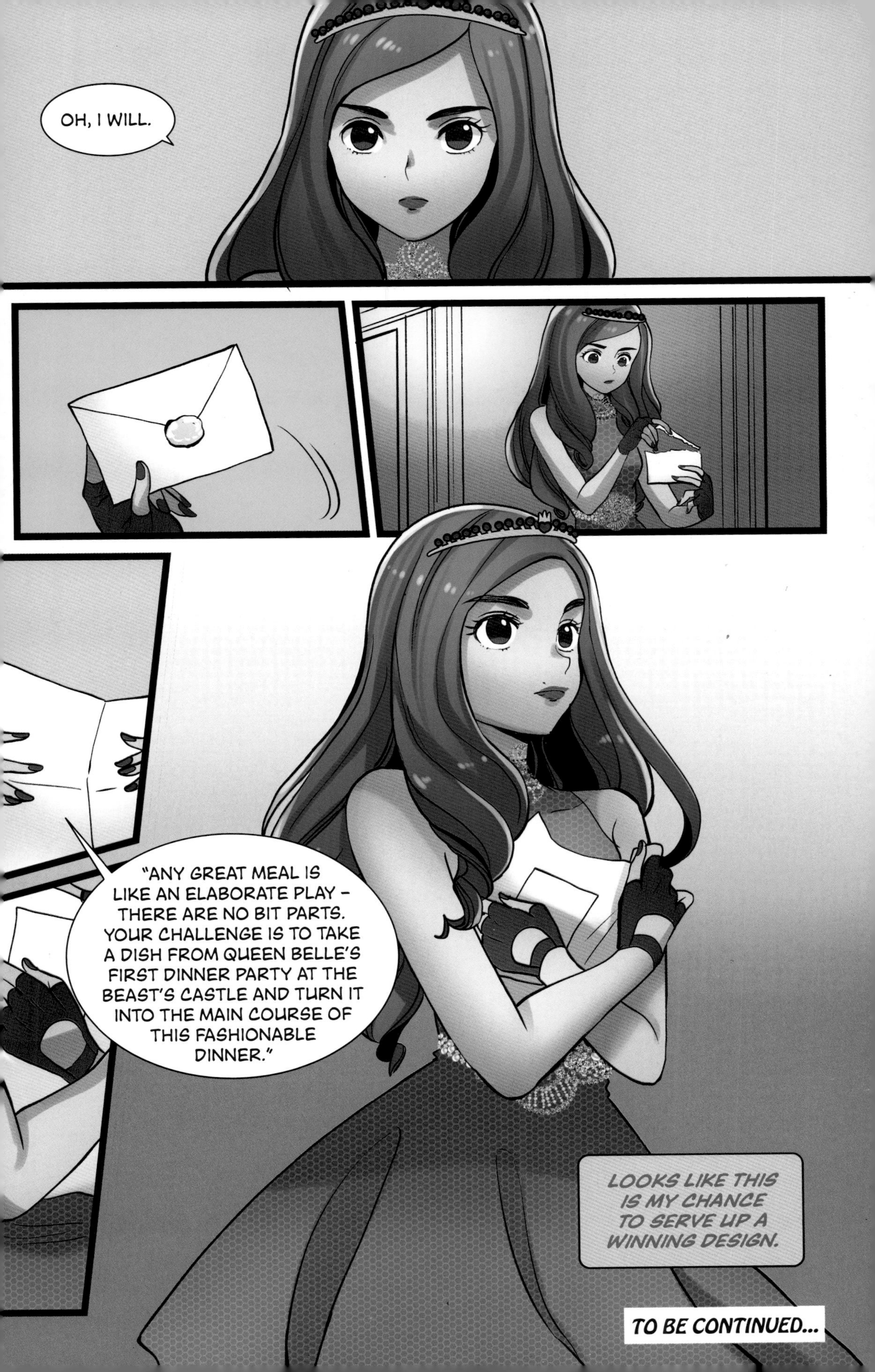
OH, I WILL.
"ANY GREAT MEAL IS LIKE AN ELABORATE PLAY – THERE ARE NO BIT PARTS. YOUR CHALLENGE IS TO TAKE A DISH FROM QUEEN BELLE'S FIRST DINNER PARTY AT THE BEAST'S CASTLE AND TURN IT INTO THE MAIN COURSE OF THIS FASHIONABLE DINNER."
LOOKS LIKE THIS IS MY CHANCE TO SERVE UP A WINNING DESIGN.
TO BE CONTINUED...

In the next volume of

EVIE'S WICKED RUNWAY

Oh no! Mia's conspiring with Chad to cheat her way to victory, and Evie's chances of winning the competition are quickly slipping away. If she loses the next round, she could be out of the contest for good!

With the next challenge calling for an inspired combination of cooking and accessory design, it'll take all of Evie's talent and creativity to win over the judges. Together she and the other VKs come up with a delicious dish for round two, and she's determined to give Mia a chance to do the right thing.

That is, as long as everything goes according to plan...

For more information about *Evie's Wicked Runway*, go to www.TOKYOPOP.com/DescendantsEvie!

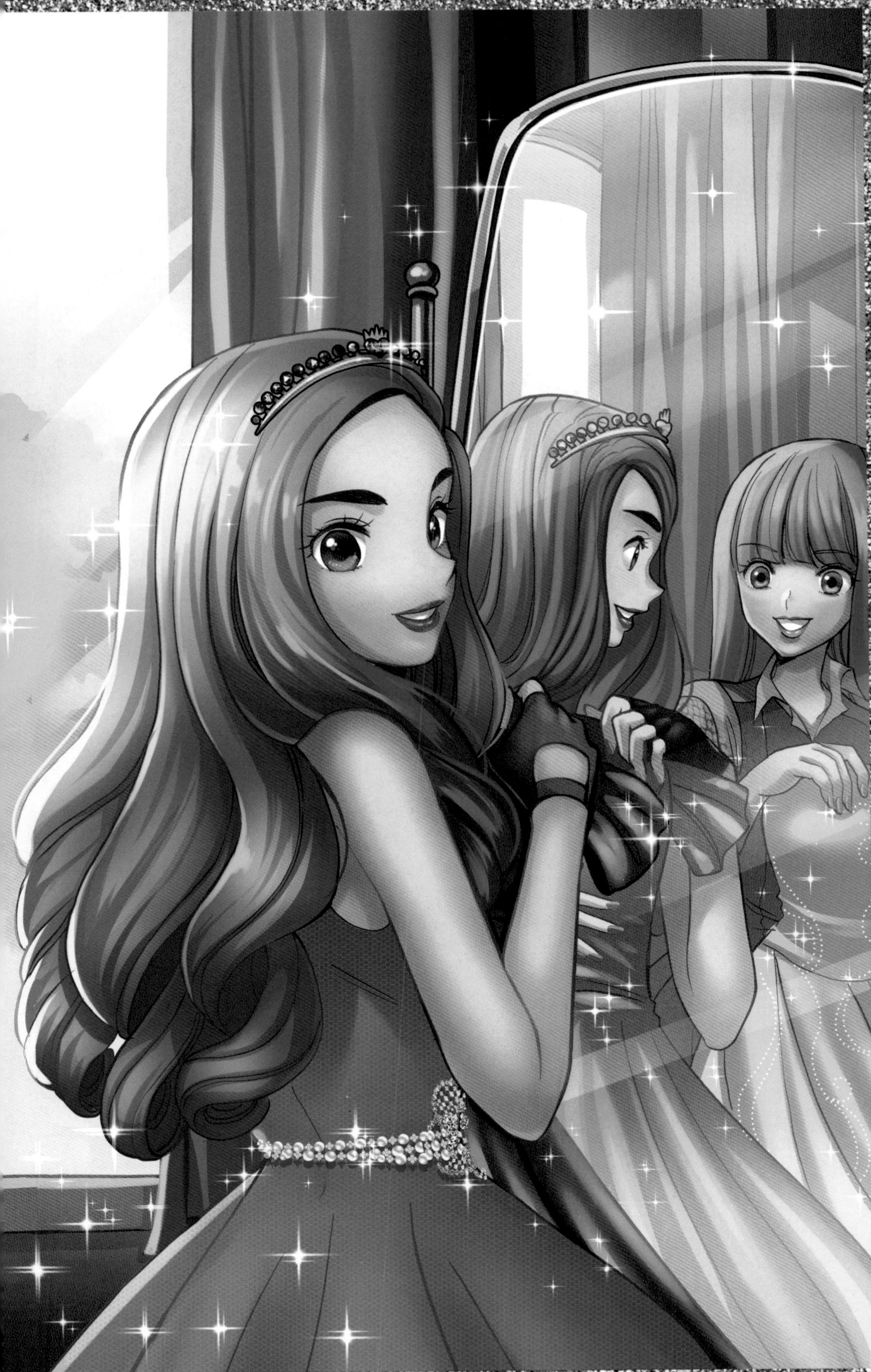

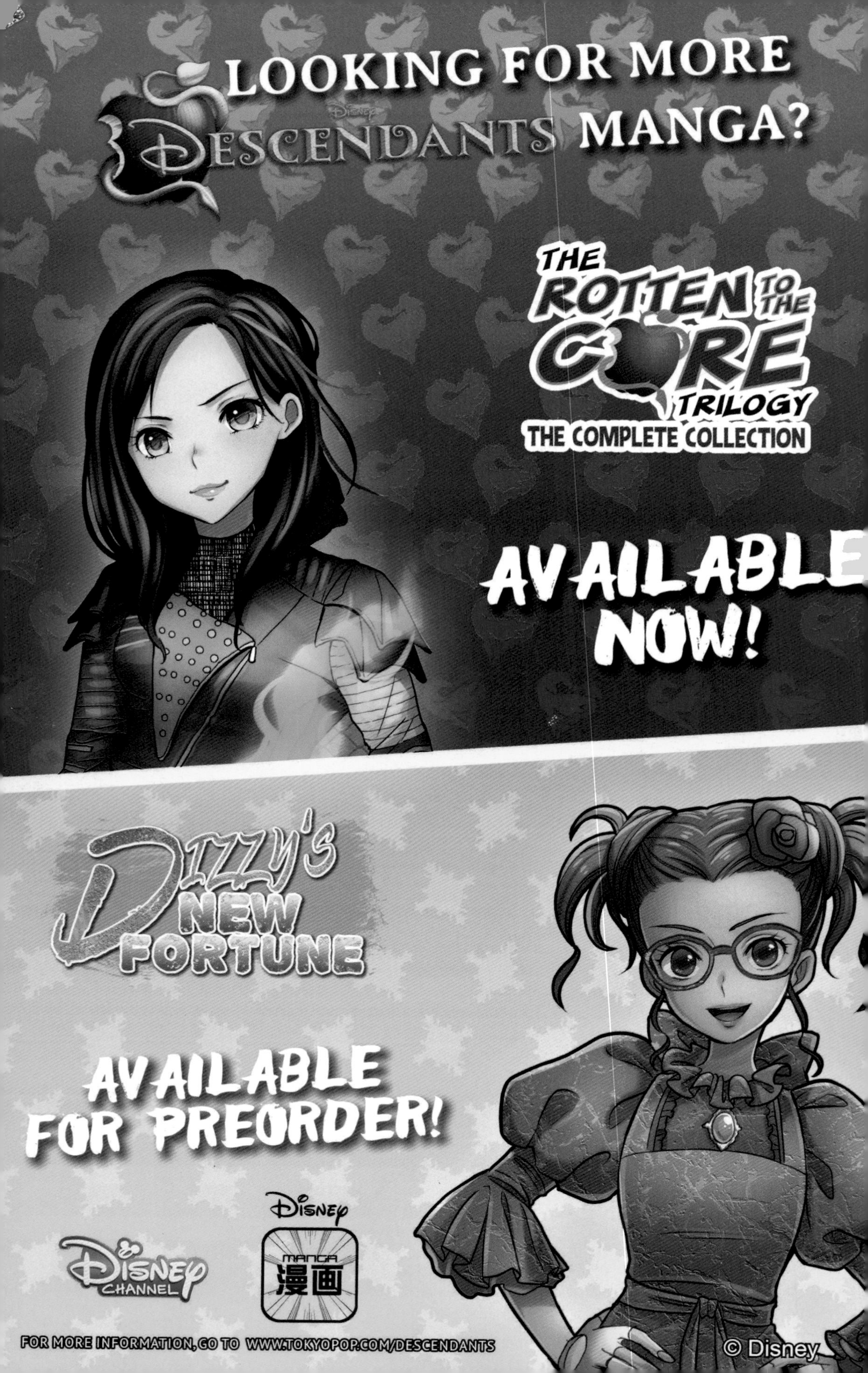
LOOKING FOR MORE
DISNEY DESCENDANTS MANGA?
THE ROTTEN TO THE CORE TRILOGY
THE COMPLETE COLLECTION
AVAILABLE NOW!
DIZZY'S NEW FORTUNE
AVAILABLE FOR PREORDER!
DISNEY CHANNEL
DISNEY
MANGA
漫画
FOR MORE INFORMATION, GO TO WWW.TOKYOPOP.COM/DESCENDANTS
© Disney

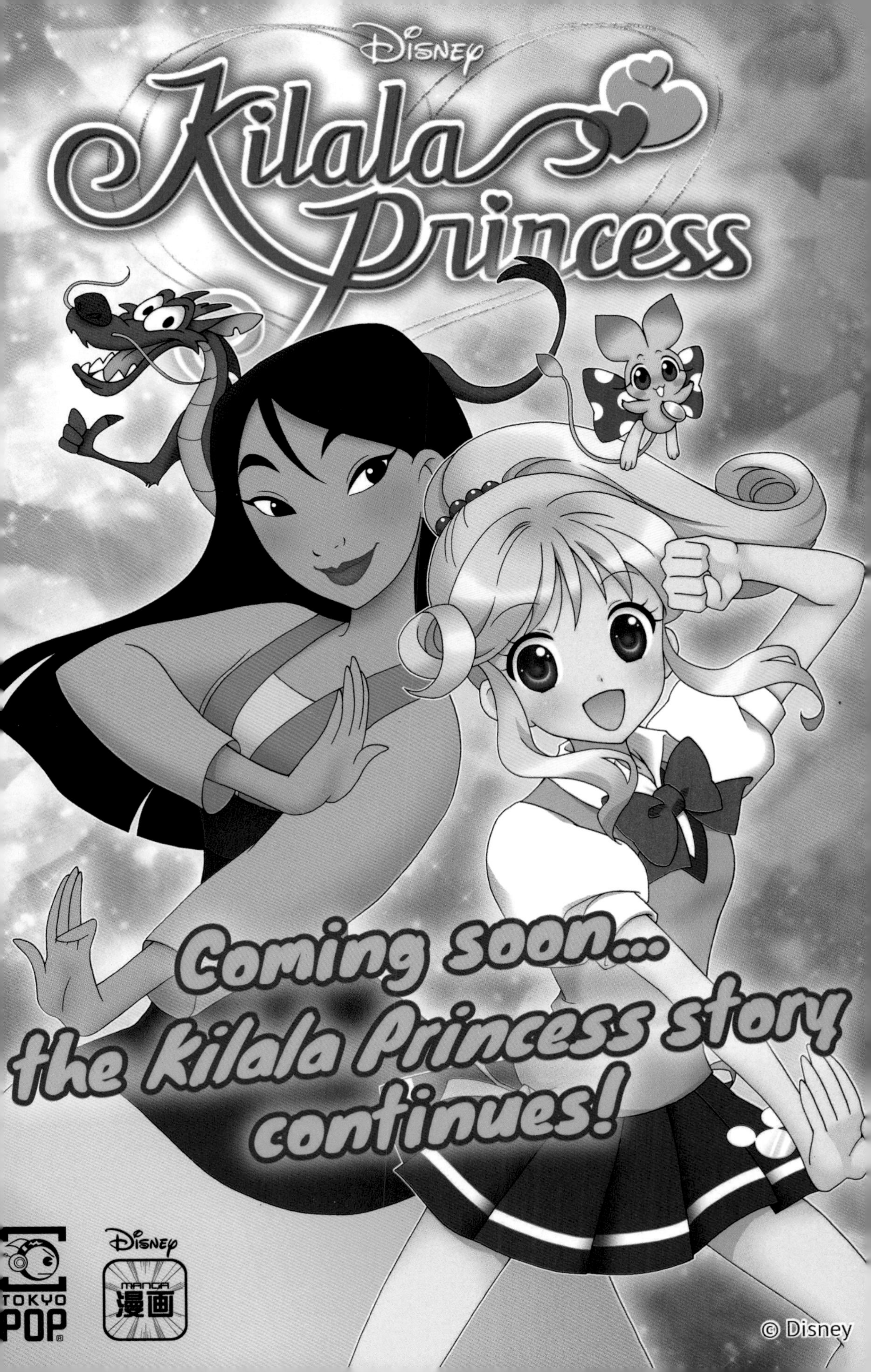
Disney
Kilala Princess
Coming soon...
the Kilala Princess story continues!
TOKYO POP
Disney
MANGA
漫画
© Disney

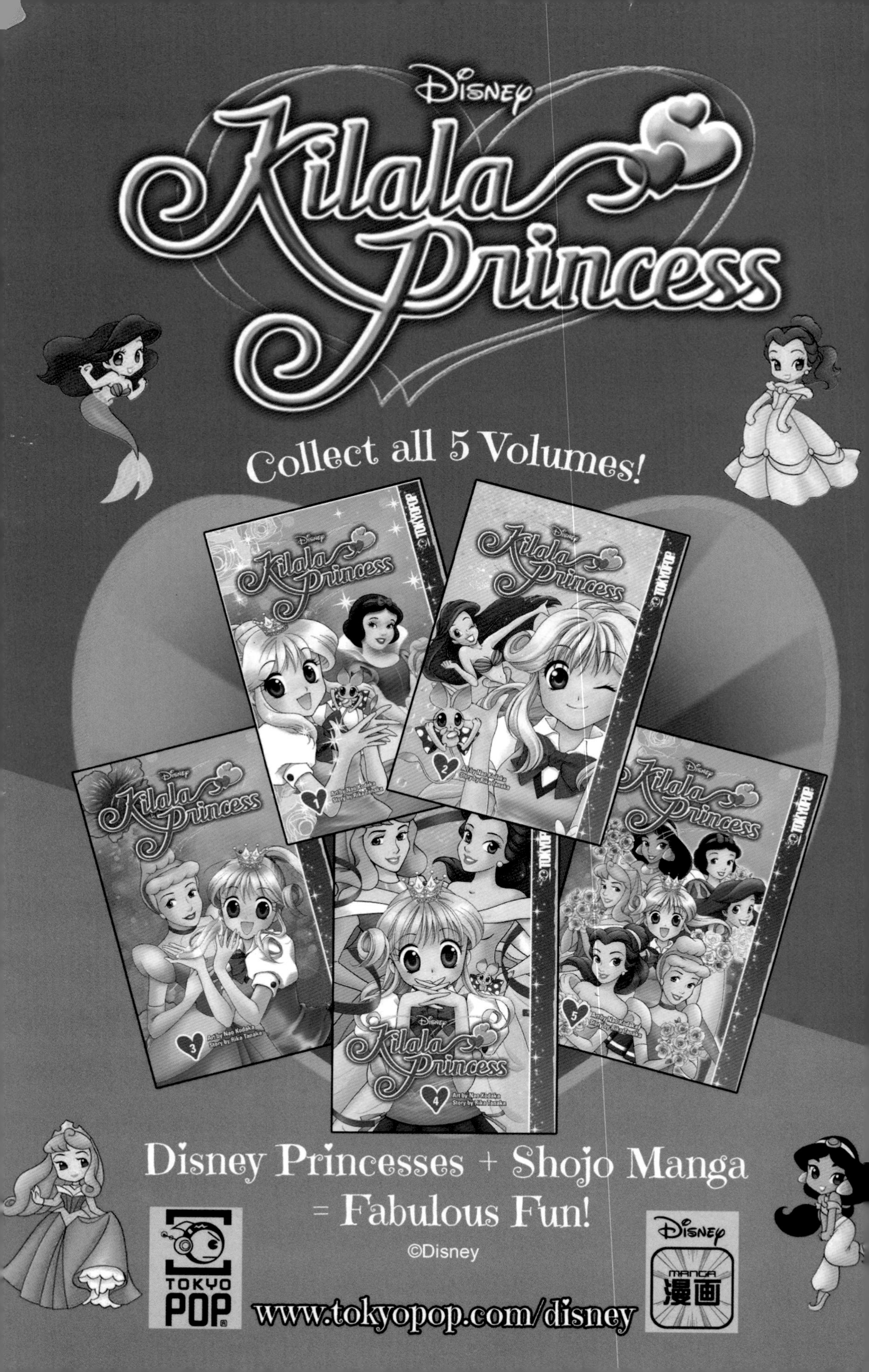
Disney
Kilala Princess
Collect all 5 Volumes!
Disney Princesses + Shojo Manga
= Fabulous Fun!
©Disney
TOKYO POP
www.tokyopop.com/disney
Disney
MANGA
漫画

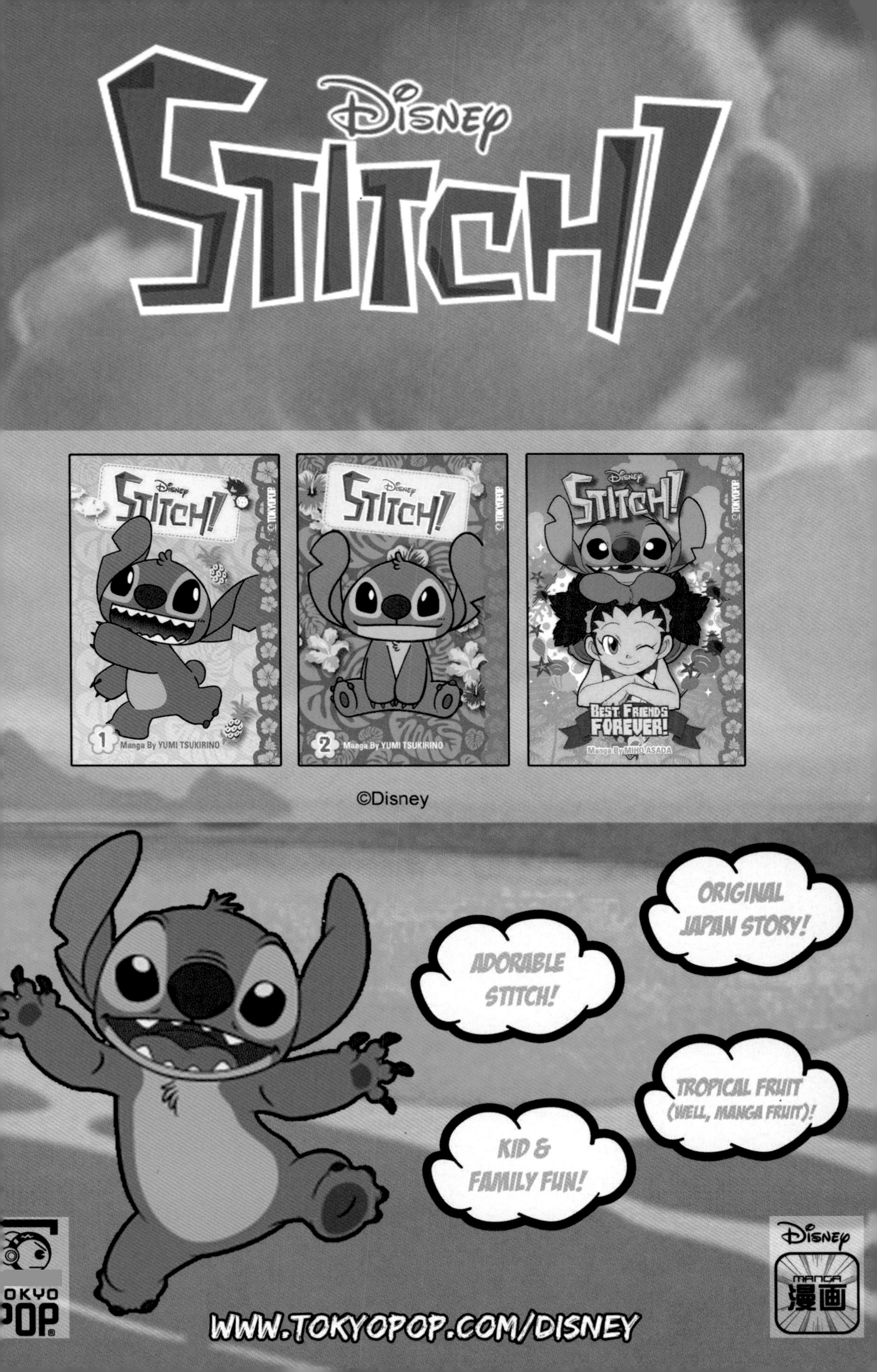
Disney
STITCH!
Disney
STITCH!
TOKYOPOP
1 Manga By YUMI TSUKIRINO
Disney
STITCH!
TOKYOPOP
2 Manga By YUMI TSUKIRINO
Disney
STITCH!
TOKYOPOP
BEST FRIENDS FOREVER!
Manga By MIHO ASADA
©Disney
ORIGINAL JAPAN STORY!
ADORABLE STITCH!
TROPICAL FRUIT (WELL, MANGA FRUIT)!
KID & FAMILY FUN!
TOKYOPOP
Disney MANGA 漫画
WWW.TOKYOPOP.COM/DISNEY

☆ **Inspired by the characters from Disney's The Aristocats**
☆ **Learn facts about Paris and Japan!**
☆ **Adorable original shojo story**
☆ **Full color manga**

Even though the wealthy young girl Miriya has almost everything she could ever need, what she really wants is the one thing money can't buy: her missing parents. But this year, she gets an extra special birthday gift when Marie, a magical white kitten, appears and whisks her away to Paris! Learning the art of magic is one thing, but getting to eat the tastiest French pastries and wear the most beautiful fashion takes Miriya and Marie's journey to a whole new level!

Manga By
MAYA

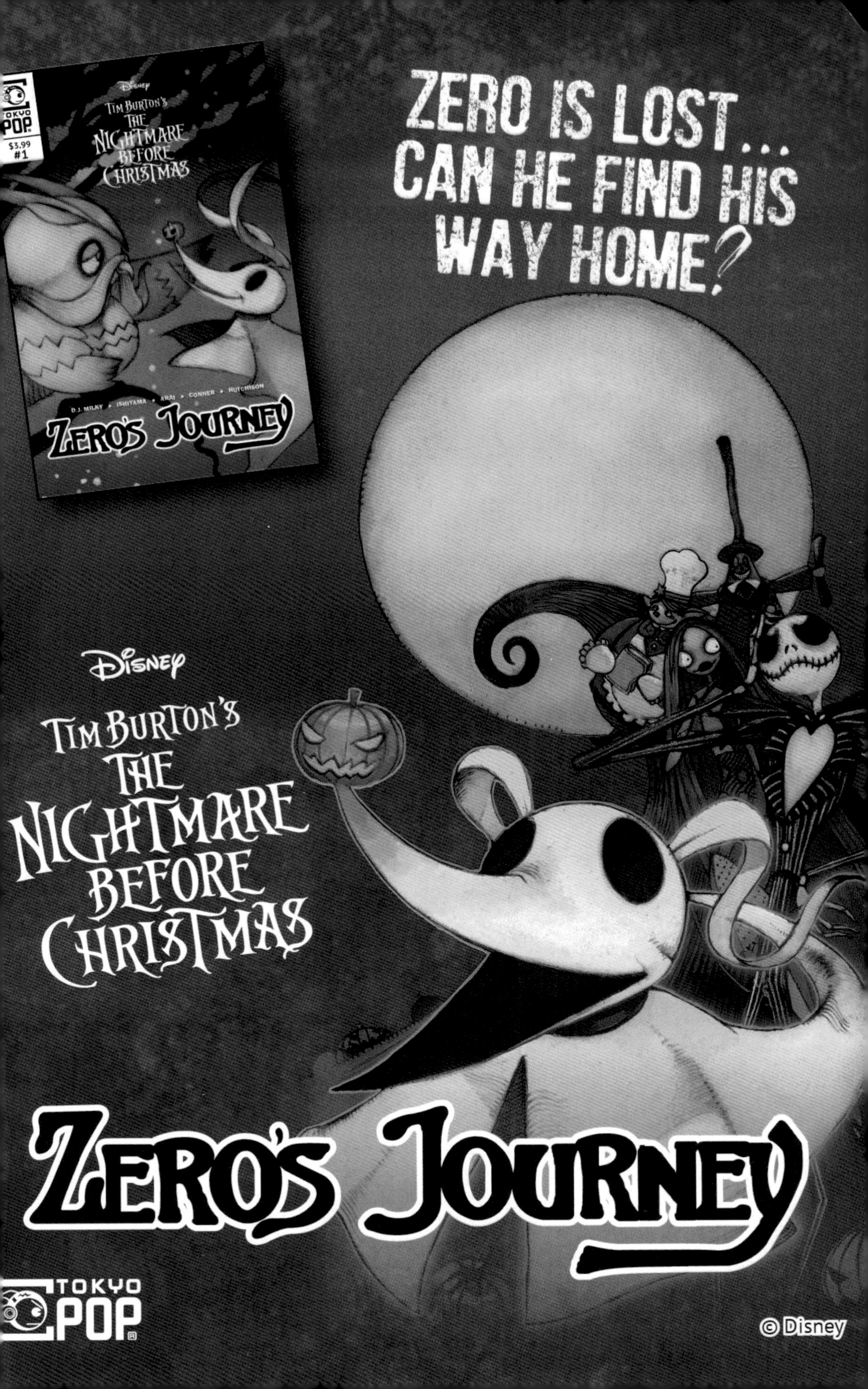

TOKYOPOP
$3.99
#1
Disney
Tim Burton's
The Nightmare Before Christmas
D.J. MILKY • ISHIYAMA • ARAI • CONNER • HUTCHISON
Zero's Journey
ZERO IS LOST... CAN HE FIND HIS WAY HOME?
Disney
Tim Burton's
The Nightmare Before Christmas
Zero's Journey
TOKYOPOP
© Disney

Find out more at
TOKYOPOP.COM/DISNEYMANGA

ADD THESE DISNEY MANGA TITLES TO YOUR COLLECTION!

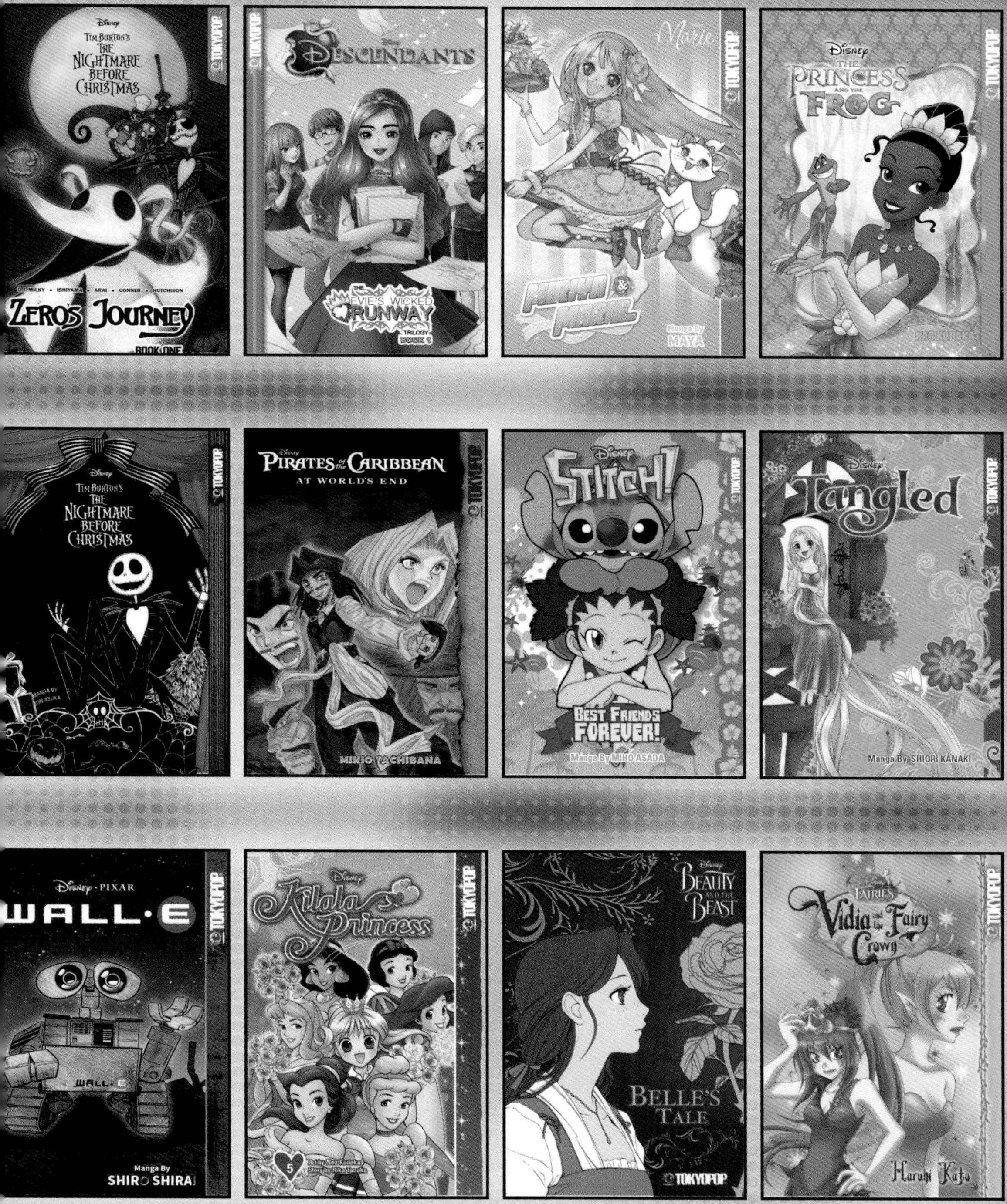
Disney
Tim Burton's The Nightmare Before Christmas
TOKYOPOP
Zero's Journey
Book One
Descendants
The Evie's Wicked Runway Trilogy
Book 1
Marie
Manga By MAYA
Disney
The Princess and the Frog
Disney
Tim Burton's The Nightmare Before Christmas
Pirates of the Caribbean
At World's End
Mikio Tachibana
Disney
Stitch!
Best Friends Forever!
Manga By Miho Asada
Disney
Tangled
Manga By Shiori Kanaki
Disney · Pixar
WALL·E
Manga By
Shiro Shirai
Disney
Kilala Princess
5
Disney
Beauty and the Beast
Belle's Tale
TOKYOPOP
Disney Fairies
Vidia and the Fairy Crown
Haruhi Kato

...AND MUCH MORE!

Disney Descendants: Evie's Wicked Runway Book 1
Written by : Jason Muell
Art by : Natsuki Minami
Inspired by the hit Disney Channel original movies *Descendants* and *Descendants*
Directed by : Kenny Ortega
Executive Produced by : Kenny Ortega and Wendy Japhet
Produced by : Tracey Jeffrey
Written by : Josann McGibbon & Sara Parriott

Publishing Associate - Janae Young
Marketing Associate - Kae Winters
Technology and Digital Media Assistant - Phillip Hong
Copy Editor - Marybeth Connaughton
Editor - Janae Young
Graphic Designer - Phillip Hong
Retouching and Lettering - Vibrraant Publishing Studio
Editor-in-Chief & Publisher - Stu Levy

A **TOKYOPOP**® Manga

TOKYOPOP and ⊙ are trademarks or registered trademarks of TOKYOPOP Inc.

TOKYOPOP Inc.
5200 W. Century Blvd. Suite 705
Los Angeles, 90045

E-mail: info@TOKYOPOP.com
Come visit us online at www.TOKYOPOP.com

www.facebook.com/TOKYOPOP
www.twitter.com/TOKYOPOP
www.pinterest.com/TOKYOPOP
www.instagram.com/TOKYOPOP

ISBN: 978-1-4278-5990-7
First TOKYOPOP Printing: March 2019
10 9 8 7 6 5 4 3 2 1
Printed in Canada.